Books of Merit

Siege 13

SIEGE
13

Tamas Dobozy

THOMAS ALLEN PUBLISHERS
TORONTO

Library and Archives Canada Cataloguing in Publication

Dobozy, Tamas, 1969–
      Siege 13 : stories / Tamas Dobozy.

Issued also in electronic formats.
ISBN 978-1-77102-204-0

I. Title.   II. Title: Siege thirteen.

PS8557.O22I8S54   2012   c813'.54   C2012-904218-8

Editor: Janice Zawerbny
Cover design: Michel Vrana
Cover image: Allan Kausch

Published by Thomas Allen Publishers,
a division of Thomas Allen & Son Limited,
390 Steelcase Road East,
Markham, Ontario L3R 1G2 Canada

www.thomasallen.ca

Canada Council
for the Arts

Conseil des Arts
du Canada

ONTARIO ARTS COUNCIL
CONSEIL DES ARTS DE L'ONTARIO

The publisher gratefully acknowledges the support of
The Ontario Arts Council for its publishing program.

We acknowledge the support of the Canada Council for the Arts, which last
year invested $20.1 million in writing and publishing throughout Canada.

We acknowledge the Government of Ontario through the Ontario
Media Development Corporation's Ontario Book Initiative.

We acknowledge the financial support of the Government of Canada
through the Canada Book Fund for our publishing activities.

12 13 14 15 16   6 5 4 3 2

Text printed on a 100% PCW recycled stock

Printed and bound in Canada

For two early and outstanding teachers—
Nancy Hollmann and Robert McCallum—
who opened all the right doors.

Both Miss Eckhart and Virgie Rainey were human beings terribly at large, roaming on the face of the earth. And there were others of them—human beings, roaming, like lost beasts.

— EUDORA WELTY, "June Recital"

Contents

The Atlas
of
B. Görbe

H E WAS THE SORT OF MAN you've seen: big
and fat in an overcoat beaded with rain, cigar
poking from between his jowls, staring at some
vision beyond the neon and noise and commuter
frenzy of Times Square.

That's how Benedek Görbe looked the last time I saw
him. This was May, 2007, shortly before I left Manhattan,
where I'd been living with my family for six months on a
Fulbright fellowship at NYU. Görbe was an ex-boyfriend
of an aunt in Budapest, though he hadn't lived in or visited
Hungary for over forty years. He wrote in Hungarian every
day though, along with drawing illustrations, for a series of
kids' books published under the name B. Görbe by a small
but quality imprint out of Brooklyn who'd hired a transla-
tor and published them in enormous folio-sized hardcovers
under the title *The Atlas of Dreams*. Benjamin and Henry, my
two boys, loved the books, with their pictures reminiscent
of *fin de siècle* posters, stories of children climbing ladders
into dreams—endless garden cities, drifting minarets, kings
shrouded in hyacinths. That was Görbe's style, not that you'd

have known it from the way he looked—with his stubble, pants the size of garbage bags, half-smouldering cigars, his obnoxious way of disagreeing with any opinion that wasn't his own, and sometimes, after a moment's reflection, even with that.

I was drawn to Görbe out of disappointment. The position at NYU had promised "a stimulating artistic environment," though what it actually gave me was an office in the back of a building where a bunch of important writers were squirrelled away writing, when they were there at all. In the end I wasn't surprised; that's what writers did—*they worked.* But this meant that when I wasn't writing I was wandering the streets, sometimes alone, sometimes with my wife, Marcy, in a dreamscape very different from the one described by Görbe. Rather than climbing up a ladder, I felt as if I'd climbed *down* one, into spaces of concrete and brick, asphalt and iron, and because it was winter it was always snowing, then rain, always torrential. I don't mean to imply that New York was dreary, only that it seemed emptied, an abandoned city, which is odd since there were people everywhere—to the point where I sometimes couldn't move along the sidewalk—all of them rushing by me as if they knew something I didn't, as if every street and avenue offered a series of doors only they could open. Because of this, because so much seemed inaccessible, New York made me feel as if I was a kid again, left alone at home for the first time, or in the house of a stranger, on a grey Sunday when there's nothing to do but search through the closets and cabinets of rooms you're not supposed to go into, never coming upon anything of interest but always hoping the next jewellry box or armoire or nightstand will redeem the lost afternoon. New York—*my* New York that winter—was a place of secrets.

Görbe was the biggest of them all. I called him on advice from my aunt Bea, who gave me his phone number after I complained about how few contacts I was making. She'd dated him, unbelievably enough, back in university in Budapest during the early 1960s. Görbe was an art student then, though he was also taking courses in literature and history and whatever else fired his imagination. He was "quiet and dreamy," according to my aunt, but also "very handsome." She compared him to Montgomery Clift. In the end, they only went out for ten months, after which Görbe dumped her for the supposed love of his life, a woman called Zella, who was majoring in psychology and who kept, according to rumour, the dream diary that would inspire Görbe's writing. Within a year of meeting Zella, Görbe left university without a degree, disappearing from my aunt's life for five years before resurfacing when his first book was published. My aunt went to the launch, wandering past posters of his illustrations, amazed to see how much Görbe had changed. Gone was the easy smile, that faraway look he sometimes had. There was something frantic about him that day, my aunt said, but he was as handsome as ever, and though he never revealed what the trouble was he seemed happy to have someone from the past to talk to. Görbe was especially bad-tempered when people who hadn't bought a book came up to him. "I was surprised to see him like that," she said. "When I knew him in university he was so different. We were hardly adults then, but we were on the edge of it—university degrees, jobs, marriages, children—but whenever I was with him it always felt to me as if we were back in the garden in Mátyásföld, playing hide-and-seek, climbing the downspout to the roof, searching for treasures in the attic." My aunt paused on the other end of the line. "Well, he's become an important man, and maybe he could help you. It doesn't sound like you're having much luck there." She paused again, and I could hear her shifting the phone against her face. "The number I have for him is quite old. He used to call me once in a while when he first left Hungary. I always got the feeling he really missed it here, that he didn't want to go, and he always asked me to describe what the city was like, the changes that had happened. I think it was because of Zella that he went." I could hear her rummaging on the other end of the line. "He hasn't called me in years."

When I finally telephoned Görbe he hesitated on the line, pretending not to remember my aunt, then grew curious when I rejected his suggestion that instead of bothering him I try to meet writers at the Hungarian Cultural Center. "I'm boycotting the place," I said, explaining how I'd gone three weeks prior to see György Konrád and afterwards spoke with the centre's director, László somebody or other, about my writing, and he'd faked interest, even enthusiasm, in that way they do so well in New York. This László person had advised me to put together an email with excerpts from my books and reviews, and to send it to him, and he'd get back to me. Hunting down the quotes and composing the email took the better part of a day, but László never responded—not to the email, not to the follow-up, nothing. "With all the time and bother it took, I could have taken my kids to the park," I said, "or gone to the Met with Marcy—a hundred different things."

Görbe laughed. It was like listening to a shout at the end of a long drainpipe. "Defaulting to the wife and kids, huh?" he said. "Listen, I hate the centre too. The programming . . . well, it's like being inside a mind the size of a walnut. And the women they have working the bar—it would kill them to smile. I never go there anymore."

"Uh . . ." I said.

"You're petty and embittered, kid," he shouted into the phone. "Running on despair. Narcissistic. Vindictive. I love it! Listen, you like Jew food?"

"Sure," I said.

"Your wife and kids, they're coming too, right?" He chuckled. "Before I help a writer I need to see what his home life is like."

It was a strange request, but it didn't take me long during that dinner at Carnegie's to see that he loved kids, *my kids*, and had a way of hitting all the right spots with Marcy's sense of humour—she was always amused by men who magnified their idiosyncrasies to comic levels—and before I knew it, before I'd even decided if I wanted to be friends with Görbe, she'd invited him to our place for dinner the next weekend. After that, with how much the kids loved him, and his attention to Marcy, we began seeing him regularly.

All of Görbe's books feature the same three protagonists: a six-year-old boy named Fritz, a girl the same age named Susanna, and a kindly court jester who's all of four years old, but whose illogical brain is perfect for figuring out the dream world and so is the wisest of them all. In the early books, the stories are about Fritz and Susanna falling asleep at night only to end up in the same dream. They spend the rest of the adventure trying to escape (with the jester's help of course). As the books go on and the children's home lives are revealed—dire poverty, Fritz's absent mother and sullen father, Susanna's illness (what in the early twentieth century was called "neurasthenia"), the cruelty of school—Fritz and Susanna decide they don't want to wake up, they want to stay asleep, and the later stories are haunted by the fear that what separates dream from reality is as thin as tissue, and once it's torn they'll never again find their way back to the jester and the endless continents of sleep. The latest book ends with the two children coming upon a strange machine that will keep them there forever—if only they can figure out how to use it.

That's the eleventh book in the series. It was published last year after we returned to Kitchener. I remember sitting with Benjamin in Words Worth Books on a snowy January day going through the illustrations and story and coming to the end, where Benjamin lingered, tracing his finger along the illustration of the dream machine, and finally said, "It was different when he read it to us." I looked at him, wondering what he was talking about, because all I remembered of Görbe's voice was the volume and rancid tobacco on his breath. It was Benjamin who reminded me that when Görbe read to him—as opposed to when Görbe spoke to *me*—his tone became quiet, it had a breathlessness to it, as if he too had no idea how the story would end and was as eager as any kid to find out. "You're right," I said, remembering those early nights in our apartment, "he did read that way," my children tucked under each of his beefy arms.

When he was done reading to them Görbe would grumble and rub his eyes like someone forced out of bed too early, which was funny because he was never available before one o'clock, and I always guessed (wrongly as it turned out) that mornings were when he did his writing and drawing. Then he'd bite his cigar and look at me and ask if I was up for a "girlie drink," which was the term he used for the awful cocktails he ordered. I think he discovered most of them in antique bartending manuals—like many children's authors he was drawn to things discarded or forgotten—concoctions such as Sherry Cobbler, Pisco Punch, New Orleans Zazerac. The bartenders looked at him as if he was totally insane.

Once we were in the bar—any bar, though mostly we hung out at a tiny place in the East Village called Lotus—anything could happen. Görbe's mouth was too big. He purposefully said things to outrage people, and most of the customers in the bars knew him on sight. He was a good fighter with fists as well as words—there was a lot of weight behind each punch, he was slow on his feet but able to withstand punishment, and only needed to connect once to knock you down. "You're right," he said to me once. "New York *is* a deserted city." He looked at the bartender. "You're a writer so you've probably seen it in the *Times*—that trembling subtext—where the critics complain that writers have failed to properly commemorate the *tragic*"—he winked at me—"event of six years ago." He called to the bartender for another Philadelphia Fish-House Punch, then continued: "What they're really bothered by is that it didn't have the effect they *wanted* it to have. Except for a few months of public tears and outrage and the constant refrain by writers trying to prove 9/11 was of enormous significance, the only difference *I* see is that people around here go shopping even more than they did before." He raised his voice and looked around the room. "It was significant to the friends and relatives of the deceased, of course, and to everyone else for a little while—a shock to the privileged and entitled who thought such a thing could never happen to them." He looked back at me. "But go out on the street now," he said. "Do you see any effect, *really*, out there? It passed right through them as if they were intangible." He sipped his drink. "Once in a while someone tries to write something profound about it, and they always fail, and the critics are always angry that they didn't do it justice. And all I can think is: Oh, New York, get over yourself!" He adopted a stage whisper: "What they can't face, none of them, is its insignificance. People died in an act of war. Wow! How unusual!" He said the last three words so loud I jumped off my seat. "It's terrible—" he pretended to wipe away tears "—now, can you please give me directions to the Louis Vuitton store?" Görbe snorted, staring back at the bartender. "It passed through them like they were ghosts," he said. "As it should have." He nodded. "*As it should have.*"

Görbe grunted and shifted on his stool and for a second I thought I saw something there, a break in the front he was putting on. "Listen, I lived through events a million times worse in Hungary—the war, the siege—like a lot of people. It wasn't one day, it was six years, and, believe me, it didn't lead to any great spiritual awakening!" He waved his hands in the air. "It happened. It was bad. And afterwards? Well, it will happen again. And in between you forget. You go back to your entertainments and schemes and obsessions and carry on. And that," he said, "is *all* there is to say about it."

Görbe rose drunkenly from his stool and bowed this way and that to the regulars, who didn't know whether to applaud or tear him apart.

His reputation for outrage extended even to the world of children's literature, which is no easy thing. When Görbe gave readings it wasn't rare to see a crowd of a hundred or more in attendance, and not the usual moms and dads and kids and teachers, but people you'd never have expected— Brooklyn hipsters, businessmen in blue suits, specialty booksellers with stacks of first editions Görbe would sign and they'd sell at inflated prices (they all had to put a wad of bills on his outstretched palm before he signed anything), and even some skeletal blondes cradling tiny dogs that trembled so bad they looked as if they were going to disintegrate. Each one was crazy about Görbe, many knew him personally, and when they lined up to have books signed he made sure to say something memorable to every one, statements so outrageous I was sure someone would burst into tears, either that or assault him. Instead they only laughed or turned to friends and said, "See! What did I tell you?" and Görbe nodded almost imperceptibly, made a flourish with his pen, and handed back the book. It seemed to me, looking at the lineup, that they loved him, and it was only later, near the end of the night, after I realized I hadn't seen one person open a book, or overheard a single comment about the writing, that I realized what was beneath it all: a fascination that was all about Görbe's appearance and character. It was him they were there for. The signings were one of those New York events you went to to prove your coolness. Worst of all, I sensed Görbe not only knew this but encouraged it, as if he spent as much time rehearsing the crazy diatribes and remarks—like some kind of comedy routine—as he did writing the books. This, too, was part of the process.

During his career Görbe had sold millions of books, gone on innumerable book tours, and the few times he invited me to his apartment in Queens I peeked at some of the royalty cheques on his desk, amazed to think he made that much and still lived in such a hole. There were only two places in the apartment that made it look as if he hadn't given up on life: the draughtsman's table where he did his work, spotlessly clean, the various tools neatly organized; and the mantelpiece where photographs of his wife, Zella, sat carefully arranged so each image could be seen in its frame. I looked at the pictures, then around the house again to see if I'd missed anything—an article of clothing, a pair of shoes—that might suggest a woman was also living there. But I saw nothing.

Görbe came into the room carrying two huge snifters filled with Crimean Cup à la Marmora, his belly brushing the doorframe as he squeezed through with a scraping of shirt buttons. "What're you looking at?" He stopped when I pointed to the pictures of his wife. "Zella," Görbe said, adding nothing more, just standing there, drinks in hand. I asked where she was. "Zella is away," came his quiet response. "In a better place." This seemed to break him out of his trance and he handed me a drink and changed the subject.

Whenever Görbe spoke about his work there was a complete absence of the technical or practical aspects of publishing. Just as when he read to my sons, he spoke as if he was a privileged reader rather than the author. He was never sure, he said, where the story was going even as his writing and drawing proceeded, always one step ahead of his conscious intentions. This was the real Görbe, I always thought, not the clown at the bar and readings, but the guy who, when he talked of his work, seemed eased of all the flesh he carried, his need to filter the world through a cigar, his overindulgence with booze and food. The real Görbe grew excited talking of clouds hollowed out by sparrows, of fire escapes woven out of iron roses growing miles into the air, of bricks made of compacted song turned into choruses conducted with wrecking balls. I'd seen him like that with my kids, and guessed that when he went on tours to the tiny libraries of Idaho and Arkansas and Nebraska he was like that too—naive, filled with wonder, released from the persona he climbed into, like some fat suit, every morning in Queens.

"You like my kids, huh?" I asked one night as we stood on the balcony of the apartment I'd been renting, subsidized by NYU, on the fourteenth floor with a view of the Empire State Building and its coloured lights. But Görbe just sucked his cigar and looked at me as if the question was a trap he wasn't going to walk into. I scratched the back of my head. "Well, you see, it's just that I was . . . Well, it's weird that you'd be so friendly to me just because fifty years ago you dated my aunt. A celebrity like you."

Görbe looked at me then as if he wanted to throw me over the balcony. "The reason I'm so friendly," he growled, "is because you're such an asshole."

I looked at him and tried to laugh.

"You're bumping your head on the glass ceiling of your mediocrity. And you're wide awake to it—why your agent doesn't return your emails; why the writers at NYU show no interest in you; why New York leaves you cold. Most people can look away from that, dream up excuses—'Oh, my agent is just busy'; 'Oh, the writers at NYU are all self-important dickheads'; 'Oh, New York is so superficial'—but not you, right? You know better than anyone you're not going to make it, and you can't hide it from yourself."

I think I spluttered. I had no idea how to respond. And then, in a moment I'll never forget, Görbe reached for my hand. It was the weirdest gesture. I tried to pull back from it, but the touch was so lonely, so childlike, it seemed more for his sake than mine, and when I gave in to it Görbe seemed to shrink, to fall into himself, clinging to me in the Manhattan night with the cavernous streets below, snow drifting past. For some reason I felt the need to say something reassuring to Görbe, to whisper him an apology for the world— "Everything will be fine, you'll see"—when in fact it should have been him apologizing to me.

It was partly because of that conversation, but mainly because of my curiosity about Zella, that the next morning I went into the archives at NYU—combing through old copies of the *Times*, *Observer*, and even the *Post*—to piece together Görbe's story. My aunt said he'd been a prominent children's author during the communist era, as far as prominence went in those days, and he'd certainly had no trouble, as far as she or any of their mutual acquaintances could say, with the Soviet authority. "In fact," she admitted, "he helped me out with his connections when I needed it." As for his books, she said they "were like a utopia." The children in them wanted to stay inside a dream, to realize a better world, and the communists liked that. "The kids were the proletariat," she wrote, "at least according to the communist reviewers." The waking world was the world as it is; and dream was the world as it could be. It was a pretty simple-minded interpretation, like most of them, but it saved Görbe. In other words, he had a good life under the Party—made enough money, had a nice apartment, ate and drank well. So nobody was really sure why he left. "As for his wife," my aunt's letter said, "I met her only once. She was just like Görbe except worse—dreamy, childish, never comfortable among adults. In fact, what seemed good in him seemed somehow bad in her. But maybe I was just jealous."

There was almost nothing in the archives about Zella. For all the publicity given Görbe—starting with his defection from Hungary, played up relentlessly in the press, and by Görbe himself as an "escape towards the dream" (so much for the communist utopia)—there was only one article that dealt at all with his wife. Sure, there was a mention here or there, a comment about them having better "food and medical care and lifestyles" in the U.S., and a statement by Görbe saying his "private life" was "private" when asked in the early

1970s about how he and Zella were adjusting to New York. But that was pretty much it. There was nothing about their home life (not even one of those lousy spreads, so common with children's authors, where some reporter visits them at home to prove that he really is a joyous family man with kids and a wife and colourful wallpaper and a house filled with constant storytelling); nothing about his career from "her" point of view (one of those pieces where the wife comments on her husband's zany writing process, his odd schedules, his fun-loving ways with the kids in the park); in fact nothing about Görbe having a wife or any home life at all. Zella's public appearances, rare in any case, stopped entirely after 1975, as did any mention of her on Görbe's part. His entire persona was public, and, as such, especially after days and days of reading about it, totally put on, or so it seemed to me, for maximum publicity.

Most amazing were the pictures. My aunt had hinted at the transformation Görbe had undergone since the 1960s, but it was beyond what I'd expected. He'd been slight, almost pixyish, at the time of his arrival in New York, and what happened to him over the years was so extreme I could only think his metabolism had been damaged. There was no way you could get that fat in that short a time all by yourself. Part of the problem early on was that he hadn't figured out how to dress for it. He was still wearing the clothes of a skinny man—narrow pants and tucked-in shirts—through much of the 1970s and '80s. It wasn't until the '90s that he adopted the black suit and overcoat whose layers smoothed his folds and bumps of flab. It was why he took up the cigar as well—his features had sunk so far into the flesh of his face he needed something sticking out like that, a flag, to remind us he was still in there. And with the physical change came increasing accounts of bad behaviour—sarcasm, insults, fist fights. I was surprised so few articles commented on how a writer of such fantastical stories, of a world mapped out with such visionary innocence, did little more than satisfy his appetite for food, booze, tobacco and outrage. There was nothing beyond that, just the immensity of his cravings, as if Görbe had become the monster excluded from his books.

That, at least, seemed to be Zella's opinion. The one article I did find on her was a page six piece from the *New York Post*, a single paragraph mostly taken up with the names of celebrities who'd attended a recent "bash" for one of Görbe's books in 1975. They gave her three sentences: "It appears the booze was flowing pretty freely. Zella Görbe, the author's wife, was acting 'erratic,' according to one guest. Before being escorted home by a private nurse, she regaled the room with stories of her husband's weight, calling him a 'fat disgusting pig' one minute, then swooning over her 'little boy' the next." There was nothing else, and however much I scanned through the information I'd gathered, returning to paragraphs and statements, there was no more about Zella's "behaviour," nothing to suggest she was a drunk, certainly nothing about a "private nurse," though I did note a number of photographs where there was a third figure present—an older woman, dressed well but very straight, always in the background near Zella. Since none of the photographs listed her among the guests, either the newspapers didn't know her name or she wanted it kept out. She looked stern, a mother figure, and the pictures made me recall what my aunt had said about Görbe when he was twenty years old: still afraid of the dark, playing hide-and-seek, climbing into the attic as if it was the entrance to a palace.

During that last month I kept my research hidden from Görbe. I worried about how he'd react. But Görbe must have sensed something, because he paid more attention to me than before, coming over unannounced with presents for the kids, sitting by the kitchen table (as much of him as would fit, anyhow) complimenting Marcy's cooking and listening to her talk half-jokingly about how I couldn't enjoy New York because I was so wrapped up in making contacts here, so obsessed with publishing in the right places, so distraught at not getting on, that the kids had started jumping on my back while I sat at the computer just to get some attention. "Ah, ambition," Görbe muttered. "Toxic as poison."

He even showed up to two dismal readings arranged by my U.S. publisher.

"Well, that sucked," he said, afterwards. "It's interesting that the woman in the audience—or I guess I should just say 'the audience,' period—didn't even bother to buy a book. With all our eyes on her you think she'd have the decency."

"The only thing worse than giving a reading is having to attend one," I replied.

"Absolutely," said Görbe. "You note that I never read myself. I just get up there and bullshit for a while. It's all they want to hear anyhow."

"More of your bullshit."

"Right. More of my bullshit." He laughed and blew a big cloud of cigar smoke. "You should think about that some time."

"It doesn't matter," I said. "I read, I don't read, it's all the same."

"That's the spirit!"

It was, I think, the only way he knew to cheer me up, though of course I didn't *need* to be cheered up. My failures were something I'd accepted, or at least stopped trying to avoid or explain. And that was the problem: the more Görbe came to my readings, or said he liked my book, or tried to get me to not take it so seriously, the more tiresome it became. I had become his foil, the failure against which he could measure his success, the person he might have been had he not so successfully managed his public persona and with it his career. Time would prove me wrong, of course—that is, I *was* Görbe's foil, but not in the way I thought—but during those weeks I was irritated by his condescension, and one night, at two in the morning, after we'd consumed more Brandy Sangarees than advisable, I turned to Görbe and said, "How's your wife?"

"My wife?" Görbe turned with the cocktail lifted partway to his lips. "My wife is none of your goddamn business."

"Oh, I see," I said. "You're the only one who's allowed to get personal." Görbe said nothing, but I could see he was ready to hit me. I felt tears come to my eyes, not because of the implied violence, but for exactly the opposite reason, for the effort Görbe had been making, in his own way, to make me see what was important, and instead of which I was trying to get to him, to bring him down to my level, which was also a way of raising myself to his. "Why are you doing this? Why are you trying so hard with me?" I pressed my face closer to his, not caring what he did. "When I called you I thought we'd meet for coffee and you'd give me the usual bullshit about writing and living in Manhattan, and I'd give you the usual bullshit about how honoured I feel to be here, and we'd never see each other again."

He grabbed my shirt and lifted me off the bar stool and slammed me against the bar—it felt as if my spine had snapped—then hauled me out of the room so fast my feet couldn't keep up, and dumped me on the sidewalk out front. Then he went back inside.

I don't know how long I stayed there, blind with humiliation. The feeling was so intense it somehow rebounded on itself and made me shameless, sitting on the pavement not caring who saw me, my clothes soaking up the slush, indifferent to Görbe's voice back in the bar telling everyone how lucky I was. I got home and Marcy asked why I was wet, and I couldn't look at her, and I couldn't look in on Henry and Benjamin asleep in their beds. I was so consumed by what Görbe had done I couldn't focus on anything.

The next morning Görbe left his apartment at ten, hopping the subway into Manhattan and then the M35 bus to Ward's Island. He was dressed as always—black suit, black tie, the overcoat, the cigar. He wasn't reading anything, wasn't looking around, wasn't muttering more than a quick hello to the bus driver. He took a seat and stared straight ahead, and once in a while he'd open a big sketchbook on his lap and make a note or doodle a picture for the next installment of the *Atlas*.

The morning started with snow, by noon it was rain, and I got off a block after he did to avoid suspicion and got soaked running back to catch Görbe checking in with the receptionist and moving down one of the corridors of the Manhattan Psychiatric Center. After he was gone, I went up to the receptionist and said I was there to visit Zella Görbe. She looked at me a bit, wanting to say something, but in the end kept it to herself. "Her husband just checked in, too," she muttered.

I crept down the corridor after him, hoping not to be seen, and when I came to Zella's room I skirted it and then snuck back and peeked in the window.

He was sitting in what seemed an absurdly small chair, all that weight on those spindly chrome legs, his coat hitting the floor in folds around his ankles.

The woman in the bed looked as if she'd been there all her life. But for some reason—maybe because she'd been there so long, removed from the stresses of lived life, taxes and sick kids and getting to work on time—Zella looked radiant, her face smooth of wrinkles, her skin white, her hair carefully arranged, to the point where I wouldn't have been surprised to find that someone came around every morning to clean her up. As I peeked in further I saw the woman from the photographs, the one always in the background, aged so much I wouldn't have recognized her except I knew she'd be there—the private nurse Görbe had been paying for who knows how long to look after Zella. For a second it seemed to me that the nurse, with her thinning hair and withered face and bent back, was somehow paying the price, physically, for Zella's radiance. Closing my eyes I leaned against the wall and listened to her and Görbe. They were speaking Hungarian. It was the first time I'd heard Görbe use the language. The nurse's name was Zsuzsa, and what they spoke of was

Zella's condition, how often the orderlies shifted her body to prevent bedsores, whether there was anything Görbe needed ("No" was his reply, though he thanked Zsuzsa for her concern), how his next book was coming along ("On time as always," was his tired reply), and whether Zsuzsa needed anything ("You've looked after me just fine," said the old woman). Then, after a short pause in which both of them seemed to be avoiding the next topic, Zsuzsa asked Görbe if he'd reconsidered "the treatment" proposed by "Dr. Norris." He replied so loudly I heard every word: "I've told you, I'm not ever going to agree to that. It's too risky." Zsuzsa's silence made it plain just how much she disagreed, or how little she believed that the "risk" was for him the only, or even the main, consideration.

"Can I help you, sir?" I was startled out of my eavesdropping by a nurse. I opened my eyes to find her standing in front of me, her hand on my shoulder as if she was worried I'd fall down. "Are you okay?"

"Oh," I said. "I'm just tired. A bit dizzy."

"Come over here." She did as I'd hoped and led me away from Zella's room to another waiting area, returning a second later with a glass of water.

"I was on my way to see Dr. Norris," I said.

"Oh, he's not in today," said the nurse. "Did you have an appointment?"

"Well, no . . . I'm a writer. A journalist. I heard he's been experimenting with some new treatment and I was thinking maybe there was a story in it."

She looked at me strangely. "Well, I'm sure I wouldn't know anything about that." She got up and smoothed the fabric of her uniform on either hip, and said, "I hope you're feeling better." I told her I was, and the minute she was gone I rose to leave as well.

It didn't take me long to look up Dr. Norris and discover he was a research physician at the Manhattan Psychiatric Center working on an experimental procedure for patients with "severe catatonia resulting from schizophrenia." I didn't have a lot of use for the article—it was filled with technical jargon I didn't understand—except it gave me the window onto Görbe I'd been looking for. Zella was schizophrenic, the disease had worsened over time, and the reason Görbe lived in such poverty was because he spent all of his money on her care, and it didn't matter to him, because without Zella there was no life for him *worth* spending money on. I sat in the Bobst Library with the research in front of me and wondered what I was doing, how I'd come to this, obsessing over the troubles of a man who'd gone through more suffering than I could conceive, and beside which my own failures in New York amounted to nothing. I wondered, too, why Görbe had not taken up Dr. Norris's offer, for it seemed to me that neither he nor Zella had anything to lose. I'd seen her on the bed, so vegetative that whatever position they moved her body into it stayed there, like a mannequin. Even death seemed better than that. So why didn't he agree to it? And I think it was this, the hopelessness of Görbe's situation, his inability to do what he knew he had to do, that made me get up and call him.

We met in a Cuban diner, Margon, on Forty-sixth Street near Times Square. It was the dirtiest place I'd ever gone to in

New York, but the food was the best, and Görbe was already into his third plate by the time I arrived. He watched suspiciously as I made my way along the narrow space between the tables and the people lined up by the counter. I'd told him over the phone I really wanted to "clear the air" over what happened at Lotus, my voice edging into an apology when he just coughed nervously into the phone and said, "Forget it, it's nothing, come have lunch at Margon."

"How's your back?" he asked, and it took me a second to realize he was referring to slamming me against the bar. I shrugged, dropped my coat, got my food, and came back just as the waitress, who knew Görbe personally, was bringing him his fourth plate.

I waited until we finished eating, talking in the meantime about nothing—the business of writing, the stories we were working on—before asking, "How's Zella?"

Görbe looked like he wanted to jump the table and grab my throat. But he was too fat, and was hemmed in by the people behind and beside him. In fact, the only way he could stand up was to upend the table, along with the food of everyone sitting there.

"I know about Dr. Norris," I said, "and the terrible decision you have to make . . ."

But it was coming out all wrong, even to my ears. It occurred to me then, staring into Görbe's enraged face, that I had no idea why I'd come here. I had thought, sitting in the library and the subway on the way up, that knowing what I knew would show Görbe I sympathized with him, and maybe I'd finally break through the front he put up, maybe he'd find in me someone he could talk to. But I wasn't really there for Görbe.

"You shut your fucking mouth," he said, pushing his chair back, bumping the man behind, who fell into his food and turned intending to say something but stopped when he saw how huge and mean Görbe was. "You don't know anything about Zella."

I slid out of my seat and stood across the table out of reach. "You're just like me," I said. In that moment it dawned on me why he didn't seek out Dr. Norris, why he didn't want Zella to wake up. "You're nowhere," I said, more to myself than him.

I left the table and went into the street. Görbe tried to get at me through the crowd but I was too fast, and he followed for only a few blocks before giving up, stopping on the edge of the crosswalk outside Toys "R" Us looking after me as I paused on the stairs to the subway. "You don't want her to wake up!" I yelled, though it's unlikely he heard me over the honking of horns, the roar of music, the shouts of Times Square. "You want her to sleep forever so she won't see what you've had to become!" But it was obvious Görbe wasn't listening to me. His gaze had gone beyond that, beyond whatever I might have been saying, all those unhappy truths, beyond even Hungary itself, where he'd been young once, and happy, and with Zella. For that was the person she would have looked for had she awakened—the self Görbe had left behind in the effort to get her here, to the best doctors and medicine, the best chance at recovery, doing whatever he could to foot the bills even if it meant turning himself into a monster she'd never have recognized. He was invisible in the eyes of the only person he cared about. Like me, he was a zero.

But I was wrong about that. Though it wasn't until the following year, in the bookstore with Benjamin, that I realized it. I had thought that Görbe, like me, was trapped in a world of failure, and we'd found each other, two men without any illusions. Except of course I was full of them, for I had at home what Görbe would never have, only I didn't know it, didn't treasure it enough, and I think this recognition was what he'd been expecting from me during our time in New York, as if his tough talk and violence could jolt me into awareness. Instead, I had gone to Margon to extend my affection—to show the monster he wasn't alone in his world—only to find that I was the monster, the only one, without the slightest clue to what affection really was.

The Animals of
the Budapest Zoo,
1944–1945

I T WAS Sándor who finally posed the question in November of 1944, when it was clear the Red Army would take Budapest from the Arrow-Cross and the Nazis. "If there's a siege, how are we going to protect the animals?" he asked, looking from one face to the next, totally baffled by the fact that everyone seemed far more interested in how they were going to protect *themselves*. "We're going to have to work double hard," replied Oszkár Teleki, director of the zoo, though Teleki was the first to run off that December when the Russian tanks entered the squares and boulevards, telling his secretary he was going to meet with the Red Army and insist that they respect the animals, and then asking her to pack all of the zoo's money into a bag, just in case.

Sándor and József were the last to see Teleki leave, intercepting him near the exit and asking whether he had plans in place for the aquarium, where even now the attendants were working around the clock to keep the water from freezing by stirring it with paddles. Both men were suspicious because Teleki was wearing an overcoat belted at the waist, an elegant hat, and was carrying an ivory-handled umbrella in one hand and a suitcase bulging with money in the other, banknotes fluttering from every crack. As well, Teleki wasn't taking the eastern exit out of the zoo—as he normally did when going home—but the western one, in the direction of Buda, of Germany, and away from the advancing Soviets.

"We should feed you to the lion," said Sándor, to which Teleki responded by fingering his collar, looking nervous, and telling them he'd be back "really quite soon." "You're not going anywhere," said József, and he grabbed hold of Teleki as he was turning from them, jerking him so hard the old man's knees gave out and József had to hold him up above the muddy cobblestones.

József was about to do something else to him then—hit him, or pull the suitcase from his grip—but when he saw Teleki's face—the bared teeth, the eyes darting back and forth, the desperation to escape—looking just like the animals did whenever there was an air raid, explosion of shells, the rattle of gunfire, flames shooting over the palisades, he let him go, knowing that the money would soon have as little currency as a fascist arm band. But if he'd looked a little closer he might have caught something else in Teleki's face, the city's future in its wrinkles and lines, a vision of what the next hundred days would be like, when Budapest's populace would be driven to looting and stealing and scavenging and murder—and there would be much of that, down by the banks of the Danube where the Arrow-Cross executed the Jewish men, women, and children after marching them naked through the snow from the ghetto; or Széll Kálmán Square after the failure of Hungarian and German soldiers to break through the Soviet encirclement, bodies piled in doorways and cellar stairs and in other piles of bodies in an attempt to shield themselves from the rockets and snipers and tanks the Red Army had stationed along the routes they knew they would take—when the dead, whether half buried in ice, the muck of the river, or the frost that settled on them from their last laboured breaths, would speak to Sándor, and Sándor would in turn relay their message to József, the thing he was more and more obsessed with as the nights of the siege dragged on, the metamorphosis at work all around them. In the early days, when József was still alert, still sane enough to ask him what the hell he was talking about, Sándor muttered about human beings turning into "flowers and animals," and held up Ovid, or some other book he'd stolen from the abandoned library in Teleki's office, and whistled quietly, reading quietly, until József fell back asleep.

It got so bad that József would need that whistling to sleep, and when it stopped, late at night, and József snapped awake, more often than not he found that Sándor wasn't there. He'd gone into the night, or disappeared, expending himself as if to prove that becoming nothing could be a transformation too. Though he was always back by morning with his dirty nails and oily face and tattered clothes and the look of someone who'd lost himself along the way.

But before all that, December turned into January. Unlike many of the other attendants, Sándor and József did not have families, and so they saw no reason to go home from the zoo except to risk dying in the streets, or being bombed out of their tiny apartments, or starving to death in the cellars that had been converted into bomb shelters. When the zebras were found slaughtered in their pens, large strips of meat carved hastily from their shoulders and flanks and bellies no doubt by starving citizens, the two men fed what was left to the lion and moved into the vacated stalls, Sándor ranting about how the zebras should still be alive and it was the looters who should have been fed to the lion.

When Márti, another of the attendants, was shot in late January as she was trying to tear up a bit of grass for the giraffe in the nearby Városliget, and somehow managed to stumble back to the zoo, she described in a sleepy voice what she had seen out there in the city. Sándor tried to get her to be quiet, to rest, pulling the blanket to her chin, but she kept speaking of the shapes of flame as a child might speak of clouds, seeing in them animals dead or dying, their souls somehow escaping the bodies trapped in the zoo, transmigrated into fire, taking revenge on the city. She said it was burning, all of it—the Western Station, the mansions along Andrássy Boulevard, the trees in the park like used matchsticks. She'd seen a street where blue flame was dancing through every pothole and crack, playing around the rim of craters, the gas mains ruptured underneath, continuing to bleed. "It was like a celebration," said Márti, before closing her eyes and falling into a sleep neither József nor Sándor tried waking her from.

The night after she died, they climbed the roof of the palm garden, which gave them a view beyond the palisades toward where the fighting was going on, now far to the west, mortars and tanks and bullets pounding the lower battlements of Buda castle, flashes of white light whenever the smoke cleared. The sky held odd things—crates falling by parachute onto the ice over the Danube; gliders crashing at night, guided by spotlights into trees and buildings; ash rising like a million flies.

Sándor tried to keep reading during those days, scrambling up a ladder to Teleki's library after the air raid destroyed the staircase, as if the books were more than a distraction, as if they were necessary to hurry his mind along, as if it was possible to stop thinking by thinking too much, by exploding thought, at a time when having a mind was, more often than not, a handicap. Of the two of them he'd always been the one given to dreams, and as they sat on the roof of the palm garden that night, Sándor spoke to József of what he'd discovered in Teleki's office, an entire library, books ancient and modern, devoted to the subject of animals—"I had no idea Teleki was such an intellectual," growled Sándor above the crackling of guns—and then began to speak of how characters in myths and stories and fairy tales turned into horses and flowers and hounds and back again, or into other people entirely, crossing limits as if they didn't exist, becoming something else. "But now, I mean *now*"—he waved his arms around as if he could encompass the last five centuries—"now we don't transform. We're *individuals* now. *Selves.* Fixed in place."

"Well," said József, turning over Sándor's ideas, "what difference does it make? They died in wars just like us."

"Maybe that's how they explained death," said Sándor, his face glazed with the light of nearby fires. "Becoming something else." He gazed down through the glass roof of the palm house. "Anyhow, we're not dead yet," he purred, flexing his fingers, József thought, as if they could become claws.

"But did they stay themselves, I mean, when they became something else?"

"That's just it. There was no self to begin with. Just an endless transformation, a constant becoming."

"So then a lion was worth the same as a human being."

"Well, I don't know about 'worth,'" said Sándor, smiling at József. "But there wasn't the same way of telling the differ . . ."

But before Sándor could take the idea any further, he was already crashing through the roof of the palm garden as the shell exploded, disappearing into the fire and shock waves and rain of glass, while József was able to scramble down before the next mortar fell whistling into the hole the last one had made, scrambling down, and then through the cracked doors of the glass building, shards raining all around, the alligators and hippos of the central exhibit too shocked to snap or charge at him, lifting Sándor's body from where it lay face down in a pool of water, and smiling despite himself when his friend began spluttering, bruises spreading across his face. Two days later, the alligators died, frozen stiff in their ice-encrusted jungle, though the hippos lived on, drawn to the very back of the tank, where the artesian well kept pumping out its thermal waters, the fat on their stomachs and backs thinning away as it fed them, all three growing skinnier and skinnier in the steam.

Later, when Lieutenant-General Zamertsev questioned József about the lion, trying to get him to reveal where it was hiding, József resisted by speaking instead about the alligators and hippos, about the destruction of the palm garden as the moment when Sándor and he realized they would have to "liberate" as many of the animals as they could. Zamertsev looked at him, and then turned to the Hungarian interpreter and whispered something, and then the interpreter said to József, "You actually thought it was a good idea to let the lions and panthers and cougars and wolves roam free?"

József knew that Zamertsev didn't believe him, that he was not accusing him of excessive sentimentality so much as lying, or maybe outright craziness, as if between the destruction of the siege and Sándor's ranting, József's brain had also become unhinged. Zamertsev was right in a sense, because it wasn't what happened to the alligators that made Sándor and József wander around the zoo unlocking cages, but rather the arrival of the Soviet soldiers, Zamertsev's men, high atop their horses, demanding that they first release a wolf, then a leopard, and then a tiger, all so they could hunt them, these half-starved creatures that could barely walk never mind run, chasing them down with fresh horses and military ordnance, drunk and laughing and twice crazy with what the war had both taken from and permitted them.

The attendants were into the champagne that night, having discovered a crate of the expensive stuff in one of the locked trunks Teleki left in his office, along with several sealed tins of caviar and a box of excellent cigars. Sándor handed out bottles and tins and matches to József and Gergö and Zsuzsi, all of them so hungry and tired of thinking about what might happen to them the following week, or tomorrow, or the next minute that they popped the corks as fast as possible and began drinking, trying to wash from themselves the cold and fear and the dead animals all around, as if by concentrating you could keep only to the taste of what was on your tongue, and think of nothing else.

It was of course Sándor's idea, the action he decided on after he'd drained his second bottle of Törley's, leaving off the caviar, looking at everyone's grubby knuckles, their wincing with the sound of another explosion or rattle of gunfire or the slow fall of flares (falling so crookedly they seemed to be welding fractures in the sky). And so it was neither love nor logic that led them around the zoo that night but drunkenness, jingling keys pulled from Teleki's walls, moving past the carcasses in the monkey house, many of them frozen to the bars they'd been gripping when their heat gave out and they laid their heads onto their shoulders welcoming the last warmth of sleep; or in the tropical aviary, the brightly coloured feathers gone dull on the curled forms, their heads dusted with frost and tangled in the netting overhead, as close as they would ever again come to the sun; or in the aquarium, where someone now gone, perhaps Márti, had broken through the glass of the tanks and tried to chip some of the fish out of the ice, whether in some pathetic attempt to thaw them back to life or to eat them no one could guess. In the end, it was less an organized act than a celebration, less motivated by reason or a goal than a delight in the moment when the cage swung open and something else bounded or crawled or slithered or flew out, the four of them downing champagne and running around, eagerly seeking the next thrill of release, opening after opening, an orgy of smashing those locks they'd worried over for years. And when it was over, when there wasn't a single cage left to open, an animal to free, then Gergö and Zsuzsi freed themselves, waltzing out the front gate straight into a warning shout, a halting laugh, a hail of machine-gun fire.

Which brought József and Sándor back to themselves in a hurry. "I'll bet it did," said Zamertsev, leaning over the table and staring at József, the shoulders and chest of his uniform covered with red stars and hammers and sickles and decorative ribbons. "And I guess that's when you got the idea of feeding my soldiers to the lion."

"It was your soldiers' horses we wanted," mumbled József, still so amazed by the last sound Sándor had made—he could imagine him tossing his head and baring his teeth and roaring so loudly it could be heard above the guns—that József might have been speaking to anybody, treating Zamertsev as though he was an acquaintance he'd met in a restaurant or café rather than someone who at any moment could have sent him out to be shot. "A lion can live a lot longer on a horse than a man, you know."

But the truth was, he wasn't so sure, for Sándor had frequently looked down upon the Russian soldiers (both from the roof of the palm garden, and later from the palisades) and licked his dry lips and recalled the Siege of Leningrad, wondering if people in Budapest would end up eating human flesh, as they were rumoured to have done there. At the time, József had not connected Sándor's actions with appetite, but with a hatred of the Soviets, because with all the dead German and Arrow-Cross soldiers not to mention civilians lying in the streets, perfectly preserved by a winter so cold even the

Danube had frozen over, there was no need to hunt the living. Sándor had made strange references to the Soviets and the Red Army as the two of them wandered around the zoo in the waning days of the siege, when most of the fires in Pest had gone out and the Russians were mopping up what was left of the enemy by marching Hungarian men and women in front of them through the streets and forcing them to call out, "Don't shoot, don't shoot, we're Hungarians, give yourselves up"; though to the west the fighting was still thick, relentless, out there across the Danube, on the Buda side of the city, where the Nazis and Arrow-Cross were holed up on Castle Hill, surrounded, running out of ammunition and food, dreaming of a breakout.

Of the animals they'd released, a few vultures and eagles remained, circling above the zoo and drifting down lazily to feed on the plentiful carrion in the streets. When they returned to their nests, Sándor would wonder what was more poisonous in their bellies, the flesh of communists or fascists. He would say things like that. They held discussions, long into the night, and József said the fascists were wrong to speak of their beliefs, the society they envisaged, as natural, for no animal was ever interested in war for glory, or compiling lists of atrocities, or mastering the world, or getting rid, en masse, of another species, and that more often than not what animals did was tend only to their immediate needs, and in doing so created a kind of harmony . . . "Harmony?" laughed Sándor. "You sound like a communist!" And he spoke of how a male grizzly will kill the cubs belonging to another male so that the female will mate with him; how he'd once heard about a weasel that came into a yard and killed twenty-five chickens, biting them through the neck, without taking a single one of the corpses to eat; how certain gulls will steal eggs from others, sit on them until they hatch, and then feed the chicks to their own young; how a cat will play with whatever it catches, torturing it slowly to death, all out of amusement. "Does that sound like *harmony* to you?" he asked József.

Zamertsev looked a moment at József, who sat there trembling in the creaking chair in the headquarters the Red Army had put up in one of the half-obliterated mansions along Andrássy Boulevard, still dressed in the ragged attendants' uniform, unwashed these hundred days, his hair matted and filthy, so shrivelled by hunger Zamertsev thought he could see the man's spine poking through the skin of a belly fallen in on its emptiness. Then Zamertsev came around the desk and grabbed József's chin roughly in one hand and said, "I'm not interested in what you think I want to hear. Politics. . . ." He glanced at the interpreter, who raised his eyebrows. "I want to protect my . . . the people's army . . . which means telling me about Sándor, what he did, what I'm dealing with . . ."

Protect the people's army. József wanted to laugh. If your soldiers had been kept in check, if they hadn't come in wanting a safari all their own, we wouldn't have had to free the animals in the first place. After that, Sándor seemed intent on prowling around the zoo as if he was an animal himself, even though József warned him to stay inside, because there wasn't a day when one of the carnivores that was still alive didn't come upon another, the polar bear devouring the wolves, the wolves taking apart the panther, the lion emerging at night.

But that's how it was then: József working hard to conserve himself, to survive, while Sándor had given up on everything—first sleep, then food, then safety—divesting himself of every resource.

Somehow Sándor had gotten word to the Russians that the lion was living in the tunnels of the subway, and when the other predators were gone—having finally eaten one other, or been shot, or wandered off—then the lion took to eating stray horses. Sándor would point out its victims to József when they went out to gather snow for drinking water, Sándor hobbling along, weakened enough by then to need the help of one of Teleki's canes, though he still had enough presence of mind to show József how it was teeth not ordnance that had made the gaping holes along the flanks and backs and bellies of the horses. "The lion must be weakened," said Sándor, clutching himself, "otherwise, it would have dragged the carcass away to where it lives, and eaten the whole thing."

"Or maybe it's too full to bother," said József, envious of its teeth.

At night, József would awaken and not even turn toward Sándor's pallet, because he knew he wasn't there. Night after night he'd awaken and Sándor would be out. Sleepwalking is what József thought at first, but when he asked about it, Sándor would laugh and say he'd been out "getting horses." There wasn't a lot to what Sándor said anymore, though truth to tell József himself was having trouble coming up with anything to say, and of saying it, when he did, in a meaningful way.

"My soldiers tell me Sándor was meeting with them," said Zamertsev. "That he was arranging lion hunts in the subway tunnels."

"You could fit a herd of horses in there," nodded József. "But it was very dark. And the soldiers were always drunk. And there were bullets flying all over the place."

"It was one way to feed the lion," said Zamertsev. "You knew about it. Perhaps even helped him?"

No, József shook his head, and then a second later, he nodded yes, and then stopped, not knowing who or what he'd helped, deciding that it certainly wasn't Sándor. Zamertsev was wrong to think that Sándor was feeding the lion, for that's what József had thought at first as well, as if the lion and Sándor were two separate things. But it was better that Zamertsev think this than what József knew to be the truth, the transformation he'd witnessed the day he'd carried Sándor to the subway entrance, one of the few that wasn't bombed out or buried in rubble or so marked by the lion's presence that even humans could sense the danger there. He'd pressed his body against the door—it was an old service entrance used by the engineers and subway personnel, wide enough to fit a small car, covered with a corrugated metal door— envisioning that awful metamorphosis.

As it turned out Zamertsev wasn't like the other soldiers, so easily led into the same trap. He sent for one of his men and told him to get a map of the old Franz Josef Underground Line, staring silently at József until the blueprints were delivered, at which point he spread them across the desk and began tracing the possible routes into and out of the subway, ignoring entirely the service entrance József had told him about. It was as if Zamertsev knew, József thought, as if he'd discerned the bits of the story he'd left out, and was even now being guided over the map by what József hadn't told him about that last night, when Sándor had crawled over and whispered to him of the effort of getting horses for the lion, of how weak he'd become, though what József really heard in his voice was a hunger so great it would have swallowed him then and there if Sándor had had the strength, if he felt he could have overpowered his friend. "I can't do it alone," Sándor mumbled. "I can't walk." When József asked if their friendship no longer meant anything to him, Sándor rubbed the place in his skull where his cheeks had been and said something about "word getting around," and the soldiers "staying away," and then paused and smiled that terrible smile, lipless, all teeth. "It's *because* I'm your friend that I'm asking you to do this. There is no greater thing a friend could do," he said, laughing without a trace of happiness.

József had looked at him then, turning from where he'd been facing the wall, hugging himself as if in consolation for the emptiness of his stomach, for the delirium of this siege without end, the constant fear, the boredom, waiting on the clock, the slow erasure of affection, of the list of things he would not do. "The city is destroyed," he said, not wanting to do as Sándor asked, not wanting even to address it, for he thought he'd caught another implication in his voice now, one even worse than what the words had at first suggested. "There are people dead and starving," he continued, "the Soviets are looting, hunting, raping, and you're worried about a lion. *Fuck the lion*," said József, "fuck everything," and he turned over on his pallet, lifting the layers of plastic sacks and tarpaulin they used for blankets. But Sándor nudged him again, and when József let out an exasperated moan and turned, he saw that his friend was already half transformed, the hair wild around his head and neck, his fingernails much longer than József's, and dirtier too, packed underneath with the hide and flesh of horses and men and what else, reduced from malnourishment and injury and trauma to crawling around on all fours. "I need you," growled Sándor, though he had lost so much by then that it came out like a cough, the cords in his throat too slack, or worn, for much noise, and it cost him to raise his voice above a whimper.

Need me? wondered József, rising from the sheets and drawing Sándor's head to his chest. *You don't know what you need,* he thought, as if there were two pulses beating in counter-rhythm within Sándor, two desires moving him in opposite directions. He held him like that for a while, feeling his friend's eyelids blinking regularly against his skin, thinking of how Sándor had run out of the zoo after Gergö and Zsuzsi, trying to gather up their limp forms, of how often they'd found him squatting in the cage of this or that dead animal, as if by lifting a wing or an arm or a leg he might reanimate them, or, as József had once observed, actually put on the animal like a suit of clothes and become it, leaving his humanity behind. At the same time Sándor had been moving in the opposite direction, trying to keep in mind who he was, who he'd been, what he cared about.

"Listen, Sándor," he murmured, frightened by what was taking place in his friend's body, the spasms that passed through it as he held him. "You have to pull yourself together," he said, "the siege won't last forever." But Sándor was already past the idea of waiting, József knew that, past thinking of what had happened and what was to come. What he really wanted, what he needed, had nothing to do with József at all, for József was already disappearing for Sándor—disintegrating into the state of war, falling apart with the capital and the zoo, with the death of the animals—and all Sándor needed to realize his own disappearance was this one last act, this final favour. But things weren't like that for József, not yet, for the presence of Sándor was still keeping him intact, as if the strength of their friendship, the history they shared, whatever it was in his character that Sándor loved, could recall József to himself. He looked at Sándor and saw what the war had done to friendship after it had finished with everything else—with sympathy, with intelligence, with self-awareness, with loyalty and affection and love—all those impediments to survival, all those things that got in the way of forgetting who you were. It was for this that József envied Sándor, for Sándor had forgotten him just as he'd forgotten that the soldiers he'd fed to the lion were men, that the bodies the birds fed on where those of women and children, that there was even such a thing as his own life, or anyone else's, and that it might be worth preserving.

When he finally rose up with Sándor that night, carrying him in his arms like a child, József wasn't sure if he could do what Sándor wanted him to do, because he was still clinging to his friend's memory, unwilling to let him go, as he would weeks later, even more so, after the conversation with Zamertsev, after the Soviet hunting party had gone out—sober this time, no horses—carrying flashlights and headlamps, determined to do it right. He had set out that night in exactly the same way, out the door, moving along, bent with Sándor's weight under arc lights and stuttering street lamps, dodging patrols that weren't really patrols but an extension of the three days of free looting the commanders had granted their troops.

By then he knew what Sándor needed as much as Sándor did—this is what József would not tell Zamertsev—and when they arrived at the subway entrance and swung open the door and looked inside, József hesitated. And when Sándor, resting his head against his old friend's chest, asked to be put down on the threshold, József laughed and said no, it was fine, they could go in together, it didn't matter. "Please," said Sándor, jerking limply in József's arms. "You've been better with your grief," he said, "better able to use it—to help make yourself stronger." With this, József finally understood what Sándor wanted, and why, and József would remember it as the moment when he finally gave in to the siege, to its terrible logic, to what Sándor hoped to become, what he needed József to witness. He said goodbye before putting Sándor down and closing the door on him. Then there was only the weakness, from carrying his friend across the ravaged city, from using up what little strength was left in closing and slumping against the door, too tired now to pull it open, knowing he would have nightmares in the years to come—nightmares of banging on it, wrenching at the handle, calling out to Sándor—only to wake to the terror of loss, alone in the dark with all he'd been separated from, as if there was no way to figure out where he was, where he began and ended, until he realized what was out of reach. It was Sándor's last gift, to József and the lion both, what he thought they needed to live, as if grief could work that way, though in the end it was only what *he'd* wanted: the death of whatever it was—affection, friendship, love—that kept him in place, reminding him of what he was and in that way of what he'd seen, when all he wanted by then was the roar and the leap—the moment when he was finally something else.

Sailor's Mouth

I was 1957 and the sailor built a plastic boat. Everything on it was transparent—plastic hull, plastic mast, plastic sail—and he lay down in it with a sack of *kifli* and a jug of water and headed south from Budapest, down the Danube, toward the Black Sea."

"Did he make it?"

"No, he was seen. His boat is in the Museum of Failed Escapes."

"There's a museum like that?"

"It's in the ninth district. A private collection. One day I'll take you there."

"How did you get in?"

"I'll tell you later." Judit shrugged, her skin dark even for a Hungarian, long hair trailing on the pillow like rays from a black sun.

Her daughter, Janka, was five years old, with the same black hair. She was standing in the doorway the first night I carried her mother home. It was the tail end of an ordinary flirtation,

Judit pretending she was drunk and her guard was down and she was doing something she didn't do for any man—show him where she lived—while I held her arm saying the streets of the eighth district were no place for a woman in her condition, all giggles and hiccups, fingers fluttering in my face. But it was really Janka I was after, having listened to Judit describe her, the life they led, their home, the food they ate, the kind of places the girl played. When we arrived, there was an old woman holding the door—the grandmother I guessed—hair covered in a lace shawl, standing stooped on the other side of the open door threatening Janka with a beating, no dinner for a week, if she didn't come inside immediately. The old woman was unsurprised when Judit and I stumbled through, little Janka trailing behind grasping after her mother's hand. I put Judit on the couch, mumbling that she'd be okay, that she was just sleepy. The old woman stared at the floor, shaking her head. "I told her never to bring anyone here."

I was supposed to have stayed in Budapest only a day, then gone on to Romania. "You stay as long as it takes," my wife, Anna, said. We had a child already, seven years old, Miklós, who was as eager as his mother for a brother or sister, it didn't matter, he'd been waiting as long as he could remember, smiling into my face as I said goodbye at the airport, telling him I was going to a place where orphanages were overflowing with children desperate for older brothers. Anna stood there also smiling, stroking the back of Miklós's hair as I spoke to him, once in a while backing up what I said, even jumping in to describe what the little girl would look like—olive eyes, curly hair, dark brown skin—the three of us picking out names—Juliska, Klára, Mária—as we waited for me to go through security.

Anna and I had been cleared to adopt years ago, when it became obvious that the magic that had produced Miklós was gone, vanished along with the conversations we'd once had (apart from how our son was doing, how much money we needed for daycare, renovations, bills), and our interest in concerts and art galleries and sex with each other—everything gone except the three or four glasses of wine we drank every night (*that* we could still agree on), though by the time of my departure for Budapest Anna was slipping even in this, and making up for it by criticizing me for drinking too much. Instead of dealing with it, our marriage, we decided, or Anna did, to become political and adopt a child.

We'd gone through the adoption course, sitting beside other desperate couples, listening to lectures on cultural sensitivity, answering awkward questions about our sex life, swearing that we never touched drugs. We'd gotten our certificate, endured the routine visit of the social worker, who slept in our guest room and concluded his assessment by saying Anna and I had a "very strong bond of friendship," which means he knew we'd lied on the sex question.

But there was no baby. More than one agency told us we were too particular, wanting a girl, preferably no older than three (though we were willing to go as high as six) from that part of Hungary called Erdély—"Transylvania" in English—ceded to Romania in 1919 by the Treaty of Trianon. This was Anna's obsession, inherited from her beloved father, an old man when I knew him, hair poking from his ears, ceiling lights bringing out the veins in his head, which he shaved with electric clippers every morning. He was always sitting in the kitchen in that awful house in North Ward, old calendars clinging to the wall with their maps of Hungary from before 1919, and then, inside that territory, the tiny Hungary of today marked with a red border. Her father was one of those angry nostalgics—Trianon this, Trianon that; *"kis Magyarország nem ország, nagy Magyarország mennyország"*; fondly recalling how much lost territory Hitler had returned between the wars—gnashing his teeth at the two million ethnic Hungarians stranded in Erdély, how they were being "culturally cleansed," not allowed to publish in their own language, schools closed, whole villages uprooted and forcibly assimilated to the south, politicians such as Ceauşescu dreaming of their disappearance, barely restrained from the genocide they would have preferred—why wait three generations if you didn't have to?—when there'd be no one left to testify that the place had never been Romanian. Meanwhile the Hungarians kept hanging on—to their language, their culture, their identity—ninety years running.

Anna's father had lived through the siege of Budapest, the subject his rants on Erdély inevitably came around to, grumbling how the Hungarians had no choice at all, between the Nazis on one side and the Soviets on the other, and at least Hitler offered to give back territory the country had lost—"Over fifty percent of our nation taken away"; "No country lost as much as Hungary did and we'd even opposed going to war!"; "the French hated us, that's the reason for Trianon, prejudice pure and simple." It was as if his vision of the siege—soldier after soldier, death after death, his own memories of being stuck in Budapest, hungry and thirsty and terrified, that parade of fatal images—spun off the inked signatures of Trianon. He and his country had endured the siege—endured what came before, and what came after— because of Trianon. Nothing could dissuade him. I heard it every time I went there, and its naiveté, its absence of even a respectable hint of fatalism, as if you really should be able to expect justice in this world, made me crazy, and, worse, reminded me of my father, who'd wanted no part of that flailing impotence and the military solution it craved—the happy days of Hitler's Reich. My father had just wanted to forget, sitting in Toronto's Szécsényi Club drinking *pálinka* and playing *tarok*, happy his son had married a Hungarian girl and that his grandchildren would one day speak Hungarian. That was enough for him.

But it wasn't enough for Anna's father, and it wasn't enough for her. She wanted an orphaned girl—first because it was so hard for Hungarians in Erdély already, and second because girls were subhuman in Hungarian culture (this was Anna's refinement on her father's beliefs, one he would never have agreed with). An orphaned girl didn't have a chance. It was an act of "cultural rescue," that's what Anna said to the caseworker when he told us there were plenty of Romani kids, kids with AIDS, even some Greek, Bulgarian, Turkish, and of course whole battalions of Romanian kids filling the orphanages in Bucharest to overflowing. "The Hungarians in Transylvania look after their own," he said to us. "If you want a Hungarian girl there's tons in Hungary." But Anna shook her head. And when the agency did find us one, there was always some problem—a form we hadn't filled out, a glitch in the paperwork, another hidden processing fee—and after that another wait from six to eight months, by which point the child was gone. Either that or we made it to the finish line, received the file—the family records, the medical reports, the photographs—and Anna took them to our doctor, who held them in the light and said, "Hm, see these shadows under the left ear, those bumps, that could be something." He tilted the pictures. "Or it could be nothing." Anna would come home and brood over Scotch and soda, and after a few days request more information, which the agency could never obtain, and finally she'd turn down the adoption. Then I'd lie in bed at night listening as Anna talked in her sleep, apologizing to the child, begging forgiveness, smashing her fists so hard against her face I had to wake and then hold her while she cried. Finally, we decided I should go to Romania, that maybe I could do in person what we'd failed to do through bureaucracy.

"In the Museum of Failed Escapes there are sails made out of tinfoil," I can still hear Judit saying, her voice slurred, on the verge of laughter. Her drunkenness, I would realize, was more an affectation than reality, all part of the act, and that any day of the week she could have drunk me under the table. "They are perfect mirrors," she continued. The sailor set them afloat one day on the Sea of Hungary when there wasn't a cloud in the sky, and they sparkled so that a man could swim unseen from one shore to the next, because the snipers were blinded by the glittering armada.

"The Sea of Hungary? There's no Sea of Hungary!"

"There is. There are many. You don't know anything about this country."

"Where are they?"

"There's a map of it in the museum. One day I'll show it to you."

There are certain retreats you make—retreats that seem to come naturally—when your marriage is spent. I saw it with some clarity in Budapest, sitting up at night, Judit asleep in bed beside me, thinking back to that moment when things were at their worst, six or seven years ago, Miklós was two or three, staring out a window then as I was staring out of one now, dreaming of what it would be like to get the whole thing over with—the arguments, the divorce, splitting up our stuff, arranging custody, and then, after that, starting all over, the initial freedom, the loneliness, followed by another relationship, followed by a marriage that would more than likely end just as this one had. The problem in the sequence, no matter how I arranged it, was me. For years now I'd been doing more and more as Anna asked—keeping an eye out for dirty laundry; for meals I could make; chores around the house; driving Miklós here and there; sitting on the veranda with her at night drinking and talking, trying to be pleasant—a hundred minor obligations and pleasures, the careful work of putting your needs to one side to make sure that everything goes well, and then collecting your rewards: a child's laugh, your wife smiling thank you, your neighbour visiting with extra strawberries from the garden. It's perfect enough on the surface, but that's all it is, containing less and less of yourself, of what you really want, until one day you realize that the only life that matters, the only place you exist, is on the inside, a world you no longer mention, filled with wants so unrealizable there's no point in even talking about them, whole continents of desire taken off the map, excised but ever-present even as your wife and child talk to you and you pretend to listen.

This, I suppose, is why on one lonely business trip I ended up leafing through the Yellow Pages looking at the ads for escort services. It seemed ideal, the intentions were absolutely clear—sex on one side, money on the other—and none of the stuff people who had affairs, and I knew a few of them, had to deal with: running a second relationship involving as many compromises as the first, the fear of exposure, the snowballing of desire into demands: "I want us to take a trip together!" "I want you to leave your wife!" "If we're to continue together we have to do it honestly and in the open!" And so these people, most of them men, would be forced to choose between a home life that was, except for the occasional irrepressible urge, the one they wanted, and a life that had no basis except for those urges. Who needed *that* kind of stress? As far as relationships went, my marriage was as good as I was likely to get, and beyond that I just wanted to be left alone, and to have sex. The call girls, prostitutes, whores, whatever you called them, provided all the benefits of an affair with none of the risks.

Except of course an ever-increasing loneliness whenever I placed another call, ushered another girl into my room, handed over another wad of cash I'd covertly put aside. Every night I spent with Judit I'd awaken at three in the morning, the worst possible hour, and gaze at the twinkling city, the Danube, thinking of how to get out of my situation, of what could still be rescued or restored and what it would take.

Then Judit would wake up, her hand would travel up my spine, and she'd tell me another crazy story about a sailor in the Museum of Failed Escapes, consoling me not so much with alternatives as with putting off the decision, not thinking about it, so that when she finished I was still in exactly the same place. She knew exactly what to do, what I wanted.

We met just after I arrived in Budapest, one night when I'd gone out hoping to lose myself in the city as I'd done on nights in countless other cities, wandering in and out of bars, looking for someone to hook up with, a businessman out for a drink, a banker from the U.K., some Hungarian guy, men who'd also taken off their wedding rings. I think on this occasion his name was Gergö, and he took me to the Tip-Top Klub, one of the city's strip bars. I was too drunk, about to get more drunk, and already listening with regret to the rising sound of morning traffic.

Judit was one of three girls we ended up sitting with, Gergö strolling over to their table and asking if they'd mind. They didn't mind, they didn't care, they were sitting in identical shorts, tight, low-cut T-shirts, drinking straight cherry *pálinka* over ice. I ended up sitting next to Judit, who turned to me with a sour smile and asked what I was doing in Budapest.

Two hours later, on the Margit Bridge, I stood in the first light of morning holding up Judit, caressed by one of those cool summer breezes that almost makes you happy to be drunk, sleepless, and still up that early. I shuffled her around to face Margit Island, then around again to gaze past the parliament with its neo-Gothic spires, at the Lánc Bridge beyond, then the Erzsébet Bridge, the green river winding itself away. All of the girls Judit had been sitting with danced at the Tip-Top Klub. I knew what "dancing" meant, and Judit knew I did, and that more often than not they danced for people like me, "men from the west," as she said, who'd get drunk, have their Visa cards overcharged, and if they didn't mind spending that much money the girls were told to offer them other things at similar rates. I knew enough about it not to ask why she did it, why she didn't quit, why we were standing on the bridge at five in the morning.

Earlier that night I'd told Judit everything—Trianon, Erdély, Anna and Miklós, the orphaned girl. It was a lame attempt to prove to her that I sympathized, that things were not good for me either, though remembering the clichés about women like Judit—those without options, unable to make the switch when communism fell, forced to cash in on their beauty, five years of work, ten at the most, before the steady slide down the rungs of the sex trade left them wasted, addicted, dead—I realized how ridiculous it was, how narcissistic.

"It's good that you're married," Judit said. One of the last casino boats of the night—those golden barges that sail up and down the Danube—pulled into dock, blaring music, lit up, filled with men and women at the roulette wheel, playing blackjack, dancing. "A child should have a father and a mother," she continued, slurring her words in that way she'd perfected, pulling up her slumping head, letting it slump again. A fleet of Mercedes passed on the bridge behind us, smaller sedans grouped around a limousine, racing along the *körút* into Pest.

"Where do you live?" I asked, hinting that it was time for her to go home.

"With my mother and daughter," she said, then went quiet.

It would be a long time before she said anything else, but by then I knew I'd be going there too, stumbling along the streets of the Nyócker, following the direction of Judit's wavering finger, up the stairs to Janka in the hall.

There was a man, Judit said, a Swede, who liked to watch her cry while she danced. He always brought a towel to soak up the tears. It was a relief, she said, to know he was coming back to Budapest, to the club, that he'd be asking for her, and she wouldn't have to pretend. He would sit there, his smile brightening, as she danced until her breasts were wet, until the makeup ran down her cheeks, until she lifted the towel to her eyes and kept it there, dancing on, her body remembering that three feet of stage with a memory all its own, until it was over and he paid her and gently wrapped up his towel in a plastic bag and left.

She laughed after she finished telling me the story. "There was a landlocked sailor who tried to cry himself to sea." Once Judit was asleep, I sat there imagining this sailor, sitting on a sidewalk in some city dreaming up the saddest stories, hoping his tears would turn into a waterway and carry him off. Were those eyes, I wondered, plucked out by the communist authority, by some guard in some horrific camp, on display in the Museum of Failed Escapes?

There were so many sailors. Judit had an endless supply. I'd lie beside her watching as she wiped the drink or me off her mouth with the back of a hand. The Nyócker was in the southeast part of Budapest, narrow neighbourhoods where the ornaments on the secessionist architecture were inches thick with grime; bullet holes still in the walls from the siege or the revolution; crammed corner stores where you dug through rotten peaches and plums, brown lettuce, yellow peppers covered in black spots; Romani children in the street staring at you with crazed smiles, bags filled with glue held in their hands like the necks of chickens; their parents wandering by, back and forth from the eastern train station, where they sent younger children to beg; men with blue tattoos, strange lettering across their backs and chests, less decoration than a series of messages only a select few, those who knew the code, could decipher; and their wives just like Judit's mother, with handkerchiefs or shawls on their heads, holding bags filled with poppy, pumpkin, hemp seeds they sold for next to nothing outside sports stadiums, metro stations, public parks; and of course the whores, not only in Rákóczi Tér, but deeper in the district, like nothing I'd ever seen, lined along the tiny streets as if someone had measured out and marked exactly the spots where they should stand, less like the girls strolling and chatting at the intersections in Montreal, Toronto, Vancouver, than some regimental line called to attention, at most lifting a cigarette to their lips, sometimes extending a leg.

Janka would come and go from the apartment where her mother and I lay in bed, never telling anyone where she was going, never asking permission, somehow always back in time for dinner, or for the bedtime story she brought up to me one time, a battered book that looked as if it had been paged through every night for years, holes punched in the spine with a knife, held together by bits of string. It was about the wind—on each page either a boat blown along a lake, a kite through the sky, pigeons up to belfries, autumn leaves—and when I read it her eyes widened, as if she'd always imagined a different story, different words, to go with the pictures.

I described it all to Anna over the phone, telling her I was in Bucharest, superimposing one set of streets over another, lying about Janka's origins. When Anna said, "Well, I don't know," when she became vague, I told her about reading to the girl, about what her mother had done for a living, how quiet Janka was when not talking in perfect Hungarian about what her village in Erdély had been like before her father's death (for a minute I thought of telling her he was killed by Romanians, but decided not to push it), which forced her mother to move to the city and sell herself. Her mother was arrested, put in jail, and Janka ended up in an orphanage. I hoped the pauses and slight reversals in my story made me sound breathless, excited, and I guess in a way I was, and not just because I was worried that Anna would catch me in the lie, but for reasons that had nothing to do with the story, or even with Janka, reasons that had come to me only after I'd picked up the phone and dialed our number hoping to catch Anna in a moment when she was surprised, receptive, wide open to the sound of my voice.

"Hm," Anna said. "I don't know . . . it's because she's five I guess. I don't like the idea of her mother still being alive." She paused. "I'm sorry I said that. It's not very nice . . ."

"Anna, I've come all the way out here to Romania. We've already talked about it."

"I know, I know. I said it might be a good idea. It felt like it at the time. What's her name? Janka? She could go back once in a while to visit. We could pay for her mother to come see her sometimes . . ." She paused. "No, it's nothing," she sighed.

"We're going to need more money," I said. "There are some additional costs . . ." I had been expecting enthusiasm, and now I was looking for something to jolt her.

"Oh sure," she said, after a quiet laugh.

"So I'll go ahead?" I said.

"Yes, you go ahead," she answered, faster now than before, as if she'd caught up to my excitement. "It's what you're there for!"

"There was a sailor. I think this was in 1967 . . ."

"Listen, Judit, I'm trying to talk to you about something."

"Just a minute," she smiled, taking the bottle out of my hands after I'd grabbed it, and unscrewing the cap. "The sailor wanted to build a boat so fast its hull would not touch the water. One night he got very drunk and built these wheels, they were like balloons, except with fins, and attached them to his car and drove it into the Tisza . . ."

"We need to talk about Janka."

"You can have her," she said, still smiling.

"Have her?"

"I can't take care of her," she said. "I *don't* take care of her, Mother does, but she's so old. Janka would be better off without me."

"Where you live, it's no place to raise a child. It . . ."

"Your place would be so much better. Filled to the roof with money."

"Look, if it's a question of money . . ."

"Always." She laughed. "It's always a question of money."

"You're her mother," I said.

She put down the bottle, and came over and looked me in the face, and opened her lips in a way that brought out her teeth. But then something slackened in her, and she grew soft, and patted the place where she'd grabbed my shirt. "Yes," she said, "I'm her mother," and then she put the cap back on the bottle and sat on the bed and hugged her knees to her chest.

"You could come out, too . . ." I was safe in saying that. I knew it.

She shook her head. "And do what?" She laughed. "It's the same out there for me as it is here." She opened the bottle again. "There was one sailor who made it, only to find that the place he'd arrived was the place from which he'd departed."

"Could you stop it with the sailor thing? This is important. It's the most important decision you'll ever make."

"Don't you want to know what happened to him?"

"No," I said. "No, I don't."

She shrugged, tracing the sailor's route with a finger along her bare thigh. "It's why you invited me back to your place, wasn't it?" I said. "For Janka? It's why . . ." I looked around the decaying apartment, the missing parquets from the floor, the balloons of yellow water stains on the ceiling. "It's why we're always here. Why I read to her." I shook my head. "You didn't expect me to believe it was for me, you bringing me here?

You could do much better than me. And I'm sure you do." I knew it was all true, what I was saying, but I still expected her to contradict me.

"Yes," she said. "Yes, I could do better than you." She laughed. "I could do it easily."

"Why then?"

She waited. "Your wife," she said. "The way you described her that night on the bridge. She sounds . . ." Judit smiled her widest smile. "She sounds like the one."

There was a sailor who built a sea of paper. That's how I think of Judit now, and how she was in those weeks when we were dealing with consulates, agencies, doctors, even civic politicians, all of them scratching their heads, reaching for paperwork, telling us we were going too fast, that we couldn't get it done, that it would take up to a year, even longer, for the adoption process—that we'd need more money, there were fees and medical tests and records to be ordered and processed, even a number of "gifts and donations" to be made. And when we weren't doing that, trying to batter a hole through that bureaucracy, then I was in some park, mainly the Városliget, playing with Janka, trying to get the girl used to me, though I think now it was just the attention she loved, attention from anybody, her mother's blessing floating along with us wherever we went—the circus, the Vidám Park, the Szécsényi Fürdö, the Gerbeaud—almost like a kind of anticipation, a perfume, some hint of a perfect future. Janka would slip her hand into mine, and smile, and ask question after question about Canada, about lakes, about rivers, about birds, about the Arctic, that would echo in me a long time afterwards. "Yes, your mother will come visit."

"What if you were to just take her?" Judit said to me one day. She was drinking even more heavily then, our hours together more and more quiet as if her interest in me was steadily draining away, the two of us leaning into the pillows, uncorking another bottle. Even her stories of sailors grew shorter and shorter, reduced to single sentences spoken at the very end of the night, when I was almost asleep, not sure if she was speaking or it was a dream. "You could take her, and I could write a letter that would let the two of you travel, and then I could work out the legal things afterwards." Judit tilted her head to one side. "But I would need the money."

"How much?" I asked. She shrugged as if she didn't know. "Twenty-five thousand dollars? That would be enough, wouldn't it?" I waited. "Thirty thousand?" Judit nodded, and I wrote her a cheque right there, the paper curling on itself like a wave. She cashed it the next morning while I went back to my hotel and, after sitting in front of the phone for what seemed hours, left a message for Anna and Míklós, telling them I was coming home, that Janka was her name.

But that's not how it worked out. Janka was standing beside her mother at the airport, crying, holding Judit's hand, the tiny flower-printed suitcase I'd bought for her sitting on the ground beside them. We were ten or fifteen minutes from boarding, and I nodded at Judit over Janka's head, saying I'd leave them alone for a moment to say goodbye. "I'll be back in a minute," I said, leaning down to stroke Janka's hair, pointing at the sign for the men's room, and then, once I was out of sight, I stood there, back against the tiled wall trying to regulate my breathing, glancing out into the crowd to see if they'd followed. Then I was gone, keeping the passengers between me and Judit, moving fast through security, down along ramps and onto the plane, looking over my shoulder every few steps to make sure Janka wasn't there, still crying, the little suitcase banging against her legs as she tried to catch up to me. Looking out the airplane window I thought I could see Janka in the terminal, back at the boarding gate, pressed against the glass wondering where I was, what happened to our plane, how long it would take before I came back, or whether her mother was still there on the other side of security or gone home, goodbye forever, the airport suddenly large and exitless and all around her.

I watched and watched for that little girl standing by the window, craning my neck as the plane reversed, moved onto the runway, took off. I sat there wishing I could go back until we were well over the Arctic, halfway to Canada, and I opened the letter Judit had written—permitting me to take Janka—and turned it this way and that. It was completely blank.

She'd known I would never take her. She'd known I'd waffle in the last minute, known it from that first night standing over the Danube, stringing me along until she got every last cent. She knew, too, that what I was really paying for was not Janka but my freedom, not just from her and Janka, but from everything that had brought me there, to Budapest, in the first place. That blank letter, which would have stopped me dead at the border, which would have gotten me arrested if I'd tried to take Janka with me, was what I'd really been after all along.

It turns out there is a Museum of Failed Escapes, and that it is, as Judit said, in the ninth district. I went there once, many years after that day on the plane with the blank letter. It had been a private collection during the eighties, nineties, and early oughts, opening to the public in 2007, after its owner, András Fabiani, died and bequeathed the property to the city. During the time it was private, entry had been limited to a tiny circle of collectors, politicians, VIPs (and, I supposed, certain exotic dancers) favoured by Fabiani, who was one of those very well connected members of the communist elite who'd profited beyond imagining when the iron curtain came down and left him and his comrades well positioned to sell state property, hand out foreign contracts, and pocket most of the money. The museum was an obsession.

Despite being public, you still needed an appointment to get in. An older man met me and the other visitors at the door. His name was Mihály, forty-five or so, incredibly well dressed, and led us from room to room in the converted apartment that was a disquieting mix of vernacular architecture and supermodern minimalism. There were three floors to the museum, each one devoted to a different medium of escape, "land," "water," and "air." After the tour, when the other visitors left, I asked Mihály if it would be okay for me to go back to level two, where I marvelled at how accurate Judit had been, because it was exactly as she'd said—all the different ways her sailors had tried to escape. Mihály accompanied me as I looked at the plastic boat, the hand-drawn map of the "seas of Hungary" (code for the lakes and rivers that crossed various borders to the west), a vial filled with the tears of the sailor who tried to cry himself to sea (the inscription said they were gathered from a failed escapee who'd been sentenced to ten years in the notorious Csillag Prison), the car outfitted with the ridiculous wheels meant to paddle along the Tisza, and a hundred other things.

There was a video on the wall showing an old guy in a sailor's suit, his toothless mouth moving endlessly, underneath it a speaker quietly playing back his words—about constellations, trade winds, shifting tides. "There was a sailor who tried to . . ?" I looked at Mihály for help.

"To talk himself to sea. To make his mouth a sail. As if his words were so much wind." The attendant looked serious for a minute, then smiled, and broke into a small laugh.

"Did you by any chance ever know a woman by the name of Judit?"

Mihály looked at me strangely. His face coloured. He shook his head. Then he changed the subject. "I worked for Fabiani a long time. He entrusted this place to me. He had nothing to do with exotic dancers . . ." Mihály paused, started over. "This is what I call 'a poetic museum,' as I said when we were upstairs." He gave me a look that said I should have been listening more carefully during the tour. "Technically, not everything in here, not every piece, was part of an actual escape," he continued. "Some were." He nodded at the plastic sailboat. "But others were escapes of a different kind . . . It was Fabiani who found all these, and who believed they belonged together. These are escapes as *he* defined them." Mihály paused again, waiting for me to say something. "The collection," he finished, "says more about *his* notion of escape than anything else."

I looked at the video screen, listening to the old sailor's quiet disquisition on longitude and latitude and how the Soviet agents, if they followed you far enough, would become lost at sea, because Marx only ever wrote about people on land.

"A woman," I finally said, "once told me about this place. Stories about these things . . ." I laughed. "Part of me thought I might find something of her here." I waited. "This was a long time ago. When this place was still closed to the general public."

"I'm sorry about that," he said, sensing my disappointment. "Was she, were you . . ?"

"I was married then," I said, not sure if this was an appropriate answer.

"Children?" he asked.

"A boy. Miklós." I smiled. "He's with cousins right now. Didn't seem all that interested in coming here." I shrugged and laughed, glancing at Mihály, who seemed to relax a bit. "He's liking Budapest," I continued, "it's his first time." I wanted to add something about Anna here, to tell him that Miklós's mother was Hungarian too, and how jealous she'd been that our son was going to Budapest instead of her, and how she'd kissed him the morning I came to pick him up, and then kissed me, too, on the cheek, before going back inside to János, their daughter Mária, and that whole other life she'd come to after the divorce. And I'd taken Miklós's hand and walked off into mine.

But before I could figure out how to phrase it, or even if it was worth phrasing, Mihály remembered something. "Did you ever hear about the sailor who tried to come back?"

"She never mentioned him," I said.

"*Her*," he said, guiding me to a glass case mounted on the wall behind which were large pieces of paper that appeared blank. Mihály told me to look closely at them, and I did, noticing how worn the paper was, as if it had been rubbed over and over with a wetted fingertip until there were only the faintest of lines, traces of red, blue, green. "She thought it was just a question of erasing the maps," he said, "and she'd find herself once more in that place from which she'd started out. I mean *when* she'd started," he corrected himself, "before she'd discovered anything of the world." He came close to the glass to look at it with me. "It's beautiful," he said.

"It is," I replied. And it was, like some transcript of dreams, written days later, when all you remember is the faintest of traces, a world already gone before it registered. But there was no surprise there, looking at it, only gratitude for what Judit had given me and what a woman like her, trapped in that life, would never be allowed—that hopefulness her sailors felt in their moment of escape, when home was still everywhere, glimmering out there, and where every mistake, every wayward decision, was for a moment erased.

The Restoration of the Villa Where Tíbor Kálmán Once Lived

"TÍBOR KÁLMÁN. Tíbor Kálmán's villa." That's what Györgyi told Zoltán the night they went AWOL from the camp, the two of them huddled in the barracks amidst the other conscripts, boys like them, but asleep, some as young as sixteen, called on in the last hours of the war in a futile effort to salvage a regime already fallen, a country and people already defeated. "We need to get to Mátyásföld," Györgyi said, "that's where the villa is. Tíbor Kálmán will give us papers." But Györgyi didn't make it far, only to the end of the barracks, to the loose board and through the fence, frantically trying to keep up with Zoltán, who always seemed to run faster, to climb better, to see in the dark. Zoltán was already waiting on the other side of the ditch, hidden in the thicket, when the guard shouted, when they heard the first crack of bullets being fired, Györgyi screaming where he'd fallen, "My leg! I've been shot! Zoli, help me," and Zoltán looked back at his friend for a second, calculating the odds of getting to him in time, the two of them managing to elude the guards, limping along at whatever speed Györgyi's leg would allow. They'd be caught, charged with desertion, executed—both of them. Then Zoltán turned in the direction he was headed, Györgyi's cries fading in the distance.

It was the end of December 1944, and that night, running from the makeshift encampment and its marshalling yard, running and running long after the military police had given up, not wanting to risk their own lives by following him east, Zoltán realized it was hopeless, there was a wall of refugees coming at him, and behind it, the Russian guns, already so loud he felt as if they were sounding beside his ears. Budapest was streaming with people fleeing from the suburbs—Rákospalota, Pestszentlőrinc, Soroksár, Mátyásföld—because the Red Army had not only arrived at these places already and taken control, but was advancing on Budapest itself.

So Zoltán became part of the human tide flowing from one death trap to another during the siege, and the things he'd seen would live on, unspoken, beneath everything he was to think and say from that point forward. Civilians used as human shields by the Red Army. Nazis exploding bridges over the Danube while there were still families and soldiers streaming across. Men and women forced to carry ammunition across the frozen river to German soldiers stationed on Margit Island while Soviet bullets and shells and bombs rained around them. He saw child soldiers holding off two dozen Russians by running up and down the stairs of a devastated building, shooting from every window, making them think there were a dozen soldiers trapped inside. Young boys crashing in gliders while attempting to fly in supplies for the fascist armies of Hitler and Szálasi, the fields littered with broken fuselages and wings and pilots contorted in positions that seemed to Zoltán the war's alphabet—untranslatable into human terms. There was a broken gas main near Vérmező that for days shot flame through every crack and hole in the asphalt—blue, orange, yellow—dancing along the road as if fire alone were capable of celebrating what had become of Budapest.

He'd seen exhausted doctors trying to save patients from a burning hospital, carrying them into the snow only to realize they had nothing—not a blanket, a sheet, even a shirt—to keep them from freezing. He'd come across the most beautiful girl, eighteen or nineteen, in one of the ruined homes filled with those too wounded to go on, staring up, whispering from the mass of bodies, injured, starving, gripped by typhus, and as he leaned in to hear what she wanted to say— "Shoot me, please shoot me"—he noticed that both her legs had been torn away.

All that time Zoltán had been tormented by the idea of Tíbor Kálmán's villa—it was like the place was imagining him rather than the other way around—it sometimes appeared in place of what he was running from, and Zoltán had to stop himself from leaping into a burning apartment, a metro tunnel, or a garden under shelling, thinking, this is it, finally, I've made it.

After a while, Zoltán began to feel protected by the villa, as if the new life it promised was his true life, and the one he was living now only an alias, false, no one real inside it, and therefore anything that happened was not really happening to him. This is what helped Zoltán survive when he was press-ganged, along with a number of other boys and young men fleeing west, into the Vannay Battalion, and ended up doing the very thing he'd hoped to avoid: fighting for the Nazis. He would have liked to remember when it happened, but there were no dates then, the end of December, the beginning of January, sometime during those hundred days of a siege that never did end for him, hauled out of the cellar where he was hiding by Vannay's men, him and the rest, given a gun and told what the Russians looked like, and from there the black minutes, schoolboy comrades falling around him, Vannay making radio announcements to the Soviets that they would take no prisoners, and the Soviets responding to this as Vannay had hoped, likewise killing every one of them they captured, which Vannay was only too pleased to tell Zoltán and the others, knowing it would make them fight with that much more desperation. Then the breakout attempt of February through Russian lines, German and Hungarian soldiers cut down in the streets as they tried to escape the gutted capital to make it to the forests and then west to where the rest of Hitler's armies were stationed, running headlong into rockets, tank fire, snipers stationed in buildings along the routes the Soviets knew they would take, drowning in sewers where the water level rose with each body that climbed down the ladder until it was up to their noses, pitch-black, screaming panic. So few of them made it. Three percent, the historians would say. The rest of the soldiers, the thousands, were killed along Széna Square and Lövöház Street and Széll Kálmán Square, piled into doorways, ground up by tanks, swearing, pleading, sobbing, unable to fire off even the last bullet they'd saved for themselves.

But Zoltán was not there. He'd gone over to the other side by then, turning on the boys he was fighting with, aged sixteen and seventeen, shooting them dead as they stared at him dumbstruck, and then saw, over his shoulder, the approaching Russians. He thought he saw a last glimmer of envy in the boys' eyes, regret at not having thought of it first, before what light there was went out forever, and Zoltán turned, feeling something fade inside him as well, his voice cracking at the edges, soft and unwavering as radio silence. "Death to the fascists," he shouted, and was rewarded with bits of red ribbon the Russians tied around his arm, and a hat they placed on his head, before sending him back into battle.

It was Zoltán's decoration as a "war hero" by the Soviets that finally brought him to Tíbor Kálmán's villa late in 1945, to the place where it seemed all his misfortune and redemption were concentrated, where he might be absolved of guilt for having made it through the siege instead of someone better—anyone at all—someone worthy of survival, like that legless girl in the makeshift infirmary, for he had done what she asked that day, scrounging among the soldiers crammed wounded or dying or dead into that corridor, found a revolver, and embraced her with one arm while with the other he pressed the barrel to her temple. If only he'd gotten to the villa in time, he told himself. If only he'd chosen the one other option he had: death. He knew now that death was preferable to what he'd done to save himself, though it was too late by then, betrayal had become Zoltán's vocation, and the woman who met him that November day in the doorway of the villa sensed it, with the tired look of someone who has outlasted her interest in life and can't understand why she's being provoked by those who insist on living. She introduced herself as Tíbor's daughter-in-law, Karola, wary enough of Zoltán and his uniform to give only the answer he wanted and not a drop more, keeping her voice to a perfect monotone, without a single nuance he might have fastened onto had he been seeking something other than forgiveness.

"I wish I could help you," she said. "But Tíbor is dead."

Zoltán stood there with his military decorations and wondered why he'd come, given that the war was over, and with it his reason for seeking out Tíbor. "He's dead," Karola said again. "He was dead when we returned here from Budapest." She pointed at the hole left by the bomb in the roof above the dining room, covered with a number of tarps inexpertly sewn together. She told him the story in a manner so offhand it was clear she was still in shock: Tíbor Kálmán had lost both hands when a Russian shell landed on the villa. He'd raised his arms to protect his wife, Ildikó, from the collapse of the ceiling, and a beautiful chandelier of Murano glass sheared off both hands at the wrist, though it hardly mattered to Tíbor by then because both he and Ildikó were dead, crushed by the weight of plaster, bricks, and several tons of antique furniture they'd stored in the attic overhead. Karola stood for a moment, as if waiting for Zoltán to respond, and when he didn't she said, "Anyhow," and he could see the effort it was costing her to repress a sneer as she scanned the medals on his chest, "you don't seem to be doing too badly."

There was something else, something other than scorn, in the way she said this, a quiet acknowledgement of what he'd come for, and at the same time a dismissal of the explanation he wanted so badly to make. "Vannay sent out radio messages to the Soviets," he whispered, and immediately regretted it, as if even now, in attempting to make amends, he was still looking out for himself. "They weren't taking any prisoners. I had to make them a sign of good faith," he said. "I was only eighteen!"

"Why are you telling me this?" she asked, and he noticed that even while talking to him she was gazing elsewhere—at the orchard, the flight of birds, a fence fallen to its side— unable to keep her eyes on anything for long.

"I killed two boys," he said. "I wanted to show that I had switched sides . . ."

"I don't know anything about what you're saying."

"You do!" he shouted. "I was supposed to have come here. Tíbor was waiting for me, for boys like me. But I couldn't get across the Russian lines!"

She shrugged. "We couldn't make it either. We were trapped inside Budapest. There were many people who suffered."

"I was part of Vannay's battalion. It was during the breakout. When I saw the Russians coming I killed two of the boys I was fighting with." He was shaking. He no longer had any control over what he was saying.

"Then you are not welcome in my house," said Karola, and for the first time since she'd opened the door, Zoltán felt her gaze rest on him, and he realized, too, that she'd been looking away not because she was disinterested in him, but because her eyes had seen too much, absorbed too much, images impossible for her to contain, which made her look elsewhere for fear of passing them on. He felt ashamed then for not being able to do as she did, keep it to himself, or expend it by shifting his gaze to where it would do no harm—the birds, the fields, the sky.

"Then you do not deserve to come in here," she hissed, and slammed the door in his face.

And so began Zoltán's persecution of Tíbor Kálmán's family, using every opportunity his status in the Party gave him—making false claims, denying them meaningful jobs, padding the files on Karola, her husband Boldizsár, their children István, Adél, Anikó, Jenö and László, citing their attendance at mass, their political support for the Smallholders Party in the elections of 1945, their open criticism of the Soviet occupation and its control of the police, factories, transit system, everything. But at the time there were so many people like this the Soviets couldn't make them disappear fast enough. It wasn't until he saw what was happening to the members of the resistance, old trade union leaders, those who'd been outspoken communists prior to the arrival of the Red Army—who had paved the way for it, but made the mistake of expecting Marxism in its wake—only when all of them were being arrested, sentenced in show trials and murdered, did Zoltán realize that the most dangerous thing of all, the most grievous of crimes, next to being a Nazi, was to have actively fought against Hitler in the name of communism. These men and women had had the courage to oppose the state, been brave enough to think for themselves, even at the cost of their lives, and it was because of this, exactly this, that the Soviets got rid of them. They were not the kind of citizens the Kremlin wanted, any more than Hitler had wanted them.

Picking off the most loyal had the added benefit of amplifying the fear, of making everyone feel equally vulnerable, because if loyalties didn't matter, if the liquidation of men and women appeared random, then survival had nothing to do with you and everything to do with grace, which arrived from the state, as mysterious and medieval as the favour of God.

Zoltán filed report after report to the Allied Control Commission, which was controlled by the Soviets, about the activities of Tíbor Kálmán and his family during the war: how they'd sheltered political refugees from Germany, how they'd helped young men escape being drafted by a government they despised, how they'd drawn up false papers for all of these. "Conscientious objectors," he called them, and it was this, finally, that elevated the Kálmáns above the common stream of citizens complaining about the occupation. It wore the family down—visits by police, seizure of property, arrests and brief imprisonments that were hints, preludes, to the sentences yet to come—and then, in a final blow, Zoltán managed to get them evicted from the villa, and to have himself, the war hero, the decorated veteran, the loyal subject of the Party, installed in their place.

That was late in 1946, the letter from the state informing the Kálmáns that their villa was being "reallocated" to "a more suitable candidate." In return, they would be given a cowshed in Csepel. The shed had held three cows and could easily fit six people, which meant that only one member of the family would have to sleep outside. So the family finally left, driven beyond exasperation, beyond fear, beyond even the love of their country. Rumour was they escaped to the west, following their eldest son, who'd left the country six months earlier. In many ways, Zoltán was happy to have been part of their forced removal, and he was delighted to think of what it was like for them out there, wherever they'd gone— not speaking the language, not making any money, not having their degrees and expertise recognized. At night, when he couldn't sleep, it was helpful to know that in some way they were suffering at least a fraction of what he'd suffered during the siege, at a time when he should have been with them, in Tíbor's care, being given a new identity and a new life.

But in the end, he had to admit, it was not the Kálmáns he'd been after, not really. It was the villa, the freedom to walk inside, to feel its mass around him.

He never forgot his first time crossing the threshold. There was the falling plaster, the bullet holes still in the walls, the water damage along the ceiling, the bits of furniture and possessions the family had left behind. There was the room where Tíbor Kálmán had died, its door nailed shut, the debris still inside as it had been when the family returned from the siege. But more than this was the feeling Zoltán had, walking down the hall, entering the rooms, that he was not yet inside, that he was still searching for a point of entry. "Another step and I will be there," he told himself, speaking into the emptiness of the home. And with the next movement, he said it again, "Another step and I will be inside." Eventually, he would exit the villa, stand in the courtyard bewildered, then cross the threshold again, hoping this time to get it right, haunted by how he'd dreamed of the place, hoped for it, imagined being safe inside these rooms, when in reality he was facing bullets and starvation and disease in Budapest. And killing people.

At night, unable to sleep, he would shake off nightmares of the siege by fixing up the place—the water damage, the rotten studs and joists, the plastering, the paint, the careful work of reconstructing the villa—as if by restoring the building to what it had once been it might finally open up to him, truly open, and he'd step inside to the life he should have had.

After the third week, he ripped off the boards covering the door to the room where Tíbor died, and a day or two later, steeling himself, went inside, staring at the mounds of rubble, the debris strewn along the floor. The Kálmán family had already exhumed and buried the bodies, touching the rubble only as much as was needed to pull it apart. After that, the family kept the door nailed shut, Zoltán had thought, because they couldn't bear to face the site where Tíbor and Ildikó died, but as he began to clear away the rubble, he discovered why they'd really left it as it was, for once the bricks and plaster and shattered beams and bits of glass were swept aside, he found the hole in the floor where Tíbor had kept his workshop, and inside, the stacks of messages he'd received during the war from the resistance, from places as far away as Cologne, and the equipment he'd used to forge identities, along with the lists of names and addresses under which Tíbor had hidden the refugees. Zoltán would use these lists to keep himself useful to the state, exposing identities one by one whenever he felt the pressure to demonstrate his loyalty. In return, they let him keep the villa. The villa with its printing press, the one they knew nothing about, his escape.

The names would run out regardless of how carefully, how slowly, he delivered them. In fact, if he delivered them too slowly the Soviets would grow impatient, demand that he tell them where he was getting his information, and then, when he refused, they'd come into the villa to find out for themselves, and his last hope would be ended.

He went looking for someone to help with the press. He met Ági later that year, as the first wave of deportations, imprisonments, and executions took place. Her father and mother had been devoted communists dating back to Béla Kun's brief dictatorship of Hungary in 1919, and were persecuted in the white terror that followed against Jews and leftists when Admiral Horthy established control over the country for the next twenty-four years. Her father had been both—Jewish and leftist—and more than once it was only the thickness of his skull that kept him from being beaten to death, just as it was his skill with the printing press that kept all three of them alive during the period of anti-Semitic laws, ghettoization, the Holocaust. "If you wear the yellow star they will kill you," he once told Ági, tossing hers and her mother's and his into the flames, "and if you do not they will kill you." He stirred the fire. "So why bother?" But he had done more than just that, drawing up papers for many others—Jews, but also members of the resistance, fellow communists, British soldiers parachuted into the capital, others who needed to escape, for one reason or another, from the powers bearing down on them—whatever he could do to subvert the fascist cause. As a result, Ági's father, like so many other communists, was arrested after the Soviet occupation on Malinovsky's orders, not so much for his vocal criticism of the Russian "liberator"—for asking what good it had done them to await liberation when it meant free looting for the Red Army, rape, robbery, extortion, the requisitioning and hoarding of the country's food for the military while the general population starved, the ransacking of the nation in the way of reparations, mass arrests, murder—but because he wasn't afraid for his life. They were to be sent to a prison camp, one of the many the Soviets had set up, in Gödöllö, when Zoltán stepped in, saying he needed someone adept at "paperwork." Malinovsky had reported to Moscow that he had captured 110,000 fascists, but as he only had 60,000, the rest had to be made up by dragging people at random from the streets and their homes, and Zoltán was put in charge of making these substitutes look legitimate.

Naturally, Ági's father objected, and so Zoltán took him aside, reminding him that the youngest women raped by the Red Army were 12, and the oldest 90, which meant that both his wife and daughter were within the normative range; he spoke, too, of the sorts of venereal diseases they could expect, not to mention how long it would last, given that some women were locked up for two weeks "entertaining" as many as thirty soldiers at a time. In the end, Ági's father agreed, and to soften the blow Zoltán made sure they were provided for, keeping his promise even after Ági's parents, having done the work they were asked to do, were visited one night by the ÁVÓ and taken away for "unauthorized forgery of government documents," and Zoltán inherited Ági.

He made a nominal attempt to save her parents, trying to get her on his side, to make her believe he wasn't really an apparatchik, that he was just using the system until he could make his escape. So he made sure she was there when he made inquiries and phone calls, made sure that when they came to the villa for her as well, agents of the ÁVÓ knocking on the door, he was there to bar the entrance, listing off his decorations and accomplishments and contacts to make it clear he, and by extension she, was "protected," though in truth, no one was protected, no matter how high up your friends were, for the most dangerous friend of all was the highest ranking, Stalin himself.

It was an act of bravery, maybe the only act of bravery he'd ever performed, though it was only due to his hope that Ági would fix the printing press hidden beneath the villa. He knew that she could repair and operate the press with her eyes closed, the old man had said as much, boasting that she'd been more than his little helper. When her father was called away on business, she'd run the whole show.

Ági was silent through it all, absolutely quiet, the look in her eyes exactly the same as Karola's had been, too hard for a girl of nineteen—still lithe, a little boyish—meeting his gaze with one in every way its equal. The war had made them old. He saw it in the way her eyes left him isolated, a lesson on shouldering what he'd done alone rather than lessening the burden by passing it on, by turning it into a secret she had to share.

It always seemed to be winter, down in the hole, Ági squatting above the trap door peering at him, listening to the clack and whir as Zoltán tried, without expertise or success, to start up Tíbor's old machinery, the presses and lamps and generators. Nothing worked. All that happened was the clashing of parts, the tearing and spewing and grinding of paper, the flickering of lamps. The generator hummed dangerously, and charged every metal object around it so badly Zoltán was continuously cursing the jolts and shocks.

Ági would leave his dinner at the edge of the trap door, listening for a moment and then hammering it with the heel of her shoe, making him jump in the midst of whatever repairs he was attempting, so that he would lose his grip on the screw or wire or flashlight and have to scramble after it in the dark. Zoltán sometimes felt she was transforming the villa by her presence. The smell of her cooking in the kitchen. The bedroom filled with the rustle of her turning in sleep. The shaded gallery, with its columns and ivy, unbearable for him because the only time a smile ever played across Ági's face was when she stepped out onto it and took in the smells of the garden and sunshine she and half the country had dreamed about in cellars and shelters during the siege, when all they had was the sound of bombs, the slow fog of plaster shaken from the walls and ceiling and floor with every explosion.

Instead of helping him, Ági reminded Zoltán, day after day, of the terrible things he'd done. She made love to him without flinching, without motion, the daughter of a man he'd killed, a woman unlawfully his, stolen, forced against her will, as if nurturing his hopelessness, his self-hate, his absent courage.

When he grew frustrated with the work he'd sit with her in one of the ruined rooms, Ági staring at the floor, not at all there. "What would you have done?" he asked, as if having told her about the press, his plan to create a new identity, to get away before scrutiny of his activities became too intense, he was now free to tell her everything, all of what that scrutiny might uncover. "What other choice was there?"

She stared at the hatch he'd left open, or the slow work of renovation he'd begun, trying to re-plaster the walls, to repair the hole in the ceiling, to paint over a half decade of water stains, her silence refusing him the one thing he most wanted: to hear someone, anyone, say that they too would have done what he did. But all he heard was the villa, rain on its roof, the ticking of radiators and plumbing, the wind playing on the windows, as if it was telling him it took a special person to do what he'd done, to have shot those boys. "No one but you could have done that," the villa said.

At other times he would remind her of those he'd assisted—the legless girl in the infirmary, Ági herself—and ask her to help him square this against the other things he'd done—to her parents, to the two boys. "How is it that I could do any good at all?" he asked. "Maybe I haven't gone so far. Maybe there's still something of me left," he said, waiting for her to speak, the villa answering instead.

When he grew angry with her silence, he threatened to stop protecting her from the ÁVÓ. Ági never raised her eyes from the floor, and he would shout that they were both going to die there, in the villa, and then he'd go back down the hatch, kicking and beating the useless machinery. "If only you would help me!" he yelled up through the trap door, letting it out before he could stop the words. "We could use this machine." But it was pointless. For years now, his job had been destroying names, not creating them.

In March of 1947 Zoltán finally ran out of names—all but one. He'd done what he could, he told Ági. At first, he'd only handed in the aliases Tíbor had given to communists, to those, Zoltán knew, who were even now active in the Party, and who'd enjoyed their fill of atrocity, and now it was their turn. When these were used up, Zoltán had moved down the list to those he knew were missing, or sick, or single. The very last names he'd handed in belonged to men who had families—wives, children, next of kin. And when those were gone—identified, questioned, arrested—when there was only the last, the one he'd picked out in advance, an address in Székesfehérvár, someone guiltier than most, susceptible to blackmail, with the means necessary to help Zoltán hide away, then he turned to Ági.

"If we're going to get away, you're going to have to help me." She made no reply. He turned, putting his hands against their bedroom wall. "I've been waiting," he said. "I thought there might be time, that if I was patient, the names would last longer than the Soviets. We could make this place mine, or ours, whatever." He took his hands from the wall. "But they aren't leaving this country. They aren't *ever* leaving this country. You wait and see! And there are no names left!"

She watched him pace back and forth, giving her a precise account of who was asking questions about him, what departments were interested, whose hands had delivered and traded memos on how he happened to know so much, on where he'd gotten the information that led to so many arrests. "The only thing that would have been worse," he hissed, "is if I'd given them no names at all."

He moved to the bed and grabbed one of her wrists. "If only I could fix the equipment Tíbor left," he said. "It would at least give me, give us, a chance to get away."

She looked at him as if she had no idea who he was.

"What's wrong with you?" he shouted. He yanked Ági off the bed then, and she stumbled after him, rounding the corner to the room where Tíbor and Ildikó had died, and down the ladder to the workshop.

He grabbed a list of names from a bench he'd built, thrusting it in her face. "Read it!" he said to her. "Read the names!"

She tried to look away.

"I got it from the ministry," he said, holding it up to her face, his other hand still gripping her wrist, "the names of the confirmed dead. I thought I could use it to make an alias. They'd never be looking for someone who has already died."

Giving in, Ági took the paper from his hand, her eyes moving side to side along one of the only records that still testified, name by name, to a whole society taken out of existence so that this new one could come into being. This is how she found it.

"Leo Kocsis," Ági whispered.

"Yes," he said, "exactly. How eager are you to join him? Because that's exactly what's going to happen, your name and my name, right here"—he poked a finger at the list—"if you don't get us out."

She let the paper fall. Leo Kocsis. Her father.

Zoltán would never remember whether Ági agreed with a "Yes" or a nod, or whether she agreed at all, only that she moved forward. In that moment he had the premonition he always had, an instinct for how betrayal might benefit him, the same instinct that had made him show Ági her father's name, knowing it was the only way to break what had formed between them. Ági worked without stopping, and was not finished before the evening of the next day. There was so much to do, so many papers, copying everything Zoltán brought to her, every sheet, without speaking.

When it was done, days later, and Zoltán was standing in the doorway, his bags packed, it occurred to him that she had not prepared an alias for her own escape, and he quietly asked if she wasn't coming along.

She stared at him.

"I'm going to Székesfehérvár," he whispered, needing to say something, to cover up this moment, this need for an apology. "I'm going to stay there for a little while." He rubbed his head. "There's still someone . . . I might get help."

Ági said nothing, only stood there in the doorway as if she had no intention of ever leaving Tíbor Kálmán's villa.

"What's wrong with you?" he asked. "You think they'll leave you alone when they come for me? You think you'll be spared?"

"They . . ." she began. "*They* have never left me alone." And she stepped back inside and quietly closed the door.

Zoltán was still standing in front of the villa minutes later, still there, silent, unable to step off the threshold, almost as if he was waiting for her to invite him back in, as if, after all this time, all he really wanted was to be welcomed into the place—as if it had never been about an alias at all.

Zoltán lingered, unable to turn decisively toward Székesfehérvár, moving along the sidewalk and glancing back, retracing five or six steps, eyes resting on the villa, long after Ági had opened the windows, brought the record player out onto the gallery, and poured herself what remained of the *pálinka*. He stood there, half hidden behind a willow, barely making out the melody of the *sláger*, watching her tilt the glass to her lips. She had the run of the place now, he realized, and he wondered if she'd known it would come to this, that for him the worst memory of all would be Ági accepted into the villa, as if his removal was all that Tíbor Kálmán's home needed to be complete, all it had needed to be finally restored.

The
Beautician

O F ALL the old dissidents at the Szécsényi Club, Árpád Holló wore the most makeup. From far away it was unnoticeable, he looked great, all *fin de siècle* elegance with pomaded hair and well-cut suits, a fresh rose in his buttonhole. But step up close, two or three feet away, and you'd see it—his face would blur for a second then snap back into focus in thick oils—and you'd wonder how deep you had to go, pushing a finger through all that mascara and rouge and foundation, before you hit a chin or a cheekbone, or if you'd hit anything at all.

It was the spring of 1993 when I betrayed him. I was twenty-one, working on my honours thesis in Central European Studies, and dating Ílona's stunning daughter, Éva, whom I still think of once in a while, walking up the street to the house I was renting with friends—her loose summer dresses, her sharp smile, her hair hennaed and waving in the breeze. She'd bend down and kiss me and we'd sit on the steps and talk about what I'd found at the Szécsényi Club library the night before.

My deadline was looming. I'd wasted the previous fall partying instead of coming up with a thesis topic. I wanted to write something about the Cold War, especially the 1950s, the terrifying Rákosi period, but every time I went to the library it seemed that everything important had been done, and even much of the unimportant stuff. Christmas came and went. I was granted an extension, then another, and finally my committee said they needed a complete paper by May if I planned to graduate that semester, which I needed to do if I was to have any hope of following Éva to Hungary, which is where her mother planned to send her, for at least a year, after her graduation from high school. I was stuck, the days slipping away, when my father suggested I speak with Holló.

When I told him Holló made me uncomfortable, my father laughed. "Of course he does. That's been his strategy for the last forty years." We were standing in the backyard of the house in Toronto where I'd grown up, and which I'd left four years ago upon starting university, a move my parents happily agreed to, since it meant they wouldn't be awakened by me coming home drunk at four in the morning, or have to watch me hanging out with friends instead of studying, or overhear Éva and me having sex in the bedroom. "He never talks about it," my father said, "but supposedly he fell in love with the wife of Ábel Cérna. That name doesn't mean anything to you," he continued. "But everyone of my generation knows it. Cérna was part of the Agitation and Propaganda Department of the Central Committee, and then high up in the Ministry of Culture. He was in charge of censorship."

My father paused, as if he was still hurting from this, and I remembered the times he'd recite from memory the verses of Ady, Arány János, Kosztolányi, and others. "Anyhow," he sighed, "when Cérna found out you can imagine the trouble Holló was in. It was then that he started wearing the makeup, pretending to be a homosexual. That's how he got out from under it."

My father didn't need to say what he said next, because I'd seen enough of it myself, the way some of his friends never really got over what they'd gone through back then, the way their survival strategies lingered across the years, even became amplified, long after they'd left Hungary and no longer needed them. There was more than one family acquaintance still hiding jewellery in cans buried under the back lawn and floorboards in expectation of the next economic collapse; who studiously avoided voting for fear of being tracked down as politically suspect when the next totalitarian regime came to power; who still denied her Jewish ethnicity since it was only that denial that had saved her during the war. But Holló and the makeup were more extreme than any of these, and my father's easy acceptance of this was disturbing as well, since it too was a form of denial.

Of course, it was easy to understand why my father, and the others who frequented the Szécsényi Club, tolerated what they would otherwise have considered Holló's perversity. The previous "caretaker" of the Szécsényi Club, Rázsoly Bodo, had been notorious for running the place into the ground, smoking terrible cigars, lecherously requesting that daughters and wives help out in the kitchen, and drinking himself to death on the *pálinka* one of the club's members,

Frigyes Bácsi, brewed in a homemade still and supplied in vast quantities. Nobody wanted to go back to *that*.

Holló took over after Bodo died. He did every job: night watchman, groundskeeper, carpenter, accountant, even chef every Saturday night at the weekly banquets and on special occasions such as the anniversary of the 1956 revolution. He accomplished a lot with very little, keeping the gardens blooming, the pond clean, the roof watertight, the bricks repointed, the furniture and appliances in good order, making the meanest *cigángy pecsenye* this side of Sopron, and most importantly stocking the cellar with the best stuff from Eger, Tokaj, and the Balaton, all without asking for more than a modest salary and a room. The club's membership was very well taken care of.

Once in a while someone would make a comment. Ílona did, early on, one of those insults that's meant to put someone in his place at the same time as it shows everyone how superior you are. She called him "Árpád Néni," the same as calling him "Mrs. Holló" in English. It happened at one of the Saturday night banquets while he was going from table to table asking everyone how the food was. "The food is very nice, *Árpád Néni*." Holló stood back from her, narrowed his eyes, and next Saturday there was no banquet, the doors to the club were closed but unlocked, so that anyone could wander in and watch Holló quietly mopping the floors and dusting tables and shrugging when they asked why dinner had been cancelled. The week after that there was no banquet either. The club executive didn't know what to do. Péter Varga, a six foot four, two hundred and forty pound guy who was the honorary bouncer at the club, tossing out drunks when they got too rowdy or lecherous, suggested threatening Holló, but this was quickly dismissed, since the risk of losing Holló forever was too great. They thought of giving him a raise, but Holló would know it was a payoff, and he was too proud for that. So finally a delegation was sent to Ílona's house, the executive having agreed that she'd either apologize to Holló or they'd rescind her membership, and Ílona, being Queen Ílona, never apologizing to anyone ever, used to getting her way in all things, swore on her dead husband's grave she'd *never* apologize. The next Saturday the club was once again humming with voices and laughter and people licking their lips with the food and drink Holló provided, when Ílona showed up demanding to be let in. But Varga barred her way, calling Holló, who came over and then looked around as if he were at a complete loss to find a place for her, everyone meanwhile singing and cheering, so happy to be back at the banquet they were oblivious to Ílona standing there, wanting in. It was the only community that mattered to her, these émigrés, where she not only knew every social code but had authored many of them. After ten minutes with Varga blocking her, and realizing how expendable, how invisible, she was, Ílona was forced to say, "Sorry." Holló inclined his head as if he couldn't hear. Ílona said it louder. Then louder again in a shout that made the whole room stop. When she said it next, almost at a whisper, "I'm sorry for what I said," Holló turned, pointed to an empty chair that seemed to appear out of nowhere, and Ílona took her place trying to rise above the shame.

She continued coming to the club, but never spoke to Holló again.

2.

With me it was not so easy. I was seeing her daughter, so we *had* to talk. But that's all it was—the barest acknowledgement. Once a week I had to go over for dinner, where she'd ask pointed questions of the other guests—Did they know that Munkácsy's paintings were growing darker and darker with time because of the bitumen he used on the canvasses? Did they know Budapest had the first metro in continental Europe? Did they know that the reason Catholic churches ring the bell at noon is to commemorate János Hunyadi's defeat of the Turks at the Battle of Nándorfehérvár in 1456?— the standard trivia of Hungarian nationalism, except that in searching the faces around the dinner table she always left me out. Whenever I spoke, she interrupted me. If Éva mentioned my studies, Ílona would say, "Yes, he's working very diligently to learn about the world," and wink at the other guests.

Across the table Éva would take a huge bite out of something her mother had made, food we both hated—*káposzta főzelék, kapór leves, lecsó*—staring at me, sitting there chewing, forcing it down. It was her way of swallowing what I had to swallow, of showing sympathy. Ílona would look at her and frown, "Please don't eat like that, *szívem*," then sigh and launch into her usual tirade, mainly for my benefit, about how she could hardly wait for Éva to graduate so she could be sent back to Hungary where they'd teach her how to behave like a lady, and where they'd find her an *appropriate* husband.

This was a frequent ritual (though it hadn't happened in my case because my parents didn't have the money): sending kids back to Hungary once their schooling was done to spend some intensive time with the language, people, and culture. But the real reason was to find suitable husbands or wives they'd hopefully settle with over there (now that communism was over)—replenishing the nation and atoning for their parents' sin of emigration—or, if necessary, returning to Toronto, where the kids would be Canadian by citizenship but in every other way as Hungarian as if they'd just stepped off a plane. It was, I suppose, what every embattled ethnicity does, though the point I'm trying to make is that I *was* Hungarian, so Ílona needn't have worried about Éva and me, if it ever came to that, which meant her threat of sending her daughter away had nothing to do with protecting the grandchildren's gene pool from defilement by non-Hungarians— *only from me.*

Ílona would mention Éva's impending trip, and her eyes would slide in my direction, then back to the guests, and I'd suddenly ask for another helping of *kapór leves*, my signal to Éva that as bad as the food was it wasn't as bad as listening to this. Ílona would sigh, as I knew she would, and tell the guests that *kapór leves* had already been served, and it was a sign of breeding, by which she meant the lack thereof, not to realize you couldn't go back to the first course once you'd moved on to the second. But I'd keep holding out my plate anyhow, then fake disappointment and return it quietly to its place, Éva turning red with the effort of holding in her laughter.

"There was a certain behaviour you used to be able to count on," Ílona would continue, "at least from people of a *certain class*. But emigration has ruined all that. They don't know anything now, despite all those classes at university."

Éva slurped from her wine with each word Ílona spoke, declaring our alliance with a lack of manners that was at once an attack on her mother's values and a confirmation of the very thing Ílona was complaining about.

I could have been a Rhodes Scholar, winner of the Booker Prize, recipient of a Guggenheim, but none of it would have mattered as much to Ílona as membership in the Hungarian Academy of Sciences. Her allegiances, her values, everything was still perceived as if it was 1940s Hungary. In fact, I would have been surprised if she even knew what a Guggenheim was. But more than any of this, it was the fact that my father had worked for the city of Toronto in road construction that really damned me. "He's not bad," I overheard her say one night to a guest, "for someone whose father is a labourer."

Dinner after dinner Éva and I stuffed ourselves with that awful food. The more we ate the more we disagreed with Ílona. When we stopped eating, or started on something that was actually good, it was a relief. Mainly we were just having a laugh at Ílona's expense, who sat amazed at how much *tökfőzelék* I could snort back when last time I hadn't touched it at all. But there was something else as well, something not so funny, and there were times I saw the realization in Éva too, that for all our coded mockery it was our own powerlessness we were putting on display, eating what we didn't want to eat, swallowing it down, when what we really wanted was to tell Ílona how terrible her dinners were—the cooking, the company, the conversation—though we were too scared to.

We had so few privileges already. I wasn't allowed in the house after 9:00 P.M. Éva was supposed to be home by 10:00 even on weekends. We were permitted, if I had to come over, to sit in the TV room, or in the kitchen and on the porch, but I wasn't allowed within ten feet of her bedroom.

Not that it stopped us. Éva regularly slipped out at night, and snuck back in late. We spent a lot of time in an old tree fort her father had built high in a maple in the back garden. We drank. We did drugs. We had sex. I'm sure Ílona knew about it, but it was the appearance of authority that mattered to her. It was an obsession, Éva told me, since the death of her father twelve years ago, and with it the loss of prestige their family once held in the community, since as a lawyer he'd handled legal matters for the Szécsényi Club, including the mess left by Bodo. Ílona had never forgiven her husband for dying so young, and for leaving her with a sizable life insurance but no way to maintain her dominance over the club, and by extension the community, other than force of will. She'd been trying to stop the erosion of her influence ever since, though it was impossible, and bit by bit it faded, first with the transfer of legal matters to another lawyer, effectively cutting off Ílona's access to insider information; then with her failure to get elected for a fifth term to the executive, probably because she'd gotten so loud since her husband's death nobody could stand her; and third with the scandal involving Holló, which left Ílona a marginal figure, forced to hold court at her own dinner table rather than the club, where she'd once been fawned on and appealed to by every up-and-coming émigré.

So, as long as this "boyfriend" business didn't get too flagrant, Ílona was as happy as Éva not to fight about it, especially since that might lead to people overhearing what they were fighting *about*.

As for Éva and me, we were lazy. She was in her last year of high school, and the thought of leaving home to live with me, or, more absurdly, on her own, was ridiculous. She would have had to get a full-time job, figure out how to cook, do laundry, pay bills, all the stuff her upper-middle-class upbringing had not prepared her for, and, besides, as far as she was concerned things weren't all that bad the way they were. Her mother was a pain, but it rarely stopped us from doing as we pleased.

If anything, I was the problem, bitching about a situation I didn't lift a finger to change, because despite my complaints about Ílona, or how Éva and I could never have sex at my place because of roommates, or the pain of fucking in the back of my car or her stupid tree fort, and despite the times I tried to convince her that getting a place of our own would be best for both of us, the truth is I was safe, and I knew it. Éva couldn't make a move, and so I could take the high road as much as I liked, and in the meantime have it both ways—partying with the roommates when she wasn't there, and professing my desire to be with her, and only her, whenever she came around, which was pretty much as often as I *wanted* her around. Looking back, I spent more time worrying about my thesis than my relationship.

3.

My days and nights were consumed with my thesis—what to write about, how the research was opening up possibilities rather than reducing them, and, worst of all, the deadline looming closer and closer.

Short of actually giving me a topic, Holló tried to help. He loaned me his desk in the club's library. It was huge, made of oak. He even cleared out several drawers, so that every day I'd at least have the thrill of squaring my notes, recapping my pens, stacking the books and journals I was looking at, and putting them away for tomorrow, as if his office was my own.

It was an amazing library. There was stuff in there—books and newspapers and magazines and pamphlets—you couldn't get anywhere outside of Hungary, stuff Holló brought with him from "the bad old communist days," or had smuggled out by "friends" when travel restrictions became looser in the 1970s and '80s, or even obtained recently from disbanded archives, estate sales, and private donations. Some of it was so rare I wondered how he'd gotten hold of it, and even just scanning the documents, without knowing exactly what they contained, I had the feeling they were more precious than most of the Hungarian holdings at the university library.

For this reason, Holló didn't allow anyone to take materials home. They had to stay at the club, he said, as if it were a real archive, though of course everyone was free to look at them, and he even granted me the special privilege of staying long into the night, after he'd gone to sleep. That's how much he trusted me. His care for that library went beyond what I'd seen at the university, a delicacy when he touched the pages, a sense of sacredness, as if Holló would have given his life to protect what was filed there, or, more importantly, our access to it.

It was this perception—as wrong as it was—that led to all the trouble.

It was already the third week in April when I came upon the journal *Piros Krónika* in a pile of recently arrived material. From what I could tell it was an in-house publication, set up by Hungary's Ministry of Culture to celebrate itself, inspire its workers, and even, in a way, reward them, showing that their efforts did not go unnoticed. Old and beat-up, its cover half-torn off, and dated 1951, the pages were so fragile I held my breath going through them, worried that a sneeze or cough would send the whole thing up in a puff of rotten paper and airborne ink. The sun was shining, and I paused for a minute before turning to the table of contents to gaze out the windows in what was once the attic of the old house, the only room large enough to serve as a library, with shelves and filing cabinets running floor to ceiling all the way around the walls, the air conditioning humming at exactly twenty degrees Celsius, the humidity hovering somewhere around forty percent, looking out over the trees and fields and hills of the back garden. Then I turned back to the journal and saw it: "The Ministry of Culture: Guardians of the Soviet Against Reactionary Propaganda," by some apparatchik called Miko Tóth.

I finally had my topic. At the time, young as I was, I thought it was the library itself that inspired me, sitting there day after day with those rare papers, aware more than ever of the importance of information, of access to it, as if there was a heroism in what Holló had done, smuggling it out, arranging for more, and beyond that the chore of taking care of it, making sure nothing disappeared, as if even shelving and cataloguing could be acts of war against an enemy whose power resided in limiting what we knew, and, with that, what we could think, imagine, and feel.

Their names were there—Holló, Cérna, Adriána—along with many others in a caption under a photo taken at the ministry, their faces as dour and anonymous as every other photo of the era. I sat there for two hours and read every sentence, some of them twice because of my sub-par Hungarian, taking pages of notes. When Holló showed up at five saying I'd have to leave early because he had a wedding banquet to set up, I was so entranced by the ideas I was generating for my thesis that I didn't even try to hide the article when he walked in. In fact, it took me a second to recognize who I was talking to.

Not that Holló was interested in my work in the slightest. After saying what he needed to say he turned and left, busy with preparations.

I sat there another fifteen minutes, wondering what to do. Would Holló miss the journal if I snuck out with it? Would he look through my papers? Would he even care that I'd discovered his secret, or was it so long ago now that it didn't matter to him? In the end, I left everything there. For all I knew Holló had already registered the arrival of *Piros Krónika* and, knowing his meticulousness, its absence would only have alerted him to its importance, whereas if I stacked it with my books he wouldn't think twice. As for my notes and papers, he never looked at them, I knew this for a fact, since they were always exactly as I'd left them the night before, my pens sitting on top of the pile. I decided it would be better to hide what I was doing in plain sight.

But I told Éva his secret. "He was a censor," I said, whispering in a darkness lit only by the cherry on the end of the joint we were smoking, weaving its orange glow in the air as we passed it back and forth. Evá's face, her reactions, were hidden. She was absolutely silent. "I can use the sources in his library, then interview him, if he'll let me. My profs will love it. They're really into that now—getting real testimony from people who were actually there. I'll have to fill out an ethics clearance form . . ."

Éva rolled over, and onto me, kissing my mouth. "Enough about Holló," she said.

"But it's important," I replied, moving aside.

"If you're right," she said, sounding hurt, "what makes you think he's going to *want* to talk with you? Maybe he's going to want to keep it with his other secrets . . ."

"No," I said, barely listening. "I think he wants me to. It's the whole library, the way he looks after it. You should see how he handles the books and papers, like he wants the information out there."

"Or something," she said, getting out of the bed and into her clothes, her movements sudden, angry. But I was too busy thinking about Holló to ask what was wrong, and as Éva left I barely acknowledged her departure, the sentences and paragraphs of my thesis as visible in the dark as the burning end of the joint. I lay there for two hours, long after Éva drove off, thinking of the questions I wanted to ask, how I'd approach Holló, telling him there was nothing to be ashamed of, I wasn't judging what he'd done, in fact I'd have done the same thing, and that this was the whole point of my thesis: the ways in which history is written not by heroes but by the most ordinary of people, with only their insecurities, their fears, and their desires to lead them on. The institutions of history, I would tell him, not only make up our society but our selves as well, and only the rarest person can see beyond that and act against the world as it's been defined for him. Yes, I was far from 1950s Hungary, but I wanted him to know I'd write as if I was inside it, setting down the words in sympathy with what he'd faced.

The problem was, I told Ílona about my project one night. We were sitting around the dinner table, Ílona once again speaking in a whisper whenever the name of a young man with a background more suitable than mine came up, or displaying her marvellous range of historical trivia at my expense, and, as usual, complaining about the state of Canadian society—its irreversible drift into liberalism, its inability to understand how little it mattered in the world, its embrace of civil rights at the expense of morality. It was at this point, hoping to pre-empt another tirade (or so I thought my motivation was at the time), that I brought up my discovery in *Piros Krónika*.

Ílona stopped talking. She looked at me with amazement, and let me go on. I was so unnerved by this that I ended up chattering faster, louder, and longer than I wanted. I told them about sitting in the library working on my thesis; I told them how strange I'd always found Holló, with his makeup and mannerisms; I told them about the moment I first picked up the journal and knew it was exactly what I was looking for; and I told them what was inside, about the names, the men and women who'd worked as censors, the sheer volume of literature suppressed. In many cases, I said, great works were lost forever, not to mention the damage to writers, some of whom even committed suicide. I worked myself into a moral outrage I'd never felt before, until I found myself snarling with condemnation, Ílona nodding along. It was only when I'd finished, when she finally spoke again, "I always knew that man—*if you can call him that*," she snorted, "—was no good," that I remembered the thesis I'd planned, though by then it was too late, because Ílona and the guests had launched into a long discussion, including personal reminiscences, of those who (unlike them) had fallen in with the Soviet program, who'd used Party membership for social and economic advantage, who'd spouted all that ideology they didn't believe in because they either wanted a step up on those around them, or were afraid not to, or had no loyalty at all to their country. When I left that night Ílona kissed me on both cheeks and seemed sad that I was leaving so early, saying to Éva, "You kids should go have some fun," and I couldn't look at Éva at all, wanting to get as far away from them as possible.

But I couldn't get away. Éva was delighted at my coup, and the two of us walked to my car, got in, and drove off. At first Éva was laughing, euphoric, fantasizing about all the things we'd be able to do now, as if one minor victory would totally reform Ílona and her attitude. For the first time I felt the difference in our ages, separated by three of the most formative years in my life, and despaired at the thought of having to wait for Éva to catch up. It was at least a half hour before she noticed I was not responding to her, and that I'd driven to the Szécsényi Club, where we idled on the side of the road just off the entrance to the parking lot, watching lights blink on and off in the various rooms as Holló went about his business. It was only then that Éva asked what was wrong.

I had no answer. It wasn't the betrayal of Holló that bothered me. Finding the article felt like something he'd planned, giving him a chance to come clean. No, it was how involuntary that betrayal had been, not only giving in to Ílona's expectations, but also taking pleasure in it, the hot thrill of righteousness, the violent solidarity with everyone at the table. I'd had no control over it.

"They say he likes boys," Éva said, nodding in the direction of the club. I looked at her. "That's what they say," she continued. "He goes off to Church Street. Seventeen, eighteen. He pays them."

"What has that got to do with anything?" I said, spilling over into exasperation.

"You don't have to get mad," she said. "I'm just telling you what they say." I looked at her for another second, then back at the club. "You're so naive," she said. "You don't think a person like that, just because he's so nice to you, and works for the community, you don't think he could do something like that? You don't think people can do good things *and* bad things?"

For a second I had no idea how to respond to her, to that screwy logic so sensible on the surface that its corruption was almost impossible to get at. "No, that's not . . ." I said. "You're missing it."

"You want a good *buzi*, nice and cultured. You don't want to hear about who he fucks."

"No," I yelled, "what I'm saying is you're wrong! There's nothing bad about sleeping with sixteen-year-olds. Or paying for it. How old were you when you first had sex?"

I knew the answer, of course. Éva went silent, and gazed not in the direction of the club but away from it, over the surrounding houses. "My mother's right about him," she finally said. "You haven't been the same since you started going there. It's all you ever think about."

"What, you think he's going to convert me?"

Éva shrugged. "I want to go home now," she said.

Holló was not around the next day, but he'd left a key. Within seconds of being inside the library I was already at work, spreading out my notes, opening books, and for the first time I spent the whole day reading and writing, not even stopping for lunch. By the time I left that evening I had the introduction written, and was starting on chapter two, a detailed account of censorship during the Rákosi era. I was onto something important, something that needed to be understood, and the sense of mission temporarily dispelled the remorse I'd felt since Ílona's dinner.

When I got home and tried to call Éva, nobody picked up. I knew she was at home, her aunt Anuska visited every Tuesday, and I thought there was no way she'd rather listen to her than me.

I was getting on my shoes, grabbing my coat, when the phone rang. It was my father. Without any preamble he asked if what Ílona was saying was true, whether Holló had once worked as a censor.

I was less shocked by how quickly the news had spread than by the worry in my father's voice. Hoping to counteract the negative portrait Ílona had drawn, I told him about *Piros*

Krónika, the work Holló had participated in, but also the thesis I was planning, as if the careful argument I'd constructed would in any way impress my father, much less change his opinion. All I got in return was a snort. "We always knew there was something queer about him," my father said. "Ílona's been trying to get rid of him for years, but nobody had to listen to her until now." He paused. "Are you sure? Is that journal a good one? Did you find the information anywhere else?" I could hear it in his voice, a reluctance, as if he, and by extension the community, would rather prove Ílona and me wrong—even if they knew we were right—than lose out on Holló's services. At the same time, if Ílona had real evidence, there wasn't a person among them, including my father, who'd stand up to defend him.

"I'm planning to talk to him directly," I said, though what I felt was not confidence but that ache in the stomach that comes from having started something now spiralling out of control.

4.

The next day Holló looked as neat as always, though instead of standing in the garden with a watering can, as he normally did in the morning, he was scrubbing spray paint off the door of the club. I could make out the words "*piszkos buzi*"—dirty fag—in faint traces across the wood. But he seemed as happy as ever, wiping his hands on a rag and smiling, his makeup slightly marred by the sweat oozing from his hairline. I'd called my thesis adviser earlier that morning hoping he'd nix the project, but he'd been so enthusiastic, no doubt because by this point he was expecting me to have given up on it, that he said it was the most interesting project he'd heard of in some time, especially if Holló agreed to the interview, and had "real potential to be published in a scholarly journal," which would pave my way into graduate school. But the excitement generated by this conversation disappeared the minute I saw Holló.

"I need to talk to you," I said, glancing again at the graffiti.

"I know," he replied, and opening the door he extended his hand for me to go in ahead of him.

I must have sat in the library for over half an hour before Holló joined me, carrying a tray loaded with tea, pastries, chocolate, and a vase of flowers. I was amazed at how he was able to keep his composure, continue with his usual style, given what was going on. While he was clattering in the kitchen I'd gone into the desk and pulled out my notes and reread them, finally turning to a blank page and staring at it, wondering if I really had it in me to go through with the interview, much less ask if he was willing to do one, or whether it was just a question now of apologizing, gathering my things, and then finding some way to undo the damage I'd caused.

But Holló wasn't interested in what *I* wanted.

He set the tray on the table between us, then stood there, prodding me to pour tea, pick out a pastry, and it wasn't until I'd done this that he sat and poured tea for himself.

"Probably you've heard a little of this story, maybe from your father." He smiled, cracks springing up in the makeup on his face. "Her name was Adriána," he said. "She was my immediate superior at the ministry run by her husband, Cérna." He paused. "It was an unusual situation."

Holló looked at me, and for the first time that morning he darkened. "Aren't you going to pick up your pen?" he asked, leaning forward. "It's very important that you get this right," he said. "It's the only way you're going to be able to tell everyone what really happened. If they're going to judge me, it's important they do so to the full extent of my crimes." I reached over, fumbling. "Pick up the pen," he said, with real impatience now, and I finally did, after brushing crumbs from my hands. "Good," Holló smiled. "There's a lot . . ." His smile faded. "I have a lot to atone for."

He continued. It went on all afternoon. I didn't speak more than five or six words the whole time, only a yes or no when he offered more tea, telling him to go on when he suggested I take a break, or grunting a bit when I shook the writer's cramp from my hand.

He'd drifted into the job after the siege, in which both his parents died, a young man of twenty, effeminate, fastidious, no university education or connections, a target of ridicule during the Horthy regime, almost executed for being homosexual by the Arrow-Cross during the winter of 1945. The truth is, Holló told me, he did not yet think of himself that way, in fact he never would, rejecting all categories. "I prefer to think of myself as a sexual adventurer," he said, winking at me and then continuing with the story. Before the war, he'd only been uncertain, confused, not even aware of what the categories were, living in expectation of women because that's what he'd been told to expect. Then, with 1939, everything changed, that moment in history introduced him to something else, the terror and intrigue of policemen and soldiers who seemed to recognize him in some way he had yet to recognize himself. Finally there was the siege. "Everything fell apart," Holló said. "The world was finally and fully shattered." His eyes were bright as he described it. "What the soldiers were fighting for was the exclusive right to pull it back together again—for whose vision of reality would prevail. But for me it was something else. It was such a short time, a hundred days or so, but I saw how much energy, how much violence, was required to maintain anything—systems, structures, truths—and how sooner or later something came along to smash it all to pieces." The siege had made it impossible to maintain anything—a politic, a community, an identity. "One day we were subhuman—homosexuals, Jews, communists, gypsies—fit only for execution, and the next we were liberated, the proletariat, the people of the future. But the real lesson in all of this," said Holló, smiling, "is that if we were only what they made us, then at bottom we were really nothing." He laughed with what sounded like joy. "And if that was true then maybe, if I was smart enough, I could take that power for myself—free to change, to invent myself, to not have to conform to *anything*." He stopped, seeing in my face a skepticism, though he was so lost in memory he thought I was questioning how quickly he'd grasped the "lesson" of the siege, when what I was really thinking was that it wasn't a lesson at all, only a symptom of what he'd gone through and how it had warped his thinking. "Well," said Holló after a while, "it started in the siege but it wasn't until I met Adriána that it all became clear."

He welcomed the security promised by membership in the Communist Party, and the relatively anonymous work for the Ministry of Culture. He was one of the many waiting for rescue at the end of the siege, desperate for the arrival of the Red Army, not realizing there would be no end to ruin, they'd been turned into its agents, harnessed to it, dragging its wreckage into the next half century.

For Holló it was the work of reading. He got to do a lot of that when he was censoring books. The primary target of his work was literature, especially the work of poets, who were heroes in Hungarian society, though there were plenty of novels, plays, and films to ban as well, along with memoirs, science fiction, children's stories, anything you could think of. "I had latitude," Holló said. "I could exercise my own responsibilities as a proletariat toward reactionary and formalist thinking."

The important thing was that people *had to be caught*, a lot of them, and he was free to pick his offenders, preferably writers who didn't belong to the Party, but once in a while a Party member too, just to keep everyone alert. "It was a paranoid time," he said, and I sensed a sadness in Holló then, something beneath the refinement he cultivated, gazing at the library as though it might vanish any second, that despite the work he'd done he didn't deserve to be there, in the company of all those books.

"At first," he said, "I tried to be careful. I picked out the really bad stuff, the ones I thought weren't worth keeping, or were offensive, as if I could somehow justify what happened to those books and their writers, telling myself they were unworthy, they had no skill, they didn't deserve to be published, communism or not." But it wore him out. Within months Holló was getting up at night haunted by the idea that one of those writers, it didn't matter which, might have gone on from the trash they were churning out to composing truly lasting work. In the office, he wanted to ask someone, anyone, to second guess his choices, to tell him he was right in thinking that writer X or Y would never amount to anything, but to even ask that, to have considerations beyond the one that mattered—whether a given book reinforced or undermined the revolution—was already to be compromised, an enemy. It was in the middle of this isolation that he began meeting with Adriána in the out-of-the-way places of the ministry—the basement storage lockers, bathrooms closed for repair, boiler rooms.

"I really don't know how it started." Holló paused. "I think it was the excitement of having something in my life other than mere survival. It wasn't her, not really." He smoothed the hair on top of his head. "We were young and stupid and I don't think either of us really knew what we wanted."

Adriána was having as much trouble sleeping as he was. For her, Cérna was the problem, another kind of censorship altogether, this man who somehow kept to himself even when they were having sex, so removed from showing what he felt, who he was, what he desired, so totally one with the Party line that he was only ever there as an instance of ideology. It had been different before the war, she told him, when there were so many different *kinds* of communist, before the Soviets arrived and liquidated those on the left who were too outspoken or brave or committed, and coerced the rest into an undifferentiated mass. "Maybe Cérna always thought the way he thought," she said, "but I never noticed it because there were always people around who thought differently."

Is that why I'm here, Holló had wondered, because I'm different? Had Adriána chosen him as a lover because unlike Cérna he was so totally an outsider in the ministry, a low-level hack, no friends or connections, someone whose comings and goings no one would even notice? Or was it because she sensed something else in him, repressed and abnormal passions, and that he was therefore less likely to arouse suspicion, to be seen as one of her possible lovers?

Adriána said she'd been watching him for weeks, which Holló understood to mean she'd been looking *into* him, whatever files there were, making sure he was safe in every way, unallied with anyone more powerful than her husband. "She kissed me first," he said, though he was already aware that it was coming, the way she sidled up to his desk, stood closer than was necessary when she called him into her office, the way she was always there, smiling, when he rounded a corner, her fingertips brushing his hand as she glided past. "I am alone," Adriána said that first time, pulling back from his lips, her gaze somewhere between authority and exposure, as if she was stepping out of her clothes right there. It was the perfect thing to say, at once a statement of how she spent her days, how she felt, and that she was acting of her own prerogative. "I'm not going to be able to wait this out," she said, gesturing hopelessly at the building. "This is going to last longer than us." He'd nodded. She stepped in to kiss him again, and he kissed her back.

They taught each other to sleep, realizing together what it required, how they could work all day doing the sorts of things they did, throwing all of that work, the beauty and truth and bravery of it, down the toilet, then meet at night, whenever Cérna was away—off to Moscow, Krakow, Berlin, Bucharest, as politics required—tossing their guilt aside as easily as their clothes, and falling afterwards into a darkness so deep it was empty even of dreams.

Holló smiled at me. "You're surprised by this? That I would be with a woman instead of a . . . what is it your girl-friend and mother say about my tastes? Instead of a boy?" He drummed his fingers on the table, then got up and retrieved a book and opened it in front of me, paging through old black-and-white photographs of the infamous communists of the 1950s until he came to Ábel Cérna.

"He was not a man to be crossed," Holló said. Then he gestured toward his own face. "This stuff here, all this"—he pointed at his eyes and cheeks and lips—"it was Adriána's idea."

She always felt they were being watched—afraid of an extra presence in the storerooms where they met; of the way Cérna rolled over and looked at her at night; of signs that someone else was going through her papers. It was in this way, Holló said, that his real work as a censor began, because as the days and weeks and months went by she made it harder and harder for them to get together. She stopped walking by his desk, calling him into her office, meeting him in the hallways. The only way to communicate became the books themselves, the ones he and his co-workers sent forward to be suppressed, and which she approved or disapproved in keeping with the policies of the time. "I came to think of the recommendations I sent to her as a kind of love letter,"

Holló said. "It was one way to ignore what I was actually doing." He looked now for the most exquisite books, those he knew would enter circulation through underground channels, with their lines of flawless prose, poetry that gave him goosebumps, the best of the best, and every single one he condemned without fail, sending them forward knowing it would give her pleasure to go through them, vouching for his decisions, thinking of him while doing it, almost like an aphrodisiac. "It was our substitute for sex," he smiled, "between meetings." It wasn't long before Holló realized his quota of censored books was increasing, that he was always in the office early, trying to get to the new stuff, to take the best from it, before anyone else.

"Of course, you tell yourself things," he continued, "stories to redeem your betrayals." At night, after work, early in the morning, he'd think of the writers who'd written these books, the hours they'd spent, the excitement and inspiration, and it felt to him like the only fitting tribute to her, the only thing those books could now realize, as if the beauty that was their aim was Adriána herself, for if they were going to be destroyed, and they were whether Holló did it or someone else, then at least they should go to that, the very thing they'd tried to accomplish and which their destruction would testify to—a love outside the ideology hemming them in, as if one secret could hide inside another, buried deep, the loss of these books covering up something else the regime had missed.

In time, it became their code. His objections to this or that book involved highlighting certain passages, circling words, putting X's through entire pages, and she noted it all—descriptions of lovers' quarrels and trysts, partings and reconciliations, triangulating the chapters, sequencing the page numbers to figure out the time and place he wanted to meet, sending them back to Holló if it wasn't going to work out, if Cérna would be in town, if there was a meeting she had to attend, asking him to "reconsider" the implications of his report, especially the bits on the ideological significance of Váci Street and Hösök Tér, and, in particular, pages four and fifty-six. After a bit of back and forth the date, time, and place would be set, and on the right night or afternoon or morning Adriána would be there, dressed in an ankle-length overcoat, a top hat, a briefcase, and Holló in a subdued dress, grey cotton, no designs, a belted coat, shielding his face with some hat or umbrella she'd left for him the last time.

Holló stopped in the middle of his story and looked at me and laughed. "The disguises were her idea. She thought we'd be less noticeable. But I wasn't so sure. . ." His voice trailed off. "I think she was more interested in exposing me to . . . various options than she was in avoiding the police." He looked into my face, saw the questions there, and smiled. "You want to know what she was. A lesbian? A man disguised as a woman who liked to disguise herself as a man?" He laughed. "I have no idea. I'd never met anyone like her, and probably never will again."

"She sounds a lot like you," I said.

"Hm," he said, nodding his head. "That's funny, because she showed me I didn't have to be *like* anything. I didn't have to be . . . consistent." Holló frowned then. He seemed at a loss for the right language with which to describe Adriána and exactly what he'd felt, or still felt, for her—I'd never seen

him searching for words before—and after a while Holló
gave up and went back to his story.

Adriána looked at him in the dress and smirked. "You
are the ugliest woman I've ever seen." He smiled, agreeing.
But he wasn't so sure. There was something in the disguise
that freed Holló to move as he'd always wanted to, before
his father had quietly battered him into adopting that set to
his shoulders, that stride, that way of turning from others
coming at you that was not really turning at all.

Adriána and Holló varied the hours they met. They varied
the code. Figuring out what they were trying to say with
their lists of banned books, their forms and reports, became
complicated, a cross-referencing of paragraphs and circled
words and page numbers. They were scared but obsessed,
and there were times, Holló confessed, when he'd forget, for
hours at a time, how to decipher it, and a panic would come
over him and he'd have to force himself not to go ask Adriána
what it all meant.

Or Adriána would not show up, and he'd sit there wondering how he'd gotten it wrong, what he'd missed. "It was
all trust," Holló told me. "I *had* to believe she wanted to meet
me, but for whatever reason couldn't. Either way—whether
she came or not—she still loved me."

It was Adriána who showed him how to apply makeup
properly. How to create shadows in his face. How to
compensate for bad lighting. What to wear under clouds,
in sunshine, when it was snowing. "For her, of course,
the disguise was easy," he said, laughing. "A briefcase, an
overcoat, a hat, and a suit with a red carnation in the lapel." It
was their fun, in whatever hotel room, vacant flat, or empty

office she found for them, something to do other than rail against the system, giggling as Adriána applied this or that cosmetic, showing him how it was done, what effect it would have, and how to get it on and off quickly, without a trace, and of course where to go buy it, the best stuff, usually through some black-market dealer who had a pipeline, God knows how, to the west. By the end of it, he said, after just two years, he could change his face in seconds, from aggressive to soft, from angry to sad, from beautiful to hideous, depending on what was needed, and with that skill he acquired even more freedom, as if going out dressed as a woman was no longer what it had been, a way of hiding, but a kind of release, even exposure, as if he was no longer bound by the fears, the rules of behaviour, even the creed of the person he'd been. Holló began to go out that way on nights when he and Adriána weren't meeting, when it was just him, and in the mornings when he got home it was almost an effort to take off the makeup, always this feeling of duress.

It wasn't long before Holló noticed others like him. He wasn't speaking about the obvious cases, he said, the men and women everyone's seen in their ill-fitting dresses and jeans, too-broad shoulders, too-narrow waists, walking down the street knowing all eyes are on them, and fitting into that too, those gazes, like an agonizing suit of clothes. No, the ones that attracted him were the beautiful, he said, who radiated the freedom he'd also begun to feel in the midst of the grey housing projects, the sooty and bullet-riddled fronts of Budapest's apartments. "Those were the ones that attracted me," he said. Everything about them seemed so perfect, the care with which they made up their faces, the perfect tailoring of

their clothes, the exact match of colours, even their movements, like actors who'd long ago mastered every nuance
of character to the point where none of it seemed choreo-
graphed or scripted. Nobody else he knew looked as free as
that. He followed them to where they went.

"They were guerrilla establishments," he said. "Spring
up. Close down just as fast." Bars. Tiny dance halls. Apartments where for one night you were nowhere in the eastern
bloc. There were people there from every part of society—
proletariat, civil servants, athletes, even a few Party officials—as if they'd managed for one night to achieve a utopian
levelling, the dreamed-of equality, that was enforced everywhere else with fists and disappearances and guns and pris-
ons. "You might have picked *that* to write your thesis on,"
he said to me, "if it had occurred to you." I looked up from
the page, saw him frowning, and for one second thought this
was a reproach for what I *had* decided to write on, though
when he spoke next I realized this was not it at all, Holló
wasn't interested in me in the slightest. He was frowning at
his memories. Mountains of flowers at a bacchanal paid for
by misappropriated Party money. Bordellos secreted away
in hunting estates once owned by the aristocracy. Male and
female escorts kept in pearls by some of the top officials. He
seemed so enraptured by what he was telling me that I found
myself wondering if I was listening to something that was
more dream than reality, if maybe the days and nights of living alone at the club hadn't turned his memories golden.

"People assume sex was somehow abolished by the Soviet
system," he said. The way historians wrote it was as if those
old wooden men spent all day in the politburo haranguing

and backstabbing each other, then put on their dark overcoats and went home to their stale wives and wiretapped phones and produced a child or two. "But the level of perversity was exquisite," Holló admitted, "maybe because it was so furtive, so hidden away, so scary."

I finished my last note on the word "perversity" and waited.

"You were expecting something else?" Holló smiled.

I shrugged. The truth is, it looked like a strategy, as if by losing himself in these fantastical descriptions he might lose me as well, leading me away from his work as a censor, and for a moment I was tempted to say I didn't believe him, that the truth was probably quieter and greyer and more desperate, all those closeted transvestites and cross-dressers and gays and lesbians meeting in dreary communist parks and housing projects and public bathrooms trying hard not to speak their names, to give anyone a good look at their faces, and when there were parties they were probably more like funerals, everyone too tired and afraid for that kind of heightened revelry.

As for Party officials being involved, and misappropriating funds for flowers and champagne, I found that totally unbelievable. He'd made the whole thing too heroic, this group of people blatantly defying political reality, and the terrible price they'd pay if they were discovered. Looking back, of course, it was Holló's final attempt to switch me from the track I was on, to interest me in something else, as if he was counting on me not believing him, on being curious about how things *really* were, and following that toward a different research topic. It was my last chance to leave it alone, him and Adriána and the makeup and the censorship, but I was too fixated on what I'd discovered to change my thesis now, and he could see it in my silence, my indifference.

He sighed. After another minute, desperate to break the silence, I asked him what happened to Adriána, and Holló glared at me as if he was going to take my head off. But then he spoke.

"It started with sloppiness," he said. "I think Adriána started sensing an indifference on my part, as if she'd opened a door and I was more interested in seeing what was on the other side than lingering with her on the threshold." She almost willed it to happen, her fear of losing Holló becoming greater than her fear of being discovered, because that would at least mean they'd been separated artificially, that whatever happened, wherever she went, wherever they put her, she'd at least know the thing with Holló was unfinished, and, in that way, everlasting.

Holló's voice was even now, with none of that rapture of before, as if all that was left was the routine end of another story of illicit love during the Kádár regime.

"She risked meeting me when Cérna was around. She went out without a disguise. She tried to get me to do the same." Adriána told him she was tired of hiding, of being afraid. She took greater chances at work, throwing herself on him when there were others around, making remarks too easily overheard. She started writing him notes he got rid of by flushing down the toilet, which was suspicious in itself, all that back and forth as if there was some problem with his bladder. It was not just the limits of his loyalty that Adriána was testing, Holló realized, but also of their entrapment, as if with enough violations, enough flagrant behaviour, she might prove there were no limits.

He got out just before her arrest, walking away from his apartment after a long night of watching shadows in the street from under the curtains. "It was no way to live," he said. "I just panicked, I guess. I put on my best dress, packed a suitcase with all the makeup I had, and never went back." They came for Adriána late in the day, November 23, 1955, he still remembered it, and she never returned, though whenever he was in Budapest he went by her place, or where she'd worked, always in disguise of course, hoping to catch a glimpse of some rehabilitated Adriána. But the only person he ever saw was Cérna, looking ever more hollow, ever more in tune with the demands of the time, and after a while there was even a new wife, as if Adriána had never existed at all.

"And what did *you* do? I mean, how did you do it?" I asked.

He smiled. "I became Árpád Holló." He looked at me and I wasn't sure if he meant an alias or he simply became himself after years of trying to be something else. "I guess you might say I didn't survive. Not in the full sense of the term." He went underground, joining others who made a living outside sanctioned channels—doing odd jobs under the table; moving from place to place without any of those securities you could only get through the government, such as a place to live, a bank account, a bed in a hospital, though there were enough doctors also leading a double life that you could get any problem looked after if you had enough money, or a nice bottle of Scotch, or a couple of chickens to barter. When I asked what he did to earn money during that time, he smiled. "I used the one skill I had outside of inventing accusations: I did makeup." Along the way, Holló learned the rest of it as well—manicures and pedicures and cutting and dyeing hair—though he was just as often forced to take whatever came to hand—gardening, carpentry, painting. "I learned a lot," he said. Mainly he worked for the people who went to the parties he'd described, who either hired him themselves, or put him in touch with others—actresses, opera singers, wives of Party officials—who had no idea who they were paying. He lived for a time in all of Hungary's major cities, Budapest, Debrecen, Sopron, Szeged, Pécs, Miskolc, Tihany, circulating through them attracting as little attention as possible, never staying long enough for people to mark him. Then, in 1956, just over a year after his affair with Adriána, he escaped altogether, leaving the country on a fake vacationer's permit to Yugoslavia, and from there, via a sickening boat ride inside a coffin, to Trieste, and, from there, to Toronto and the Szécsényi Club.

Holló finished speaking. I said nothing. "You know the rest," he finally said.

"Didn't you miss Adriána?" I asked, though what I really wanted to know, but didn't have the bravery to ask, was why he hadn't tried to find out what happened to her.

"Sometimes." He smiled, then grew thoughtful. "What I miss most about Adriána," he laughed, "is the times she wore suits. She'd wear them to bed. I stayed in the dresses. I miss how open she was to that. As if she knew what she'd awakened in me." Holló lightly tapped his empty teacup on the table.

I nodded, looking at the pages of notes I'd taken, then wondered how it was going to go when Ílona, my father, and the rest found out what I'd written. Nothing about Holló wearing makeup as a mere disguise. Nothing about him being just like they were. Nothing, really, about Holló having entirely average (whatever that was) appetites. It was a record of exactly those things they'd always suspected about him and talked themselves out of, and whose revelation would make it impossible to ignore his "obscenity," "perversion," "immorality," and all the other phrases Ílona would use in her campaign against him. Those who wouldn't object to him being gay, or whatever he was, would certainly object to the work he'd done as a censor, or, worse, hide their objection to his sexuality under objections to his past, his politics. When I looked up from my notes Holló was sitting there unmoving, a smile still on his face, the room receding into darkness as evening came on, heightening the noise of cars in the street, the city rumbling, children calling after each other as if in preparation for summer.

"I'm tired," Holló finally said. He waited for me to speak, then for a moment it looked as if he was wrestling with something—disbelief, exasperation—but it was soon over, he suppressed it, and returned to his tired but elegant manner. "I've made no secret of who I am," he continued.

No, I shook my head in agreement, he hadn't. Instead, he'd allowed *them* to make a secret of him, obscuring what was blatantly obvious, and, for them, so objectionable, with a mollifying fairy tale, since they could only take what Holló offered if they could ignore who was offering it. The fact was, he didn't need to hide—they'd done the hiding for him. And I didn't know who was worse, people like my father, so complicit in that, or like Ílona, who wanted Holló exposed even if it meant impoverishing the community. Or people like me, I realized, who were doing exactly as Holló wanted.

I looked at the notes I'd taken, at Holló sitting there waiting for my reaction, at the whole chain of events from my father telling me to come to the library, to the hours in Holló's company as he guided me through the holdings, to the day I found *Piros Krónika*, the dinner at Éva's, our argument, the spray paint on the door, everything. There was no way Holló couldn't have known what I'd find—he knew everything about the library down to the last misprinted word. He *wanted* me to do this, to write my thesis, to expose him, and I was angry at being manoeuvred into this position, for the way he'd kept me from discovering *Piros Krónika* until three weeks before the deadline for my thesis, for making me not only responsible for destroying him, but worst of all complicit with Ílona in the process.

"Why?" I asked. "Why do you want this?"

I'm not sure what response I was expecting. Maybe I thought he'd push aside the tray between us, maybe with enough force to send it crashing to the ground, and then yell something—that he was sick of not being seen, that he'd been working at the Szécsényi Club for over twenty years and not once had anyone acknowledged who he was, that all his life he'd been invisible. But Holló didn't do any of that. He was as composed as ever, putting down his cup, folding his hands in his lap. "I don't want anything," he said. "I'm telling you this because you asked. For your thesis."

"If this gets out," I said.

He shrugged. "Nothing will happen." He seemed so sure of himself I was at a loss to come up with a warning equal to it. "It's not like it's the Rákosi era," Holló laughed.

5.

From there, the days accelerated. Half the time I was in a daze, wanting to quit the whole project, desperately trying to think of another thesis. The other half I was at the club, working like a demon to get the thing written by deadline, hopeful that it would happen, that I'd actually get my degree, that I wouldn't have to face the prospect of temporarily withdrawing from the program to work some awful job just to get money for another semester of tuition. I wanted to graduate and follow Éva to Hungary, scuttling Ílona's plan—which relied on my laziness and poverty—to keep me from her daughter.

Holló would come into the library once in a while to water plants, adjust the thermostat, do the dusting, and he'd peer over my shoulder and nod, his face perfectly neutral, composed, but still projecting this awful power, as if he was guiding my hand through every paragraph. As for the thesis committee, they were overjoyed with the proposal I handed in, commenting on the "clarity and rigour" of the argument, asking for minor editorial changes, signing their names to the ethics form required for the interview with Holló that had already taken place, then telling me I had two weeks to get the whole thing in, eighty to a hundred pages, most of which, by that time, was already written.

The dinners at Ílona's were more frequent now. I was invited every other day, including the sacred rite of Tuesday evening, in the company of Anuska Néni, whose optimism about the situation with the Szécsényi Club and Holló seemed even more sinister than Ílona's hostility. She was old, at least eighty, and Éva told me she was fêted every Tuesday because she was rich, and Ílona her only remaining relative, which should have been an open-and-shut case of inheritance except that Anuska Néni was also, unfortunately, a philanthropist. She'd donated money to the Szécsényi Club in the days before Holló, as well as to the Church, various anticommunist newspapers, the Conservative Party, and pro-life organizations. Ílona's greatest fear was that when Anuska Néni died the money would die with her, frittered away in one last gesture on her pet causes.

"You know, I think a change would be good for the club," Anuska Néni said, looking at me kindly. "Oh, there are a lot of people who will say Holló has done a good job," she said. "But, you know, the place has been one way, *his way*, for a long time, and it's good to see things done differently once in a while." She smiled. "That's what's so great about living in a democracy." She rocked back and forth at this for a little longer than normal, and I had the urge to grab her shoulder and make her stop.

Following this, Ílona asked how the writing was coming along. I told her the thesis was days from completion. She nodded and said she'd love to see it when it was done, and I nodded back and said everyone would be able to see it, given that all theses presented in the history department were bound and shelved in the library. There was a pause then, and

I quickly added that of course I'd give her a copy. Éva smiled at me across the table, and Anuska Néni looked around at all the smiling faces and then smiled herself, more broadly than anyone, clearly not sure what was going on, her eyes darting back and forth to make sure we didn't stop smiling before she did.

After dinner Éva and I went out, with Ílona's blessing, and Éva was so thrilled at how well things were going that she straddled me in the driver's seat after we parked in one of the darkened lots by the lake, saying that now for sure Ílona wouldn't send her to Hungary. "You could go to graduate school, and we could live together. I'll be eighteen by then and my mother won't be able to do a thing."

I felt Éva's weight, her breath close, but all I wanted was to get outside, into the darkness past the grass ringing the parking lot, down to the lake and the wind driving the waves onto the beach. But I didn't know how to climb out from under her without making it look like rejection. "What about Holló?" I said. I told her I'd spoken with my father, who said the community was in an uproar, some of them had even gone to the club to confront Holló, who sat in total silence, smiling at them as if he had no idea what they were talking about. "That place is Holló's life," I said. "If they get rid of him . . ."

Éva sighed. "Who cares? That's not even what I'm talking about. Haven't you been listening?"

I pulled the handle on the door. The summer air rushed in with a fragrance of water, the tarmac of the lot, the night-blooming flowers in planters all around, and I slid from under Éva and stepped out as if I was rising from some contorted sleep, stretching, breathing deep, and walked down to the shore.

It didn't take long for her to join me. The wind was warm that night, sending up a fine spray from the lake.

"You know what Aurél Bácsi told my mother?" Éva said, standing so close I could hear her hair whipping in the breeze. I shrugged. She continued anyhow. "He wondered who was going to serve him *rántot hús* every Saturday if Holló wasn't around. Or where he was going to go for a nice glass of *aszú*. Or what he was going to read without Holló stocking the latest edition of *Népszava*." She didn't laugh. "Then you know what Aurél Bácsi said? He said he didn't believe it. He said Holló probably did some low-level work for the Party when he lived in Hungary just like everyone else. He said you were probably just making it look bigger than it was so my mother would agree to you dating me."

I turned to Éva. "What business is it of his, you and me being together?"

"Everyone knows about it. My mother talks."

"I didn't realize we were a community concern."

She put her hand on my arm. "People like your father. They've been on your side." She waited. "Until now. They think the thesis is just your way of sucking up to my mother." She paused again. "A lot of them agree with Aurél. Some are even making comments about the two of us trying to ruin the place."

I looked out on the lake, thinking of my father, of our recent conversations, how hesitant he'd been, asking careful questions, giving little in the way of replies, as if he was weighing not so much the believability of what I was saying—he believed me, I was sure of that—but whether *everyone else* would believe it, or how the information would have to be presented to save my reputation, which was of course his reputation as well. Maybe, I thought, watching stray headlights play over the dark waves from a nearby overpass, he was also thinking of how to save Holló. But saving both of us was impossible, I saw that, and in that moment my father's dilemma was mine as well.

"My mother swears she's going to prove to everyone that what she's been saying about Holló is true." Éva shuffled her feet on the sand. "If you help her."

"What I don't understand," I said, "is what your mother's motivation is. She loves going to the club as much as anyone."

"The club is the only place my mother is visible," said Éva. "That's the most important thing—making them pay attention to her."

I turned, and saw that she was hugging herself against the breeze, her eyes fixed on something at the shoreline. "I was thinking this could work out so well for us," Éva said. "But maybe that's not right." She looked up at me. "I don't think you should do it if you don't want to."

Then I did just as Éva wanted, I put my arms around her, and with that I thought it was decided. I would hand in the thesis because Éva wanted it, and because Holló wanted it too, an end to deception, an acknowledgement of who he really was, whatever the cost. But the truth is the decision had been made long before, and all I was really doing, that night by the lake, was pretending, squeezing the situation for every last bit of drama. I was going to get that degree on time, no matter what, even if it meant exposing Holló, turning all those rumours into fact, and destroying what he'd built at the Szécsényi Club. I wasn't going to give Ílona the satisfaction of separating me from Éva.

6.

Everything that happened after that night played out like a script. My father called later, once we returned home, Éva asleep in my bed in complete defiance of her mother's rules, while I tiptoed into the bathroom with the phone and listened to my father say that Holló had finally taken a stand, refusing to let him into the library to look at the research materials I was using, saying they were "reserved." When I asked my father why he'd gone there in the first place, he let out a short laugh. "It's not that I don't trust you," he said, "but I wanted to see them myself, to see how explicit they . . ."

"My Hungarian isn't that bad," I snapped.

My father sighed. "Mainly it was an excuse. I wanted to see Holló. How he's holding up. People are really starting to boycott the place now," he said. "Ílona's been phoning around, paying house calls, getting everyone agitated. Holló showed me where someone threw a brick through the window."

"Is he upset?"

"No," my father said. "He doesn't seem upset at all. It's like he was expecting or even enjoying it in some way. You know what he said?" I waited. "He said he had half a mind to let whoever it was come in and destroy the place. To show them *they'd* miss it way more than *he* would."

"Yes," I said, quietly. "He's probably right."

"Of course he's right!" my father yelled. "Those idiots are *all* going to miss it. What do they think, Ílona's going to come in and take over and make everyone happy like Holló does?" He snorted. "She's called a general meeting," he said. "You know she's going to ask you to be there. And if you're not able to prove what she's been saying there's going to be trouble."

"I know," I said, my voice firm with the decision I'd made.

"Are you sure?" he asked. "Because," and his voice dropped to a whisper, "you could leave, you know. There's no reason for you to go through with it. You could take another semester, write something else. You could even take some time off, go somewhere."

"Like where?" I asked.

"Your mother and I were thinking of your uncle's place in St. Catharines. Sanyi would love to have you. You could spend the summer there."

"No," I said. "I don't think that would work for me."

There was a moment of silence on the other end. "No," he said. "I guess you're right." I thought I heard him whisper something about Éva—or was it Ílona?—but his voice was too soft to hear.

Neither of us knew how to continue.

"I'll talk to you later," I said.

"Sure," he answered, his voice distant. "Sure, sure."

I went to the Szécsényi Club early the next morning, dragging my feet along the sidewalk, up the steps, through the front door, to find Holló in the library looking absently through a series of books and magazines. His makeup was smeared, as if he'd put it on while standing in a moving train. He nodded hello, forced out a smile, and indicated the stack of books with his hand.

I nodded back and looked at them, half a dozen journals, a novel, a book of poems, and, most amazingly, a journal written during the 1950s—in the original. "Wow," I said, despite myself, paging through it, noting the dates, the archaic handwriting, stopping to read the pages Holló had marked with sticky notes, then looking back at him in shock, and sitting down to read the entries, all dating from 1953, by Antal Balogh, a novelist who'd fearlessly petitioned the censoring of his work. The entries detailed his meetings with Holló, whose inability (or unwillingness) to change the verdict understandably infuriated Balogh, who spent pages describing their meetings, and exactly what he thought of Holló and the whole Ministry of Culture. It was a remarkable document, irreplaceable, and I was so amazed by it I completely forgot Holló was there, until he said, "If you don't need these, I can put them away."

I looked at him, unable to respond, and put down the journal on top of the other material Holló had gathered for me, like some kind of death wish on the old man's part, wanting to create as total a case against himself as he could. "If you don't want them," he said, "if they're extraneous . . ." Behind Holló's careful words I could hear what was really going through his mind: *If you're too scared to go through with this, if you aren't brave enough to do me this favour . . .*

"No, I'll use them," I answered, reaching for the journal again. "How did you get this?"

He smiled. *Good.* "Antal Balogh committed suicide early in 1954," he said. "His mother delivered that to me," he nodded at the journal, "in person."

The way he said it, so easy, I wondered if I'd heard correctly. "What did you do?"

Holló stood there impassive, not a twitch to betray what he was feeling. "Nothing," he said. "There was nothing I *could* do, except have her arrested." He laughed bitterly. "But I let her get away with it." Holló closed his eyes. "Balogh's books, his novels"—his nostrils widened—"they were really beautiful. Sentence by sentence. I can still remember some of them." He opened his eyes. "I forwarded them to Adriána. They were destroyed." *You have to do this for me. I'm tired of keeping this to myself.*

"I see," I said. But I didn't see, not at all, only Holló standing there in all his terrible peace, and I wondered if Balogh's mother had seen the same thing, his passivity, his refusal to take action, his feigned optimism, and whether it had sent the same shudder, half rage, half hopelessness, through her.

"Well, I'll leave them then," he said. "Your paper is due in a week." *We're going all the way.*

"Yes," I said, but I wasn't looking at or even speaking to him then, I was lost already, back in that rush of words Balogh had written during the fall and winter of 1953, so close to his suicide but still taking care to make sure his story came out right, each word in its place, each breathless clause brimming with invective, a magical current that must have finally run dry, because I couldn't see why anyone who wrote this well, regardless of whether he was published, would quit life, as if it should have been enough, his sheer talent, his genius, even if he was its only witness.

In the days that followed I didn't see Éva at all, nor anyone else, as I raced my thesis to the finish line. It was, I now realize, a way of avoiding people, anyone who might speak to me about Holló. I sat in the club's library writing and writing, taking apart the sources, putting them back together, perfecting the transcript of the interview.

Éva and I did speak once on the phone. She understood that I needed to get this done, though there was an extra anxiety there too, something she wasn't saying, but when I asked what it was, Éva said we could talk after the thesis was finished.

Sometimes Holló would come into the room, completely unconcerned with what I was doing, moving around the furniture with his duster or vacuum or cloth as if the place had gone strange, he no longer lived there, had no idea how dirty it was, cleaning the same places over and over. He, too, was desperately waiting for me to finish. Like Éva, he wanted it over with.

But of all of them, Ílona was the most impatient. At ten o'clock, the night of the twenty-eighth, she pulled up to the curb as I was walking home, motioning for me to get in. "*Szerbusz*," she said, stinking of booze, patting the seat beside her. I looked back along the road, then at her. Ílona scowled. "I need to speak with you," she said. I glanced over my shoulder at the club, feeling sick, and shook my head.

"But I don't need to speak with you," I finally said.

She smiled tightly. "That's right. All you need to do is *listen*." The car idled noisily, Ílona shaking her head free of some drunken lassitude, trying to make her words, what she was going to say next, sharp and to the point. "Éva loves you," she said. "She really does." She leaned so far toward me across the passenger seat her head was almost outside the door. "You know I'm telling the truth. And you know, too, that if she does love you, then what *I* think doesn't matter." The leather of the car seat creaked. "It's taken me a long time," she continued. "But I'm prepared to acknowledge that." Her eyes glinted with street light. "I'm *prepared*." I waited there on the sidewalk. "You can walk home if you like." She shrugged, leaned back, gazed out at the sky. "It's a nice night. Early summer."

I heard trees rustling along the street, saw the city's light and smog turning the sky a hazy orange, distant office buildings glittering to the sky, smelled a summer almost fresh enough to make me forget I was in Toronto. When I looked back, Ílona was staring over the steering wheel as if she meant to go, though the passenger door was still open.

"You'll get it," I said. "He's practically forcing me to give it to you."

"Oh? Why do you think that is?" she asked, still gazing out the windshield.

"Because he's as sick of you as I am," I said. "Of all of you."

"Well, it's not really about what he wants, or what we want, is it? It's about what's right."

I slammed the door, and continued walking, and it was several minutes, long after I'd rounded the corner, that I heard the roar of her car as it blew by me along Harbord.

The first thing I did on getting home was call Éva, who answered on the first ring, strange noises leaking into the mouthpiece that suggested she was somewhere else, not at home, and I could swear there was a bird crying somewhere in the background.

I told her about my encounter with Ílona. For a while Éva said nothing, the silence on the other end broken by that same piercing cry.

"Where the hell are you?" I asked.

"The tree fort," she answered. "There's a nest up here somewhere. I think I'm disturbing it."

"Oh," I said, not surprised that she'd be up there, even at that time of night.

"She bought my plane ticket," Éva finally said. "She just went ahead and did it."

"Plane ticket?"

"To Hungary," Éva said. "It's still two months to graduation, but she bought it anyhow. I leave July first." She waited before continuing. "She says it's my graduation present."

"You're not going to go." I'd intended it as a statement, but the way it came out, so hesitating, it might as well have been a question, and I wondered why I hadn't said, "I'll follow you," instead.

Éva waited again. The birds screamed. "It's only for a year. You'll be done your thesis and have your degree. You could visit me," she finished, supplying the words I should have said.

"You're not going to go," I repeated, trying for more emphasis, though because of the repetition it ended up sounding strange, accusatory.

Her voice hardened as well. "Sure. It's always up to me, isn't it?" she hissed. "If you're so willing to put an end to this why don't you ask me to move in with you? Right now. I'd do it, you know." By now, she was shouting into the phone. "We could be done with my mother once and for all."

"No, that's not it." I wanted it to sound like I was pleading. "It's all going to work out. This is just your mother's way of threatening me so I'll expose Holló. Once I do that, she'll cancel the ticket."

"No! *You* don't get it!" she said. "This is not about Holló." And with that the phone went dead.

7.

But it *was* about Holló, nothing but, and Éva's mistake (or so I thought at the time) was in thinking it could all be separated out—my thesis from Ilona's vendetta from our relationship—but they were all strung together like a series of explosives. To tamper with one was to tamper with the whole.

The next day, April 29, I called the Szécsényi Club and asked Holló what he'd no doubt been expecting me to ask ever since he'd told me the story of Adriána. It was a special favour I wanted, something that went against the one rule of his library, and for some reason I lied (even though I knew Holló was perfectly aware of what was going on), saying the examiners wanted to see not only my paper but the rest as well, every one of the sources I'd used, especially the issue of *Piros Krónika*, as well as the pamphlets and articles and of course Balogh's memoir, since none of these were available from the university library. They needed to make sure my bibliography was legitimate.

In reality, the examiners didn't want to see any of it. Like most professors in that situation, all they wanted was to get it done with, to read my thesis as quickly as possible, ask a bunch of questions during the oral defense, then give me a grade—as painlessly as possible—and not think about it for one second more. It was really Ílona who needed to see my sources, and Holló knew it.

Which is why he was silent only for a second on the phone, and then, in his unhurried way, he said it wasn't a problem, he'd make an exception in my case, provided I returned everything within a day or two. "I'm sure nobody will come around looking for those particular books," he said.

I told him I'd be over later. I couldn't hide the anger in my voice, almost snarling. I was doing exactly as he wanted, all his dirty work, and he didn't have to lift a finger, just sit there watching Ílona jerk me around, knowing I was too invested in keeping Éva to do otherwise. I suppose that was the worst of it, Holló relying on exactly the same motivation Ílona was relying on, as if they were working together, as if they'd colluded in bringing me to this impossible choice—Holló or Éva.

I went to bed after that, thinking I'd go to the club later in the day, pick up the stuff, and deliver the essay to the university tomorrow, right on schedule. I was putting it off, I knew that, disconnecting the phone, climbing between the sheets, covering my head hoping I'd awaken to find the dilemma gone. It was a sweaty sleep, and I spent more time waking than dreaming, always just below the surface, fighting ripples of anxiety. Then I was up, into my clothes, long before I'd planned it, and out the door.

Holló was waiting for me when I arrived. He entered the front hall as soon as I stepped across the threshold, a large box in his arms.

He was not smiling, he did not say hello, but he didn't look unhappy either. He was just neutral, standing with the box as if he was hoping I'd relieve him of it so he could get on with the day.

He held it out, arms fully extended, and I stood there, unable to take it. He thrust it at me again. "It's what you came for," he said, and his face was terrifying, all that makeup blurring my vision, only this time it wasn't coming back together, it was sliding apart in an ooze of pigment and oil and powder.

"I gave you a lot of chances to get out of this," Holló finally said, though it seemed to me, oddly, like an apology.

"I know," I said, confused.

But the moment I took the box and held its weight, Holló's face resolved itself, losing any sign of weakness or passivity, as if he'd known all along it would come to this, the troubles of the last few weeks, confirming some impression he'd formed on human nature long ago. His nonchalance, his easy acceptance, these weren't because he thought he could count on anyone's loyalty, mine or that of the people in the club, or even on the smooth course of Ílona's malice, but because my betrayal, the herd mentality of the membership, the dark egotism of Ílona, was exactly the world as he knew it. For him it had been inevitable, all our actions beyond our control, and he'd prepared carefully for it.

I can't remember whether I was angrier with Holló for misleading me, or with myself for feeling so relieved, holding that box, at having the choice taken away.

"Don't you ever feel bad about what you did?" I asked. "Not even for a second?"

Holló shrugged. "Ask yourself, how many books have you reread in your life? I'll bet you're always looking for the next one, aren't you? Just like the rest of us." He waited for my response, but there was none. "The great thing about writing," he whispered, "about art, is that you can always make more of it. It's not like I destroyed the recipe for antibiotics."

"It's not just the books," I said, stunned by the coldness of his answer. "People put their whole lives into their art. It's not just paper, film, whatever you want to call it, you were destroying!"

"Anyone," he said, stepping toward me, "who mistakes life for a book, who thinks his life ends when his works end, is an idiot. Not one word of it will last, *not one*. And the moment is everything. I learned that very clearly back there."

There were so many responses to this I couldn't make a sound. Instead, I shifted the box to one hand, unable to stop looking at him.

"But this one I did for you, not me," Holló continued. "You don't understand the sacrifice now, what I've given up, what's been lost here, and not just by me, but you will later."

He spoke as if he'd taken a terrible risk, as if one day I'd realize the danger he'd faced so I could learn the lesson he'd wanted to teach, that one day I'd come around to thanking him for freeing me from Éva, and Éva from me, for she had been secondary all along—to my thesis, to my relationship with Holló, to my need to prove myself to her mother— though I'd only appreciate the salvation long after, when it became clear Éva would not return from Hungary and I would not follow her there, when Ílona's vendetta was dismissed for the lack of proof only I, with my research and thesis, could have provided. It may have been an imperfect peace at the Szécsényi Club, but it was still peace, and it depended on nobody *having to know*, nobody being irrefutably confronted with, who and what Holló was. For Holló it meant survival itself, and that's exactly what he was, what he'd always been—a survivor—and I finally understood that our responsibility to others sometimes requires us to bury knowledge, even destroy it, though we've been told, over and over, that there's nothing worse.

But I wasn't thinking of that then, only of what I'd lost, Éva and my thesis and my father's respect, and I turned with the box and left Holló and walked in the direction of my parked car, down Harbord Street. After a block I peeled back the flaps and spilled it, the ash of books and pamphlets and the memoir and my essay, all of it irreplaceable, poured out onto the sidewalk.

Days of Orphans and Strangers

JENŐ KÁLMÁN was a tough guy. He could move an oak desk or filing cabinet or armoire without bothering to unpack what was inside. He had a temper as well, and his voice could blow a door off its hinges whether he was yelling in English or Hungarian or even German, which was a language Jenő spoke fluently, though try as he might he had no memory of how and when he'd learned it. He'd flown back to Hungary once, in 1960, without a passport, evaded the communist guards at the border, went to his stepsister's place, beat the crap out of the brother-in-law who'd in turn been beating her, stopping only when the brother-in-law promised never to harm her again, and then returned to Canada carrying a suitcase full of *cseresznye pálinka* off the plane.

But László was not scared of Jenő, and he made a point of showing how unafraid he was by laughing and saying "you're cracked" whenever Jenő claimed that László was not who he said he was, which Jenő did quite often. "The only reason you're so obsessed with who and what I am," László would say in front of the family, "is because you're adopted, and you want to pull everyone else down to your level."

Jenö's last name was not really Kálmán, nor did he know what his last name was. He'd been adopted, or "found" as his stepbrother István put it, during the siege of Budapest, when István's father, Boldizsár, went out scrounging for food and came upon the teenage boy sitting against a wall holding a giant loaf of bread and a sack of yellow peppers. Boldizsár took Jenö back to the family, holed up in a cellar trying to avoid the explosions and fires, and discovery by the fascists and Soviets, both of whom were using civilians as shields during their fire-fights. From then on they'd always had enough to eat, Jenö heading out every morning and returning with all the food they needed. When something was required, he got it.

Jenö couldn't overcome László because in his own way László was just as tough as he was—not so much physically as *on the inside*. His poker face, his stoic fortitude, his ability to laugh in the most anxious of circumstances, resulted from the fact that he'd watched his wife, Mária, get raped by members of the Red Army during the siege. As the Red Army came closer and closer to where the family was hiding, László and Mária went out to find a new place for them all, and it was this that caused the tragedy, for there was no one else to come to Mária's aid while the soldiers held László down and forced him to witness the whole horrific thing. From that point on nothing and nobody ever struck László as fearsome again—not even Jenö.

But Jenö disputed the rape story, and he was the only person in the family who would have dared. He was the one who'd disembarked from the boat that brought them to Canada and decided that New Brunswick was *not* the place to be, told them to wait on the dock, and returned an hour later with a bundle of train tickets to Toronto. Jenö said László had not only *not* been married to Mária, but Mária had not even been Mária. She was a German woman with whom László had escaped from Germany—their *mother*, in fact—meaning that László was not László either, but a German boy who took on the name and then invented the story of being married to Mária in order to hide what really happened to her, and this only to confuse the hell out of Jenö. This meant that he, Jenö, and László were actually brothers. As for Krisztián, the son of László and Mária, who'd been only a few months old at the end of the war when his mother was supposedly raped and abducted and killed, and only a year and a half old when he came west with his father, he was obviously someone else's baby that László had agreed to raise. What Jenö couldn't figure out was why the family was so intent on hiding these facts, why his stepsiblings—István, Adél and Anikó—were colluding with László in keeping up his story.

The rest of the family cringed but didn't say a thing, though sometimes they spoke amongst themselves wondering if it would be best to agree with Jenö, except that he would know they were doing it from the sound of fear in their voices. So they remained silent, and Jenö said, "Ah, you're useless," and stormed out the door, only to return at the next family gathering and spout his accusations all over again.

László didn't speak often, but when he did he'd point out that Jenö was so interested in the story of Mária—so obsessed with it—only because it was something from László's past that exerted more power over him, and the rest of the family, than Jenö did. "You don't like coming up against something stronger than you are," he said, smiling with such fury even Jenö thought twice about what kind of comeback to make.

"I've heard you speak German in your sleep," he finally said.

"Never!" shouted László.

"Yes, you do," Jenö shouted back. He pulled from his pocket a Dictaphone and waved it in front of the family gathered at the dining room table. "Since none of you have anything to say on the subject," he said, "I suppose you won't mind listening to this?"

They'd been speaking in Hungarian, but when Jenö hit the play button (despite the objections stuttered by László) what emerged—in between the snores, the tossing and turning, the sound of Jenö crawling along the floor to get as close to László as possible—was pure German interspersed with sounds of panic—groans, hollers, mewling—from whatever memories László's dreams were regurgitating.

"That's not me!" shouted László, standing up from the table in a great rattling of glasses and plates and cutlery.

"It *is* you!" shouted Jenö. "I've been telling everyone you speak German in your sleep for years!" Every time they went camping or hunting or stayed overnight somewhere, Jenö heard it, but László and everyone always said he was crazy. So Jenö decided to buy a Dictaphone. Now, he described how László exhausted himself on their last hunting trip for moose, tramping miles in search of the biggest antlers long after everyone had quit. By evening he could barely hold the shots of *pálinka* they put into his hand, and soon fell asleep. Later, Jenö was awakened by Krisztián crawling into his tent to complain how he couldn't sleep beside his father's shouting and pleading. "I'd heard you do it a thousand times," said Jenö, pointing at László, "and I was going to make sure everyone else finally heard it too."

He nodded at the Dictaphone, and for a second more the family listened to the sentences running beneath the tape hiss. "I know what you're saying," Jenö said. "My German's just as good as yours. But just to be fair maybe someone else here, Heléna, should translate it and prove to everyone that's really German you're speaking, like it was your native language. Once we've settled that then maybe you can answer some questions about Mária and what really happened during the siege."

The family turned to Heléna, the daughter of Anikó. She began, slow and halting, to translate the words coming out of the speakers, at least as far as her Bachelor of Arts in German Language and Literature allowed. She spoke of the siege of Budapest, what it was like to have been there. She sounded dreamy and vague, skipping a difficult word or verb tense here and there, channelling a message across the most tenuous of connections. The beginning of the story was the most garbled, as if László had been so traumatized by what he'd seen, by what happened to Mária, that he was lost in the language needed to express it. But gradually the story became clearer. Heléna spoke of László's disorientation, not knowing where the soldiers had taken Mariá when they were finished with her, or how to get back to the cellar where his family and infant son were hiding. She spoke of his decision to strike out in the direction of Mátyásföld, a suburb to the east of Budapest now churned to mud and broken brick, bombed homes, populations hiding or scattered or dead, overrun by the Red Army. That's where home was, the ancestral seat of the Kálmán family, a sprawling villa surrounded by orchards.

The Dictaphone told the story of László's journey there, the weeks during which he avoided Soviet patrols. They were really just bands of men in uniform wandering aimlessly, firing off shots, taking what they could—watches and sex— threatening, crying, crazy with war. He hid in cellars, ran and dodged, was taken in by women.

The women's names made the biggest impression on the family that night. Heléna translated them from dream-speak into Hungarian—Rózsa, Ibolya, Lilike—as if the siege of Budapest had made allowance for a flower here and there— rose, violet, lily—in a city whose main part was wreckage and fire and bodies.

Rózsa was the first to find him, letting László think he was taking care of her while she restored him from what had happened to Mária, his failure to defend her. Rózsa didn't live anywhere. As she put it, she lived wherever she happened to be. It was a way of staying alive, inhabiting only the place she found herself, calling it home for an hour or afternoon or night and then moving on, never returning to the same spot twice. She had a way of making László feel secure even as they huddled behind half-exploded walls, beneath viaducts, in the shell of a burned-out tank, as if she knew an enchantment for turning ruin into shelter.

The second woman, Ibolya, lived in a furnished apartment that had survived a direct hit, the rest of the apartments falling down around her place. She and László risked their lives going up and down the swaying staircase that led to her home. Inside there was antique furniture, leather-bound editions of poets, and even plants—vines and leaves and flowers Ibolya tended by taking as little water for herself as was necessary.

The third woman, Lilike, lived in a closet. When she pulled László from in front of the tank he felt as if he'd fallen into a box. It was hot in there, oppressive and dark. For three weeks they sat on a floor so small their legs twined together, so that after the sounds of battle stopped they moved in unison for a while, as if all four legs belonged to both of them, as if they were fused.

From here, László exited Budapest onto the dirt track to Mátyásföld, the ransacked villa, and the bodies of Tíbor and Ildikó, his grandmother and grandfather.

A second after the Dictaphone stopped, Heléna stopped too.

"Those were the things that happened to me after Mária," said László finally, the room otherwise silent. "It took me so long to find the way home."

"Now why would you need to recount that in German?" asked Jenő, the only one not in awe of the story.

László replied that he spoke German quite well, demonstrating it right there by quoting from Rilke, and said he'd lived for two years in Vienna after escaping Hungary.

Jenö replied, "I see. So you lived in Vienna, and you learned the language so well—*in two years*—that it's what you prefer to speak in your dreams."

The evening left Jenö confused, as everyone could see. László had dreamed in German, but the dream perfectly fit the story everyone had been telling about him, the siege of Budapest, and Mária. Jenö went home that night, spent a few hours thinking about the impossibility of reconciling the German with the story, and at one in the morning phoned Heléna. He reminded her that he was aware of what Uncle László had done for her over the years, paying the tuition her mother, the widow Anikó, could not afford. But she also owed Jenö. Or had she forgotten the time he'd come over for a visit and discovered that her landlord was jackhammering out part of the foundation? Recognizing the noise, like a crack of thunder, for what it was, he'd hustled Heléna and her cousin Sári out of the building before the place came down, burying the landlord. Had she forgotten that? Had she forgotten how he'd stuck his arm into the mouth of that German shepherd who'd lunged at her during a family camping trip, shoving his arm further and further until it choked and was forced to spit it out? "My chewed-up arm could have been your face!" he said. "Have you forgotten that?"

"It's one in the morning," she said, not fully awake. "I'm having a hard time remembering anything."

Jenö began pestering her. But growing up the fifth of five children, struggling to overcome her immigrant roots and father's early death, getting a degree in languages and embarking on a career in the diplomatic corps, Heléna had discovered she was tough too.

She'd tease Jenö, saying things like "Well, I may have mistranslated a verb here or there, which would have influenced the meaning of such-and-such a sentence," to which Jenö would roll his eyes, reminding her that he spoke German too and there was nothing wrong with her translation.

"Did László or did László not go through all that during the siege of Budapest?" he asked.

"Well," she replied, "maybe you and I misheard what he was saying, or let a few sentences escape us. After all, he was talking pretty quietly, and in his sleep, too."

"Come on!" he yelled.

"Why is Jenö so obsessed?" Anikó asked Heléna, worried about what might happen to her daughter if she continued to toy with him.

"He's adopted," Heléna said. "He's adopted and we're one of those families where knowing where you come from and who your ancestors were and the exact nature of your connection with the culture is very important."

"Did they teach you that in university?" Anikó asked. "In one of those classes on multiculturalism or something?"

"Let's talk about Dad," replied Heléna. She said it fast, by reflex, and her mother was already turning away in rage and shame as Heléna recalled how her father's surname, Cukor, had been Zuckermandle before his grandfather, like so many Jews at the turn of the century, decided to blend in by changing everything—names, religion, history, even the features of their grandchildren by encouraging their sons and daughters to marry Hungarians.

"You're not Jewish," said Anikó, visibly shaken. "I've told you many times. To be Jewish it has to come through the mother's line, and I'm pure Hungarian. So even they—

I mean the Jews—wouldn't consider you Jewish."

"My point exactly," said Heléna, thinking of what it must be like to be Jenö, watching his children and wife in the yard, all of them connected to mothers and fathers, brothers and sisters, aunts and uncles—to each other—except him. In some way, Heléna decided, Jenö's desire to expose László was not because he wanted him to be lonely as well, but because he wanted them to be alone *together*.

So Heléna decided to do something. She was a diplomat after all, and as she'd written in one of the essays required by the application process, she'd always viewed diplomacy as more than a government job. It was a way of negotiating without the threat of war and violence, creating out of conflicting laws and customs a new story everyone would listen to.

She invited the two men on a camping trip where she hoped they'd work out a history acceptable to them both. Jenö agreed, thinking he'd brush Heléna aside once they were there and begin the slow psychological torture of László that would end in him revealing the story Jenö had always wanted to hear.

But László was suspicious. "Why do you want us to go camping?"

"It would be a good way for you and Jenö to work out your differences."

"I don't have any differences," he said. "The differences belong to Jenö."

No matter how she described the beauty of the hike, or of the campsite she'd chosen, he refused. "Camping! Where did you ever come up with such an idea?"

"Our family has always gone camping!"

"Yes, the family *together*. Years ago when I was a lot younger, and you and Krisztián were kids!"

Heléna ended up camping with Jenö alone. She didn't tell him about László's refusal until they were on the side of a mountain, thirty miles from the nearest road.

Once the tent was set up, the fire started, Jenö asked when László was going to arrive, and Heléna had to tell him that, well, actually, he wasn't. Jenö had a fit then. He started shouting about how cowardly László was—even as he knew it wasn't true—how László was always one step ahead, how he kept tricking Jenö, and that he would like once, *just once*, to finally get the jump on him. Then he kicked over the fire, pulled up the tent, and scattered their sleeping bags and cookware and food everywhere. Heléna let him do it because it was better he vent on the equipment than on her.

"He was too ashamed to come," she said.

"Ashamed?" said Jenö, stopping in the middle of twirling the axe, which he was planning on hurling into a lake a hundred feet away.

"And scared," she continued.

"Scared?" He lowered the axe.

Heléna then went over the history as she knew it. She let Jenö know just how much of an impression he'd made on her, on the younger cousins who'd grown up on stories of the things he'd done, hoping to make him understand that it connected them more strongly than any blood relation. She spoke of how Jenö had single-handedly saved the family during the siege of Budapest, especially after Boldizsár grew too weak to accompany him, how he left the family in the cellar to go out alone, returning bruised and cut and beat up, but always with enough food and water for the next day. She spoke of the way István, Adél, and Anikó described the trek back to Mátyásföld, Jenö scouting ahead, and dealing with what he found, before returning to lead the family on. She spoke of how after days of scurrying, and evading what even Jenö couldn't overcome, they arrived at the villa, only to find László alone there, sitting in a dark, rubble-strewn room, his hands still dirty from burying Tíbor and Ildikó in the yard.

"László is afraid of all the things you did for the family that he couldn't do."

No, Jenö shook his head and looked at her sadly. That wasn't what happened at all. "Mária and László had already gone out by the time Boldizsár brought me back to the cellar that day," he said, "so I didn't know what he looked like. In fact, I only heard about their story, the rape, afterwards, once we were back in Mátyásföld, as if the whole family had agreed on this giant lie. But I'll tell you this: the person we met in the villa did not at all resemble the László I would later see in family photographs from before the war. That is, before Boldizsár got rid of the photographs, telling us he didn't want Krisztián to be reminded of the mother he'd lost, since Mária was in most of those photographs too. Of course that was probably a different Mária as well." The siblings tried to convince Jenö that László's experiences in the siege had had a catastrophic effect on him physically, that they'd altered his appearance, but Jenö refused to believe that anything, no matter how traumatic, could change a person's hair from brown to blond, or straighten his nose, or make him grow a foot in height.

"So either László is a miracle of science," Jenö said, "or an imposter." They were walking through the long grasses at the edge of the lake now. Heléna was scanning the ground for the camping equipment he'd tossed away. Jenö, meanwhile, seemed unconcerned with recovering a thing, or making camp, or nightfall, or the storm that was building. "You're wrong, Heléna. László is not afraid of me. In fact, if it wasn't for László I wouldn't even be a member of this family."

Heléna looked at him, then turned in the direction of the wind, which was beginning to carry off their possessions, the tent ballooning like a parachute, dragging off one of the sleeping bags snarled in its strings, disappearing over the lake. God only knew where Jenö had thrown the map, much less the compass, the food, and Heléna moved along in a panic, picking up bits and pieces as the ground grew wetter and light faded from the sky, Jenö tagging along as if they had all the time in the world.

He was also talking more than she'd ever heard him talk. Except for the obsession with László, Jenö had always been quiet, saying only the minimum of what needed to be said and adding nothing else, even when the family tried to bring up exceptions and contradictions to the iron-clad rules and opinions whereby he operated.

But that night he was having a hard time focusing on what was in front of them, on her futile effort to recover the things he'd tossed away, not even keeping his eye on where the two of them were going so they could find their way back. He was lost in recounting the things that had befallen him during the siege. Jenö said he remembered nothing of his life from before, only that he was sixteen, there was blood on his head, and that whatever had hit him had bounced off and hit him again, a number of times, on the shoulders, the chest, the front of his legs. It almost scraped the clothes right off his body. But he found more clothing, food too, though he didn't remember doing that either, only that what he needed was somehow always there, and when it wasn't, when it seemed he'd finally come to the end of his bewildered wandering in the midst of shells and flame and strafing and men in various uniforms shouting languages into his face, when he'd finally sat down to finish his last loaf of bread, a man's kindly face appeared in front of him (though Jenö wasn't even sure if he remembered this, or if it was just something he'd *come to remember* through the repetition of the family story about how Boldizsár had found him).

Boldizsár had offered Jenö shelter in a language it would take the boy years to comprehend, and knelt down, stripped off his shirt, and ripped it into strips he wound around the boy's fractured skull, taking him to where the rest of the family were hiding.

The wind was whipping around them now, and Jenö reached down and plucked up a bag of trail mix strained out of the air by a bush, offering some to Heléna before taking a handful himself.

Jenö never did figure out where he'd come from, but the Kálmán family, once they saw how little he remembered, never asked again, behaving as though he'd always belonged to the family. When he went into the streets, desperate to repay them for their generosity, their accepting him, he always felt it was his last chance, if he didn't return with something he'd find the door to the cellar closed, the family gone, as if his scrounging, his ability to find food and clothing and whatever was needed was the necessary gesture, the offering, that kept them there, awaiting his return. He never went back before he found something, braving any danger if it meant putting his hands on eggs, cheese, rations in the pocket of a fallen soldier. "I have something, I have something, I have something," he'd whisper to himself, running back to where the Kálmáns were hiding, frightened at the thought of being cast back into the city, which seemed a projection of his memory, as if the world had become the ruins of what was left in his head.

"It was on the third day of that," said Jenö, sitting on a rock at the edge of the lake, "that I began to feel as if the things I was finding had been planted there for me." From then on there was a second presence, but always invisible, on the periphery of things. It seemed to be anticipating his movements, running forward, hanging back, always in advance of where he didn't yet know he was going to turn, or look, or enter.

"Listen," said Heléna carefully. "I don't mean to interrupt, but we're going to need to figure out how to get back to the car. Our stuff . . ." She pointed in the direction of the landscape, where ahead of them, stretching low and flat, was the lake, with its grasses and mud. "And it looks like it's going to rain," she said, gazing up.

Jenö looked around and shrugged, continuing the story. As the days wore on, he began to discern a pattern to the way he found things, the presence growing ever stronger, or so he thought, as if once in a while there was a shadow, a movement, the quick withdrawal of a hand, just before he noticed the package or crate that contained what the family needed that day. After a while he realized it was not a force that was making him so lucky in his search, but a person. That's what it was—a person, looking out for him. He knew it then, and after that his trips into the chaos of Budapest became easier, the city no longer inhospitable, a place where he had to prove himself against impossible odds, but secure, where he could do the most daring things, take incredible risks, because there was someone to catch him when he fell. "I was always brave after that," said Jenö. It was amazing, he told Heléna, what the world was like for the brave, how confidence carried you through situations that swallowed others alive, as if the belief that you would not only survive but prosper was enough to make reality conform.

"That's why I think it was László," he said. László was the only person Jenö had ever met who was braver than he was, unafraid, secure in his fate, unwilling to change who he was and what he did regardless of circumstance. It was László who made sure Jenö was found by Boldizsár. László who planted every bit of food, every article of clothing, every drop of water Jenö found. László who set it up so Jenö would never have to recover his memory, that he'd be taken in by the family, that he would have a future of such respect and admiration he would never be driven to search too hard in the darkness behind him. And this was why, Jenö believed, László convinced the family to play along in denying that they were related, so his kid brother would never learn the circumstances—horrific as they were—that preceded the day Boldiszár found him, and that included the story of what really happened to Mária, their mother.

"You're telling me László was following you around Budapest, predicting where you would look, and, like, dropping off care packages before you got there?"

Jenö gazed at her, and when she saw the expression on his face, Heléna whistled and turned back to her search, despairing at all the items she saw now, blown by the wind, dancing on the horizon, too far for her to recover. She could imagine how the rest of the story went in Jenö's head—László somewhere in front, paving the way for his younger brother, setting up everything so that by the time László arrived to wherever he was headed the danger had been dealt with, or brought down to a level he could handle. By the time they got back to the villa, László had already tipped off Boldizsár and the rest, visiting them one night after Jenö had fallen asleep to explain what he was doing, what they must do in return for the way he'd kept them alive—pretend for the rest of their lives that he was the same László as the young man in their family pictures from before the war (God only knew what had really happened to *that* Lászlo), who'd had a wife called Mária, also featured in the photographs, who was raped and kidnapped by the Red Army. So when they arrived at Mátyásföld everyone but Jenö was ready to receive László among them, as easy with his presence as if they'd known him forever, the lost son miraculously returned to them after horrific trauma.

"That's the craziest thing I've ever heard," said Heléna, stopping her search, wondering how long they'd survive in the night. "You and László look nothing alike."

"Really? What about our noses? Don't you think they look the same? And his chin? He almost has a cleft there, which, if he did, would make him look more like me."

Heléna watched him, and what she saw was a longing so powerful it had transformed reality. It made Jenö more powerful than the world, for he truly believed there was always someone looking after him. It was as redemptive a craziness as she would ever witness, and for a long time Heléna stood in awe of it.

"I don't know how we're going to last out here," she said, edging closer to Jenö.

"We'll last," he laughed, putting an arm around her, and in the same motion yelling "Hello" to László, who it turned out had changed his mind, and was even now marching across the grasses toward them, his backpack full of food and shelter, a map and compass gripped tightly in his hand.

Rosewood Queens

I'LL NEVER KNOW what Aunt Rose liked better: finding the pieces she was searching for, or the looks on the faces of the dealers when she said she didn't want to buy the whole set.

"Excuse me?" they'd ask, eyes flickering as if they were having a seizure.

"You heard me," she'd reply. "All I want are the kings" (or the rooks, or the queens, or the bishops, or whatever she was after that day).

Most of the time, the dealers just laughed. "Lady, you buy it all or you buy none of it." And she'd laugh too as if they were old friends and reply, "All right," and pull out her wallet and pay for the whole set. Then she'd open the chessboard and lift out two kings, holding them to the light saying, "Look at that, Mariska—the famous Templar rosewood," and we'd examine them for a while before she sighed, put them in her bag, and turned to leave.

"Hey lady," the dealers would shout, "what about the rest?"

She always gave them a wicked grin. "I only wanted these," she'd say. "You can throw the rest in the garbage."

I'll never forget their expressions then, it was the saddest thing, those old men in their dusty stores filled with stuff they'd found at estate sales and flea markets and container auctions, men who knew the value of the forgotten treasures of the world, and whose pride and self-esteem rested in their expertise. They were devastated—you didn't do that, take something that rare, that fine, and just toss it—staring at the remains of the set, useless now but too beautiful to throw away, knowing it would sit on their shelves forever, lifted down every six months by a collector who'd whistle, "Wow, Templar rosewood! Too bad it's incomplete," and look at the dealer with a mixture of accusation and pity.

"Have a nice day," she'd say, and waltz us out of there.

This was thirty-five years ago, when the woman my father told me to call "Aunt Rose" lived across from us on Michigan Avenue in Kitchener in one of those neighbourhoods still there in the hundreds, crumbling brick houses built cheap by the government for soldiers returned from the war. They were tiny, only two bedrooms, though in the past they'd housed families of five or six. My father, Miklós Berényi, known locally as "Mike," worked at the vinyl factory down the road, making "skin," as the men referred to it, that went into car seats and handbags and cheap furniture, before a fire in the early 1990s destroyed the plant and put him on early retirement and disability because of what the burning fumes did to his lungs, wheezing another six years, carting around a portable oxygen tank, dying. My mother had left years earlier—"Did us the favour of taking off," as my father described it—when I was too young to have any memory of her other than those created by the few photographs she left, kept in an album on the shelf above my father's bed, which would have been a place of importance except it was always covered in dust, untouched except once in a while by me.

In the photographs she always seemed to be staring at my father as if waiting for an explanation. It was a look I'd come to share, and which I'd also see on Aunt Rose, as if all three of the women in my father's life wanted the story of his ecstasies and silences, of the way he danced and joked and sang, then sat with us at dinner, lost in some private nightmare he'd as suddenly sink into as come out of, interrupting the conversation that had been going on for an hour to ask what we were talking about, who was involved, what the details were, and we, exasperated, would have to tell it all over again.

When I asked my father if he missed my mother, he always said, "Why anyone who's been married once would ever want to be married again is a total mystery to me."

It was one of the many things he didn't speak about. No matter how I pressed, even when I was older and confronted him head-on, saying it was important, I needed to hear about the past, my father either muttered that I should drop it, or started making up stories he knew were too ridiculous to believe, or grabbed me around the waist and said it was a time to dance a *paso doble*. His response always depended on his mood, manic sometimes, but more and more depressed and withdrawn as he grew older. Either way, I never got the truth. His parents had died during the siege of Budapest, that's all he said, and he'd come to Canada at sixteen, an orphan, having lied to immigration officials about his age, and worked at whatever he could—painting houses, road construction, tobacco farming, and finally in the vinyl plant because it was a union job and meant stability even though he hated unions.

It was probably because of his silence that I fell in love with reading, the only way of replacing the information he should have supplied, all those picture books and travel journals and histories on Hungary I checked out of the library, though there wasn't a lot in English, picturing what my life might have been like had my father stayed there, the two of us in that dirty beautiful capital, strolling the bridges across the Danube, lost in the war-torn corridors of the ninth district, sitting in the faded elegance of the New York Kávéház.

My love of reading was encouraged by Aunt Rose. She worked at the University of Waterloo in the art history department, and had moved into a house on our block when she was starting out like so many other junior professors who had fashionable sympathies with the working class (whatever that is), before tenure and promotion took them to more affluent neighbourhoods—Mary Ellen, Westmount, Beechwood—places with quiet streets, where every year the city sent a suction truck to clean up the fallen leaves, where you didn't have to worry about what your kid would meet with at school. Unlike them, Aunt Rose never left. She loved Michigan Avenue, though Michigan Avenue didn't always love her, especially the wives of the men she danced and drank and played pool with at the local bar, Henry's, who gossiped about her for the decade and a half she lived there, not so much because she was loose or anything, since Aunt Rose, at least during the years I'm talking about, only slept with my father, but because she was "slumming," picking her way through the community as if it was a hobby, drawn to those with the worst stories, physical scars, damaged beyond repair by poverty or hard work, sitting with them sipping bar Scotch and listening.

Aunt Rose started seeing my father the winter I turned five.

The first time she came to our house she was carrying a tape recorder, one of those black boxes with the white and red buttons. My father disappeared with her into the kitchen, where they spoke quietly for a while, sitting at the table wringing out a bottle of wine, my father not speaking so much as nervously coughing into the microphone after each of her questions. It was too low for me to hear though I'd crept as close as possible, desperate for information, something to explain the pictures in the book on the shelf above his bed, photographs not only of my mother, but distant places— Nyíregyháza, Debrecen, Budapest—and men dressed as soldiers, priests, magistrates, women young and old sitting in some eastern European orchard shelling peas, or in front of a church in their finery, or seated on a horse-drawn carriage, the entire history of who he was and where he'd come from and by extension me. Later on, when I was older, he'd tell me a few names, or point out who was an aunt or grandmother or nephew, sometimes even lapse into the longest most boring genealogical explanation, but not a word about how the faces and times and places all hung together. "It's just history," he'd say. "Dead stories."

About half an hour into the interview, Aunt Rose leaned over and kissed my father. It was as if she'd put something into his mouth and he wasn't sure whether he wanted to spit it out or swallow it whole. "I won't do this!" he yelled, jumping up from the table. "I can't!" He rose and stormed out. Aunt Rose stared at the tape recorder a minute, and turning caught sight of me. She came over, smiled, touched my cheeks, and followed my father out the door. They were out there on the sidewalk a long time. I was crouched on the threshold watching, dark figures under the street light at the end of the driveway, steam bursting from their mouths, and then my father stopped in the middle of what he was saying, shook his head, and came back and gathered me in his arms and put me to bed.

Later that night, I snuck out of my bed and crept down the hall to my father's room, as I always did, since he slept too soundly to ever come to me, whether it was a glass of water I needed or protection from a nightmare. I climbed up on his bed in the complete dark, feeling around on the comforter, searching for some trace of him or a clue to where he'd gone. I started crying, softly at first, but it grew until Aunt Rose rushed in and found me in the middle of the bed, curled up, hysterical. She took me in her arms, though I was demanding my father, and soothed me with whispers and carried me back to my room, lying down beside me. I never found out where she'd come from, or why it had taken so long for someone to get to me, and why that someone wasn't my father, but when the light came up the next morning she was still there, snoring lightly, reeking of whiskey. It felt right somehow, her presence there, as if the punishment of sharing that sliver of mattress all night, the hangover and bad sleep, was the price she paid for entering my life. After that, when I woke at night, she was the one I started to call for, the one I knew would come.

And so Aunt Rose became a part of our lives. She didn't care what Michigan Avenue thought of her, floating above the gossip, and with the way she danced and laughed and cooked, the way she kissed, both my father and me were happy to have her around.

I knew she was good at kissing. I saw it on the nights I crept out of my room and peered over the banister, memorizing the way she stood on her toes, touched her lips to my father's, the two of them drinking and dancing to the music on the radio. There was this one CBC program they listened to, *The Neon Dancehall*, between ten and midnight. My father could dance to anything, he knew it all—the waltz, the tango, the foxtrot—his lanky body strange and graceful in the worn millworker's clothes that were the only clothes he wore. He said he'd learned to dance "on the trip across the Atlantic," in the ballroom on the ship, as a way of dealing with the boredom. When I asked if there was a woman involved he always just winked at me and said "Ssshhh," or, if he was in a bad mood, said nothing at all.

It was this "gift," as Aunt Rose called it, that kept her coming around after that first night, that plus the intensity that overcame him whenever she was around, carrying her laughing up the stairs over his shoulder, running out at midnight to get us all ice cream, the way he was unable to walk past her without kissing her on the back of the neck, behind the ear, under the line of her jaw. "You beautiful man," she called my father, a phrase that made him laugh, with his patched clothes and packs of cigarettes, his days of stubble, the nicks and bruises he got at the factory, too macho to report the injuries to the medical office.

Neither of them was young, both were in their mid-forties, though you could see they hadn't left it far behind, the impatience with which they held each other, the look in their eyes that said they'd only recently become cautious, that they'd been burned badly enough by past relationships to have developed rules against the risk of opening up again.

So when my father stopped in the middle of a dance and suddenly said he was tired, or paused in telling a joke and passed a hand over his face, or lost the thread of a sentence— "The thing I hate about Charlie Parker is that unlike the swing bands he made it impossible to . . ." pausing there, "impossible to . . ." then went silent—Aunt Rose would either not press him on it, or come out with something weak. "What's wrong?"

"Nothing," he'd say, irritated. A few minutes later he would say goodnight and goodbye to both of us, taking off his shoes with a grunt, and heading upstairs in a way that made it plain he didn't want anyone—not Aunt Rose, not me—coming after him.

I wonder now what would have happened if they'd gotten together earlier. Maybe Aunt Rose, with her knowledge and empathy, might have broken through to my father in a way my mother hadn't been able to, or there might have been time afterwards, when it was clear there was no breaking through, for Aunt Rose to have taken me with her, since I would have been her daughter.

I don't know what deal the two of them made, but at 3:30 Aunt Rose was always waiting for me after daycare at the home of a local woman, or, as was the case later, school, and we'd go back to her house. She must have requested the same teaching schedule year after year, doing her marking and course preparation in the evening at a beautiful Biedermeier table while I sat doing homework, or reading, or watching TV. At eight, it was time for bed, we'd walk along the hallways lined with shelves on which she kept her chess figurines, up the stairs into what I now think of as my real room, set up when she first started taking care of me, the day she led me by the hand and opened the door with a flourish, hoping it would coax me out of the crying fits that started the minute I left school and didn't end until my father showed up the next morning, coming for me straight off a night shift. The walls of the bedroom were filled with antique pictures, set side by side so tight you couldn't see the wallpaper. I don't know where she found them, they were *fin de siècle* children's illustrations, horses in Swiss army uniforms, standing on their hind legs, gazing through telescopes, riding in air balloons, piloting submarines. There was a bed painted with sleeping maidens. A cut-glass chandelier hanging from the ceiling, spinning diamonds of light across the ceiling. It seemed less like a room than a place from which I could go anywhere, into whatever fantasy I chose, though all I really wanted was for it to simply be a normal room belonging to a normal girl with a father and a mother.

Long after Aunt Rose was gone from my life, I'd remember her stories clearest of all, as if that's where she too belonged, off in some fable rather than reality. She worked on collectors, she said, the men and women in history— kings, baronesses, industrialists, eccentric heirs—"and their influence," as she wrote in one of her articles, "on what we now think of as the canon of great artworks." They were the people who'd decided what it was important to keep, she told me, though it seemed during those nights that what really interested her were not the people who'd set the standard, but the others, whose collections she'd come upon by accident, along the margins, on some side track where history wasn't written, the bits and pieces of research she couldn't draft into her books and essays.

She told me about Count Afanasei Naryshkin, the eighteenth-century Russian nobleman who collected "experience," sending his serfs on "expeditions" and "travels" and "challenges," some fatal, then installing the survivors, or their remains, in his dacha, where they could be questioned again and again by his friends on what it had been like to face a Siberian tiger bare-handed, to have wandered the length of Afghanistan in nothing but a loincloth, to have been the one and only survivor of Professor Artyukhin's wondrous but ultimately flawed "flying machine" in the Himalayas. Those who could answer did so, the rest of the stories had to be guessed, with a fair degree of accuracy, from the corpses.

She told me of Frithjof Damkjær, the cloth merchant who lived in Copenhagen in the first half of the twentieth century, and claimed to have amassed over "a million types of death." After he passed away, his eldest son, Thormod, went into his father's home to draw up the estate, and was never heard from again. His daughter, Silje, went next, trying to figure out not only what happened to her brother (though she was secretly glad that, as primary heir, he was out of the picture), but also what kind of wealth her secretive father had hoarded away. Her body was found days later; the cause of death looked a lot like the depressurization an astronaut might experience on rupturing his spacesuit, though of course the doctors at the time had no idea. One by one his children died, along with a number of solicitors—one looked like she'd been mauled by a swarm of Howler monkeys; another was found covered head to toe in radiation burns; another had been hacked to pieces with some kind of cutting weapon that cauterized the wound as soon as it made it; another was found dead "by bula-bula," a death of such savagery the papers refused to describe it. As for Thormod, since his body was never found it was ruled a "death by misadventure."

She told me of Sister Ingrid Van Buren, the seventeenth-century nun who collected "acts of charity," renouncing a life of aristocratic privilege by donating her dead husband's estate to the orphanages of Amsterdam, entering a nunnery, taking a vow of poverty, always volunteering for the hardest jobs—scrubbing floors, stripping varnish from pews, walking twenty miles a day dispensing food and clothing to the poor, and in the end travelling to India to live among the lepers, contracting the disease, her body rotting away, and yet still continuing to work among them to her last breath. After she died they found a logbook among her possessions in which she'd recorded every single charitable act, including some she'd performed as a young girl, as if it had been a lifelong project, rows of dates and times kept in meticulous order, including sum totals she'd calculated during the last days of her life: Fed the hungry: 2, 015 times; Clothed the naked: 3, 582 times; Ministered to the sick: 4, 871 times. The priests and nuns looked at the book as if it were obscene, as if her vocation had not been the cloister at all but the opportunity to accrue as many selfless works as possible. There was something greedy about it, and they drew back from the figures and columns, remembering the times she'd pushed others aside to get at some sick or dying person, the lengths she'd gone to make sure the worst assignments fell to her, the two or three hours she slept a night, unable to tear herself from the work. The logbook was her collection—Aunt Rose had seen it—no different from an album of stamps or hockey cards.

There were dozens of others. She said that for many of these collectors there came a time, after many years, when everything faded to unimportance, as if contrary to what most people believed collecting was not the amassing of things but a way of cutting yourself off from them, focusing so exclusively on one object that all else—your clothes, your food, your job, your friends, your lovers—fades. Sometimes, she said, they reached the point where even that, their one thing, their sole focus, abandoned them, as if they'd finally arrived in that place they'd always wanted to get to, even if they hadn't known it starting out, where nothing mattered at all. "Some of them," she said, "would start giving it away then—the precious jewellery, the holy books, the sacred relics."

She was talking about my father, of course, how his one focus, those unspoken memories, made him insensible to everything else, all the good things that might have been his, and how that obsession, too, would one day seem irrelevant and leave him with nothing, not even remorse over what he'd squandered.

I got a sense of this, her coded prophecy, on those evenings when Aunt Rose put on her special dinners. There was expensive wine and prime rib and pie. At the end of the night the subject would always circle around, over the *diges-tif*—which was always Unicum, that bitter stuff brewed by Zwack and Co. that Aunt Rose picked up on research trips to Hungary—to what I came to think of as their game. It seemed pathetic to me, not so much when I was a kid but later, the way they pretended that the last thing they wanted, ever again, was to share their homes or lives with someone else, making fun of married life as if the false confidences and camaraderie of cynicism could make up for the attachment my father was too scared to risk. "Who loves you?" she'd laugh, setting down his food. He'd gaze at the plate: "You keep feeding us like this, honey, we'll be fat as pigs." "Just imagine," Aunt Rose would lower her voice, imitating one of her mother's sayings, "how much you'd pay for all this amazing food at a restaurant." "I wish I'd learned to cook!" my father would reply. "It's one of my great regrets!" "Next Christmas we'll buy a turkey big enough to last a week," she'd say, "just the three of us sitting around living like kings. What do you think, Mariska?" My father tilted back in his chair, "Now that," he said, "is what I'd call living!"

At one of these dinners, my father did something I'll never forget: getting up from the table, he lurched drunkenly against a shelf of figurines and caught them as they fell, picking them out of the air one two three four five as if they were suspended there, holding them between his fingers afterwards, staring, as if he was more amazed than any of us at his reflexes, at the fact that he'd managed to do it.

"See, Mariska," Aunt Rose said, "it's nice to have a man around." But she didn't seem very confident then, gazing at my father in bewilderment, as though she not only hadn't expected him to catch the pieces, but didn't want him to, as if watching them shatter on the floor would have been preferable to him standing there amazed at his capacity to save something. The thing she was after, the thing she wanted from him, it would not happen until he was no longer surprised by that—his capacity to step forth, reach out, and take hold.

She was sick of the game they played.

I'd see that look on Aunt Rose's face many times over the years, nights I'd awaken to her sitting on my bed staring at me, as if I was a problem for which she had no solution.

"Go back to sleep," she'd whisper. "I'm just checking on you."

But it was impossible, closing my eyes while she was looking at me like that, and as I got older they became the times we really talked, as if the late hour, the lights off, gave us permission to broach subjects otherwise left alone.

"Did you ever want kids, Aunt Rose?"

She sighed and shrugged, muttered something about her "first husband," one of "those pseudo-radical academics," she called him, "about as far from your father as you could get, a narcissist who didn't realize that having an 'open relationship' applied to the wife as well as the husband," and then something about the "dedication" required for "making it as a woman scholar. Men have wives at home who take care of the kids," she said, "but I'd never have that, and without the time to work I wouldn't have gotten anywhere." She shrugged again, looking at me. "And I'm too old for that now." She continued sitting there a while, the room filling with whatever I was expecting her to say, something to do with my father, that it wasn't what she wanted but what he *didn't want* that was in the way—not just between the two of them, but between her and me—his inability to risk loss, to lay claim to anyone or anything. She said nothing, and I knew, even then, that it was her way of trying to protect me from disappointment, from what she had already predicted would and would not happen between them, though if she stayed quiet long enough, unnaturally enough, I might hear it anyhow—the silent admission that she didn't need kids because she had me, because I *was* her own—and that this withholding of what I wanted her so badly to say would, long after, be both an admission and my protection from it. Had she spoken the words it would have led me to form an even greater attachment to her, which would only have further confronted my father with what he was too afraid to have, driving us all apart. Though the truth is, her not saying it had exactly the same effect, at least for me.

I was nineteen when their relationship ended. But I was on my own long before that, in the way you're alone when your parents haven't yet realized how separate your life has become, how innumerable your secrets, though I was still nominally at home, nights when I wasn't out with friends, with boys, in deserted playgrounds, drinking, smoking dope, giggling as we rode merry-go-rounds, swings, even the slides, as if childhood joy could be restored with something as simple as booze. More often than not part of me was hoping my father would find me—I would make a point of going out when he wasn't working nights—that he'd walk square shouldered into the field or playground or bush party and catch me with Jim MacDonald, whose hand was up my shirt, and break his arm or teeth. But he never showed.

Then there was Marc Lancaster. He was the one dealer Aunt Rose couldn't crack, never once looking distressed when she left behind the remains of a chess set. He dumped them into a bin and sold them for a quarter each, kids coming in to replace some pawn or rook gone missing from the game back home, and which was pure profit since Aunt Rose had already paid for the full set. I don't know how many times I stood there with her, trying to appreciate a bit of jade or tortoise shell or walrus tusk carved into the shape of a rearing horse. "Master Diederich made truly sublime knights," Lancaster would say. "His pawns look like something a dog spat out, but knights, they were his forte." Sometimes he tried to give her the chess pieces for free, but Aunt Rose refused, and the best he could do was keep a constant lookout for things she was interested in. He even travelled to Europe in the summers, always bringing back some treasures just for her.

His shop was different from the other places we went to, neat and orderly and regularly dusted. There was none of that smell you get in pawnshops or standard junk stores, the scent of something people have lived with for too long, on which they've spilled one too many beers, smoked one too many cigarettes, lain one too many children sweating sick with flu. His place was a shop of wonders. There were original copper etchings of the collections of Albertus Seba, pictures of two-headed snakes, rare shells, Amazonian plants and butterflies laid out as if it was possible to collect every detail the world had to offer. He owned a cabinet of curiosities that belonged to Alexander Von Humboldt, beautiful with its ebony veneer, its floral marquetry, the nooks and crannies still rich with dust from the eighteenth century. One time he even showed me one of Joseph Cornell's boxes, which I spent an hour looking at, filled with vials and clippings from old maps, Lancaster leaning over my shoulder saying Cornell was a collector masquerading as an artist.

Unlike the other shop owners, he was impeccably dressed, in bespoke suits, with that perfect drape of fabric picked up in London and Paris and Milan during the summers, and worn with the kind of carelessness that makes clothes look even better.

I loved him. I couldn't help it. He was younger than Aunt Rose and my father, though still quite a bit older than me. Compared to what I knew of the world, or the little bits of Hungary my father let slip, or Aunt Rose's anecdotes, so odd as to be unreal, Lancaster seemed a window onto what I *could* know, all that was still obscure but tantalizingly out there, a real life that I might actually encounter beyond the books and stories I was already bored with.

"Why not have a game with me before you defile the set?" he'd smile, flirting with Aunt Rose. He'd reach under the counter and pull out a bottle of cognac and wag it side to side. "We could have a drink. Your daughter here could keep track of the moves." When he winked at me his eye stayed closed for longer than it should have.

"She's not my daughter," Aunt Rose said. By then I was too old, or too disheartened by their refusal to marry or move in together, to care.

"Whatever," he said, shrugging. "What do you say?"

"I hate chess," she replied. "It's a stupid game."

He stood back. It was the only time I'd see him at a loss. Aunt Rose smiled: "It's one of the reasons I like collecting the figurines," she said. "I like breaking up the sets." She shrugged. "Chess is a stupid idea: a totally logical world with only one possible outcome."

"There are two outcomes," I interrupted her. She looked at me surprised, and then smiled, already nodding at what I was going to say. "There's winning, and there's stalemate," I said, but instead of smiling back at her I was smiling at Lancaster.

"There's also forfeiture," she whispered, frowning at both of us.

Lancaster would show up everywhere we went that last year. He always appeared with a chessboard tucked under his arm. Even when Aunt Rose took me shopping, the two of us wandering the sidewalks of Uptown, where I so rarely went, picking out the clothes I loved back then—leg warmers, jodhpurs, gauchos—somehow he was always there. I thought he was stalking Aunt Rose, though neither of us was particularly alarmed, since he seemed slick but harmless. To some degree she encouraged it, inviting him to sit with us, to set up his chessboard, then making a move or two before she waved him away, laughing, "No, really, it's so boring." She'd motion for me to get up, and I'd look back and Lancaster would be sitting there smiling at me, pointing at the chessboard, inviting me to take up the game Aunt Rose wasn't willing to play—at least not entirely.

If my father noticed, he said nothing. He was indifferent to Lancaster, didn't know the guy, wouldn't have recognized him on the street, never made a single comment when his name came up between Aunt Rose and me.

It was a whole half year before I got up the nerve to walk into Lancaster's store one evening, come up to the counter, and tell him I wanted to play.

He was looking through a box of old jewellery, his fingers scraping the bottom as if looking for a hidden compartment. "You ready to play chess?"

He turned over the sign in the front door, twisted the lock, and motioned with a finger for me to come into the back room, where there were two couches and a couple of easy chairs arranged around a low table covered with empty wine, whiskey and beer bottles that he swept into a box. He dragged the arm of his linen shirt across the table to clear away any remaining crumbs or ash, then pulled a chess set off a shelf and set up the figurines. I sat down, sinking so far into the sofa it felt as if I was going to fall out the bottom.

Lancaster showed me how the pieces moved, basic strategy, took my hand and placed it on each pawn, rook, knight, and together we moved them along the white and black squares. "Would you like a drink?" he asked, and when I nodded he came back with two glasses of red wine, proposing a toast to "all the pieces left over" by Aunt Rose.

It took me a second to get up, struggling against the pull of the couch. But I did it, leaning over to place my mouth on his. And then he was the one who couldn't find his feet.

We did eventually play, not just that night, but across many nights, huddled in that room half undressed, drinking wine, and laughing. I didn't bother to hide it from my father, walking out the front door, through the overgrown yard with its piles of bricks and firewood and the two old trucks my father must have been interested in enough, who knows when, to put up on blocks and cover with blue tarps against the rain. I went along Michigan Avenue, my intentions plain for the neighbors to see, hoping they'd tell my father I was out at all hours, and finally arriving at Lancaster's shop.

Lancaster was self-involved enough to think I believed the things he said: that he'd inherited enough money to do as he pleased, and what pleased him, he said, were "Beautiful things." We were on the couch when he said this, our bodies wedged beside each other, a quilt protecting us from the cold that winter in the uninsulated back room. "Beautiful things," he said, running a hand down my breasts, lingering on my belly, between my legs.

He never once asked what I was interested in, either thinking he already knew, or not caring, though I wouldn't have known what to say if he had, only that I liked hearing about the places he'd gone, descriptions of Rome, London, New York, the view from the Eiffel Tower, pubs along the Thames, Saint Peter's Basilica, the Schönbrunn, and the things he showed me, things that never made it onto the shelves of his store, already sold before he'd bought them, placed into registered packages sent out after hours. But what I loved the most, what he never stopped tempting me with, were the descriptions of Budapest, the city my father refused to speak about—lights along the Danube as casino boats and barges from Turkey and Bulgaria and Greece drifted in the night; the neo-Gothic architecture of the parliament buildings, like the whitened bones of a fallen bird; the grime of the ninth district and its alleys twisting onto some new bar, cellar restaurant, another statue of some failed statesman; the New York Kávéház and its chandeliers and steam and ghosts of a hundred writers and artists perished in wars, concentration camps, the interrogation rooms of the ÁVÓ and SS. They were the places I'd fantasized about long ago, when I was a girl checking out books from the library, but now I could ask questions of someone who'd actually been there, an emissary from my dreams. It was all my father had denied me, my heritage, a sense of self beyond the vinyl factory, the black-rimmed snow along Michigan Avenue at the end of winter, the phony room at Aunt Rose's.

Our relationship didn't last, of course, and it's easy to see now that beyond the stories, the exoticism that had more to do with recovering my father than any attraction to Lancaster, I really had no use for him. He was still part of that town, a mouthpiece for its banal escape fantasies, still someone I could get to by walking along Michigan Avenue.

I was staying at Aunt Rose's the night everything fell apart. We were supposed to have dinner, Aunt Rose flitting around the place more excited than usual, setting candles on the table, putting a bottle of champagne into the fridge, working hard at getting the roast just right, far more preparation than she normally did. When I asked what the occasion was she only winked at me. "Your father and I have been together for many years," she said. "He spends more time here than he does at home."

I nodded. It was true. But I didn't tell her it was because to have her at his place, night after night, was to let her in, and as the danger of that increased over the years he was always in Aunt Rose's bed, which meant she was shut out completely.

My father never showed up for dinner. Aunt Rose grew silent as the minutes ticked by, until finally she shrugged, told me to sit down, and I sat and ate in the midst of that empty banquet, watching her lean against the wall by the front window drinking glass after glass of wine, occasionally reaching into her pocket to clutch at something, drawing out her hand as if she'd been bitten by whatever was in there.

He never showed. The grease congealed around the roast. Aunt Rose finished the bottle and opened another. I did my dishes, then watched TV, and finally went to bed.

I wasn't asleep long, maybe a couple of hours, when I heard the crash.

They were downstairs. She was yelling. I snuck down the back stairs and peeked from around the banister. My father was standing in front of Aunt Rose, who was on the couch, one hand in her pocket. My father looked angry, wearing his work clothes, which were dirtier than normal, staring at her hard. "It was overtime. I can't afford to say no to overtime. You know that."

"Mike . . ." She glanced at the telephone, but then changed her mind about what she wanted to say next. "It's not the money!" she hissed. "It's not just a dance once in a while, or someone to babysit your daughter, or a fuck, or your endless unchanging no surprises idea of security." She made the last comment as if it was a revelation to her as well, as if she'd just realized it, since for a long time it had been yet another thing that attracted her to my father.

"You don't know a thing about my security," he yelled. And he swept his hand along one of the shelves of the room, scattering chess pieces across the floor. He stood there as if he had no idea what he'd done, as if the action came first and the idea of it afterward. The chess pieces were everywhere, like tripwires.

Aunt Rose did not get up. My father stood there, trapped among the chess pieces, not daring to move. "Do you even know what your daughter does?" she asked.

"You don't get to ask me that," he said. "She's *my* daughter."

The way he said it, "my," made Aunt Rose wince. "She *might* have been mine, too," Aunt Rose whispered. Her hand came out of her pocket gripping something.

My father never noticed. He was looking at his hands too, inspecting the knuckles. "If it's what I think it is. If it's *who* I think it is . . ."

"Then what?" she said. "Find him, find all of them, and kill them?"

My father looked at her. He was helpless, shaking with rage at his impotence, but with something else as well, the desire to find a way out when there was none.

"It would be so much easier to do that," she said. "Dance instead of talk, fight instead of figure out, labour instead of work. Passion is always easier, isn't it, Mike?" Her voice was quiet now. She rubbed the back of a hand against her forehead. "But that's all there ever is, just passion, laughter and rage and intensity and whatever it is in your mind that takes you from me in the middle of the afternoon, during a conversation, that makes you sit in the bathroom hissing at people, who knows how long dead, threatening them—"

"She's not your daughter," my father interrupted her. "She's just a deal we made that went on longer than it should have."

"You think this . . ."Aunt Rose closed her eyes. She waved her clenched fist at the room. "There was no deal, Mike," she said.

He shrugged. "I told you about Hungary."

"No, Mike." She got up and went to him, chess pieces crunching underfoot, and took him by the hand. "Did you forget what happened that night? You couldn't get out a single sentence." She held his hand. "You never told me about Hungary."

My father looked away. He was scared. "Quiet," he said, "you'll wake her."

"Oh, fuck you, Mike."

"That's right." He smiled, and it was horrible because although his words were hostile he was ranting like a man being led down a corridor toward something he'd rather not face. "Fuck me. That's what we've been doing these years. And that's all it's ever going to be. You will never be my wife, and she will never be your daughter. Never!" It was the most hurtful thing he could have said, but I do not think he was trying to hurt Aunt Rose, not really. He was just terrified of where she'd gotten to, trespassing on his isolation from where he'd always hoped to keep her, the careful dance of the last fourteen years all gone to waste, when he would have happily gone on that way with her—dancing—forever.

"You're right," she said, and her voice had gone quiet too, but soft in a way my father's was not, without the hardness that puts edges around a whisper. "If I could have had you I'd have gladly taken the rest," she murmured, opening her fist on a tiny velvet box, from which she took a ring and placed it on my father's finger. He stood there, shocked, unable to move his hand out of hers. She kissed him then, as soft as her voice had been. "Goodbye, Mike," she said, and she turned and brushed past me on the stairs.

My father stood there, staring after her, staring at me.

"Goodbye," he finally said, and I could not tell which of us he was talking to, but he motioned to me, and as we left I heard Aunt Rose run down the stairs as if she wanted to say something else. I never heard what it was.

She was gone in a week. I remember going back to the house, standing outside as the movers arrived. But she wasn't there. I watched as they carted out the bits of my old bedroom, and as I stopped myself from rushing up the steps to make them put it all back I finally understood what had happened in those pawnshops over the years, the pieces Aunt Rose left because as beautiful as they were they weren't the one thing she loved the best.

I did not stick around for long after that either, five months. Then I was gone, too, not with Lancaster, but on my own. They were not easy, those first years, though things grew easier afterwards, once I figured out all I had not been able, or permitted, to figure out when I still lived on Michigan Avenue. I even got to Hungary, though that was decades later, after my father had died, lungs rotted out, indifferent to my occasional visits home, as if in leaving I too had died and this phantom who came back once in a while to visit was not the girl he'd help raise but an intruder into that place he'd drifted to, one that must have looked like peace to everyone else, no more yelling or rages or wild nights. But peace was not where he was at then, or at least not peace in the usual sense, just an indifference so profound nothing mattered at all, not even me. He rarely spoke, simple requests only: "Pass the salt"; "Don't forget to put gas in the car"; "Sure, I'll see you next time"—nothing about where I was going, who I was with, what my life consisted of. I was young then, and I didn't want to deal with parents anymore, nor any of the people I'd left behind on Michigan Avenue, coming and going as quickly, quietly, and as rarely as possible.

In Hungary I managed to learn a bit of the language, enough to comb through the National Archives and libraries. You see, I had followed in Aunt Rose's footsteps, but only in order to follow my father's. I retraced his life back to a time before Canada, before his transatlantic trip, an orphan of sixteen having seen too much during the siege of Budapest. I found an address on the back of one of his photographs (though the date that accompanied it was from long before the war), an apartment in the seventh district, which later became the Jewish ghetto, and saw pictures of what happened to the people who lived there (had my father been one of them, or had his family left by then?)—emaciated bodies in the streets, frozen to death in rubbled buildings, hanging by their hands, wired to wrought-iron railings on the wrong sides of stairwells. I read the essays and memoirs and journalism. I learned of the rapes of women by the Red Army, men standing on women's faces while their comrades took turns, girls young as fourteen locked in rooms visited repeatedly, and afterwards the gift of a bayonet slashed from crotch to throat. I read of children forced to walk in front of detachments, their small bodies big enough to absorb the bullets. I read of the camps their parents were sent to, digging holes in Siberia, bodies cut down by malnutrition, frost, sadistic guards chopping off fingers, and, later, when the thaw came, the earth refusing to harbor them, their bodies resurfacing in old coats and jackets, pockets stuffed with faded folded pictures. It was too much, it was enough, and in the end it still wasn't the specifics of what my father had experienced. But I understood why he couldn't talk about it, and why, with all that happened there, with whatever he'd gone through, an entire world lost before he even knew what the world was, he'd struggled to lose even more of it, even the memories, never repeating what he'd experienced for fear it would grow ever more vivid in his mind. I would never be sure if his inability to let go of that meant he couldn't hold onto anything else, or if, in fact, it made him terrified of holding on.

It was the only clue I obtained to Miklós Berényi. I found nothing else except stories, sitting there night after night as fascinated by it as Aunt Rose had been, filling up pages and pages with a history that was also mine, since his remoteness had become my own. This was my "research specialty" now: the passing of trauma from one generation to the next.

I was at a conference, giving a talk on exactly this, when I ran into Aunt Rose again.

She'd aged almost beyond recognition, another of those professors emeritus you see at conferences, full of the ease that comes when the bad work—students, marking, committees, faculty rivalries—is behind you, when at last there's only the work you love: research, writing, and the endless debate.

"Hi, Mariska," she said, stepping up to the bus stop outside the hotel where I was waiting for the shuttle to take me to the conference. She was peering from under an umbrella, this old lady withered to four feet tall, and it was a minute before her eyes gave her away, still full of that energy, and without thinking I threw my arms around her. She smiled tightly, patting my shoulder. "I've been watching you for a half hour," she said.

"I didn't even . . ." I started to say something but couldn't finish. There was too much. I pulled the program from my bag. "I haven't looked at the presenters yet, otherwise I . . ."

"You've been doing what I would have done," she smiled again. "I've never been fond of looking back, either. But your father was better at avoiding the past than either of us. Maybe we should have left him alone about that."

Her left hand was gripping the umbrella, and I looked at it instinctively and saw the gold ring. She caught the glance and shrugged.

"I'm sorry," I said, and in the rush to cover up my embarrassment I blurted out my sense of guilt. "I should have visited you. After you moved away. I thought of writing . . . A few times I thought I should try."

"It's okay," she said. "You inherited that honestly: leaving, never going back. It's important that some things end." For a second I wondered if she was talking about herself as well as my father.

"Well, we're here now." I tried to laugh. "Do you have plans for dinner?"

She shook her head. "No," she mumbled. "I won't have plans."

"So why not meet, then," I said, taking her hand, "after the conference today?"

"It might be nice," she said.

The shuttle arrived and I boarded it thinking she was coming too, but when I looked back she was standing outside smiling and nodding at me while the other passengers got on, and soon the shuttle was on its way, and she was still standing there one hand raised, not quite waving, having said all there was to say.

Of course we never met up that night. We didn't even try. Aunt Rose was checked out by the time I got back to the hotel, just as I'd predicted. "She left you this," the concierge said, pushing over a tiny package I knew, even then, would contain two queens, one black, one white, that I would hold up to the light in my hotel room, tracing the intricacies of their design. There was a receipt inside from a local shop, where I would go and return them the next day, walking along with the box under my arm thinking of all the shop owners all those years ago facing their useless chess sets, seeing in them what Aunt Rose must have seen in my father—that fragmented beauty terrifying in its uselessness, in its demand that you protect and preserve it even while it offers you nothing of itself.

When I got to the store I stopped outside, holding the box. I lifted out the two queens again and peered into the box, pushing the cotton wadding aside with a finger as if I might find something else. There was nothing, of course, and never had been, only two queens desperate for the affections of an absent king, trying to conjure him into existence, and losing each other along the way.

The Encirclement

AT SOME POINT during the lecture Sándor would get up, point a finger at Professor Teleki, and accuse him of lying—and Teleki would gasp and sputter and grow red in the face and the audience would love it. But it wasn't an act, and Teleki had approached Sándor many times—either personally or through his agent—to ask him what his problem was. He even offered him money, which Sándor accepted only to break his promise and show up at the lectures again—to the point where audiences started expecting him, as if Teleki's presence was secondary, playing the straight man to this hectoring vindictive blind guy who was the star of the show.

Yes, Sándor was blind. Which only made it more incredible, especially in the early days, that he'd managed to follow Teleki all over North America, from one stop on the lecture circuit to the next. "How the hell can a blind man," Teleki yelled at his agent, "get around the country so quickly?" Nonetheless, Teleki could see it: Sándor in a dark overcoat, black glasses not flashing in the sunshine so much as absorbing it, his cane tip-tapping along the pavement through all kinds of landscape—deserts, mountains, prairies—and weather—squalls, blizzards, heat waves—aimed directly at the place where Teleki had scheduled his next appearance. It was like something out of a bad folk tale.

But once Teleki started bribing him the vision changed, and he always pictured Sándor sipping mai tais in the airport lounge before boarding with the first-class ticket Teleki's hush money had bought him, chatting amiably with businessmen, and flirting, in a blind man sort of way, with the stewardesses, though this was as far from the truth as the first vision had been, as Sándor himself explained.

They sat in the bar of the Seelbach Hilton in Louisville and Sándor, with a casual seriousness that always drove Teleki crazy, told him he hadn't spent a cent Teleki had given him, that every single trip had been accomplished through the "assistance of strangers." All he had to do, Sándor said, was step out the door, and instantly there were people there, asking if he was okay, if there was anything they could do to help, if there was something he needed. When Teleki said he found it hard to believe that such spontaneous charity could have gotten him from Toronto to New York, to Montreal, Halifax, Boston, Chicago, Calgary, Los Angeles, Vancouver, and Anchorage, in that order, on time for every single one of his lectures, Sándor replied, "You can believe it or not, but that's exactly what happened." He'd downloaded Teleki's itinerary, grabbed his coat and suitcase and cane, and walked out of the door into the care of the first stranger he'd met,

and from there, "Well, things just took care of themselves."
Teleki looked at him, then around the Seelbach, wondering
if he could get away with strangling him right there.

The point at which Sándor would usually rise from his seat—
various people supporting him by the elbows—was when
Teleki began to describe the morning of January 18, 1945
in Budapest, the minute he'd stepped off the Chain Bridge,
and the order went out to blow it up, along with the Hungarian and German soldiers, the peasants and their wheel-
barrows full of ducks, the middle-class children and women
and men, suitcases packed, still streaming across it. By then,
the bridges were a tangled mass of metal, holes gaping along
the causeway, cars stuck in them, on fire, bodies shredded
by Soviet artillery tangled in the cables and railings, thousands of people trying to force their way across in advance
of the Soviets, trampling and being trampled on, cursing in
the near dark, forced over the sides into the icy river, mowed
down by fighter planes, Red Army tanks, machine guns,
while behind their backs, in that half of Budapest, the siege
went on, fighting from street to street, building to building,
the whole place ablaze.

"Tell them how you grabbed two of the children whose
parents had died coming across the bridge," Sándor would
yell at him at this point. "Tell them how you held them to
your chest, telling the Arrow-Cross officer you couldn't join
the siege effort because your wife had just died. Then tell
them how you abandoned those kids in the next street. You
tell them that!" Sándor jabbed his cane in Teleki's direction.

"That never happened!" Teleki would shout back. "I never did that."

And the audience would hoot and laugh and clap, egging Sándor on.

It was always something different, another part of the story sabotaged. When Teleki got to the part about how he'd gone up to the castle and "volunteered," as he put it, to join the defence under Lieutenant-Colonel László Veresváry, Sándor stood up—someone had handed him a bullhorn—and did a high-pitched imitation of how Teleki, after abandoning the children, had run into an Arrow-Cross soldier who saw that he was able-bodied, and told him to get up to the castle. "B-b-b-b-but, I'm just looking for fooooood," whined Sándor. "I-I-I-I left my kids a block over, and I was about to go back for them. My wife, you see, she died when they blew up the bridge . . ." And here Sándor fell into a fit of such flawless mock weeping that many in the audience turned toward Teleki and copied him. "But the soldier forced you up to the castle anyhow, didn't he?" said Sándor, suddenly serious. "Giving your ass a kick every few feet just to make sure you got there."

"I have no idea what you're talking about," said Teleki, trying to look cool, "and if you don't stop interrupting my talks I'm going to have a restraining order put on you."

But Teleki's agent advised him against this. How would it look, he asked, if Teleki, the great professor of twentieth-century middle European history, award-winning author of biographies and memoirs, survivor of the siege of Budapest, were suddenly afraid of the rantings of a blind man? Besides, the lawyer had explained, it would only provide more publicity for Sándor, which was the last thing either of them wanted. He finally suggested—and he was surprised that Teleki hadn't considered this himself—that he get his act together and take on Sándor directly, since he was after all a historian. Or was he?

Teleki looked at him, wondering whether his agent had been to one of his lectures lately. Had he seen what went on up there? Sándor was killing him, and on the very ground where Teleki was supposed to be the authority. On the other hand, looking again at his agent, Teleki realized that maybe he didn't want him to get rid of Sándor, that maybe—no, *probably*—his agent was actually happy with the way things were working out, eagerly calculating his percentage from the recent "bump" in ticket sales.

"What I mean," said the agent, "is find out who this Sándor guy is. Isn't that something you do? Root around in people's pasts?"

Teleki had not known how to respond to that. Sándor Veselényi was his name. That's as far as they'd gotten during their first few meetings. And he couldn't just walk into the nearest archive and pull out a file by that name and voila there would be everything from the baptismal record to the accident that caused Sándor's blindness to why he'd decided to make it his life's work to humiliate Teleki. No, it would take years to do that kind of research, just as it had taken years to gather material for each of the biographies and memoirs Teleki had written, to put together the lecture that was now, unfortunately, thrilling audiences more than ever, and which he was contractually locked into.

Not that it wouldn't have been nice—Teleki was the first to admit—to get up at the lectern and to lay it all out the next time Sándor opened his mouth, flashing the PowerPoint slides of Sándor in his fascist uniform, a member of the Arrow-Cross, or better yet of Father Kun's murderous band, so unlike the Germans in their rejection of efficiency, in really going out of their way, even to be inconvenienced, as long as it meant slaughtering the Jews *just right*. And for the *coup de grâce*, for a nice moral twist at the end of the story, something about how Sándor had been blinded by his own desire to seek and destroy, perhaps a shard of glass from an explosion he'd rigged in one of the buildings in the Budapest ghetto—whole families tied up inside.

But Teleki had no information on Sándor—only on himself. He'd get up there with his black-and-white slides, his laser pointer, his tongue tripping up, bogged down, boxed in by English, a language so clunky compared to Hungarian, and try to tighten up his story even further, to make himself appear even *more* authentic, only to have Sándor hobble in on the arms of two businessmen, a mother of three, four old men in outdated suits, and two guys sporting Mohawks. His entourage was growing.

Teleki spoke on, trying to keep his voice from going falsetto. He focused on the crowd—the usual assemblage of academics, writers, journalists, immigrants, students, amateur historians, senior citizens—and pointed to the picture of himself in the uniform of Veresváry's garrison, expected to keep the Soviets from capturing Buda castle, where the SS and Arrow-Cross commanders were wringing their hands in the middle of the siege, encircled entirely by the Red Army, trying to figure out what to do. At night, young men, really just boys, would try to fly in supplies by glider, Soviet artillery shooting them out of the sky. Teleki struck a solemn tone when he told the crowd that the place they were supposed to land—Vérmezö—could be translated as "Blood Meadow."

When Sándor stayed silent, Teleki grew braver, and he told them of what it was like in the final days of the siege, the desperate order of the castle with its German and Hungarian armies, the soldiers too frightened of punishment—usually a bullet in the head—to voice what was on their minds: why SS Obergruppenführer Pfeffer-Wildenbruch hadn't gotten them the hell out of Budapest, why they were clearly sitting around waiting to be slaughtered. Worse still was being under the command of Veresváry, whose soldiers were men like Teleki—refugees or criminals or labourers pressed into service—for whom Veresváry was always willing to spare a bit of whipping from the riding crop he carried around, brandishing it over his head as he strode along the trenches they'd dug and were defending, as if the Soviet bullets whizzing around him were so many mosquitoes. Veresváry would sentence men to death for cowardice, then commute the sentence, then brutalize them so badly over the next several days—screaming and kicking at them while the fusillade continued, a horizontal rain of bullets and mortars—that the men would eventually stand in the trench, ostensibly to take better aim at the enemy, though from the way their guns hung in their hands it was little more than suicide. They stood there until half their faces suddenly vanished in a splatter, or their backs bloomed open, red and purple and bone. This seemed to satisfy Veresváry, who praised them as they fell, pointing to how they slumped, knees buckling, heads thrown back, and said to the rest, "There was a soldier, you chickenshits. There was a soldier!" as if the definition of soldier was impossible without the past tense.

"Was that why you came up with the plan to do away with him? To undermine and to betray and to murder your commander?" asked Sándor, standing up.

"You must be thinking of someone else, Sándor."

"Sure you did. You went from soldier to soldier and then, when you had them onside, you turned around and betrayed them to Pfeffer-Wildenbruch, telling him you'd heard whispers that there would be a mutiny."

"That's the biggest lie I've ever—"

"Look at the next picture. Look at it."

The audience turned from Sándor to Teleki, who stood there, mouth agape, the remote control in hand, his finger poised above the button, wondering whether Sándor was bluffing, or whether he'd somehow managed to hijack his PowerPoint, slipping in a different set of slides.

"Let's see it," someone in the audience yelled, and everyone laughed.

Teleki hit the button and there they were: all those arrested on charges of treason, five battered men with rotting clothes and unshaven faces standing against the blackened walls of the castle district, loosely grouped together, as if they were not yet accused and looking to slink off before it happened. It was the picture as Teleki remembered it, in exactly the place where it always appeared.

"There you are. You're standing just to the left of Pfeffer-Wildenbruch. That's you right there, you dirty stinking fink! You sold out all your comrades!"

Teleki turned, squinting at the photograph, noting with eye-opening surprise that the guy there did resemble, in a way, what he might have looked like fifty years ago, after seventy or so days of siege—malnourished, frightened to death, desperate.

The audience applauded.

"The guy can see photographs!" said Teleki to his agent. "He's a complete fraud!"

"Why didn't you say anything at the lecture?"

"I did! But nobody could hear me! They were too busy applauding!"

His agent shrugged. "Maybe he saw the photograph before he went blind. Maybe somebody described it to him."

"Come off it," Teleki said.

"So how come he knows so much about you, then?"

"He doesn't know anything about me! All that stuff . . . he's lying!"

The agent looked at him with a raised eyebrow.

"What? You believe him now, too?"

"The only thing I believe in is sales," replied the agent, recovering quickly. "And sales are excellent," he said. "How would you feel about playing in bigger venues?"

"I'm not 'playing'! I'm trying to inform people, to teach them something!"

What Teleki noticed next was that Sándor's entourage seemed to be growing, as if the people who helped him were no longer dropping him off at the lectures and going their way, but sticking around, as if something in Sándor's words, the depth of his conviction, had brought them into contact with a higher cause, a belief system. Great, thought Teleki, just what I need: Sándor becoming a guru.

In addition, it seemed as though Sándor was now doing almost as much talking as Teleki was—bellowing on, jabbing the cane in Teleki's direction, the group of people immediately around him more vociferous in their approval than the rest. By the end of the night, Teleki noted that he'd spoken only three minutes more than Sándor.

But it was not just this that made Teleki decide, then and there, after twelve fingers of Scotch on the balcony of his hotel room, to pack it in, but also what Sándor had said. For the first time since the beginning of their conflict he was seriously doubting whether he knew more about the siege than the blind man, or whether, in fact, his very first guess had been right after all, and that Sándor, far from being a disabled person, was some spirit of vengeance, one of those mythic figures who were blind not because they couldn't see but because they were distracted from the material world by a deeper insight, by being able to peer into places no one else could see. Of course, remembering how he'd watched Sándor walk into pillars, or trip over seats, Teleki laughed and dismissed the thought, though it always came back, forcing him up from sleep, the extent of Sándor's information, the way he could retrieve things from the abyss of the past.

For when Teleki had described the last few days in the castle, how Veresváry ordered them to draw up surveillance maps using telescopes taken from the National Archives, plotting the streets in the direction of western Buda, Sándor had nodded in his seat. When Teleki said that rumours of a breakout had been swirling for days, Sándor rose up, but said nothing. Nervously, Teleki had continued, saying the German soldiers, during the Second World War, never surrendered, preferring the death of fighting on, of retreat, rather than captivity, for they'd been told of the horrors and torments of Siberia, as if it was possible to imagine a place where death was salvation.

Teleki was sent to Pfeffer-Wildenbruch with the maps they'd drawn up. At this point in the story, Sándor began rubbing his hands together, waiting for Teleki to repeat what Pfeffer-Wildenbruch had said that day as he took the documents from Teleki's hand, staring right through him as if he wasn't in the room, as if there was only the Obergruppenführer himself, alone with the choices he couldn't make: "If I give the order for a breakout," he mumbled, "everyone will die."

It was here that Sándor finally chimed in, mimicking the reply Teleki had supposedly given: "S-s-s-surely not everyone."

Teleki reached for the volume adjustment on his microphone, continuing on with what Pfeffer-Wildenbruch had said to him: "You'll probably be one of the first to die."

"I-i-it's a fitting thing, sir—" Sándor interrupted him again.

"I did not say that!" shouted Teleki, turning the volume all the way up.

Someone handed Sándor the bullhorn again. "To face the enemy directly is a fitting thing, Obergruppenführer, sir. Without flinching."

Suddenly Sándor began to play both roles, turning this way and that to indicate when Pfeffer-Wildenbruch was speaking and when Teleki, the crowd watching raptly, oblivious to the "No, no, no" Teleki was shouting into the microphone.

"Meanwhile," said Sándor, now in the role of Teleki, "while the men are proving their bravery, we could do *our* duty and escape using the sewers under the castle."

"Our duty?" Sándor carried off Pfeffer-Wildenbruch's fatigue perfectly.

"I-i-i-it would not be cowardice," Sándor stuttered, again playing Teleki. "Such words belong to narcissists, those who worry for their reputations, for how history will regard them. No"—Sándor shook his head as Teleki might have—"we must look beyond our egos, our timid wishes for glory. The war effort needs us . . . needs *you* . . . to survive this. You must sacrifice your pride for the greater good." Then, in a flourish, Sándor removed his glasses, shifting his eyes side to side as Teleki had done so many times behind the lectern. "Obergruppenführer, sir, I've heard the men speaking of a plot on Lieutenant-Colonel Veresváry's life. In the sewers, you will need men you can trust . . . to prove my devotion I will give you the names of the conspirators . . .

"And so," Sándor now said, returning to himself (or what Teleki was increasingly thinking of as the *role* of himself), "while men died by the thousands in the breakout, our friend here"—he indicated Teleki—"was splashing through the sewers."

The sewers. Here, Sándor's knowledge was just as extensive. It was called *Ördög-Árok*, "devil's ditch," a name in keeping with what was to greet them, descending into waters swirling with suitcases, soggy files, fragments of memoranda, whole suits of clothing from which men and women seemed to have dissolved, a wooden statue of the Virgin face down, her hand entwined with the much smaller one of a body trapped in the waters beneath her. They ran into loose bands of SS. They waited below while men tried scaling the rungs of ladders to sewer grates above, poking their heads out, followed by the crack of a sniper's bullet, the body falling back and knocking off all who were clinging to the ladder below it. They entered aqueducts that grew narrower and narrower, Pfeffer-Wildenbruch sending Teleki on ahead (or so Sándor said) into places he could move along crouched over, then only on his hands and knees, and finally on his belly, each pipe he went into smaller than the last, until he was overcome by claustrophobia and panicked, inching backwards on his stomach and chest like some worm reversing itself—only to find that Pfeffer-Wildenbruch and his party had already moved on, leaving him behind. It was at this point that he ran into two soldiers accompanying Hungarian commander Iván Hindy and his wife, who was still wearing the finery she put on every day, as befitted her position, the hems of her dress drifting out around her as she whispered to the men on either side, trying to keep the mood light, the company agreeable, even as the screams of men rang up and down the sewer. They were holding her by either elbow, but it seemed as if she was holding them, especially the soldier whose arm was in a sling, as if the sound of her voice could keep them going, as if in allowing them to hold her she was lending them strength.

As Sándor's story went—and it was a compelling story, Teleki had to admit, so much so that even *he* wanted to hear how it would end—Teleki was reluctant to accept Hindy's order to bring up the rear of their little party. When Hindy, seeing his reluctance, suggested that he could take up the front then, Teleki again demurred. "Well, where would you like to be?" Teleki said he would prefer to stay in the middle, alongside Mrs. Hindy, and everyone laughed, their echoes bouncing off the walls and water until he realized they'd stopped caring, that he was trapped in a group of people tripping along cheerily to capture, trial, execution. "M-m-m-maybe we should try another few of the sewer grates," he said, pointing up, waiting for a break in the laughter. "Would you prefer to go first or second?" Hindy asked, and when Teleki said second they laughed all over again—except for Mrs. Hindy, who reached forward (Sándor reproducing her movement for the benefit of the audience), and tenderly stroked Teleki's cheek.

It was decided that the uninjured soldier would go first, since he was the heaviest and needed two men to lift him within reach of the first rung of the ladder. He would see whether there were snipers present, and draw their fire away from the manhole, hopefully without getting his head blown off. Next would come Teleki, whom the commander could boost up alone, and who'd then help, from above, with the delicate job of heaving up the injured soldier, as well as the voluminous Mrs. Hindy, and finally Hindy himself.

The soldier nodded, taking a long swig from a bottle of Napolean brandy he said he'd found floating in the sewer, then stepped onto the hands held out to him and reached up for the ladder, crawling up it quickly and pushing open the grate. *Click.* There was the sound of a firing pin hitting a dud cartridge. Looking up, they saw the soldier staring directly into the barrel of a Soviet gun, though in the next second he'd thrust the bottle of brandy into the Russian's face, rolled quickly out of the hole, and ran, the Soviet soldier giving his head a shake, and then chasing after him. Within seconds, Hindy was holding out his hands for Teleki, who looked at them, placed his foot tentatively into the knitted fingers, then boosted himself up, only to have Hindy remove his hands the instant he'd grabbed the rung, leaving him dangling there, too weak to pull himself up and too afraid to fall back into the sewer, from which there would be no second chance at escape. Hindy and the injured soldier were laughing again, but not Mrs. Hindy, who was telling them to stop and try-ing to reach up, to help him, only to be met by Teleki's gaze, desperate and pitiless, as he placed his boot squarely in the middle of her upturned face and pushed off, feeling her nose crack under the sole. Then he was up the ladder, rung over rung, and out the manhole and running, while they called after him to help pull them out.

Sándor stopped, intending to continue, but the audience had begun booing in Teleki's direction, the sound growing louder and louder until he left the stage.

Strangely, Teleki slept very well that night. There was something about surrender that was incredibly calming, as if the loss of desire could compensate for defeat. But by the middle of the next day he was squirming again, for his agent was sitting across the table from him in the café sliding across one article, feature, and editorial after another, all of them reporting on the "creative sabotage" of his lectures. In keeping with Teleki's recent luck, the writers devoted far more space to Sándor than to him, mainly because none of them had been able to dig up a single thing about his nemesis. They were fascinated by this blind man tapping his way out of nowhere to deliver his long apocalyptic monologues, setting the record straight and exposing the liars. In these articles Sándor was a moral force, and Teleki a con man.

"There's one here that speculates on whether you guys are working together," said the agent, pushing across a copy of the *New York Times*. Teleki glanced at it for a second and then quietly told his agent he was quitting.

"Quitting!" the agent responded. "You can't quit!"

"I think I just need to disappear for a while," said Teleki. "Once this dies down we can talk about what to do next."

"We? There is no *we*," the agent told him. "Not if you quit!"

Teleki looked at him, and in an instant realized what had happened. "You've been talking to Sándor, haven't you? What, you're representing both of us?"

His agent looked out the window, then back at him. "You know how often something like this comes around? A sleeper like this?"

"Tonight's my last show," said Teleki, rising from the table.

It wasn't like Teleki to fulfill a contract—or any other kind of promise for that matter—if he didn't want to, and yet he found himself fighting the impulse to just walk away. Maybe he wanted to prove to Sándor that he wasn't afraid, that he couldn't be so easily chased away, that he could take whatever was thrown at him. But there was a more dangerous realization as well, and all that afternoon he seemed on the verge of confronting it only to get scared and turn away, channelling what he felt into a rage so acute that more than once he was seen talking to himself, having imaginary arguments with Sándor from which he always emerged with the decisive victory. By nightfall though, shortly before he was due onstage, Teleki finally admitted to himself that Sándor's descriptions of the man using two children to get out of military service, or exposed by Pfeffer-Wildenbruch as a totally expendable soldier, or being mocked by Hindy and his men for cowardice, was not without a certain comfort, as if there might be something to gain from having your stories turned inside out, from having the hard moral decision—whether to lie or tell the truth—taken away from you.

And when Teleki finally took the stage that night, standing on the podium, he was no longer the showman of six months ago, when Sándor had first turned up at his lectures, nor even of the day before yesterday, when he'd tried to defend himself. There was something serious in him now, as if having come to the end of all this, having failed to defend himself, he was beyond loss, free, unconcerned for his reputation.

It was in his eyes, the need to survive, irrespective of honour or glory or anything else, as if he was once again looking at what Sándor had begun to describe, standing to interrupt Teleki five minutes into the lecture: the worst of what happened in the siege, all those men forced to take part in a breakout that should have happened months earlier, and which was now little more than a mass human sacrifice.

He remembered the morning, February 11, when a rumour went round that the radio operators had begun destroying their equipment; remembered the illusions many of the soldiers clung to: that only Romanians were guarding the breakout point, that they'd run the minute they saw the horde of fascist soldiers; that it would be no more than a half-hour march through the empty city to the place where German reinforcements were waiting; that, absurdly, the Russians were no match for the tactical brilliance of the Nazi and Arrow-Cross commanders. Like Sándor, Teleki knew that Veresváry had assembled his men at the Bécsi Gate before the march, that they were hit by a bombardment out of nowhere, their bodies ripped open, dismembered, even before they'd had a chance to set out. He could have followed Sándor word for word in recounting what only a very few men—a mere three percent of the 28,000 who set out that day—could recount seeing, or refuse to recount, crushed as they were by recurring nightmares of that three kilometres of city, so overwhelming that to begin speaking of it would be to never speak of anything else again. Mortar fire along avenues and boulevards. Flares hanging in the sky overhead. Soldiers screaming in a rush of animal frenzy, all semblance of reason gone as they realized the Soviets were stationed along the route—that they'd prepared for the breakout, that tanks and rockets and snipers were in place to kill every single one of them—now crushed into doorways, stumbling in the dark, crawling over comrades missing arms and legs and begging to be shot—one last mercy for which no one could spare the time—pushed on by those behind them, a river of flesh squeezed out between the buildings bordering Széna and Széll Kálmán Square, into a night kaleidoscopic with shells, tracer bullets, flares, *panzerfausts*, the light at the end of machine guns flashing without pause, a city shattered into ever more impossible configurations—a maze without discernible routes, choices, even the certainty of dead ends.

There was a pause in the auditorium at the end of this. Then Sándor, gathering himself up, began to speak again, his glasses aimed at Teleki. "This is what you saw when you emerged from the sewers. This is what you'd supported—you and the men like you—so eager to champion Horthy when he signed with the Nazis, and then, when he was deposed for wanting to break with them, to shift your support to Hitler's puppet, Szálasi, and the Arrow-Cross. Honour! you said. Bravery! The nation above all! But it was always someone else who paid for this allegiance, wasn't it? Not you. You slithered out of every situation, every duty you so loudly insisted upon, all those high standards and noble causes you so loudly proclaimed—always the job of someone else. And at the end of all that, in the aftermath, when you saw the breakout, realized what you'd done . . ."

"You went blind," whispered Teleki into the microphone. "You went blind."

"I'm talking about you!"

"No you're not," said Teleki, and he pushed back the lectern and walked off the raised platform and up the auditorium steps to where Sándor was standing, who drew back as Teleki approached. "This story you've been telling is your own, Sándor."

"It's yours!" Sándor shouted. "You know it's yours!"

Then Teleki, in the most inspired performance of his career, threw his arms around the blind man whispering, "It's okay, it's okay, it's okay," just loud enough to be picked up by the microphone pinned to his lapel.

He had tightened his hold until Sándor stopped struggling, and all the while he'd continued to whisper soothingly of how this was Sándor's public confession, how he could not have described the things he'd described unless he'd seen them, or known the things he knew unless he'd been there. He said he knew Sándor could still see, and that what had darkened his eyes was not physical in nature, but moral. Sándor had shouted and hollered and tried to fight him off, but Teleki merely continued to hold him, and the audience had inclined their heads, finally, in sympathy, as if they'd never for a second thought of Sándor as anything other than a refugee from himself, using Teleki's lectures to disclose his conscience in the only way he could—obliquely, by projecting his guilt and shame onto someone else. They even clapped when Teleki finally let go of the exhausted, defeated Sándor and taking him by the hand led him from the hall, down the steps, out the back exit off the wings of the stage, where the blind man flung Teleki's hand away, told him he should be ashamed of himself, and stormed off as fast as the tentative tapping of his cane would allow, tripping over the first curb he came to. Teleki smiled.

And he'd continued smiling late into the night, wrapped in his robe in the hotel, drinking the champagne his agent had sent up along with a note of apology Teleki never read, already knowing what it said. He gazed out over the city and wondered what Sándor might be doing in it now, who he was with, where he was headed. For that was Sándor's way, Teleki had realized, incapable of functioning, of getting from one place to the next, unless there was someone, preferably a crowd, to help him, as if his blindness was a way of restoring people to some sense of community, as if by helping him they were ultimately helping themselves, as if there was another map of the world, not of nations and cities but intersections of need, of what draws us together.

Sándor's world, Teleki thought. *His*. And he wondered for a moment what it was like—all those people working together—having long ago learned to count on nobody and nothing, groping his way all alone through the darkest of places.

The Society of Friends

LUJZA GALAMBOS was the lover of both Frigyes and Aurél, but her death solved nothing, the two men continued to fight over her until the end of their lives. For instance, Frigyes would lend Aurél an outboard motor, which Aurél never returned, though he complained about it, telling Frigyes it was without a doubt the shittiest piece of equipment he'd ever attached to the back of his boat, sputtering so bad it felt like he was sitting on "a goddamn earthquake," sending up blue clouds so noxious there was "no point," he said, "in even thinking you're anywhere outdoors," and guzzling so much gas it was a wonder he hadn't run dry the first time he used it, stranded in the middle of some lake rowing half the night just to get home.

Frigyes took back his gift, repaired it, and returned it to Aurél, who yelled at him that it still wasn't working right. "You give me this motor, you say it's fixed," Aurél shouted, standing in Frigyes's driveway holding the piece of equipment as if he wanted to throw it in his face, "but then I have to buy new spark plugs for it. Why can't you ever just do something properly?"

Frigyes smiled. "Perhaps you would allow me to take you out to dinner as a way of apologizing." It was just the sort of gesture—so sweet, so kind—that drove Aurél crazy.

But Aurél wasn't listening. He was gazing up at the bedroom window where Lujza was looking down on them, a sheet draped around her shoulders, smiling and waving. Frigyes followed his friend's gaze, then waved at Lujza too, and when she blew both of them kisses the two men glared at each other, though what they were really doing was angling their faces just so, trying to catch more of that windblown affection than the other guy.

The next week Frigyes went over to Aurél's and offered to pay for the spark plugs. Aurél told him he'd not only have to pay for the spark plugs but also the time it had taken to go buy them. When Frigyes asked how much, Aurél said, "Twenty-five dollars an hour. That's how much I'm worth. It took me four hours to get them out, go to the store, find new ones, pay, come back, put them in." He held out his hand. Frigyes smiled, dipped into his wallet, and pulled out a hundred dollars. "These are all twos and ones!" Aurél yelled. "Don't you have anything bigger?"

"It's all I've got. Let me make it up to you. I'll mow your lawn."

"Last time you mowed my lawn you left big clumps of grass everywhere!"

"Then I'll fix the transmission on your truck."

"Last time you did that I had to go out and buy new

transmission fluid! There isn't a mechanic in the world who'd make his customer do that!"

Frigyes smirked, deciding not to mention that no mechanic in the world would have done all those repairs for free.

Frigyes and Aurél were friends of mine, DPs like me, escaped from Hungary in 1956. We spent a lot of time together at the Szécsényi Club in Toronto, especially in the early days, playing *tarok*, bowling in the wooden lanes out back, trying to tell the most hilarious joke, the two of them always fiercely competitive with each other, though in those days it was part of the camaraderie, the fun, no hard feelings. I still have pictures of them, kept in a shoebox—Aurél and Frigyes drinking Metaxa at a picnic table; Aurél and Frigyes standing in front of some trout they'd caught; Aurél and Frigyes dressed as shepherds on the *puszta*—old colour photographs now faded to a golden haze, as if to commemorate how inseparable they'd been, long before Lujza arrived, long after her death. In those last years they became an old bickering couple eating at one of Toronto's two Hungarian restaurants, everyone would see them there, Frigyes treating them to appetizers, sometimes several main courses, wine, to which Aurél would respond, loud enough for everyone to hear, "Well, that was pricey. It cost five times what I normally spend at a restaurant, if we'd gone to the place *I* recommended. So I guess you owe me four more dinners." After all, he hadn't *asked* Frigyes to take him somewhere so expensive. It was the sort of insane logic, a complete lack of gratitude, that would have caused most people's brains to melt, though the truth is it was a torment tailormade for Frigyes, who rolled his eyes and shook his head and then smiled that sickly smile and treated his friend to four more dinners.

After arriving in Canada Aurél became a game warden, and for the rest of his life would go out hunting regularly—for grouse and duck, but also deer and bear when the season was in, not to mention fly-fishing—and everyone cozied up to him, hoping to get his secrets, the best places to find game, methods of tracking, how to properly train a *vizsla*, the sorts of flies he was tying. They wanted his advice, and if you poured him enough wine, and if Lujza encouraged him to help the people who hated her, he just might have given it, maybe even invited you along.

Frigyes was a bootlegger. It's what he'd always been, in Hungary and Canada, famous for the *pálinka* he brewed in some secret still he always hinted at but no one apart from Aurél had ever seen. It had medicinal properties, or so it was said, helping to cure arthritis, asthma, impotence, as long as you made sure to drink at least one shot, but preferably more, every single day. For Lujza, Frigyes even made a special batch of *pálinka*, the few who'd tasted it said it was less like a drink than heaven itself distilled into a bottle. To the last day of her life, Lujza swore it was what kept her young, carrying it around in a silver flask Aurél had given her—an heirloom that had belonged to his father and grandfather and great-grandfather and still bore the family crest—and which he insisted had magical properties that transformed Frigyes's "rotgut" into the miraculous potion Lujza was almost constantly sipping. Of course you could never tell with Lujza if she was being honest in calling Frigyes's *pálinka* still "the fountain of eternal youth," or heavily ironic, since more than once she told my wife, Vera, that the secret to her appearance was "a combination of avoiding work as much as possible and pickling myself with alcohol."

If the problem with Aurél was his lack of generosity, the problem with Frigyes was his chaos. He was notoriously undependable, no one knew when they'd get their delivery of brandy, if it would show up on Friday or Saturday as promised, or even in time for the baptism, wedding, dinner, or whatever the event was. But when Frigyes *did* arrive it was always with a laugh and more than you'd ordered or he was willing to accept payment for—double the number of jars, some of the very best quality (with the exception of the stuff he made only for Lujza).

It was Lujza's arrival in Toronto, in 1958, that made everything that was good in the two men's relationship—Aurél's intensity, Frigyes's impulsiveness—turn into everything that was bad. It was then that Frigyes began telling everyone what a great woodsman Aurél was, singing his praises up and down like some herald in those old etchings of King Mátyás's royal hunting parties; it was then that Aurél started criticizing Frigyes, and no longer in a funny way, saying the only reason he was such "an agent of anarchy" was so that people would be even *more* thankful when he finally showed up, providing his little extras like some great benefactor.

As for Lujza, nobody could really place her, which was unusual, since almost everyone who came to Toronto in those days came because they knew *someone*—a family member, an in-law, a classmate from school—who'd come before, and who was there waiting when they arrived, offering a place to stay, help getting around, contacts for jobs, introductions at the Szécsényi Club. She arrived with nothing, knowing nobody, no father or brother or husband. In those days she had exactly two suits of good clothes, none of the finery the men would later bankroll, and her hands were chapped and worn and fidgety, her hair carefully combed and pinned back but not styled, her face already developing the kinds of wrinkles it would take weekly spa treatments and plenty of Frigyes's *pálinka* to arrest and then erase. Throughout her time in Toronto, Lujza made no attempt to correct the rumours that grew up around her.

In the first year she sat for hours with Árpád Holló, who ran the Szécsényi Club, dressed in one of those two outfits that would have looked refined on the streets of Budapest— high heels, tight skirts, complicated blouses—but in Toronto just looked trashy. (Later, with the money the two men lavished on her, she adopted the style of 1950s and early 1960s European film stars, such as Corinne Marchand in *Cleo from 5 to 7*, or Anouk Aimée in *8½*.) Nobody knew what Holló and she talked about, but they talked, laughing quietly, pouring brandy into their coffees, and once in a while Holló would nod in the direction of someone entering the club and whisper a word or two into Lujza's ear. It was understood, early on, that she was looking for a man, that was the first rumour, but if anyone ever mentioned it in Lujza's presence, she'd turn to them and say, "Actually, I'm looking for *more* than a man," as if one just wasn't enough.

When the scandal broke, late in 1959, that Lujza was seeing both Aurél *and* Frigyes, everyone said Holló had introduced them, since they were both regulars at the club. The story went around and around, how that slut, Lujza, just couldn't get enough, *at her age* (she must have been thirty-five then), of men, of chocolates and roses and money, of *sex*, and that by stringing along Aurél and Frigyes she was ruining one of the purest friendships anyone had ever seen, not to mention stealing two of the community's most eligible bachelors. Lujza responded by putting on extra perfume, swinging her backside a little more when she walked, addressing the husbands of other women by briefly caressing their cheeks, not long enough for the wives to jump in or make a comment, but long enough to make their men blush.

Lujza's sluttiness dated far back, that's what everyone said, from even before she'd left Hungary. She'd *always* been too free. Some said she'd made her way into the Hungarian fascist party, the Arrow-Cross, by sleeping her way up the hierarchy. There was even a picture that went around—I saw it briefly—one of those grainy things cut from a wartime newspaper, of her standing with some politicians and generals and scientists at a gala, all of them in arm bands, resting her head against the shoulder of Otto Kovács, who'd been one of the Nazi physicists trying to build Hitler a "super-weapon." Lujza responded to this rumour by showing up at the next club banquet dressed in black, there was even some leather in her outfit, and was heard saying to one guest, "You remind me of my old lover, Otto. He was very sweet for someone who was planning to end the world." She smiled as if reliving a distant memory. "He said he wouldn't be able to save me, but he'd keep me company until the end." You could never be quite sure if she was lying or telling the truth, though for me it was all lies, driven by a fury at how stupid the rumours were, how far from what she'd actually lived through and suffered and that had brought her to this place, this community so impoverished in its imagination that she was going to show all of us how character assassination should really be done.

The rumours always featured the siege of Budapest—how somewhere in the midst of that disaster she'd joined one side, the fascists, then switched over when it became clear the Red Army was going to win. It was said that during those terrible days she'd joined a cell of radical Bolsheviks who preached free love, as a result of which she'd slept with a thousand soldiers, and eventually become the lover of the Hungarian man who took on the name Maxim Zabrovsky and after the war served as a high-ranking officer in the Hungarian secret police, the ÁVÓ. "Oh, those days of 'free love,'" Lujza would say, her voice husky with nostalgia. "Of course, it worked better for the men than the women. We ended up pregnant; or got beaten up for sleeping with the wrong person, including other women, which the men didn't like; or farmed out like whores, except of course we didn't get paid. 'Do it for the revolution, comrade.'" She snorted. "Have you ever heard anything so idiotic? But we believed it back then, the 'revolutionary potential of sex,' all that garbage." She sighed. "The men did whatever they wanted. They had the time of their lives."

Others said that Zabrovsky was just a stop along the way for Lujza, who slept her way so far up the chain that when 1956 rolled around, and it looked for a while like the anti-Soviet revolutionaries would succeed, she left for the west. "Yes, yes," she said, sitting beside Aurél one night during a

dance at the club, "there was a faction among the revolutionaries targeting me because I'd collected the seed of so many
Soviet officers I could breed another Red Army." She was
very drunk when she said this, leaning across the table and
weaving in front of us like a charmed snake. Aurél pulled her
back and glared at everyone, daring us to laugh or say something, and when no one did, he quietly collected her, Lujza
was crying by then, and led her gently across the ballroom
and out the doors. I can still see him in his tuxedo, Lujza elegant for all her drunkenness, leaning on his arm in her white
dress, a gauzy scarf across the small of her back and trailing
from where it was wound around her wrists.

I only ever saw her lose control like that once more, at
the end. Normally she seemed supremely confident, secure
in her power, ironic but always gracious, never for a moment
bothered by the whispers buzzing around her.

As far as the rumours went, the women were the worst,
since the only thing they loved complaining about more than
how bad it was being married to Hungarian men—their tyr-
anny, the way they expected dinner and sex and never lifted
a finger with the children, their chronic infidelity while vio-
lently insisting on virtue from their wives—was a woman who
dared to do all the things they wouldn't. Looking at her I could
imagine why Aurél and Frigyes endured Lujza's inability to
choose between the two of them. She carried an impression of sex wherever she went—homes she entered, streets
she was on, whether the occasion was a baptism, first holy
communion, or a Christmas party—there she was exuding
it, close enough to touch, to taste, but always unattainable.
I knew her for over fifteen years and it was always there, it

didn't matter how old she was, she just adjusted, figured out different ways to carry it, varying the hairstyles, the scarves and dresses, that kept her sexy even after what was beautiful about her vanished.

Vera put it perfectly one day after she noticed me watching Lujza at church, scowling as I tried to deny it: "She doesn't wear too much perfume, and her clothes are elegant but not revealing," she said, staring out the windshield. "It's her freedom. It attracts and repulses you. You want her to be like us—controlled—but you also *don't* want that." Vera waited a second while the wipers swept back and forth. "Don't worry," she said, "it's the same with us women. We tell stories to try and tame her, to put her in a box, but the more we tell the more she rises to the challenge, the bigger she seems, as if there's no limit to her freedom."

It was true, Lujza had this liberty in her own body, an intimacy that enveloped you even if all she was doing was introducing herself, smiling hello, shaking your hand. I knew it more than the rest, since Vera was one of the few so intrigued by the rumours that she tried to get close to Lujza, thinking the truth must be even more exotic than the stories, only to end up going beyond that intrigue, as envy turned to sympathy, and becoming her one true friend.

Lujza carried it right to our house, the black chatter that followed her. She carried it like a mark of honour, clipping along the sidewalk in heels, a colourful scarf wound around her head, dark sunglasses, cigarette between her ruby lips, as if she was worth every bit of attention. "Hello, Bence," she'd say, strolling through the gate. She was always polite with me, respectful, though I knew she could be otherwise if she chose, there was something fearsome about her even at her friendliest. But there was something else, too, a weariness and solitude, and it made me wonder if what was so frightening about that ferocity was not that it was held back but that it was *always taking place*, only inside, bursting out once in a while as sarcasm because she knew of no other way to let anyone see it. "Is Vera home?" she'd ask, and if not for the smell of *pálinka* billowing from her mouth, the question would have been innocent.

I used to listen to them sometimes, from the basement, or the study, Lujza's presence making Vera brave, indifferent to where her voice carried.

"I couldn't divorce him, Lujza. What would I do? How would I make money?"

"You'd take *his* money, of course," Lujza said. "Though I don't know why you'd want to do something as stupid as go out on your own."

"You're out on your own! And you've got Aurél and Frigyes looking after you." Vera waited then, as if expecting Lujza to reveal her secret, how she did it, her control over the two men, but she said nothing. "You're not like us," Vera said. "We're invisible compared to you."

"Of course you're invisible," said Lujza. "You're invisible because you've let yourself be looked at, *fully* looked at. You should never allow anything but a glimpse." Her voice quavered as she spoke, as if it was a statement of fact rather than a recommendation, as if she envied Vera her transparency, and what she asked next sounded like a lullaby meant to soothe herself. "Vera, tell me that story, when you knew you were going to give birth to Krisztina."

Vera sighed, not hearing her at all, "I don't know how it could be otherwise." She began to talk about me in the way she sometimes did—how I'd come home from work and tell her she had no idea what work was, that whenever she needed money she just wrote a cheque and that was that. She told Lujza what she told me—that I was the one with no idea, never having washed the same floor for decades, or spent as little as a week looking after kids, or sacrificed a lifetime to the fluorescent light of grocery stores, the terrifying boredom of doing it over and over, then waking up to do it again. "For Bence," she said, "there is only one *real* job, the kind he does at the office, doing things that matter in the world. He makes the money, *his* money."

I could hear the clock tick. Neither woman spoke. Finally Lujza hissed something I'll never forget. "It must be nice," she said, "to think of this home when you're away from it—to know there's such a place that has so much of you, your story, your history." She waited. "The real story, I mean, not like the ones people invent for me."

"I don't tell stories," Vera said.

"You do," said Lujza. There was no bitterness there, only fact, the momentary return of the flippancy she showed at the club. "Why else invite me over here? It's okay, Vera, I don't mind. Your company is useful to me."

"Tell me," said Vera, as if this was the cue, as if she'd been waiting for it all day, as if there was nothing else she'd ever wanted to hear. "Tell me, tell me."

I could hear Lujza pouring some of Frigyes's *pálinka* into their coffees, but when she spoke her voice was tired. "Last week, Erzsi told Magdi—Holló overheard them and repeated it to me—that I survived the siege of Budapest by whoring around. I'm sure you've heard that one before. But you know what Holló did?" Lujza tried to laugh. "He's such a troublemaker. He told them I'd confessed as much to him. That selling myself is how I looked after my mother and father and brothers and sisters. I got food for them that way, and protection. And they believed him! So you know what I did?" When Vera said nothing, I imagined her shaking her head. "I told Frigyes, and you know what he did?" Again there was nothing from Vera. "He stopped working on Erzsi's roof. He just stopped. One day. Two days. She kept calling him. He wouldn't answer. She tried hiring other workmen. They said they'd come, but they never did, Frigyes made sure of that. Remember how it rained last week? Half of Erzsi's living room got washed away. Then Frigyes came over and fixed what he'd started. He made his point. The next time Erzsi came to the Szécsényi Club, Holló asked if she'd heard about how I'd had sex with a whole regiment of the Red Army, and she told him she didn't want to talk about it." Lujza was almost shouting the last part of the story, though there was nothing triumphant in it.

"She didn't?" Vera laughed too. This was why she invited Lujza over, the real purpose behind their friendship, Lujza's enchanted life, the secret of how she'd managed to resist convention and still be happy, how she'd kept that sense of mystery leached from women like Vera by the time they hit forty. I saw it on my wife every night, standing by the sink, hands covered in suds, staring into windows with the night behind them, reflecting Vera back at herself.

I left them that afternoon, crept down the stairs and out the back door, making sure they didn't hear. Vera's vision of me wasn't at all accurate. I saw nothing glorious in my work, my life, only the day-to-day grind of trying to minimize humiliation and hide from the knowledge, more insistent every year, of how expendable I was, as quickly replaced as retired, and in the meantime trying to salvage a bit of self-worth to stay afloat on like wreckage. One way to do this was to fight with Vera, and it had nothing to do with the actual terms we used, like weapons—who made the money and who wiped the noses and who mopped the floors and who put in the fence posts— these were just things we said to make ourselves visible, though what they really did, and I knew this without knowing how to stop it, was make us indifferent to each other's entrapment—bitter, estranged, kept together by a habit of mutual grievance that became the one certainty the two of us would carry into old age. The truth is, I envied Lujza too.

The ones I didn't envy were Aurél and Frigyes. In the years before Lujza's arrival, they'd come over to help make *kolbász* in my shed, mixing great batches of ground pork with paprika and garlic and pepper and even a little jalapeño (Frigyes's innovation). They'd come over to make beer, wine. They'd help me put in new windows, drywall, plumbing, concrete. None of us Hungarians hired a contractor—*ever*—you had to do it by yourself or with help from the community. Often, this meant a lot of fights—all of us men set in our ways of doing things, ordering each other around, shouting as to whose methods were the best—and a lot of resentment over who'd done who more favours, worked harder, not seen sufficient returns. Sometimes I think it would have been better just to hire the contractors.

I'm speaking of the last time Aurél and Frigyes ever helped me do anything. This was 1965, seven years after Lujza's arrival and six years after she took up with the two men. We were putting in a new fence. It was careful work involving string stretched around the perimeter of my yard giving the precise heights and angles of the posts, holes dug to exact depth, specific consistencies of cement, poles covered in layers of tar—enough work to have us arguing and taking tools from each other's hands and sweating in the heat after only ten minutes.

I was standing by one of the holes we'd dug, holding up a post, when it started.

Frigyes wanted to give Aurél the rest of the beer he'd been drinking because Aurél had long ago finished his and was visibly sweating in the August heat. He accepted it from Frigyes, took a long swallow, and said, "It's warm as piss. You give me this beer, but it's disgusting." He took another long swallow, finishing what was left. "It's always the same with you, isn't it?"

Frigyes frowned, then brightened in that way of his. "Just a minute. I'll get you another, a cold one," he said. He looked over at me. "You want one, too?"

I could feel it coming. I'd seen it often enough by now. So I let the post rest against the edge of the hole and said I'd go get us the beers instead.

"That would be better, because then—" Aurél said.

"No, no," Frigyes interrupted him, and turned to me. "You've worked hard, you're sweating like a dog, let me get them."

Aurél stepped in front of me, poking his finger into Frigyes's chest. "You always do this. You get mad at me when I don't come to you for favours—'Why didn't you bring the car to me to fix?' 'Why didn't you get me to help with the roof?' 'Why are you making wine with that guy and not me?'—but then when I do come to you, you fuck it all up! You don't do it properly, or you give it to someone else to do, or you're late or don't show up! Even this, going to get me a beer, you're going to fuck that up, too." He jerked his thumb at me. "Let Bence bring us the beer," he said.

Frigyes looked at Aurél. "What did I screw up? Was it the truck? Why didn't you tell me? I'd have come over and fixed it again."

"You did come over to fix it!" shouted Aurél. "But that's not the point."

"What is the point?" Frigyes asked, just as loud.

"The sour cream," said Aurél. It was voiced in such a way that there was no doubt Frigyes knew what he was talking about, that all of us knew what he was talking about, and Aurél just stood there in silence, as if he didn't need to elaborate, as if Frigyes's memory of the grievances he'd caused was equal to Aurél's own, stretching back right to 1959 when they'd both bought flowers for Lujza at the same time and she'd accepted them both, stepping between them when they started to argue, saying, "If you fight over me I'll throw all the flowers out, and both of you with them."

"The sour cream?" Frigyes looked at me, then at Aurél. "What sour cream?"

"When you came over to fix the truck you went into the kitchen and you ate all the sour cream. You know exactly what I'm talking about!"

"So I ate the sour cream," Frigyes said.

Aurél made his hands into fists. "You're always doing that!" he howled. "You do these things all the time, these"— he shook his fists—"these millions of things, in my home—*my home*, do you understand?—and they—" he took a step toward Frigyes "— they add up!"

"So I'll buy you sour cream next time I come over," replied Frigyes, not backing down.

"Fuck. The. Fucking. Sour. Cream." Aurél yelled each word, wanting to make sure we heard the sentence clearly, and then he swept all of Frigyes's tools off the workbench into a wheelbarrow full of fresh concrete. I jumped back, as some of the tools were still connected to extension cords running to an outlet off the side of the house. Frigyes just stared at the tools while Aurél stormed off to his truck, started it up, and sped away.

Most of the tools were ruined. But we managed to clean off the rest. It took over an hour, and by the time we were finished I had no desire to go back to putting up fence posts. The whole time Frigyes had been whistling away and smiling.

By the time we'd finished, Vera had brought out beer, and Frigyes turned to her and asked if she knew of a place nearby where he could pick up a container of sour cream.

"Safeway. Two blocks that way," she said.

As he pulled away I took off my cap and used it to wipe the sweat off my head. "I wish those two would just argue about what they're *really* arguing about."

"They love Lujza too much for that," she said, gazing after Frigyes's departing truck. "The last thing they want is to make a big public scene, and cause more trouble for her." She waited for my response, but when I said nothing she turned and went back into the house.

She was wrong, I knew it, but I had no proof.

Despite the arguments the two men had, everyone knew Lujza was under their protection. Whenever one or the other of them turned up at a dance or wedding or picnic, Lujza was usually there with him, and people kept quiet and pretended they were an old couple, and after they left brought out the knives and tore holes in Lujza's reputation.

This protection was the only thing Aurél and Frigyes did in mutual agreement, though the truth was that even here they were competing. It was maybe their greatest competition. If one of them was coming to an event with her, the other would stay away. It was a system Lujza devised, letting them think they were saving her from shame or awkwardness, when really she was just managing their violence, which otherwise would have ended in murder.

I was eavesdropping again, as Lujza described her strategy to Vera in that tired way she had. "I told them in no uncertain terms that I have one absolute rule: no violence, ever. One broken tooth or black eye or dislocated shoulder—*even the rumour of them*—and I'll be gone from this place as quietly as I arrived. They know how fast I can disappear."

"Did they listen?" Vera said.

"Of course not!" said Lujza. "So I left for a whole month. Don't you remember?"

Vera waited a minute, thinking. "Was this . . . was this in the summer of 1962?"

"August," said Lujza.

I remembered that month, too, always the worst in Toronto, the heat and humidity settling around your neck like a hot anchor. Word went around that Lujza had mysteriously vanished. In the weeks that followed we'd see Aurél and Frigyes sitting quietly in the cool of the club's bar, their heads bowed over the table as if they were less men than photographs blending in with the half-light and grimy stools, cold bottles between them. It looked like they were looking after each other again. Nobody knew what was going on, but before we'd figured it out it was September, Lujza was back, and the two men were stalking each other like before.

"The stories you people tell about me," Lujza said. "I'm not sure Aurél and Frigyes don't in some part believe them."

"I don't tell stories," Vera said.

"You do!" yelled Lujza, slamming her hand down on the table.

"I don't," said Vera quietly, "not anymore."

"I don't know," said Lujza after a while, her voice breaking. "Maybe Aurél and Frigyes just worry about me. Do you think so?"

I never heard Vera's reply. It was too quiet.

Shortly after this, Aurél learned to tango. Lujza loved the dance, and she was an expert, and Frigyes knew it as well. In fact, Frigyes said he was the one who'd taught it to Aurél, to which Aurél replied that he'd learned the dance *despite* Frigyes's half-assed instruction, though it was probably the memory of who his teacher had been that gave Aurél's moves such fury, tossing his head and puffing out his chest in arrogance, as if trying to prove that anyone who danced *this well* couldn't possibly have learned it from Frigyes. Lujza won every dance competition the club ever put on, with one man or the other, since they refused to dance with anyone else (except, of course, with each other).

A year after that, Frigyes learned to hunt and fish, because Lujza mentioned how nice it was that Aurél kept stocking her freezer with "tasty game." He went on and on to anyone who'd listen about how great a teacher Aurél had been, though whenever he heard about this Aurél just snarled and told the story of how Frigyes had lost one of his best fishing rods by accidentally throwing it into the river during a cast. "It was an old Remington bamboo-cane rod. Irreplaceable. He bought me a Bowline instead. Well that's no fucking good!"

They cultivated themselves ferociously. Both men had to become familiar with the latest in French and Italian fashion, sitting in their respective homes scratching their heads over magazines picked up at a specialty newsstand, and then outdoing one another with orders for this or that blouse or dress or shoes from New York, Milan, Paris.

They grew flowers. You'd see them at opposite ends of the local garden centre loading up their pickup trucks with fertilizer. Both their gardens failed, but Lujza always came to see Vera with a bouquet of the thin, colourless flowers the two men left on her doorstep.

The only time Lujza allowed them to appear together was at the monthly bridge tournaments at the club, to which she'd always come alone. Lujza loved the lockout convention when playing bridge. Frigyes tried to master it, but every time he did, Aurél countered with the Neapolitan white cat double response. When Frigyes, trying to make him happy, also took up the Neapolitan white cat double response, then Aurél switched to the salamander double, and beat him every time, which made Frigyes laugh and Aurél furious. Lujza, meanwhile, clung to the lockout convention, which in the end neither man managed to play in a way that pleased her.

It went on year after year, the men playing out their violence indirectly, though they felt free to threaten or do worse to anyone who slandered Lujza.

What happened with Erzsi's roof was just one of a million reprisals. It happened all the time. Tíbor Hajdu disappeared during a fishing trip with Aurél. They found him forty-eight hours later huddled by a tiny campfire off some forgotten logging road, covered in mud and mosquito bites, claiming Aurél abandoned him after he'd made a crack about Lujza selling herself for a loaf of bread during the siege of Budapest, which meant, of course, that Aurél was the only one who could find him, patiently tracking Hajdu along the forests and swamps he'd run through in his frenzy to find the way home. Despite it all, Tíbor and Aurél did go fishing again—Aurél's expertise was just too good to refuse—though Tíbor never again mentioned Lujza.

Anikó Horvát's car burst into flame one day while idling at the corner of Commercial and Broadway. No one could prove a thing, but some said Frigyes had been seen around her place one night after Anikó—who was in love with Aurél—had announced she was a much better woman than "that whore Lujza," and to prove it was challenging her to a year-long courting war over Aurél, with the winner being the one who got him to marry her. It was understood that Lujza was already the winner before the competition began, and that Frigyes sabotaged the car because he didn't want to risk losing her in marriage to Aurél.

I wonder if they didn't collaborate on some of these. Because when they weren't with Lujza they were together, Aurél and Frigyes, hanging out at their homes or the rifle range or a lake or the club, Frigyes constant in his gifts and favours, Aurél constant in his acceptance and criticism. Most people thought they kept after each other out of mistrust, a need for surveillance, keeping tabs, making sure neither one did anything that would give him an edge in Lujza's affections.

Everyone said she was stringing them along, she'd created a perfect system. But I knew it wasn't true. In fact, Lujza had gone too far, she was trapped, she couldn't choose, because to choose one man would have been to kill the other. They had her as much as she had them.

But this devil's bargain was the symptom, not the cause, of what killed Lujza. She died in 1975, February 23, after visiting Vera for the last time.

She looked awful that night. Her makeup and clothes had been put on in a rush, her face a smear of lotions and powders and jellies, the bits and pieces of her outfit clashing so bad I could see her in the half-dark of the winter afternoon from a full block away. But there was nothing sad in her behaviour that night. She was more full of life than ever, sweeping through the garden gate, kissing me on both cheeks, swaying up the front steps in that way she had, compensating for her drunkenness by moving even more provocatively.

I followed after her, drawn by the glint of her flask raised in the light above our door, Vera already reaching for her coat.

"It's funny," said Lujza, sitting at the kitchen table, "just this afternoon I remembered a fairy tale my mother had told me as a child." She hiccupped slightly and covered her mouth with a gloved hand and shook her head to get the hair out of her eyes. "There was once a young man—that's how it always started." She grew serious, thoughtful, suddenly sober. "He owned a hundred beautiful women. Not all at the same time, of course. One by one. When one of these women grew old (because the young man never aged) she'd throw herself graciously on the garbage heap. Well, it wasn't a garbage heap, though that's what my mother called it, it was really a hill of bones. She threw herself on it to make room for the next one. The young man also had a young wife. She too was young forever. Her problem was that none of the hundred women were immortal like her, their prettiness didn't last, so none of them took him away for good. He kept coming home for *túrósgombóc* and *lekvár*." Lujza laughed, pulled out the flask, and poured two drinks, but Vera didn't touch hers. "So finally the wife sent for me and said I should search for the most beautiful woman in the world." Lujza smiled, closing her eyes, remembering. "I travelled to so many places, Vera. I saw so many things—some beautiful, some horrible. The stories they tell about me, they're nothing, they don't even come close. It took me all this time to realize that the woman I was searching for—it was me! There was no reason to have left in the first place." She sighed, patting her hair. "I was still sixteen, seventeen, and my mother was still telling that fairy tale. I kept waiting for some woman, out there in the world, to grow old and throw herself on that hill of bones so my father would come home for *túrósgombóc*." She took a drink.

Vera looked at me for help, but I just widened my eyes and shrugged.

"Lujza," she said, quietly, "you're drinking too much. You're not making any sense." She carefully pulled Lujza's cup out of her hand. "Let me call Frigyes or Aurél to take you home." When Lujza said nothing, staring at the place where the cup had been, Vera got up.

She left me there with Lujza. There was an awkward silence. I saw Vera's cup and raised it to my lips and drank it in one gulp, bringing it down to see Lujza glaring at me across the table. "Aurél and Frigyes," she snorted. "Fuck both those assholes." She dragged her cup back from where Vera had put it, but didn't drink. "They don't love me, neither of them, not for a single minute." She turned her cup clockwise, counter-clockwise. "Have you ever seen anybody so alone?" She grinned at me. I wasn't sure who she was talking about. "Aurél is so cheap," Lujza said, "that he can't say no to anything, no matter how much he hates taking it. And Frigyes is so insecure he doesn't exist if he's not the hero who does everything the best." Lujza's face was grey under the glaze of makeup. "I got everything I wanted out of those two, and I never had to scrub a floor, or toss shit-stained underwear into a washing machine, or listen to somebody tell me

I had it easy because they brought home the money, so wipe those snotty noses, cook dinner, and spread my legs." Her laugh then was the most horrible I've ever heard. She drained her cup. "Those two—they made me so happy!—they were just darlings!"

Vera came back saying Aurél had agreed to come. Lujza nodded and rose unsteadily from the table. "I think I'll wait for him outside." She looked around the kitchen now like someone in real distress, and wiped the back of her hand across her forehead. "I'm so sorry," she said. "I shouldn't have come over tonight." When she looked up she was smiling, really smiling. "Thank you, both of you, for listening to me."

Vera helped Lujza with her coat. A flurry of snow burst in through the opened door. The wind was blowing, bending the tops of trees. Lujza seemed delighted to breathe it in, and then she turned to me. "When I leave, Vera will tell you to put on a coat and come out and stand with me until Áurel shows up." She kissed both of us on the cheeks and stepped out.

By the time I'd gotten my coat and gone out she'd disappeared.

That was the last time we saw her. Ten minutes later Aurél caught up to me, circling the block. We went everywhere that night—to her house, the club, all the places Lujza might have been, even some places she would have avoided, before I finally talked Aurél into going to Frigyes's house. But Frigyes was gone—Vera had already called him—out searching.

It was still dark by the time I got home, but it was already morning. Vera opened the door (I'd forgotten to take a key) in her dressing gown, but I could tell she hadn't slept, and while I stood there stammering, listing the places we'd gone, thinking it was something I needed to do immediately, before coming in, she peered out the door, craning her neck to see over my shoulder, her eyes so wide it was as if she was trying to take in the remaining light.

For the next few days, Vera hoped Lujza would never be found. She hoped her vanishing would be the occasion for more stories. That she'd waltzed off to new adventures. New men. Finer clothes. Riches. The usual dreams. But four days later they fished her out of Lake Ontario. For some reason Lujza was not wearing the clothes she'd worn that last night at our house. She had on a black cocktail dress, some pearls Frigyes had bought, and a large hat, its peacock feathers matted and encased in ice, that she'd tied with string under her chin as if she was afraid the tides would carry it away, the strap of a purse tangled around her thin forearm. There was a letter inside leaving her entire "fortune"—that was the word she used—"to all the esteemed members of the Szécsényi Club of Toronto." It was written in Hungarian.

Holló hired a lawyer to sort out Lujza's effects. It was also Holló, gossipy as ever, who let everyone know what day the lawyer was planning to go to Lujza's to take an inventory. By the time he got there a crowd was waiting on the front steps of the semi-detached house Aurél had put a down payment on in 1963, and Frigyes had paid the rent on ever since. Carefully, the lawyer opened the front door with the key Lujza had folded into her waterlogged will. The lawyer asked everyone to stay back, not to come in. He needed to take an accurate inventory, without anyone tampering with (i.e., stealing) "the personal effects of the deceased." For a while everyone did as asked, but gradually one person stepped over the threshold, then made room for someone else, edging in a little further, and soon they were tiptoeing between the twilit rooms, looking at the books and paintings, then touching things, poking around in the roll-top desk in the hall. It wasn't long before they were actively searching.

We were there, too, Vera and I, standing on the front doormat, gazing in as the lawyer came down the stairs and ran around trying to get everyone to keep their hands off Lujza's things, when Anikó suddenly shouted that she'd found something, and everyone stopped what they were doing and gathered around her, forming a circle the lawyer couldn't get through. It was at this point that Vera told me to wait, she'd be back.

Anikó had found a ledger, one of those old-style account books, a black hardcover with silver lettering, tabs along the side. As the crowd formed, Anikó began reading what was written in it, notes that were somewhere between a list and a diary, recording each of the things Frigyes or Aurél had done for Lujza, including place and date and time, and beside these were figures, a code that repeated over and over with only slight variations, consistent for each man but with considerable differences between them. "It's the sex acts she performed for Aurél and Frigyes," said Anikó. Erzsi took up the book and tilted it, her eyes snapping open, and she said it wasn't code at all but tiny X-rated cartoons. The book went around, everyone took a look, though there was more than one person who didn't see it—people fucking. Eventually Anikó got the book again and paged forward, then lifted her face in false horror and said, "Look, here, now there are three figures having sex, not just two!" and a dozen hands started grabbing for the ledger.

I can't remember whether it was Aurél or Frigyes who, shouldering past me into the house, ripped the book out of her hands. Vera had phoned them, but they were already on their way, and in five seconds they accomplished what the lawyer had not managed in a half hour, grabbing everyone, women included, by the scruff of the neck and tossing them out.

The last thing I saw, before Vera and I left as well, was the two men sitting on the couch with the ledger between them. They were running their fingers over it as if they might erase the dirty fingerprints of all those intruders, as if they could make the record of their relationship with Lujza pristine again. But looking closer I saw that Frigyes was nodding, and Aurél was hissing at him, his finger moving faster and faster in pointing out this or that, as if the more Frigyes agreed with him the less proof Aurél felt he had. Vera and I walked down the street and got into our car in silence. She'd seen what Aurél and Frigyes were doing too, and as the car traveled west we felt our togetherness as if we were separated by a hair, which was nothing compared to the miles of concrete those two men had put between themselves, and putting it there cemented their relationship forever. Lujza had been right after all, she was just the medium, a crushed telephone, through which they communicated their love for each other. All the way home I had them in front of me, Frigyes and Aurél, pointing to the ledger and arguing over which of them had loved Lujza the best.

The Miracles of Saint Marx

ONE OF THE WEIRDER PEOPLE to surface during the era of Hungarian communism (and it was a time of much weirdness) was a priest by the name of Monsignor József Szent-Mihály. There were a number of rumours concerning the man—that he was a fugitive in disguise; that he was a government agent rooting out anti-revolutionary groups; that he was somebody who just really, really wanted to be a priest—but none was more fantastical than the one about the book he was writing.

The title of the manuscript (according to rumour) was "A Chronicle of the Miracles of Communism," and it contained stories of such impossibility that people couldn't stop recounting them—from Nyírábrány right across to Sopron. Naturally, this chronicle was a serious concern for the communist authority, for Marx had spent the better part of his life arguing that there were no such things as miracles—that we, and only we, made up our fate. And our fate, in fact, was to realize exactly this: that the collective was all and the individual nothing—never mind what the capitalists and Christians said—and that it was the job of the state to help everyone remember this (with brutal force if necessary) because without it there would never be a better world.

But the stories were so interesting!

For instance, there was the story of Vasily Baazova, one of those unfortunate men in the gulags who were designated as "cows" by their fellow prisoners. These cows would be approached, told that an escape was being planned, and invited along. Then, once the prisoners had made their getaway and were out on the barren landscape with nothing but snow and ice for hundreds of miles, these cows would be killed and eaten by the other prisoners, who obviously hadn't had the chance to pack sandwiches for the trip. The search parties sent out from the gulags would find their corpses drained of blood and cut open, their kidneys gone—since blood and kidneys are the only parts of the human body you can eat raw, and since lighting a fire to cook the rest would have given away the escapees' location. In this case, however, Vasily somehow managed to fend off the attempt on his life and get away, living for six weeks on the frozen steppes (which was five weeks longer than the other prisoners lived), drinking melted snow and eating pages from *Das Kapital*, which he'd only brought along as fire starter. When the patrols finally caught him, they couldn't believe it, so he offered them a few pages, and after a bit of argument they agreed to try them, only to find that Marx's writing was actually quite good, with a taste somewhere between *kotleti* and *bitochki*.

Then there was the one about Ivan Baryatinsky, who was kicked out of the Party for refusing to accede to the will of the state, and afterwards spent the next three decades wandering the streets of Moscow with placards strapped to his chest announcing how Lenin, and then Stalin, had failed to practise Marxism. Miraculously, he was not only left in peace to do this, but his situation always elicited sympathy from those he met, who defied the authorities by feeding and clothing him. Stranger yet, anyone who came into contact with Baryatinsky couldn't help but continue to extend this sympathy to others, so that wherever Baryatinsky went there was a sudden flowering of human fellowship, like a trail of roses left by a saint.

There was the story of Beryx Baboescu, the mechanical engineer charged with coming to grips with "the Romani problem" in Romania, which meant getting them to give up their itinerant ways and settle down and begin labouring like everyone else for the state. Baboescu's solution, in a visionary moment, was to create the blueprints for what he called "The Mobile Town of the Proletariat," houses and stores and factories, an entire village in fact, mounted on stilt legs, powered by enormous batteries and cogwheels, that would follow the Romani wherever they went, so relentless in its pursuit that it would wear them out, forcing them to accept defeat and settle down. Shortly after presenting his plan to the Soviet Council, Baboescu was taken somewhere "for his own good," but almost immediately there were sightings of his mobile town all over the Romanian countryside—reports of forests mown down by its passage, large depressions where the stilt legs had left their imprint in sand, stone, asphalt. Even worse, it was reported that the Romani, instead of being harassed by "Baboescuville," ended up realizing—after fleeing in terror for some months—that it was exactly the sort of place they were looking for, the sort of place where you could settle down but still get in a bit of sightseeing. And so they ended up moving in, taking up residence, travelling the country in a little utopia that was so much closer to what Marx had envisioned that everyone else in Romania wanted to live there too. It became such a source of shame to the communists—whose towns and cities could never live up to comparisons—that it was all they could do to threaten and imprison and execute anyone who mentioned it.

The story that was to occupy agent Flóri Nándorrfy of the Hungarian secret police—otherwise known as the ÁVÓ—was her *own*, the one Szent-Mihály would come to call "the Nándorrfy Network." At the start, though, her job was simply to find the priest, and his fellow counter-revolutionaries, and stop these subversive stories once and for all.

Insofar as Flóri was concerned, she was famous too, though to a much lesser degree. Back in 1945, at the end of the Second World War and the siege of Budapest, she'd infiltrated the so-called Vannay Battalion, a combat unit put together by László Vannay, a right-wing fanatic who decided to support the Nazis even when all was lost, rounding up a bunch of old men and boys—none of whom had proper combat training—and sending them out against the Red Army. It was suicide of course, and when Vannay ran out of old men and kids, he'd get more by raiding the cellars where civilians were hiding, enlisting those who could fight by showing them his pistol and offering them a choice between two deaths—one immediate, one probably later. As the official records had it, she'd disguised herself as a boy, infiltrated the battalion, and helped the Red Army dispatch a number of its more "dedicated" agents, contributing in her small way to the eventual defeat of the Nazis and the Arrow-Cross Party, and winning for herself a number of commendations and decorations and a plum job assisting with the Soviet spread of terror once the war went cold. It was in this capacity that she was assigned to Szent-Mihály. It was, as Comrade Maxim Zabrovsky, her superior, put it with a wink, the sort of "tactical betrayal" she "excelled at." Flóri agreed, for it was exactly this reputation that had kept her alive, useful to the state, though not alive and *well*, for she had been drinking for years by then, quick nips during the day, and entire bottles by night.

She couldn't remember when the rumours of the Monsignor and his chronicle first began, and this was itself a problem as she started out, winding her way through the reports, vague reminiscences from men and women and even children who said they'd seen the book, even held it in their hands, or spoken to people who'd done so, or heard its contents read or recited (even, she discovered, in the way of bedtime stories)— for without a point of origin she could not measure their distance from the truth. Mainly, she found herself in the usual bars and outlying villages, broken-down places, filled with people the Soviet had always prided itself on helping, but for whom their arrival—preceded as it was by bullets and fire, by soldiers killing and dying, by cities in flames—had only been another event in the ongoing cycle of deprivation. She tried to look the part, and she needed to, because everyone was suspect now, you couldn't count on your unimportance, your expendability, to save you, not in a time when people were imprisoned and sent to work camps and executed to maintain a sense of arbitrariness, when anyone at any time could be picked up without a reason, as if the state's caprice could keep consciences clean. These people could no longer sit around complaining about the local councils or the soldiers or the politicians as they once had about the emperor, the nobles, the bourgeoisie. She infiltrated them by appealing to their sense of wonder—speaking of things so distant from reality they seemed to have no bearing on the state—so that when they told her what she needed to hear they had no idea of the magnitude of their offense. She made sure they saw how drunk she was, slurring her words and gazing around in disorientation, so that they could also believe she was in the midst of a blackout, an episode she wouldn't remember—that she was, in fact, one of them.

But the drunkenness was real. Looking back, the memory of those times would appear to Flóri not as a series of dates—discreet occasions—but as one long moment, a smear of occurrence, filled with faces any one of which she could have picked out, accused, had imprisoned, making up the reasons and evidence as she went along, even after the fact. It was how she'd been working for the last two or three years, an agent of arbitrariness herself, bent on folding the world into her personal chaos.

"Yes, I've heard of the book," the man told her, fingering his collar. "I've heard of you, too." She looked at him, surprised, but he was already on his feet, moving into the mass of people going crazy in the bar—because it was already two in the morning now, those hours after closing time when drink opened onto hallucinations, transgressions of law, of not only what was permitted but what was conceivable. Some were dancing, alone or in pairs or in groups of four or more, including one man doing a soft shoe under that soggy part of the roof where the rain came in—and by the time Flóri heard the man's voice again she was sitting on a toilet watching the dirty water inch up around her shoes.

"The Vannay Battalion," she heard. A whisper. Flóri shook her head, unsure if it came from the stall to the left or right, or whether it had come, as it had so many times before, from somewhere inside her skull. And, as quickly as that, out came the rest: "You were hiding in the cellar during the siege. It was your parents who cut your hair, thinking that if you looked like a boy you might escape the fate of so many women then—the Red Army coming in, sore, tired, traumatized beyond morality—and the free looting they were granted by their commanders didn't only extend to pockets and suitcases and wristwatches, did it? But Vannay came along first, forced you to join up, and he did something to your parents that made sure you would never tell him who you really were. But you revealed yourself in the end, didn't you?"

By this point Flóri was already up, drunkenly and unsuccessfully yanking on her pants, stumbling out the door, ripping open the stall beside her, then all the others, gazing overhead, running her eyes along the floor. He was nowhere, not a footprint or a strand of toilet paper or a running tap to mark that he'd ever been there.

In the days that followed, Flóri kept her flat cap down over her eyes, moving between the homes of people she'd seen in the bar, not many of whom (like her) remembered what they'd been doing that night, at those hours, never mind the person whose face she described. But Flóri had some of them arrested anyhow, and so they opened up with all sorts of information, none of it useful or true—talking and talking just to say something, to avoid the admission of guilt that came with keeping silent.

How could he have known what happened to her back then, during the siege? There were no real records, no photographs, no eyewitnesses, nothing. And while there was suspicion among the members of the Party as to the extent of her "infiltration" of the Vannay Battalion, that suspicion was more the standard relationship between people, especially in the Party, than anything derived from evidence. Yet he knew.

At nights she stayed up thinking about his face, sketching it again and again on a pad of paper. At first, she thought his face looked weathered, stripped away, disfigured to the point of being less than what it had once been, as if his skin and bones bore out the wasting that takes place in a person as they become legendary, when identity becomes the property of true believers rather than the self, but as the days went on and she moved along the track of stories and possible sightings she thought back to how he'd looked in the bar that night and changed her mind. The face was less than it was only because it had been added to—as if he was wearing bits and pieces of the faces of others, as if he'd carried away with him a trace of those he met, others like him, on the periphery of a state that wasn't supposed to have a periphery, that was supposed to have abolished it—taken what was best in them, but without absorbing it, as if it was possible to give them room, to maintain them as they had been, in that place where he had the most to lose himself—his appearance. Flóri realized he'd taken something of her as well—the secret of her time with Vannay—something she was determined to get back, and then to destroy once and for all by destroying him. Except of course that in some way he'd already given it back, for in allowing her to revisit the siege, even if only with him, he'd also allowed her to testify to those she'd betrayed, to speak their memory rather than hide it behind science and ideology and booze—even from herself. The miracles and fantastic stories that surrounded him were only camouflage for what Szent-Mihály really offered, the most ordinary of escapes.

She was at mass the second time they met—or, more accurately, made contact, because once again he was gone before she was aware of him. This was the time—the early 1950s—when Cardinal Mindszenty, Primate of Hungary, had been arrested—threatened, starved, refused sleep for days on end, had broken glass forced up his ass, made to sign documents he'd repudiated in a public letter prior to his arrest (saying anything he signed while in the hands of his interrogators would be invalid, the result of "human weakness")—all because he'd refused to cede churches and schools to the communist authority. It was the time when the Party sent agents (known as "snitches") to mass to transcribe the sermons of priests for use in show trials afterwards. A time when being Catholic meant you couldn't be in the Party, couldn't rise in the ranks of the communist aristocracy, couldn't get a decent job. A time when people often met this way, in churches makeshift or in ill repair, according to a schedule that somehow arrived to them, along routes so twisted you couldn't imagine the landscape it had been carried through. But of course the Party knew of them, and so the Monsignor knew Flóri would be there, not so much recording every word as figuring out what she would say the priest had said. She was sitting in a pew when someone slid an envelope over her shoulder. By the time she'd grabbed it, glanced inside, and quickly folded the flap back in alarm and wheeled around there was only a little boy, staring up, clutching the coin the Monsignor had given him for passing on the information, proud of finally having something to put in the collection basket.

Her story was inside it—*the whole story*—including snapshots of the boys she'd helped kill when she'd turned on the Vannay Battalion—all written out in the form of an accusation. Later that day, in the room where she was staying, Flóri let the letter and photographs slide from the bed, remembering what it had been like inside that building, trapped with the Red Army all around—she was only sixteen years old, and the three boys were fourteen, seventeen, and eighteen—firing weapons they were already experts at reloading. There had been some German soldiers in there to begin with, all three injured, two of them dying the first day after crawling over to lean against the doorways. Why the doorways she couldn't say. The third one lived for three more days, sitting there demanding water, and reminding them, as often as possible, about the number of Soviet soldiers outside, the sorts of weapons they had, what those weapons could do to a human body. But most of all he kept repeating how they were going to die. "It's what we all deserve," he laughed, holding his hand over the gash in his stomach. Even worse were the horses the Germans had brought in there, up the staircase to the third floor, so starved they had barely enough energy to kick holes in the walls, to tear with their teeth at each other and anyone else who approached, before the soldiers outside managed to kill one with a rocket, and the other two with a single bullet each. "I brought them in case we needed to escape," the third soldier laughed. "So we could get on them and ride away." The stink of corpses was unbearable. But in the early days, when their stomachs were still big enough to feel hunger, they ignored the smell and searched up and down the horse carcasses, observing the thin line that separated meat already gone sour, rotting, poisoned, from meat they could keep down, carving it out and tossing it into the fire and then swallowing the blackened lumps hot as coal. Then it was back to scrambling across the heaps of masonry and concrete, iron rods and fallen chandeliers, releasing a volley of shots from one window, then another, then up or down a flight of stairs, passing another member of the battalion who was doing the same thing but in the opposite direction, the stairwell ringing with the voice of the German soldier sapping what frantic energy they still had, "You're going to die. You're all going to die." Within days they'd stopped jumping over the bodies in the doorways, the horses in the salon, first stepping on them carefully, then running across, until they had to stop looking at what was beneath their feet, making the way so clotted and slippery.

She never would remember if it was Gyuri or Gerö who found the manhole in the cellar, calling them down to help lift off the cover. Descend down that iron ladder, and then what? she'd thought. Only to come up somewhere else in the city, places just as bad or worse, the siege dragging into its fiftieth day, whole blocks so pulverized by ordnance and fire your feet stumbled on rooftops fallen into the street, trying to figure out where a corner had been, an avenue, the place you'd once lived. Down that ladder and then what? Gerö was in the middle of asking who was going to go first when the body floated by. The body of a woman, naked, face down. Her fingers entwined with the fingers of another hand, smaller, attached to a corpse trapped somewhere in the water beneath her, drifting this way and that, turned away from the air, from what was happening in the world above. Then Flóri heard gunfire, shouts in Russian, closer to them than ever before.

She would always try to forget what happened next—turning from the boys while ripping off her Vannay insignias, running to open the door for the Soviet soldiers before anyone could stop her, watching as members of the Red Army charged through, gunning down Gyuri and Gerö and János. Afterwards, as the soldiers looked Flóri over, her back to the wall, hands empty and raised above her head, she mumbled incoherently in Hungarian and the little Russian she knew about how she was Jewish, how her parents had been members of the communist faction of the Independence Front, how she'd been captured by Vannay's men, made their prisoner. She said she'd been waiting for days to be liberated by the Red Army. As it turned out, the soldiers didn't really care about what she was saying, except for the part about how the boys had "treated" her while she'd been their prisoner—making her demonstrate this part of her alleged captivity over and over again that afternoon—and she was to cling to the story even when it was obvious no one cared, that it was only her present usefulness the Party was interested in.

Now she picked up the pictures and looked at the faces. Did Szent-Mihály carry bits and pieces of their expressions as well? She looked at them closely, and tried to remember a time when it would have been difficult to turn on these faces—on any faces—to betray them. And then she wondered how Szent-Mihály had found out about what had happened, reading through the letter again, carefully examining the photographs, turning them over to read the dates on the back— Gerö Tolscvay (February 12, 1947), Gyuri Kelemen (February 12, 1947), János Szabó (February 12, 1947).

1947. They should have been dead for two years by then.

Flóri stared at the pictures again, flipping them back and forth, reaching for the bottle of *pálinka*, noticing how little the boys had aged and yet how much, comparing them with the faces she remembered from the moment the Soviets trained their guns on them. Then, taking up the bottle, Flóri was out of the room, out into the frigid winter without shoes or a coat or any knowledge of how to retrace her steps, holding the letter and pictures and turning this way and that on the streets, as if randomness itself, the loss of maps, was the only way of getting near Szent-Mihály, as if what she needed was to forget how much she wanted to find him— how much her happiness depended on it.

"What if I told you they were alive? That they'd all survived?" Flóri looked up from where she'd eventually fallen down, feeling the weight of something on her chest, the large coat he'd taken off and wrapped around her, snow hanging from eaves overhead, the priest rubbing his hands together as if it was that easy to wash them of everything. "What if I told you they're alive today only because of what you did—because the Russians left them for dead after becoming distracted by you and what you . . . offered them—that they were only wounded, unconscious?" She was shivering under the coat, her teeth clenched to keep them from chattering. "What if I told you that everyone you've gone after since then, all of them, only survived *because* you turned them in?" He opened a file and held the photographs before her eyes, face after face after face, all of which she remembered as she remembered the faces of the boys, that look on the other side of goodbye, when the waving's done and you've given yourself over to what's coming. "Mária Ligeti—the sole survivor of a prison train derailment," he said. "Erzsébet Hauser—if she'd been arrested two days later she would have been charged as part of the White October conspiracy." He pointed at another picture. "Péter Horváth—turned out, unbeknownst to him, that he was a loyal comrade who'd infiltrated a reactionary network." The Monsignor smiled. "They were looking for someone to play that role; Péter went along with it." He laughed, and it sounded to Flóri as bright and as warm a thing as she'd ever heard. "I like to call them the Nándorffy Network." He patted her once more. "You're in my book: Flóri the miracle worker." He rose. "Look them up if you don't believe me."

It seemed to take a lot longer to get to the hospital than it did to get lost. Other than that, Flóri retained no memory of it. Was she found, or had the Monsignor taken her there? There were policemen, then the usual calls through the usual channels, and then long nights of questions, a revolving door of men who came and went with their stock phrases and ideological tilts of the head. "It's not normal that someone gets away from us," they said, sitting by her bed. Not officially, she thought, though in a second amended this to, not normally, and then amended that, spoken aloud, to, "He hasn't gotten away." The interlocutors (as they called themselves, though they were really interrogators) looked at her then, and she frowned back, returning the expression of revolutionary seriousness they wanted rather than the bourgeois delight she felt, and was increasingly feeling, at what Szent-Mihály had told her. "I know where to find him."

She didn't, of course. But they didn't know that, their doubts tempered by her record of rooting out reactionary forces. So upon her release they gave her two days to come up with him—two days, not enough time for her to disappear as well. Flóri went home from the hospital and threw out every bottle—empty, half drunk, totally full—tossing them one by one into the garbage chute in the main corridor, and listening to them shatter as they rebounded off the tin walls on the way down. Then Flóri packed a suitcase, prepared her maps, her free train passes, everything she would need, and then she slept. Upon getting up, she made a phone call, listing off the names—Gerö Tolscvay, Gyuri Kelemen, János Szabó—and the approximate ages, ignoring anyone who was too young or too old, and then collected those addresses that seemed to fit the men she was looking for. As she walked out she looked at the calendar, noting that it was Friday, which meant she had until Sunday to find the priest or follow him into hiding, and reflected then that this didn't at all seem coincidental, as if the Monsignor had known how much time they'd give her, how much time she would have to make contact with the three boys she needed to find, to pry from them the secret of their escape and vanishing, and then to use it herself.

But the feeling of lightness she had that morning—as if she'd been freed of her fatalism, the sense she'd had, carried for years, that where she'd ended up, the things she was doing, were as inevitable as her betrayal of the boys—this was not to last. Because within a day Flóri was seeing strange faces peering at her from doorways, men called Gerő Tolscvay and Gyuri Kelemen and János Szabó for whom there was no spark of recognition in seeing her. None of them looked anything like the faces she remembered, or the ones in the photographs Szent-Mihály had given her and which she'd lost staggering through the town that snowy day, so that by Saturday afternoon Flóri turned into one of the tiny bars on the outskirts of Miskolc and began ordering one shot of cherry *pálinka* after another, staring up at the roof as if by following the cracks she might find a hole in tomorrow, Sunday, when she'd agreed to be waiting in her room at the appointed hour with the information on how to get to the Monsignor and his chronicle. She was still following those cracks, now multiplied with the double vision of drunkenness, when the bartender gently said it was time to go and she slid off the seat onto the floor, continuing to gaze up as if at constellations, trying to read something in the glitter of the lamp hanging from the ceiling. They ended up looking at her insignias carefully, and then pretending to hold her with the greatest dignity, by the elbows, while escorting her out—though what they really did was simply lift her off the floor and dump her outside.

Then came the long night, Flóri sitting on the bed awake, too lost to go in search of more to drink, or to do anything other than resist sleep, shaking her head every time it came over her. Then came the morning, so clear she knew there'd be no forgetting it, the slow onset of the shakes, the fears magnified by whatever it was the alcohol did to her brain, synapses firing and misfiring, the sudden shudders of an ever-worse imagining. When there was a knock on the door she crawled under the sheets to get away from it.

It was Szent-Mihály who lifted them off her, peering down and asking how good it had felt, over the last weeks, thinking that the boys and women and men she'd helped kill in one way or another were all still alive. The priest stared at her with eyes so tired, his face more crumpled than she remembered it.

"There's no Nándorffy Network, is there?" she said, pushing the hair out of her eyes. "You made it up." In response, the priest shrugged, so casual it seemed as if the presence or absence of miracles—and of the book that was rumoured to contain them—was a matter of complete indifference to him, though at the same time she detected no cynicism in his manner, rather the sense that the book was not important in the way she'd thought it was—that his project, one he would risk his life for, was conceived along entirely different lines.

"I must look tawdry to you," he said, not so much sitting down as dropping into a chair. "Like a common criminal," he continued, shrugging again.

"The Church is a criminal organization," she said, finding comfort not so much in the idea as in the return to a definite position—a script whose beginning and middle and end she knew by heart.

And here he described for her some of the things he'd seen (though how he'd gotten to see them she could only guess): state dinners where servants walked around the Party members with trays of champagne and caviar, everyone dressed in the best possible clothes, twirling through ballrooms; hunting lodges for members of the inner party where they were attended on by butlers and maids and where they rode out in traditional hunting regalia across land kept from everyone else by barbed wire, shooting their guns and collecting their game like Viennese aristocrats; prostitution rings that catered only to the most refined of Marxist tastes. "But of course," he continued, "since the money and property for these belong to the state all these people can turn and say, 'But I have nothing, my pockets are empty, I'm as poor as you'—and meanwhile living like kings."

"What those people do, what they've done, is not really communism."

"We say the same things about bad popes—that what they did wasn't really Christianity." He leaned forward. "But wasn't it Marx himself who said there is only history—only the things that *were actually done*—to guide our thinking? All the rest"—he fluttered his hands in the air like birds—"*real* Communism, *real* Christianity, these are just metaphysics. Daydreams. Bad excuses."

"We've done some good things."

"Most people do," he said, "here and there."

She looked at him, and he laughed, saying, "They're not so different—the two systems." He watched her rise from the bed, and reach for the bottle of *pálinka*. "I'm not really a priest," he continued, shifting his gaze to the window. "It's just a way of operating." He paused. "But you haven't answered my question. It was nice for you, for a while, thinking differently about yourself?"

This was when they, the ones Flóri had been expecting, entered the room.

What Flóri would remember, what she would take away from what followed, was not the surprise of the policemen as they shifted their focus from her to the priest and back again, nor the scrape of quick feet on the floor, the scuffle of bodies, the detaining and slaps and the forced march out the door, nor the grudging respect on the face of Comrade Zabrovsky at how she'd once again managed, in the last second, to turn the tables. Rather, she would remember the shock on Szent-Mihály's face, and the way it was directed not at the arrival of the ÁVÓ but at her, as if what was unexpected was the fact that she had known they were coming and yet not warned him beforehand. "I thought you'd see what I was telling you," he said, as they pulled and kicked him from the room. "Remember—I told you to find them! Why would I have done that if . . . ?" He was gone.

In an instant Zabrovsky was back in the room, commending her with his usual sarcasm: "Excellent work, Comrade Nándorffy. But there is still the matter of the book . . . the so-called 'chronicle.' Of course it is the true threat, more than the priest. Reactionary, capitalistic, metaphysical. Where is it?"

But Flóri was only half listening, for it was here, in realizing how wrong Zabrovsky was, that she finally understood what Szent-Mihály's purpose had been in telling her to find the three boys. He knew she would fail, and perhaps, in that moment of failure, to find not those three people, nor the rest, all of them long dead, but that place inside herself she'd likewise lost, buried deep, forgotten it even existed—replaced by a cynicism that allowed her to stand there as the police kicked in the door and hauled people like him away. And it had worked, she *had* felt better in the last few weeks, even as she was being asked question after question, overcome by a feeling of lightness she no longer believed existed, as if it was possible, after all, to think that individual action—laziness, charity, vigilance, indifference, greed, envy, love, ambition— even the smallest of gestures, a moment's shift in attitude, could add up to something else, better or worse.

"Comrade Nándorffy, need I mention your responsibility to the state?"

What state? she thought, gazing left and right. This was not about the state, either serving or rising in it, not about churches and soviets and aristocracy and other forms of government, but the place where history was made—in the way you faced everyone else—for it was not miracles Szent-Mihály had been offering, but himself, making people laugh at what they all knew was untrue, returning them from the dream state and its history to the moment they created—the moment in which they lived.

"Comrade Nándorffy!"

"The book got away from me," she finally said. "It's out there."

The Selected Mug Shots of Famous Hungarian Assassins

MY COUSIN'S NAME in Hungarian was Imre Ászok, but as "ászok" is Hungarian for "aces" that's how he was known, fighting anyone who called him otherwise.

He'd keep me awake, nights when he stayed at our place, with the most fantastic stories. His father, Jancsi Bácsi, was crazily successful, an importer of high-end European cars (BMW, Mercedes, Audi, Porsche), and often away on what he referred to as "business trips," but which my mother called "parties"—weekends at clients' homes in the Turks and Caicos, Paris, the Swiss Alps, Hong Kong—scenes into which it was best not to bring a three-year-old.

That's how old Aces and I were—I was only three months younger than him—when he began staying over, inching under my bed every night in his sleeping bag thinking he could cry there without being overheard, determined even then to be tougher than everyone else. Later, when he realized that as long as he was talking he could control his homesickness, he'd invite me to join him, and the two of us would fall asleep face to face in the middle of his last murmur.

I could tell from the frown on my mother's face whenever I asked that Aces was never left with us for a good reason, and that it wasn't for her sister- and brother-in-law, but for Aces himself, that she took him in. His parents were away too much for him to be left with a stranger, she reasoned. Once in a while she'd let something slip, "I'd go visit when Aces was two, and he was wearing this diaper that looked like he'd been in it for days." Or she'd say something like, "I hope Jancsi is having fun sipping margaritas," when Aces was caught shoplifting and she had to go speak with the manager at the drugstore; or meet with the teachers who said that while Aces was smart when it came to what interested him (wars, revolutions, assassins), he was incapable of concentrating on anything that didn't (school in general); or take him to rugby practice because, as she said, Aces needed "something in life he was good at too."

Me, I loved having Aces over. I missed him when he wasn't there, and told my mother so, making up things he'd said—how much he loved her *paprikás*, how our house was as much a home as his own, how we were "brothers." Whenever I begged to have him back, my mother would always mutter about how Jancsi and Annabella should be grateful for all the "free babysitting" they were getting even as Aces walked through the door holding his little overnight bag, looking bewildered and lost, before my toys and TV and bike rides brought him out of it.

At twelve, thirteen, fourteen we were still underneath that bed, leaving a window open so we could risk cigarettes, drinking from mickeys of rum Aces smuggled over, even smoking the pot he'd started to sell after he was fired from the Stainesly Marina for trying to make a flame-thrower out of a gas pump. By this point his stories amused me, and I had to exercise extreme self-control not to laugh out loud, because Aces still took them as seriously as ever. "Gyula Hegedus," he'd whisper, moving closer, our faces inches from the bottom of the bed, "learned the secret art of Mongolian judoka from Tsakhiagiin Tömörbaatar, who later worked for Stalin and the NKVD during the Mongolian Great Purge! Tömörbaatar's specialty was killing Buddhist lamas, who were no slouches either when it came to martial arts—so you can imagine the action sequences! But Hegedus left Hungary long before the communists showed up, working for gangsters in New York in the late 1930s. Mostly, he did killings. But he had brains, too. He was the first person to see an opportunity in introducing heroin into the music business." Aces twisted in the dark to fish a photograph out of his jeans. I looked at it in the dim light, old and crumpled, a black-and-white snapshot of a kind I'd seen a million times—an unsmiling face, slicked-back hair, a white shirt, dark suit, eyes glowering with the intent to murder the photographer—pretty much like any other photo of Hungarian men of that generation. But on the back was a list of the ways Hegedus had killed people, along with two columns, one for the *proven* number of times he'd committed this or that assassination, and one in brackets for the *probable* number: "With garrotte 15 (42)";

"Gunshot 34 (112)"; "Hand to Hand Combat 2 (93)."

"Can I keep it?" I asked.

"Are you kidding?" he snorted, snatching back the picture. "Hegedus is the Wayne Gretzky of Hungarian assassins."

There were others, of course. Aces even had women in his collection, such as Elke Gábor, who while in the employ of the Hapsburgs swallowed poisons in ever-increasing doses until she became immune, which brought her to the attention of the tsar's secret police, the Okhrana, who borrowed her from Emperor Franz Josef to infiltrate the anarchist organization *Отравителей*, which had stymied them for years, their agents always coming down with gastric cramps that despite the best Russian doctors deteriorated into full-out haemorrhaging and death. Like Azef and Bogrov, Gábor became a famous provocateur and double agent, joining radical organizations and killing Russian noblemen, which gave the Okhrana just the excuse they needed to crack down on those communists or anarchists or Jews whom they then blamed for the murders. In Aces' picture Gábor looked about a hundred years old, her face ready to slide off her skull, as if the poisons had damaged her after all, though she was only fifty-two when it was taken, weeks before her execution by the Bolsheviks in 1918. Aces wouldn't let me have that photo either.

By far the most disturbing pictures were the children, some as young as eight, who Aces swore were some of the most effective assassins in human history, exploiting the myth of childhood innocence in order to evade suspicion while carrying out the most brutal murders. "Here's Emile Vaskó," he said, flipping me a photo from where he was leaning against the chain-link fence in the schoolyard. "He killed other children—*exclusively*. They called him 'Stalin's loyal little soldier.' He was sent to Vienna, Paris, Rome, London, to befriend the children of ex-Bolsheviks and then kill them. It was retribution for their parents being traitors to Stalin. The amazing thing is Vaskó always came back to Russia." I looked at the picture, disturbed and fascinated.

Being with Aces meant security. No one ever went near him—he had a reputation for being crazy—which meant no one came near *me*. Behind us stood the old school with its cracked bricks, the guys' bathroom where you would find Aces smoking in his favourite stall; the cavity under the stage where Aces made a nest for himself with old comics and a *Playboy* and some pillows stolen from the kindergarten class; the tin duct that twisted above the ceiling, and which Aces found a way into, the two of us hunched over, shoes laced together and slung around our necks, sliding along the flimsy tin surface to keep it from reverberating.

"Vasko built his own weapons." Aces whistled with respect. "He had great names for them; they sounded like toys: 'the tarnished star'; 'the portable crypt'; 'the pocket bomb.'" Aces looked at me, then pushed himself off the fence with a sudden jerk. "That card you can keep."

The stories I loved so much—the Okhrana, Stalin's purges, Hapsburg politics, New York gangsters—went silent whenever I visited Aces' house. Even at that age—five, six, seven—I didn't like the place, and felt sorry for Aces having to live there. It was decorated straight out of some homemaker's magazine—minimalist chrome and leather furniture, dried flowers arranged in enormous urns, polished concrete floors, abstract paintings jumping off the walls, rustic cabinets artfully scarred—rooms so defined by space, by emptiness, that you were constantly picking up after yourself, scared to leave behind a hair. It was the polar opposite of the unruly mess at my house, my mother screaming at us to pick up our books and Lego and bicycles, and where I felt as if I were wading through a burst reservoir of toys, always something interesting underfoot.

But while the décor was minimal, everything else in Aces' house was pure anarchy. I would say that of all my cousin's losses the worst was simple clarity, the map of days most kids need to figure out where they're waking, where going to sleep, a parent always there at the promised hour, dinnertime set in stone, someone on hand to help with the homework. The truth is, Jancsi rarely came home from work before midnight, and often Annabella joined him out there, wherever he was, in the darkened world beyond the living room window where Aces was often found waiting for them by the babysitter (the few times he wasn't staying at our place), sneaking out of bed to peer into the street beyond the glass. But worse than this were the promises made—I was there enough times to experience it—Jancsi Bácsi always agreeing to what we asked, that he'd take us to the amusement park, skiing, a movie, congenitally unable to say no to anyone whether he actually wanted to do what was asked or not, only to then not show up as expected, or to change the plan in the last second. Later on, when things had really soured, I remember Aces saying about his father and mother: "Any answer is only a temporary answer." Aces' home was always a whirling chaos, and he didn't even have the comfort of being at the centre of it.

We'd wander through the house and sometimes Jancsi Bácsi would show up with his squinting eyes and quick smile, ready to make fun of us. "Well hello," he'd say, catching sight of me, "how's the long-distance runner doing? Managed to run a mile yet? Non-stop?"

He mentioned it whenever I went there: my first track meet, I was six years old, dead last in the cross-country race, gasping, my hand over a cramp, stopping to stumble along, starting to run again, stopping, running again, long after everyone else had finished.

"Everyone had already gone home and you were still running, ten feet and half an hour from the finish line," he laughed.

But this was a minor humiliation compared to what Aces went through.

I remember one time we took Aces' car to a wedding banquet in Whistler. Halfway there, along the Sea-to-Sky Highway, Jancsi roared out of the dark in his Mercedes and passed us on the inside. From there, the two of them—father and son—spent the next twenty minutes shifting lanes, veering between the mountain on one side and the sheer drop on the other, until Jancsi laughed and sped off between two semis travelling side by side. Aces tried to follow, but one of the trucks honked and shifted, cutting us off, and he had to hit the brakes, sending us skidding in circles, spinning between a wall of rock and the chasm.

I couldn't count the number of times I had to lose a chess game against Aces because every time he played his father and lost, Jancsi Bácsi would force him to go through the ranks before giving him another shot at the title. Aces had to play his mother, me, my mother, and my father before Jancsi would play him again. It would take weeks. Sometimes, to tease him, Jancsi would finish a game by saying, "Well, that's the last game we play, Imi. I think I'll retire as champion."

It wasn't enough for Aces to lose; he had to be reminded of it. When he was fired for not delivering his newspapers on time, Jancsi would always bring it up at the next family get-together—"Can you pass me the salt sometime soon? It's not a newspaper, you know"—as if humiliating him would produce the best results. Things only got worse once it was known that Aces was selling drugs. "Sorry there's no wacky tobacky in the cake," Jancsi said at the family celebration my mother prepared for Aces' graduation (unlike me, he never finished high school, but my mom coached him through the GED exam that finally got him his diploma), "but news of your graduation already makes me feel like I'm hallucinating."

That night Aces asked to stay at our place, but he didn't invite me under the bed.

It was the cards that eventually got Aces into trouble. We were in grade nine when it happened. My mother was in the kitchen writing a letter, and I was sitting there doing math (which I always needed help with), when Mrs. Connolly walked in without knocking and threw a packet of photographs onto the table. My mother glanced up from her letter, leaning forward to see where Mrs. Connolly had come from, whether she'd failed to hear the knock or if maybe our front door was missing. "Tard cards," Mrs. Connolly said, nodding at the photographs as if she couldn't bear to touch them a second longer. "Do you get it, Mária? *'Tard* as in *re*tard."

I managed a glimpse as my mother scooped them up, and recognized among them a photograph of John Harrod, brain-damaged from birth, and notorious for bursting into song as he lurched along the pavement, much to the amusement of the neighbourhood kids who'd follow him requesting songs. John would belt out Springsteen's "Streets of Fire," or The Doors' "Riders on the Storm," or Michael Jackson's "Beat It," his singing a great garble of words you could only understand if you knew the lyrics to what he was howling. He'd also do this dance, though it was more like a series of spasms, his arms and legs flailing at us as we followed, just out of reach, laughing and making requests until we got to his house, into which John would escape, and from which his older brother Sebastian would run, trying to catch us.

My mother looked through the photos, back and front, shaking her head in disgust.

"Your nephew," Mrs. Connolly said, as if my mother had no right to be offended by what she was looking at, "has been making those. Trading them with friends."

"No way!" I said. I was right—Aces had never taken part in tormenting John Harrod—and if anyone would have known about him making such cards it would have been me.

"I'm not speaking to you, am I, young man?" said Mrs. Connolly. No doubt somewhere in there—I'd have bet on it—was a picture of Chester, Mrs. Connolly's youngest, born with Down's syndrome, though he was in his late twenties by then, with the unfortunate reputation of trying to kiss every kid he came across whether they wanted him to or not. I'd been kissed by him several times when I was younger, and we'd trained ourselves to be alert for him after mass, at the mall, along the beach, where he'd leap from the shadows and hug you and drench your face in saliva.

"I think it's despicable that he's taken all those poor people with their problems and turned it into a perverted game." She picked up one of the photographs between her thumb and forefinger. "Have you read what's written on the backs? Stuff about what their 'marketable skills' are—tying shoelaces! swimming without drowning! singing the 'ABC song'!—and even 'career highlights!'" Mrs. Connolly let the photograph go. It drifted back and forth and landed on the floor. "I wanted you to hear it from me. I've spoken to Father Hammond, I've notified the school board, and Constable Eckart will be coming over to take a statement. He says Aces is 'a person of interest.' That boy's staying with you now, isn't he?" She looked around, sniffing the air.

"No, he's not," my mother sighed. "He's at home. You can go ahead and speak to the police. I don't think he has anything to do with it. He's not interested in those kinds of pictures," she said, nodding at the stack. "Take them with you when you go." And with that my mother went back to her letter, not even looking up when Mrs. Connolly slammed the door.

But my mother looked up afterwards, narrowing her eyes. "I want you to know I believe you," she said to me. "Aces is not the smartest boy around, but he's smarter than that. He knows if he did what Mrs. Connolly says he'd never be allowed back into this house."

I picked up the stray card, stuffed it into my back pocket, and later that night I opened my bedroom window, reached out for the edge of the roof, swung my legs onto the garage, and was running across it, down the nearby cherry tree, and into the street.

It took half an hour to get to the police station. It was quiet by then, that time of night, only two other people seated in the front room, one of them holding an ice pack to his eye, and the other, dead drunk, trying to keep from slipping off his chair.

"I'm here to see Constable Eckart," I said to the night clerk. He looked up from the *Buy and Sell* he was reading and raised an eyebrow, then picked up the phone and held his hand over the keypad without dialling, asking what my business was. I rubbed the back of my head. "The 'tard cards," I said. The night clerk shrugged and punched in four numbers.

Constable Eckart was there in seconds, holding open the door to a hallway that looked as if it disappeared into another dimension. He stared hard at me a minute, then beckoned with his finger, leading me a short distance into the building before turning off into a glass-walled room containing two chairs and a table. I sat in one and he sat in the other. There was a fat manila envelope in the middle of the desk that Eckart put his hand over the second he was done taking down my address, phone number, and names of my parents.

"What do you know about these?" he asked.

"They're mine," I said. There was a minute of silence, and I was so worried he wouldn't believe me that instead of waiting for his response I dove right in. "I find retards really funny," I said. "My cousin has these cards . . . of Hungarian assassins, and I thought it would be hilarious to have cards with retards on them."

"Uh-huh," Constable Eckart said, incredulous. "So you made these . . ."

"'Tard cards," I said.

"'Tard cards," he echoed, and the way he said it I half expected a wedge of raw lemon to fall from his mouth. "You made them to trade with your friends."

"Sure," I said. "But I take full responsibility."

"Of course you do," he nodded. Then, after staring at me another minute, Constable Eckart did something totally unexpected: he reached into the manila envelope, drew a card at random, and hid it behind his hand. "What's the real name of the re . . . the special-needs person who's known by the alias 'The Molester'?"

That was an easy one. "Chester Connolly," I said instantly.

Constable Eckart frowned, reached into the envelope again, pulled out another random card. "What," he said, "is Cordelia Steen's 'Career Highlight'?" The look on his face, it was like he was going to punch me if I got it right.

I sat there paralyzed, going over everything Cordelia had done, flashing through rumours and stories, knowing I had very little time to get it right. "Stealing a glue stick from the drugstore and sealing her lips shut thinking it was lipgloss." For a minute I thought I'd gotten it wrong, my heart skipping erratically. Constable Eckart scowled at me before reaching into the envelope again. "Name Stanley Holden's—" he said.

"Stan the Stall Man!" I cried.

"*Stanley Holden*," Constable Eckart continued. "Name his 'marketable skills.' In order."

"In order!" I couldn't help but protest. "I've made so many of those," I indicated the envelope, "how am I supposed to remember them in order?"

"Just name them then," Constable Eckart snarled.

I looked at my hands, flat on the table, thinking of how Stan had been caught with another special-needs student, Horace Threadgill, their pants down around their ankles, fondling each other in a bathroom stall. "Milking cows," I finally said. "Polishing microphones." I stared at my hands thinking of how it went, the joke that never got old, every time Stan walked by us in the school hallways. "Putting those little stickers on bananas."

Constable Eckart got up and slapped me in the face, so hard I had to grab the table to keep from falling off the chair. Then he left the room.

My mother didn't believe it for a second, but she didn't protest either. She came down with my father, the two of them sitting in another glass room across the hall as Constable Eckart went through my confession, shaking his head, every so often glaring across at me, even pounding his fist on the desk once and pointing at my parents and yelling something that made the two of them nod in shame. Afterwards they gathered me without a word, and out we walked into the parking lot, the car, home, the two of them leaving me to go put on pyjamas, brush my teeth, get into bed, to lie in the dark hoping my mother would come in and admit she knew what I'd done, stroke my hair, tell me to sleep. But I knew I didn't deserve it, that in being able to answer Constable

Eckart's questions I was as guilty as if I'd made the cards in the first place.

There was no trial. Maybe Constable Eckart figured it was a waste of money, or realized he could punish me without bothering a judge, which is exactly what he did, forcing me to wear orange coveralls while I mowed lawns, cleaned bathrooms, and helped load the bus at the local Hollyoak Centre, a halfway house for "special-needs people," as I was henceforth to call them.

But that wasn't the worst of it. The worst was that Sebastian found out about the 'tard cards and was waiting for me every day to get off work. Luckily, there were a hundred exits from the centre—out around the pond, through the woods in back, over the fence by the dumpsters—so it was easy enough to ask one of the residents, Bernie Aldridge, to go and check where the "mean-looking guy" was waiting. What I didn't count on was that Sebastian would eventually figure out this tactic and give Bernie a quick history lesson on 'tard cards, why I had to wear an orange jumpsuit, and the importance of loyalty to your own people.

So one day he was waiting for me on the other side of the fence around the dumpsters, grabbing my hair the moment I landed, jerking me to my knees and holding me there. I remember staring at the broken glass on the asphalt, worried (of all things) that it would tear my pants and my mother would never let me hear the end of it, with Sebastian's voice hissing in my ear. Meanwhile, in the background, Bernie was laughing and clapping his hands.

"You know what John does after you little fuckers chase him home?" I tried to shake my head, but it was impossible with the grip Sebastian had on my hair, and anyhow I doubted he was interested in my answer. "He locks himself into a closet. And you know what I have to do?" The hiss had suddenly become a shout, and Sebastian shook my head like a bag of marbles. "I have to sit there and listen to him sing. It takes forever! And when he's done I have to clap, and only then, when I've clapped enough, does he unlock the closet and let me take him out." I could see it, Sebastian carefully creaking open the door, a wedge of light falling on John kneeling in the dark, tears streaming down his face, still murmuring a song to himself, almost totally inert as his brother carefully embraces and helps him out.

"I'm sorry," I said, tears coming to my eyes, though I'm not sure if I was crying because I was really sorry or just afraid for my life.

But Sebastian never got a chance to judge.

He let go of my hair. I looked up. Aces had him in a headlock. They struggled along the asphalt, shoes scraping back and forth, Aces howling that I was innocent, and Sebastian that he was going to kill both of us, and then Aces screamed at me to run, aided by Bernie, who was just screaming period. It seemed like good advice.

I never found out who won the fight. When Aces got home he looked like he'd been hit by a garbage truck, wincing with every step, tape on his nose, one side of his face puffy and green. When I saw Sebastian again, at the grocery store with his mother, he looked just as bad. We almost smacked into each other rounding an aisle, but before I could hide Sebastian stared right through me as if I didn't exist. It was the last I heard from him, though there was plenty from others, ex-friends of my parents, people at church—averting their eyes, smiling tightly, whispering as we passed—as if everyone in town was convinced I'd taken the blame for Aces, and so it was also my job, and my family's, to take the shame.

As for Aces, he left it alone—no commiseration, no thank you. But he did give me the assassin cards when he left. That was in 1987, the year I graduated from high school, the two of us standing on the pier below the Seahouse Resort, where the school held the party, both of us drinking from a bottle Aces had bought, walking through the liquor store as if at seventeen he owned the place, plunking the money on the counter and staring at the clerk just daring her to ID him. We were watching the sun come up, already hungover, listening to the splash of waves and clang of rigging in the morning breeze. He reached into his jacket and brought out a plastic bag. "For you," he said. "A graduation present." He was staring into the distance, clenching his jaw, as if giving them away pained him. I was surprised to see the photographs inside, having forgotten them, and was about to ask Aces why, at seventeen, he was still hanging onto these, but then thought better of it for the usual reasons.

I showed the photographs to my father a year later, after we heard that Aces had one night, without consulting his parents, packed a suitcase, left behind a business card, and walked out the door. The card said, "Aces, 604 485 9380," and nothing else, in shiny black font on a matte black background, so indistinct you had to tilt the card back and forth to catch the light and make out the numbers. "My nephew has finally gone nutso," my father said, picking through the photographs, "if he wasn't nuts already." He held up one of them. "This is Endre Huszár, my great-uncle. And this is Elke Papp, my grandmother." He turned over the photograph. "As far as I know," he said, "she never killed anybody by 'pyrotechnical blowgun,' whatever that is." He handed them back. "Your cousin's going to end up in a padded room or at the bottom of a pit."

I kept the photos. Whenever we tried calling the number Aces had left—the area code was for Texada Island, British Columbia—we received only a long silence, followed by the short beep for leaving a message. Sometimes, after I left one, Aces would call me back to talk about the "harvests" he was doing in the mountains. He sounded tired, and when I asked what they were harvesting—as if I didn't know—he said it was "a cash crop," and that much of his day was spent "trimming, weighing, curing," and then he'd go into a long tirade about how much he hated mould, specifically *Aspergillus*, though he was not a big fan of *Clostridium botulinum*, *Penicillium*, or *Stachybotrys* either. Finally, he asked if I still had the cards, whether I was taking care of them, and if I'd shown them to anyone (this last question was asked with such hopefulness the sound of it stayed with me for years). I said they were on the top shelf of my closet. Then, maybe because he was so far away, I told him what my father had said about the assassins all being family. Aces just laughed. "I've been doing some research here on my days off," he said. "They have a little archive in Powell River. One day my dumb-ass uncle is going to have to wake up."

Following that telephone call I took the photographs down and stared at them until everything turned white at the edges of my vision, but they still didn't become real. I looked at them everywhere that summer—on lunch breaks at the mill where I had a student job as a broke hustler; in my girlfriend, Mary's, bed, the two of us smoking and lifting them to the light; even in the Westview Bar, which was the only place I could get into under age, on Saturdays at the weekly jam, drinking clam eyes with friends and passing them around and laughing, feeling the whole time as if I was betraying Aces (though of course I was doing exactly what he wanted). By the end of summer the pictures weren't in good shape, but everyone had seen them, and for a long time afterwards friends would mention them when I came home to visit, almost as if the assassins were real, or they'd transformed them, in the way we sometimes do with memory, into people who'd once lived and breathed.

That fall I left for university in Victoria, and Aces moved from Texada to Los Angeles, sending another card, exactly the same as the last one but with a different phone number, to his parents and me in the mail. I forgot all about the pictures.

Forgot about them for years. I did a BA in Victoria, an MA in Montreal, then moved to Hungary for two years, so that by the time 2009 rolled around Aces and I hadn't spoken or written to each other for almost a decade. What finally recalled the pictures to me was accidentally coming upon the book *Hungarian Assassins, 1900–2000* in the Art Gallery of Ontario bookstore, and opening it to find the photographs my father had identified as Elke Papp and Endre Huszár, but who'd had other names—the names they were given in the book—in Aces' childhood fantasies. *Hungarian Assassins* presented the photographs recto and verso, so I could see the statistics Aces had carefully typed on the back of each photo. There was no mention anywhere in the book of words like "imagined," "made up," "delusional," never mind "simulation," "forgery," or "bogus." There were only paragraphs about composition, lighting, film stock, the anonymous photographer's "contemporaries," and straightforward thematic analyses.

I bought a copy and took it home to Kitchener and spent the next few days tracking down the author, an "independent scholar" by the name of Christine Banks, whom I finally got in touch with by email through her publisher, asking where she'd gotten the pictures from, and why she hadn't addressed their authenticity. She replied within days: "Thank you for admiring my work [I hadn't said I admired it]. It's always heartening to hear from fans [I hadn't said I was a fan]. As to your questions, I thought long and hard about the issue of 'authenticity,' but it just seemed so twentieth-century to me, you know? What's real, what's fake—I mean, who cares? It's art. As for the photographs, they were collected from archives throughout the United States, most of them in the little towns where the assassins went into hiding, took aliases, or lay low for a while before disappearing. I've appended a list to this email. Might I ask what your interest is?"

I never responded.

Instead, I called my mother and asked what she'd done with the bag of photos when she'd renovated my old room. "I still have them," she said. "They're with your other stuff in the basement. Do you want me to send them to you?" I told her I did, but before that I wanted my father to go through the pictures—all the pictures—and identify which ones were relations and which were friends or acquaintances or strangers.

My mother called back the next day, and from the exasperation in her voice I could tell she'd had a fight with my father. They'd sat up until midnight going through the pictures and arguing about who was who. "They're definitely our relatives," she said, "but your father's got it wrong when it comes to names and faces." I could see their argument as she described it: "That isn't your aunt Elke—that's Aces' cousin by marriage. I met her once in 2002 when they came to Canada. What's her name?" My mother stared at the picture. "I remember—Cili Vashegyi! Apparently, she killed someone once," she said. Aces' mother had told her about it, something to do with a first marriage, an abusive husband, a scratch from a poisoned hairpin, never proven in court. My mother turned the picture around. "Here it is: Poisoning 1 (53)."

My father took the picture from her hand. "That's Elke Papp," he said.

My mother fanned out the photographs on the table. "*This* is Elke Papp. Didn't she supposedly spit gasoline on a Russian soldier in 1956 and set him on fire?"

"Shit," my father replied. "I forgot about that. Actually, she spit it through a pipe . . . out the window so she wouldn't be shot by snipers. But it's such a bullshit story, I didn't even believe it when I was a kid." He laughed. "Family apocrypha."

"I met your grandmother," she said. "She was definitely capable of burning someone alive!"

I listened to her recount their conversation, a different argument for each photograph. "Just send them to me," I sighed.

Meanwhile, Aces mailed me his third black card, with a telephone number in Toronto. From what Annabella told my mother, he'd lived in the States for a number of years, "travelling here and there," which she gathered from the libraries in Wyoming and Montana and New Mexico that kept calling her to ask if she knew someone by the name of "Imre Ászok" who owed thousands of dollars in overdue fines for books such as *The Secret Order of Assassins: The Struggle of the Early Nizari Ismai'lis Against the Islamic World*; *Secret Societies of the Middle Ages: The Assassins, The Templars & the Secret Tribunals of Westphalia*; *Conversations With an Assassin: Reflections on Modern Society*, and many others, to which Annabella replied saying Aces was an adult and she had no intention of covering his fines.

In the previous year Aces had been kicked out of the States, and had brought a woman with him, Anna Kovács, who was "masquerading" as his wife. That's what my mother said: "I don't think she's his real wife. They didn't get married in a church or anything. I think Aces just helped her to become a Canadian citizen."

"Maybe he loves her," I replied.

Aces had been in love before, with at least one girl I could remember, Katie Smith. She was the daughter of Leo Smith, one of the top managers at the pulp and paper mill. For some reason, Leo had liked Aces, hiring him on the university student program the summer before I worked there, even though Aces had dropped out of high school. Leo and Aces would go target shooting in the gravel pits up the north shore logging roads, Aces trying hard not to speak the script running through his brain—how each of the wine bottles, beer cans, and cardboard boxes were actually assassination targets. "Good one," Leo would shout, looking through the binoculars and clapping Aces on the back. Meanwhile, Aces was thinking, "That's one less crazy communist dictator for the world to worry about."

But Leo's daughter, Katie, was more exposed to Aces' craziness. Aces would show up hanging headfirst from the roof and gazing into her second-floor bedroom until she turned and caught sight of him and screamed. He'd take her out in his car and veer off into the alley that ran under the east-side power lines, racing along, trying to show her he was adept at executing a "Rockford" manoeuvre at high speeds. He'd take her to a dance at the Mercury Ballroom and look around as if he could see in the dark and ask if there was any guy there who'd ever looked at her funny, or made crude remarks, or treated her badly. "Tell me his name," he'd say. "Tell me all their names."

I wasn't there that night in the ballroom, but I could see her answer, gazing at Aces cruelly in the dim light, the smell of spilled beer and rye and Coke, the scrape of chairs as drunken kids fell to the floor, the blare of canned music. "Sure," she said. "Lance Banks over there." She pointed him out. "Ryan Olsen." She pointed again. "He called me a cunt once," she said, noting how it made Aces hop from his chair.

"Then there's Alex Johnston, by the beer counter. He told me I could suck his dick any time I liked." She peered around some more. "Oh, yeah, Bruce Norris over there. Another dickhead. And George Hazelton, Jerry Alsop, Judson Astor. This one time, they wanted to do a four-way. Can you imagine that? It'd be like a porno."

I went to visit Aces in the hospital a few days after he'd regained consciousness. The first three fights had gone well, but they'd worn him down, and it was on the sixth one, when Jerry Alsop was kicking him repeatedly in the head, that Aces realized, with a tinge of disappointment, that he probably wasn't going to get a chance to take on Judson Astor. "But more than that," Aces told me through the stitching on his lips, "I was sad because I knew this was Katie's way of breaking up with me." I had to look away from Aces then, turning my face to the window, afraid I'd see him cry. "I've got to find some way to get her back," he whispered.

He was serious. He loved her. It took me two anxious days to figure out what to do, knowing I had only as long as they kept Aces in the hospital. The next day, when my mother stepped out, I went into her jewellery, stuff that seemed famous to me from the stories that surrounded it— which aristocratic branch of the family had worn these rings, how this necklace was recovered from a collapsed apartment in the war, why the emeralds in this pair of earrings were traded for a wedding dress—until I found exactly the thing.

I tracked Katie down that night, waiting in the parking lot for her to close up the clothing store where she worked, watching as she turned the "open" sign to "closed," pulled in the rack of sale items from the sidewalk, cleared the till, turned out the lights, turned on the alarm, then lowered the grille, at which point I got out of the car and walked over.

"What do you want?" she said, glaring at me. It was the exact opposite reception I got whenever I went inside the store, where my mother had been buying me clothes for years—stuff to wear to St. Joseph's for mass, to concerts and better restaurants—and where Katie always remembered everyone's names, plus an anecdote or two, to make them feel welcome, though she always walked past you without saying so much as hello when you ran into her anywhere else.

"I have a message from Aces," I said. "It's really important."

She looked at me as if I was crazy. "What the hell does *he* want?"

"It's right here," I said, reaching into a pocket, then another, hoping it didn't look rehearsed, and finally coming out with a piece of paper. I cleared my throat, noting how the hostility in her eyes had been replaced with apprehension. "'Dear Katie,'" I started. "'I hope you don't mind me sending my cousin like this, but I know you're probably afraid to see me given the condition I'm in, and because of what happened. I want you to know that I'm grateful that you gave me the chance to defend your honour. We haven't been going out very long—well, I'd call what we're doing 'going out' anyhow—but I think my actions at the dance made it clear how much I love you. I have sent my cousin to deliver this message because I wanted you to know as soon as possible that I will never stop loving you no matter what, and the minute I'm well enough I'm going to finish the job I started on Saturday night, and when that's done, when Jerry and Judson have hauled their broken bones over to your place to apologize, then you and I can finally get married.'" At this point I pulled out the wedding band that had belonged to my mother's father—a beautiful orange-gold ring that looked like a twist of tiny flowers and leaves—and knelt in front of her, trying to look awkward, and said, "Will you marry my cousin Aces?"

Katie looked at me in horror. "You guys are totally fucked!" she said.

"He's not sure, however," I continued, "that he can wait until the wedding night to consummate the marriage."

Within three days Katie was gone. I heard she'd quit her job suddenly and gone to live with an aunt in Halifax, where she was planning on attending university that fall. Aces was heartbroken, but he was safe, and that was all that mattered to me.

Once I found out that Aces was in Toronto I called and said I really wanted to see him and Anna. Aces faltered on the other end, saying it was really a long drive, maybe I should reconsider the cost of gas, the lunch I'd have to stop for along the way, the endless traffic on highway 401. He didn't want me to come, which of course only made me all the more interested.

I was not surprised when Anna Kovács met me at the door wearing the sort of long, low-cut dress you'd see in movies about 1950s cocktail parties. From the moment she opened her mouth, it was obvious she was from California, and from the moment Aces entered, the way she looked at him, it was obvious she had as little interest in loving him as Katie had.

"She's the great-granddaughter of Elke Gábor," Aces said after we'd sat down to the dinner he'd made (barbecued steak, plus salad), pointing at Anna with his knife. "I couldn't believe it," he said. "There I am, sitting in my place in L.A. (I had a great apartment there for a while, man), when I get a call from this librarian, saying Billy . . . well, one of my associates, had gone into the L.A. Public Library and mentioned that I was doing research on Hungarian assassins, and since it's her research obsession, too, she was actually calling *me* to see if I could help *her*." Aces grinned, and Anna leaned over and kissed him. "Things just took off from there," he laughed.

"Aces needs someone to help find those little libraries he goes to, don't you, honey?" Anna turned to me and smiled one of those smiles where it was clear she knew I didn't like her, and instead of expecting me to smile in return was looking for something else, a wince, a series of blinks, some sign of the wound she'd gouged into me by the way she turned her lips. "At first I thought I was crazy getting involved with Aces, with the kind of work he does, but it's exciting."

"My people really liked the idea," Aces said. "They'd give Anna directions to the places we were supposed to go, and all I had to do was drive. It was a legal thing, they said. If the two of us only knew half the plan each, it would make it easier for the lawyers if we got caught."

"You aren't by any chance related to an art historian by the name of Christine Banks?" I asked Anna, and then, without waiting for an answer, said, "What year did you guys meet?"

"June 2007," she said. Two years before the Banks book was published.

"How are you doing?" Aces asked, changing the subject as if he knew exactly where my questions were headed, and wanted to stop before we got there.

"I'm a prof." I laughed. "Every day is the same."

"Already looking forward to retirement?" Anna said, smiling that smile again.

"Absolutely," I replied.

There was a long silence. "Well . . ." Aces began, rubbing the tops of his thighs.

"Tell me about your great-grandmother," I said to Anna.

"Just a minute," she answered, and left the room.

Aces looked like he was finally going to give me that beating I was afraid of as a child, but he just shrugged. "They caught me in Nevada," he said. "I never saw it coming. We get out of the car in some parking lot. Anna disappears into the Ramada, says she's got to go to the bathroom. It's night." He raised his hands over his head to suggest the dazzle of Las Vegas. "And suddenly there's cops everywhere. Guns. Padded vests. Face shields. The works. I'm down on the ground, a boot pressing on the back of my head." He lowered his hands and shrugged. I knew the rest of the story. He'd been thrown in jail, then, through some finagling by his father, got transferred to a kind of holding tank, really a halfway house for illegal immigrants and foreign nationals who'd committed crimes the police thought were more annoying than significant, too much trouble to prosecute, and then Jancsi Bácsi's lawyer convinced the police that Aces was too stupid to have been the brains behind all those drugs in the trunk of the car, and eventually Aces was kicked in the ass back over the border and told that under no circumstances would he ever be allowed back into the U.S.

"I liked living in America," Aces said. "It was easy to get guns." He shrugged. "It was also easy to get arrested. They have more police than I've ever seen." He tilted his head and gazed at the ceiling, and I noticed a new tattoo, a series of tiny devils rising up his neck to his left ear, their tails linked like the little plastic monkeys we played with as children.

Anna returned, slapped an envelope down on the table, and took a drag on her cigarette, wincing as the smoke went in her eyes. Reaching inside, I took out a photograph as old as the pictures Aces had shown me so many years ago, and then, in the real shock of the night, realized it was another photo of Elke Gábor. It was unmistakable. I glanced at Anna, still staring at me, and was unsure if her squint was because of the smoke or something more pitiless.

"I got that from my grandmother," she said. Whatever the truth was, I knew she hadn't gotten it from Aces, because I still had the original picture in my possession.

"Tell me about your great-grandmother."

And she did, for the rest of the evening—the Okhrana, the poisons, Отравителей—filling in the details according to Aces' original version, but also adding personal bits—the children Gábor had, how they were spirited out of Russia just in time for the revolution but too late for Elke herself to get out, their emigration from Hungary during the Kun dictatorship. It was all there, wonderfully imagined, and the feeling that she was telling the truth followed me west along highway 401, into Kitchener, and right to my door, where with the turning of a key it vanished. Who was Anna Kovács? What did she want with my cousin?

I started working on a plan, but nothing came of it, because the next time I called Aces, only two days later, an automated message told me the number had been disconnected, and when I called information to get his new number there was nothing. I even drove to Toronto and went back to the apartment but the place was empty, cleaned out, the landlord already showing it to another couple. Naturally, he had no idea where Aces had gone, and he handed me three letters that had arrived for my cousin, saying he was hoping someone would get in touch so he could pass them on.

They were three notices from three different archives, all of them in such tiny towns I'd never heard of them—Smuteye, Alabama; Hot Coffee, Mississippi; Why Not, North Carolina—all saying that they'd made a mistake with his request, that upon "further digging," an "uncatalogued file" had turned up "pertinent to [his] request for information on Gyula Hegedus," and though the contents were "too precious to send by mail" they'd be happy to "photocopy the contents upon receipt of a fee payable to the Why Not Public Library."

I must have sat for three hours reading and re-reading those letters, as mystified by them as I had been with the Banks book. It was only then, in those late hours, that I realized what Aces had been doing all this time, starting from his earliest days, underneath my bed, dreaming through his tears.

He had not gone home after his expulsion from the U.S. After Jancsi Bácsi had bailed him out and sent money for a ticket, the old man went down to the bus depot to wait for the Greyhound, watching as the last passenger left, climbing the steps to scan the empty rows of seats, only to be told by the driver that a young man and woman had gotten off in Richmond, at the first stop after the border. From Richmond the two of them had made their way to Toronto, then disappeared again after I showed up and Aces knew I'd once again interfere with his life, taking from him what he wanted in another of my selfish attempts at help.

What did he want? It wasn't until I went back to Vancouver that I was able to make myself certain of it. But I needed to. I drove to Jancsi and Annabella's house in West Vancouver, stepping through the gates, up the steps, wondering what there was for Aces to come home to.

Jancsi Bácsi met me at the door. "Quite the marathon coming up those steps, isn't it?" he said, laughing. "God, I'll never forget that race, how slow you were. Everyone's done, you're still slogging through the mud. Nothing has changed for you, has it?" He winked at me as if he was the keeper of my secret humiliations, there to remind me just in case I forgot. But for some reason I felt sorry for him now, standing there, both of us knowing what our meeting was about—his abandonment of and by Aces—and I tried not to show how pathetic it was, this memory from over thirty-five years ago, that it was all he had on me, the best he could come up with.

"Where's Annabella Néni?" I asked.

"New York." He shrugged. I nodded, but he didn't wait for me to add anything, because his confident smile flickered and faded as he came to the only question that mattered, the one he'd been waiting to ask: "You saw Imi?" With the way he said it, so quiet, I realized how hard it must have been for him to face that empty bus, to have confronted once again the one failure that made all his successes look like nothing. I nodded, not giving him anything else. "How's he doing?" he pressed. "This woman he's with, is she . . . ?"

"I don't know," I replied. "I guess that's what I'm here to figure out." Jancsi looked around, not sure what I was after. "Did you ever get mail from Aces when he was away?"

The old man shrugged. "Sometimes. I knew he needed money, so I'd send him some. He never asked for it." Jancsi said this with real regret, though I wasn't sure if it was because his son no longer turned to him in moments of need, or because his independence left Jancsi alone on one more battlefield. "When the money arrived he'd send back a postcard. Nothing on it."

"Did you keep them?"

Jancsi nodded. "They're upstairs."

Aces' room was exactly as I remembered: small, spare, remarkable only for the number of books on the shelves, and the four pictures on the wall above the desk, all from the siege of Budapest, early 1945, pictures of haggard men and women wandering bombed-out streets, dead horses half buried in rubble, planes crashed into buildings. "I'd forgotten these," I said to Jancsi.

"The siege. When Imi was young he was always asking me about it," the old man said. "He loved those stories. All of us stuck in that cellar—me and my brothers and sisters, mother, father, aunts, uncles—all there together with no way out. It was the most terrifying time of my life, but Imi wanted me to tell the story over and over." It sounded as if Jancsi would have liked to tell the story one more time. "Here they are," he said, fetching the postcards off the desk.

I went through them, front and back, in about twenty seconds. The backs were easy, since there was nothing on them other than a few stamps and Jancsi Bácsi's address. They were about as complete a rejection of his father as it was possible to make, not only because he refused to acknowledge the money Jancsi sent, but because of the images of the small towns—the dozens of unknown places—where Aces was dreaming into being the only family he'd ever known, the only one in which he'd ever felt welcome.

I could see him in those tiny archives, sometimes only a room in a basement filled with bursting file cabinets, an old computer beside stacks of papers slowly being entered into a database, the sorts of places where it was not uncommon to come upon something startling—a clipping, a reference, a local history no one had heard about. I could see Aces waiting for the librarian to disappear, then reaching into his jacket and pulling out a photograph or forged letter, crumpled and stained to look authentic, and sticking it into one of the cabinets. It was a secret infiltration, a mythology slowly built up in these tiny rooms where oversight was lax, but from which the stuff he planted could filter into the larger system, archives in New York, Los Angeles, Washington, D.C., in a process Aces sped up by requesting the documents he'd planted the next time he came through town, forcing them into existence, the librarians always laughing, saying, "We have nothing like that," but promising to look into it, and then, days later, they'd call or write, their voices always apologetic, filled with awe, "It turns out that we do have something on a Hungar-

ian émigré who lived hereabouts and killed himself back in
'72." And before you knew it a scholar like Christine Banks,
hungry for a new research field, would trace the information
back to Smuteye, Hot Coffee, wherever, and publish a book
that made it all official.

I gave the postcards back to Jancsi. "It's my fault, too," I
said.

"What?" he asked.

I was thinking of Jancsi and Annabella, my mother and
father, and of Anna and me—all the people who had abused
Aces' trust either by abandoning him, or taking him from his
family under the guise of hospitality, or exploiting his obsession for criminal purposes. But worse than all of this was that
Aces no longer cared about our motives, past or present, didn't
care about who was real or fake, only that they stick with the
program, as Anna seemed to be doing, maintaining his illusions as long as he kept up his end in their drug deals. It was
all he needed us for now, and if we didn't comply he was finished with us as easily and totally as the closing of a file or
dossier in the secret archive that was his only real family, his
only real home.

The Ghosts
of Budapest
and Toronto

MÁRIA DIDN'T DIE in the siege of Budapest. No, she suffered the fate of so many women— *millions of women*, according to historians— who were raped by the Red Army during their "liberation" of eastern and central Europe. For the survivors of this ordeal—women and girls and grandmothers and sisters and any other kind of female the troops could get their hands on—there was a second ordeal once the first was over, and that was the look of shame and disgust in the eyes of the men—husbands, lovers, sons, nephews—who'd been powerless to help them, and for whom the women remained a continual reminder of how they'd failed. Of course, there was also the look of those men who *had* tried to do something, but this was even more haunting, for some of them had their brains bashed out with the butt ends of rifles, or were shot five or six times, or received so much in the way of injury that the look they gave you afterwards was, for the women, like gazing into a mirror.

Mária's husband, László, never did find out where the soldiers took her after they'd finished doing what they did, holding him down while they did it in such a way that he had the best view in the house, screaming and struggling so fiercely they finally had to knock him over the head. He returned to consciousness, Mária was gone, and no matter how he searched for her afterwards, paying visits to the Allied Control Commission offices, looking through lists of the wounded, the arrested, the dead, even wandering the neighbourhood where it happened and questioning every tenant or soldier or policeman he came upon, hopeful for just one witness, László got nothing but the same blank stare so many others received in the search for missing women after the war—all those families who eventually found peace by pretending that their wives or mothers or daughters had really died, burying them in proper ceremonies, their caskets and urns empty of bodies and ash; or that they were still alive, somewhere out there, emigrated to the west, enjoying happiness and prosperity; or that they'd never existed at all, removing their photos from walls and scrapbooks and family albums and tossing them into the fire. As the weeks and then months ticked by, László came to realize that what he feared the most was not Mária's disappearance but her return, that he would somehow have to find the words that would both console and still let him continue on beside her. So what László finally did, after a year had gone by, was mutter something to his father, Boldizsár—whose health was failing by then—about it being 1946 and the country in ruins and the Soviets not making any plans to leave, and the next day he gathered up his and Mária's son, Krisztián, and headed west, intending to write of his whereabouts to the family once he knew what it was. When he finally settled in Canada, he told everyone that Mária had died from the wounds inflicted upon her by the soldiers, and hoped he was right. As for Krisztián, then aged two, László waited a decade and then simply said, "Your mother died in the war," and let the kid's lack of memories do the rest.

The problems began three decades later, in 1975, by which point the rest of László's siblings—István, Adél and Anikó—had also left Hungary for Canada, and settled into low-paying jobs, and raised children who they hoped would do much better than they had. It was Adél, two years younger than László but still fifty-one at the time this all happened, who first caught a glimpse of Mária at the intersection of Yonge and King, where Adél worked as a janitor in an office building. The rule in the family was that Mária wasn't to be talked about, mainly for Krisztián's sake, but also for László's (though both Adél and Anikó sometimes wondered why they'd worked so hard to spare László, since it was Mária, not him, who'd truly suffered). Yet this sighting was so unnerving Adél just had to bring it up—"I saw the strangest thing the other day; I'm sure it was Mária..."—at which point István, older than László by a year, yelled out, "This is great cake!" as if he could change the subject. But Adél caught his signal in time and went into a long phony coughing fit that made everyone jump up to help her and forget what she'd just said.

Adél, who was twenty-one at the time of the siege of Budapest, had seen what happened to women afterwards because she saw what had happened to Mária when she finally turned up, very much alive, six weeks after László and Krisztián left for Canada. She was in the care of Béla Kerepesi, a decorated war hero and communist, who sent word to Boldizsár that the family should come see her, also warning them that her memory had only recently returned, that she was "still fragile, almost broken," and needed to be treated gently. Boldizsár mulled it over for a few days, then called together István, Adél and Anikó to give them the news, insisting that the rest of the family should not know about this—Mária's survival—at least not yet, not until they'd gone and seen her and determined the extent of the damage, and under no circumstances should they tell her where László and Krisztián had gone. When they finally had gone to Béla's place, everyone acted toward Mária as if nothing had happened. It was easier to do this than try to imagine what sort of sympathy such a person might need. In fact, on that day three decades later, when Adél glimpsed Mária buying a hot dog from a vendor at Yonge and King, she saw that her sister-in-law was still wearing the look she'd worn back in 1946—like someone trying to catch a departing train. Immediately Adél stopped what she was doing, wiping dust off plastic ferns in the lobby of the Bingeman Building, and rushed outside and called to her, but Mária only looked around in bewilderment and then rushed on.

The second person in the family to see Mária was István. He was standing on a subway platform when the doors opened and she brushed by him with a plastic bag full of what looked like apples. István stepped into the car, waited as the doors closed, and then with a shudder realized who he'd just seen. As the subway pulled out of the station, his face was pressed to the glass, and his hands to either side of that, white and bloodless and mashed against the window as his eyes veered crazily from left to right searching the darkened platform for her face.

Finally, Anikó saw Mária in a Persian carpet store, or, more accurately, she heard her voice. It seemed like every time she peeled back the corner of a carpet to see the one underneath she caught Mária's low tone, speaking in Hungarian of course, haggling with a vendor over his prices, but when she dropped the carpet in surprise and looked around, there was nobody in the place other than the merchants and the other ladies who had no better way of spending a Thursday than by looking at things they couldn't afford.

The truth was, Mária was angry at the fact that the man behind the stall was charging five forints a kilo for what were clearly rotten apples, using the usual trick of displaying the ripe ones up front, but then filling your bag from the half-rotten pile under the counter. After a while, she began to shout and stamp her feet loud enough to scare off the other customers, at which point the vendor decided it wasn't worth it and gave the five forints back, waving her off with the usual curses about being a whore and her mother being a whore and her grandmother being a whore and all the rest. It was at this moment that Mária felt an inexplicable shame, not because of the vendor's language—she, like most of the women who frequented the market, was used to that—but because of the odd feeling that someone else, someone who knew her intimately, was watching. She hurried from the covered market, walked along the *körut*, down toward the Danube, where the breeze coming off the water streamed away the ghost that had suddenly latched onto her. After twenty minutes she felt armoured in the present again, protected not only against the ghost, but against the past, what she called "the other Márias"—the one whose father had died in the First World War and whose mother had died in the second; the one with the torn thighs and face; the one who'd been taken away in a Russian military truck for more of the same but had escaped when they stopped at a checkpoint; the one who'd then wandered the city until she was discovered by Béla, a soldier who nursed her back to health, who provided medicine and doctors and therapists during the long year of her physical recovery, and who, despite having fallen in love with her, delivered news of Mária to the family patriarch, Boldizsár, when her memory returned, and then convinced her to stay with him when it became clear that the Kálmán family was not prepared to deal with the silences and weeping and raging violence, when it became clear that they did not want her. They crowded her, these Márias did, making claims on her body as if it was common property, but there was only room enough for one, and Mária, *this* Mária, was determined to make it her own. She was the wife of Béla Kerepesi, a decorated war hero, a wonderful man, and a member of Rákosi's inner circle, one who was spoken about in the Party as "the future of communism in Hungary."

But it was the *other* ghosts that Mária had the most trouble repressing—those people she'd once known, those gone or dead or escaped, especially Krisztián, her son. Unlike the Márias, these ghosts were not there to claim her, but to remind her, with their silences and empty gazes, that despite being ghosts they were more present, more real, than she was—that Mária was empty, that she'd become someone else too completely and too easily to say there had ever been a real Mária to begin with.

When László stepped through the door, Adél and István and Anikó would stop talking about how they'd seen her. They would stop talking altogether, as if they had nothing to talk about at all, and had been eagerly awaiting his arrival, the conversation-bringer. Naturally, László would be disconcerted by this, not being an especially talkative guy, and would wrack his brains for something with which to break the silence.

This often took the form of his retirement, since László was frightened by the time it had opened up for him, releasing odd impulses kept in check by the work he'd done for the last twenty-five years—collecting garbage for the city—impulses he hadn't even known were there. Now, it was all he could do to keep from drinking, from eating himself to death, all he could do to keep from looking at the magazines on the top rack in the corner store. Where had these appetites come from?

Of course, he never told any of this to his brother and sisters, who wouldn't have understood. Instead, he asked them what hobbies he should pursue. But there was something odd—something suppressed—in their responses. For instance, he mentioned bowling, something he'd done as a teenager, heading down to the outdoor alleys with their hand-carved pins, the balls you had to hurl as hard as possible to make them go up the curved wall at the end and roll back along the trough. But when he mentioned that he was considering signing up at a place at Spadina and Eglinton that had a seniors' discount, István looked at Adél and back again. "Spadina and Eglinton . . ." he began, "subway stop there . . . uh, not a great place for an old man to be going to alone. I mean, it's, well . . . you never know who you might run into."

László looked at him. He was used to István's halting manner, but this explanation was so cautious it was nonsensical.

The other thing László thought of doing was enrolling in a cooking course, something he'd only learned to do marginally well after leaving Hungary and having to raise Krisztián by himself. "There's that place near where you work," he said to Adél, "that college. They have an adult cooking course Krisztián's been telling me about."

"You cooked very well for Krisztián while he was growing up," replied Adél frantically, "and it's terribly ungrateful of him, after all that, to tell you to take a cooking course. If he has some bitterness over your cooking, why doesn't he just come out and say it?" she continued, glancing quickly from László to Anikó and back again.

László couldn't believe what he was hearing.

"And the other thing you don't want to do," added Anikó without even waiting for László's next idea, "is to shop for Persian carpets. There's no way they're going to match with the décor in your apartment."

László didn't stick around after that, scratching his head, grabbing his jacket, and heading into the city, despite the combined efforts of István and Adél and Anikó to make him go straight home, or, better yet, if he was serious about needing a hobby, selling his place in Toronto and relocating, say, to Kitchener or Kingston or Guelph, where István had heard there was really good fly-fishing. "Ever thought about doing more fly-fishing?" István said, to which László didn't even bother replying, except to shake his head and say, "Maybe *you* need a hobby—all three of you."

Anikó was convinced that the ghost of Mária was seeking out László in order to exact revenge. "How do you know she's not looking for *us*?" István asked, angry that Anikó had never for a second thought of herself as sharing in László's guilt. "Remember how we let Béla take her off our hands? We did nothing to help her. We never even told her we were planning on following László!"

"I don't remember that. "

"We did," answered Adél. "You wanted it kept from her more than any of us. You said she couldn't travel in the condition she was in. That's what you said."

"I was trying to protect the family! What do you think would have happened if she'd had one of her hysterical fits at the border?"

"You said we should listen to Béla and let him take care of her."

"That was Father's idea."

"Your and Father's idea! And you were the one who talked Mária into it."

"That's a lie! I remember she laughed and cried every time I visited her in Béla's apartment. You wouldn't believe the craziness. I visited her more than anyone else. It was the two of you who said there was no point in inviting her to come back to Mátyásföld because we were all leaving anyway."

"Béla was a communist by then, and so was Mária! They could have given us away!" shouted Anikó, thrusting her face in front of Adél's.

"We left her no one to turn to but Béla," whispered István.

After his sisters left, István sat in his chair and dreamed of the technology he might have had back then—Hungary in the mid-1940s—Polaroid cameras and photocopiers and tape recorders, so that he could have kept all the images and letters and conversations from that time not as they were remembered, but as they actually were. Because only he, of the three, would admit that they were guilty, that they had, each in his or her way—and however helpful or benign their motives now appeared—contributed to the distancing of Mária from the rest of the family—the slight, polite resistance they'd put up when Béla, sensing how there was no place for her at Mátyásföld, offered to keep Mária indefinitely; the regular bits of money put aside so that Anikó could go visit her with the food and clothing Mária no longer needed; the false admiration they showed on hearing that Béla was a rising star in the Communist Party; the pretence Boldizsár devised, and that they agreed upon, telling Mária that László and Krisztián had simply disappeared one day in 1946, whether they fled to the west or were arrested no one could say, so that she would stay with Béla knowing he had the best chance of finding them. The old man was hysterical when it came to Mária, forcing the three of them to swear on a Bible that they'd keep her whereabouts a secret from the rest of the family, "from László and Krisztián and Jenő and Angyalka and Cornél and Tívadar and Margó and . . ." On and on he went, listing every relation near and far, as if the information would only be safe if the three of them heard and agreed to every single name, leaving not one crack, not one solitary leak, in the conspiracy—which, of course, was impossible. "If any of them find out," Boldizsár said, "they might tell László and he'll be tortured the rest of his life out there in Canada, with no way to get back, no way to get her out. Or someone will want to bring Mária with us across the border, and you know we can't risk that with the condition she's in. Or they'll want us to stay because of her, and that's suicide with the way the ÁVÓ is coming after us, with the way that bastard, our *good friend*, Comrade Zoltán Erdész, is persecuting the family. We have to forget about her, there's no other way."

It's true that she would regularly trash the room when they came to visit—tearing paintings from the wall, throwing glassware, even ripping the bedding into thin strips—and that it took all three of them to hold her down, and that only when Béla came back into the room did she seem neutralized, content, docile. But all of these were still excuses, ways of justifying the family's abandonment of her. They should have looked after Mária, should have made the sacrifice, instead of being so lazy, so eager to escape Hungary, that they convinced themselves that leaving her was the right thing to do.

For István knew that her trauma was only part of it. After the war she had a look to her that was terrifying, a hunger for solace so absolute it left you looking for ways to escape. She took to draping her hair over her eyes, whose glitter was not an emanation of light but its disappearance, vacuumed up, coalescing to two sparks before being swallowed. That was part of it, but there was also the family's inability—especially on the part of Boldizsár, whose dictates were absolute—to admit that in dumping Mária they were compromising their principles. Instead, they used Béla as a convenient excuse, as if it was Mária who wasn't living up to the things the family believed in—the glories of Austro-Hungarian monarchy, political conservatism, national autonomy. It was she who was consorting with a communist, the enemy, and was thus a disgrace and liability. In any case, István thought now, it was clear she'd seen Hungary's future better than anyone, and that in the absence of family she'd followed her intuition, surrounding herself with the sort of people who'd look after her, leaving no want unattended, for the next forty-five years.

It worked out better than anyone (except Mária) could have imagined. Béla would wrap her in furs as he went out at night. The driver would bring the car around, whisking her off in a manner that was all too western, as if the Budapest she inhabited was not the city everyone else lived in, as if she, too, and not just the Kálmán family, had escaped to something better. Mária looked so good, in fact, that when Adél saw her next—as she was coming off a night shift, itchy with the disinfectants she used on toilets—it occurred to her that maybe she was not seeing a ghost at all. Mária looked radiant, what with her furs and jewellery, a face and hands untouched by work or worry.

Adél went home and phoned István and Anikó, asking them whether it was possible that Mária too had emigrated to Canada, and struck it rich, and was looking far better for the passage of years than anyone had a right to expect. "You're crazy," replied István; and Anikó said, "You've been putting your nose too close to the disinfectant."

Try as she might Adél couldn't convince them otherwise, even as she pointed out that traditionally ghosts only haunted those who had been responsible for their deaths, or who had caused them the greatest misery while they were alive, rarely appearing to those they hadn't known. Yet here was Mária holding sidewalk conversations with taxi drivers, and God knew whom else. "No, no, no," said István. "What we've got to figure out is how we're going to get rid of her, exorcise her from our lives."

Mária, for her part, would have liked to do what István, Adél and Anikó did—gone to a Catholic priest, who put them in touch with an exorcist, who in turn said the sighting of a ghost was highly unlikely, and a product of their guilt, and that what they needed was a solid hour each in the confessional. He added that he dealt with devils, and so wasn't qualified to help with ghosts, even if marrying a communist meant that Mária was most likely visiting them from hell. "Try holy water," he said. "A crucifix above the door, and one around your necks." He thought a moment more. "And prayer, of course. As much as you can fit." The three of them shook their heads and held a long argument about whether it was possible to follow the priest's advice.

For Mária, however, there was no such argument, she knew she couldn't observe any of the rituals. It would compromise Béla to put up a single crucifix, not to mention the risk of visiting a priest to obtain holy water. If the regime ever heard about it—if word reached Rákosi—Béla would be given a one-way ticket to Moscow, and from there who knows? House arrest. Siberian work camps. A starring role in a show trial. No, if she was going to keep the ghosts away it would have to be through some method other than the charms and totems of Christianity.

But there were so many ghosts! Anyone in her position would have had their hands full just beating back the past, but on top of it to be constantly running into the Kálmán family—to watch Adél in her janitor's apron staring after her on the street; and István in his dirty overalls on the way to tending the gardens of those who were as wealthy as he'd hoped to be after leaving Hungary; and Anikó in her Westminster Mall uniform as she went from table to table in the food court clearing away the trays and plastic cutlery and greasy plates left by those too lazy to clean up after themselves. Looking at them, Mária was amazed and terrified by her spectral knowledge, the realization that they'd been too frightened of communism to realize that the free market had its own forms of humiliation, of hardscrabble poverty.

She should have helped them while they were still in Hungary, Mária thought. She should have used Béla's connections. But the Kálmáns were so incapable of accepting her charity, so ashamed of dealing with her, that the gifts she provided would only have been further torture to them, especially Boldizsár, the grand patriarch, who'd already lost his wife and would die, just prior to the family's departure, from the thought that he was too weak to accompany them, defeated by his own anxiety over being defeated. They left the minute he was in the ground, starting out straight from the cemetery. All along, Boldizsár had kept piling on the reasons for why the family should let Béla keep her, why she should be abandoned—playing up his old age, his weakness, his need for sleep and peace and quiet, in order to prepare himself for the trek to the west. In fact, he was the reason she'd agreed to stay with Béla, the sight of Boldizsár as he looked away from her, the failure she reminded him of, his inability to protect a family he felt responsible for. She could shrink him with a glance, as if the sight of Mária's face stripped him of the beliefs that let him function in the world, and in a rush brought home his helplessness, his dependence on chance, his incapacity to even *know* his fate, much less influence it. In the end, Mária couldn't stand how sorry she felt for him.

Still, there was more she might have done, not just then, but later, once the communists came fully into power. She might have gotten Boldiszár medication for his heart and nerves, and maybe then everyone else would have stayed, because she'd shown Boldizsár the loyalty they'd been unable to show her. She could have left food for them on the doorstep, or had it delivered anonymously. She might have arranged it that they got better jobs. Or asked Béla to stop their harassment at the hands of the ÁVÓ—especially that bastard Zoltán Erdész, who wanted the villa for himself—for their past political allegiances, their Catholicism, their refusal to join the Party. But she'd never done any of this, and most of it was conjecture anyhow, things as they might have been. What she regretted most was that she'd felt too unprotected—from what had happened to her, from the past—and too busy getting that protection to realize that with the loss of the family she'd lost a far more crucial link, for they were her only point of contact with László and Krisztián. At night, as the driver guided Béla and her along streets, or when the two of them strolled down the *rakpart*, she wondered whether his arm around her waist, or holding her hand, was strong enough to keep her from one day wandering after those ghosts, just to see where they went. But she knew that to let go of Béla was to risk fragmentation, the falling apart of what she'd barely shored together, and which was held in place only because of him, a frame around her disintegration. Béla knew none of this, of course, only that it was possible to fall in love with someone because you could never replace what she lacked, and because of this feel a constant desire to fulfill her.

"We shall eat here tonight," he said, taking his hand from Mária's eyes and leading her past the decaying exterior of a building into rooms of light and wine, walking backwards as he held her hands, allowing her one short glance at where she'd come from.

The family breathed a sigh of relief late in 1957 when Juliska sent Anikó a letter informing her of Mária's death, since it meant the lie they'd been telling Krisztián all those years had at last become the truth. Juliska had been caught trying to escape from the country two years prior and was rehabilitated, as best as was possible with someone who'd never been a Party member to begin with, and now shared a three-bedroom flat in Óbuda with three other families. Once in a while one of her letters would be missed by the censors in the post office and make it through to the west.

She wrote that Mária and Béla had not survived the revolution of 1956. Before the tanks had come rolling in—when it almost looked, miraculously, as if the partisans had succeeded in getting Moscow to capitulate—the two of them had been dragged from their mansion on Andrássy Boulevard and had guns put to their heads, or so the letter went, and reading it Anikó had no reason to doubt it, at least at the time.

But the night they went over to László's, she paused in the vestibule while István and Adél took off their coats and boots, and told them that while waiting for the College streetcar she'd seen Mária enter Chez Queux on the arm of a gentleman, and had decided to call out to her just as they reached the door.

"I wanted to see if you were right," Anikó said, turning to Adél. "I mean if Juliska got it wrong," she continued in a hoarse whisper. "And Mária turned! She saw me well enough, but then the gentleman she was with—he was so young and handsome *he looked like Béla!*—called to her. The look she gave me! As if I was hardly worth noticing. As if I was a beggar on the street. Then," she hissed, "the doorman opened the door for them. Both of them! He treated Mária as if she was as alive as you or I."

"She's kept her looks, hasn't she?" asked Adél.

"Have you two gone insane?" murmured István. "We're at László's!"

"It's hard to feel happy for her," continued Adél, looking at her hands, lined with years of handling mop handles and cleanser. "Getting to eat in places like that."

"Are you coming inside or what?" asked László, coming out of the kitchen to greet them, holding aloft an uncorked bottle of Egri Bikavér.

It was the imploring figure of Anikó that Mária continued to see as Béla poured the wine and lifted his glass to the light and tilted it this way and that, pointing out how it coated the glass, how it flowed back. Mária was thinking she would have liked to invite Anikó inside the restaurant, that there was something in the pitiful way she'd stood holding her purse, hunched over with what looked like osteoporosis, as if her skeleton had had enough of holding up her body and decided to curl up and go to sleep inside her flesh. Life had not been kind to Anikó, and so why shouldn't Mária be kind to her, just this once, never mind that the old woman (she thought of her that way, though there was a time when they'd been the same age) was not dressed for Chez Queux? Béla, meanwhile, had stopped watching the splash and play of wine, set his glass aside, and followed Mária's look out the window, wondering what he could say that would complete her sense of loss, make her stop looking beyond him for what was missing.

After all, 1956 was still two years away, and Béla could not have known it, but they'd pack an incredible amount of life into the twenty-four months before they died, always appearing in public as the Party advised them to do, in solemn grey, clothing tailored from the finest materials but always made to look nondescript, so that no one would guess how well they were really living. In the next few weeks, it was in fact their clothing that would consume Mária's attention. He would come upon her frantically going through the closet as if there was something in there that would make her stand out even less than she already did, a disguise to throw off the pursuit of ghosts.

For they were pursuing her more than ever now. There wasn't a day Mária didn't turn a corner and find herself face to face with Anikó or István or Adél, their faces no longer betraying fear or aversion, but envy and lust. More often than not they would try to approach her, no longer content to remain on the periphery, as if they'd decided that Mária wasn't empty after all but full enough to fulfill everyone.

Anikó was the worst, the neediest, and more than once she called out, "Mária, it's me, Anikó, remember me? Your sister-in-law. You look very fine in that overcoat. And what's that beautiful perfume you're wearing?"

At other times, the three ghosts appeared together, as if they were attempting to set themselves up in front of and behind her, cutting off all avenues of escape. But Mária knew that she would always be able to get by István, with his overwhelming guilt, since he always gave way in the last second, allowing her to jump into a car or bus or a restaurant too fine for them to follow her inside. He was the weak link, though even he attempted to get her favour, once offering a bouquet of red carnations, the official flower of Party bosses and apparatchiks, adorning every one of their corsages and buttonholes.

"What do you want?" she once asked Adél. "How can I possibly help you?"

Adél stood there, finally put on the spot, stopped in seeking what she wanted by the fact that it had been offered to her. She hadn't considered how ashamed she'd be to ask for all the things Mária had—the clothes, the food, the luxuries—all the things Adél believed Mária could provide for them. But now, the only thing Adél could say was "You should never forget your family; especially when they're in need." And almost as soon as the words were spoken she looked up, afraid that clouds would close in, that buildings would shake, that the ground would open up. By the time the dizziness passed, and she wanted to beg forgiveness, Mária was gone, having fled, tears and all, down one of the streets of the fourteenth district, collapsing after an hour, sitting on the sidewalk and speaking to no one in particular about all the things that had been in her power to do for the Kálmán family in 1947. The things she hadn't done.

It was Béla who found her. He asked the driver to take him everywhere, and so he had, through the twisting alleys of districts seven, eight, nine; across the *körut*; and into district fourteen, where they found Mária crumpled into a ball under an art nouveau building, huddled there wondering why the February wind was no longer able to sweep everything behind her. Gathering her into his arms, Béla realized that the need to banish what Mária had been seeking was no longer a question of how much he wanted her to want him, but a question of keeping her alive. So for the next several days he listened to what she said in her sleep, in the fevers that overtook her sometimes for hours, and whose hallucinations played vividly across her face. Her intonation varied so much it sounded less like a monologue than a roomful of souls. Had Béla been even slightly religious, anything other than the atheist he was, he might even have thought there were ghosts massing inside her, that she was channelling voices from the other side.

Chief among these was István, who finally lost his temper with Anikó and Adél and their belief that Mária's death had been misreported, that she'd somehow immigrated to Canada and was among them. Their envy of her good life, and attempts to speak with her, to flatter her, to curry favour, sickened him, even after he'd agreed to help. "She wants us to leave her alone," he told them. "She's made that very clear!"

"I don't know how she did it," replied Anikó. "She never had any more on the ball than any of us, but she came over here and got rich, and we came over here and we are lucky to have a roof over our heads!"

"C'mon," István said. "Heléna's in university. Krisztián's a professor. Maybe we didn't do so well, but our children have a future."

"What about us?" yelled Adél. "What about our future?"

"What makes you think you deserve one?" howled István. "What makes you think any of us deserve one?"

The next day Anikó and Adél were back on the street, dressed in the best dresses they'd managed to find inside a box of clothing they'd long ago given up on wearing, dresses they cut along the seams and resewed to fit. Because this time there would be no fooling around with Mária—they were bringing Krisztián. They showed up at his office at the University of Toronto and put on the elderly aunt act, telling him they were out for a walk and decided to see where he worked, and wondered whether or not he was interested in treating them to lunch on his big university professor's salary. They chose Chez Queux, and marched him along, pretending to hold onto his elbows for support.

When they arrived they saw that a table had been reserved for them, and for Mária too, who was over by the window wearing a dress of the whitest silk, with the usual handsome man leaning across and holding her hand and placing a dossier between them.

After the waiter brought them to their table, Adél and Anikó turned to Krisztián and asked if he'd like to meet his mother, both their eyes swinging in the direction of the couple. Béla meanwhile had had enough of the voices and names issuing from Mária for the last two weeks, of watching her being torn apart, and decided that the only way to dispel them would be to find out what had happened to each and every one, her lost and absent relatives, even if it meant finding out, once and for all, that what Mária was missing would be missing forever, and that, because of this, he would only ever be what she loved second best.

"I searched everywhere," he whispered consolingly, taking her face in his hands in the hope that his touch would make her eyes return from the distance she'd been staring into, tears streaming down her cheeks and along her jawbone and dripping off her chin. But she would not focus on him, and finally he had to stand, and pull the pictures from the file, and get between her and the gaze she was directing across the room at a young man and a couple of old ladies. "They didn't make it," he said. "None of them." She finally looked at him in panic. "I'm sorry," he said. "There were a lot of people who didn't get across." He wanted to say more but didn't know what, and instead he shifted his feet, holding the pictures he no longer knew what to do with, wondering for the first time if Mária's visions were not so much guilt but a way of wondering what life might have been like if she'd left, gone west instead of staying with him, spinning fantasies of the next forty-five years of the Kálmán family's existence.

"He didn't make it?" she asked, reaching for the picture of Krisztián as if he was there, as if she might with a curled finger again caress his face, even as she knew that what she was seeing, for the first time since Béla had found her huddled in the street, was not a ghost but an image. "I wanted so much to know he was alive," she said, "to know he had a happy life." Béla nodded, and said "Yes," and then slowly put the photographs back into the dossier as the curtains blew in through the window and what ghosts there were withdrew forever. Because Adél and Anikó *had* withdrawn, frantically apologizing—"She was there! A second ago! We saw her!"—trying to keep up to Krisztián as he stormed out of Chez Queux and away from them, wondering if either of his aunts had any idea how often he'd sat in bed as a boy, how often he still did, haunted by what wasn't there—the memory of a face, a touch, the voice you most wanted to hear—as if absence could live on in you like a ghost.

The
Homemade
Doomsday
Machine

B OBBY WANTED to build a device that would end human civilization. It had to have a fuse.

He was nine years old when Otto Kovács visited us with his prototype, which I still have, sitting in front of me on the kitchen table. Bobby himself—*that* Bobby—is long gone.

Before Kovács there were trips to the wrecking yard, the letters Bobby sent—to the Chalk River Nuclear Reactor (requesting "mail order isotopes"), ComDev (asking, just for the sake of theory, if you could build a guidance system that was lit with a match), the New Mexico Allied Atomic Project (wondering how things were going in the "capacity-for-destruction department"), and the Federal Mining Research Institute (querying how deep an explosion would have to be in order to "trigger massive tectonic cataclysm")—and the books, articles, blueprints, diagrams, whatever you want, that he bought, ordered, or borrowed from the library, stacked on his desk, the shelves in the kitchen, the floor by the toilet, everywhere.

I can't tell you how many times I drove to the Toews Wrecking Yard, along Wellington, left on Grand, Bobby popping out of the car to run up the steps of the dirty trailer where Vic the proprietor kept his "head office." Vic would look up from the latest issue of *Playboy* and smile at Bobby (only six years old at the time) and say, "I just got an old Ford Pinto—a doomsday machine if ever there was one," and then lock up the office and show Bobby and me around.

It always made me nervous, watching Bobby climb into those wrecks—torn metal everywhere, burns along the interior, the smell of gas—not that he ever asked for permission. He'd crawl through a shattered windshield while Vic and I tore stuff off the outside or grabbed at fallen bits of motor underneath, bringing whatever it was to Bobby for inspection. That day, Vic managed to pry off a door. "This would be good for shielding," he said.

Bobby looked at it. "It needs to be made out of lead."

"Of course!" Vic said. "I know that!" He winked at me over the top of Bobby's head.

"Victor," said Bobby. "Cars are never made out of lead. First of all, it's a very heavy metal, and would therefore suck gas like no one's business. Second of all, it's incredibly pliable, which means if you ever got into an accident you could basically kiss your ass goodbye. Now, I know Pintos are notoriously dangerous cars, what with the whole bursting into flame thing, but I doubt very highly that Ford would be so stupid as to build them out of lead." Bobby paused to let his words sink into Vic's head. "At the same time, I must admit there's a certain poetry in using one's imagination and simply pretending that such a door would provide adequate shielding. But make no mistake, Victor, poetry, no matter how poetic, is not going to be worth jack when the doomsday machine goes off and fries everyone within a globular radius of 24,901.55 miles."

Vic stared at Bobby for a minute, mesmerized. Then, when my son went back to looking through the yard, he looked at me. "Fuck, I love your kid," he said.

That didn't last long, a year or two at the most. Bobby was quick to figure out that our basement assemblages, stuff I welded together with a hand-held torch, were all fantasy, and that going to Vic's wrecking yard to look for parts was, in his words, "like looking for the Manhattan Project at the bottom of an outhouse." So, while Bobby understood rationally, he had *emotional* trouble with the fact that you couldn't build sci-fi machines out of household detritus, and that maybe he should turn his attention, like other boys his age, to soccer or hockey or baseball. He was quite good at sports, maddeningly good in fact, where he could score and pass and make plays even while none of it interested him a bit, and it showed, on his face, in his body language, the way he shrugged and turned away from the play even as the puck or ball he'd hit went into the net or out of the park.

No, the thing that really broke him up was the failure of our doomsday machines, and so his mother, Rebecca, and I had words.

Rebecca insisted he had Asperger's syndrome. She'd taken him to a therapist who'd run four three-hour tests, and there was no doubt.

"You took him to a therapist?" I shouted into the phone. "Aren't you supposed to have my permission for doing something like that?"

Rebecca said she knew I'd disagree, so she just went ahead and forged my signature on the forms, which is of course exactly the sort of thing I divorced her for, and why I happened to get primary custody of Bobby, and why I'm continually tormented by fantasies of ripping off her head. It was also why I was powerless to do anything more about it: she had nothing left to lose where she and Bobby and I were concerned.

"The therapist," she continued, "concluded that for sure Bobby has borderline Asperger's, which is now actually included in the broad spectrum of autism disorders . . ."

"I know what Asperger's is," I said, trying not to sound bitchy. "It doesn't fit at all. Those people are introverted freaks. They turn their backs to you when you're speaking to them! When they're speaking to you! They say goodbye through the palms of their hands. They can tell you the exact train schedule between Kitchener and Sault Ste. Marie for the months of August through February, but don't know how to ask a checkout girl to give them the price of milk."

"He's borderline!" replied Rebecca, getting agitated, as she always does, whenever she's contradicted. "Right now he's a kid, so it's not so noticeable. But the therapist said that as he gets older, and social interactions become more complex, he's not going to be able to keep up."

"Crap."

"Jesus, have you ever listened to him? He sounds like some smartass twenty-year-old! No kid talks the way he does. And all that stuff he's into—he's memorized it to the last detail."

"Rebecca," I said, adopting the grandfatherly tone I used when I wanted to send her into a screaming frenzy. "Bobby's the most popular boy in class. What do you mean 'borderline'? He's even got girls working on his goddamn doomsday machine." I couldn't believe we were having this conversation, talking about Bobby as if he were some kind of outcast loitering on the edge of the playground, when in fact I'd pick him up from school and always there was a crowd of kids listening to everything he said, hanging on every word, running errands, even offering him their toys, and then calling at night, on weekends, one parent after another wanting to arrange play dates, sleepovers, birthday-party invites. "Everyone wants to do everything for Bobby," I said to Rebecca. "Our kid isn't one of those invisible loners. He's Charles fucking Manson! The only person who doesn't worship him is you."

"That's because he doesn't like to come here," she said, accusingly.

"You think that's my fault? I spend all my time trying to get him to like you."

She burst into tears and hung up the phone.

I called the therapist. Or, rather, I called the therapists, looking them up one by one in the phone book—anyone that had "child psychology" or "educational counselling" or "learning disabilities" beside his or her ad in the Yellow Pages—threatening each of them in turn, "Do you realize the trouble you could get into for treating a boy without the consent of *both* parents?" until finally one of them, Maryse LeBlanc, said, "You don't need to threaten me, you know."

"Does Bobby have Asperger's?" I said, not bothering to apologize.

"What is it with you people and Asperger's?" she said. When I asked what she meant, Maryse replied, "Your wife, what was her name?" I could hear papers being shuffled. "Right, Rebecca. She just would not get *off* it! Asperger's, Asperger's, Asperger's. She came in here with books and articles and . . . you name it!"

"You don't think Bobby has Asperger's?"

"I think *Rebecca* has Asperger's," she said, and when I laughed, Maryse took heart and continued, "Bobby, I think, is a genius. Off the charts on every test." For some reason, Maryse was now breathing hard. "He is the most amazing young man I have ever met."

This sounded more than a little excessive. "'Young man?' The kid's six years old!" I waited for her to respond to me, but Maryse said nothing. "Do you realize he's trying to build a doomsday machine?"

I was thinking this might put the brakes on Maryse a little, and she remained silent for a long time, but then: "Well, Mr. Howe, if anyone was ever to succeed at something like that, I'd say it's Bobby." She laughed. "Can you say hi to him for me? And let him know that if he ever gets that machine built I'd love to join him in his post-apocalyptic world."

Everyone always assumed there'd be some kind of world after doomsday—that the Earth, in some shape or form, would go on—and there'd be this lucky few whom Bobby would save and take with him into the next phase of human history. But Bobby kept this list of names—if it even existed—very close, and it was painful watching the assumptions of people like Vic and Maryse crumbling as they joked with Bobby about being notified of the apocalypse, a kind of nervousness creeping into their laughter as they waited for my son to offer some reassurance that he wouldn't abandon them along with the billions of others when he finally lit that fuse. What made them think they'd be saved, that he'd want them around? I always wondered. The fact is, they needed Bobby to love them, and he knew that's what they wanted, and he withheld it on purpose, watching them squirm, trying to please him in some way.

The only one who didn't squirm was Otto Kovács. But, then, he had no intention of leaving the world, much less humanity, intact. There wasn't going to be any new phase of human history in *his* apocalypse. No friends saved. No elect. Not even himself. I still wonder if that's what fascinated and disturbed my son so much about Otto, why they started writing letters back and forth: here was someone, finally someone, who didn't care whether Bobby liked him.

Which brings me right back around to Rebecca. I always believed, and still believe, that Bobby wanted to make the world better, wanted to destroy what *was* in order to bring about what *could be*, and that this idealism was obvious in everything he did, including his relationship with his mother, whose problems with Bobby could be traced exactly to her failure to understand this. He was, after all, the reason Rebecca and I got divorced, which began on that Monday morning in 1991 when we sat down to breakfast. Bobby watched as the two of us grumbled at each other over how little milk there was in the fridge, who should and shouldn't have gotten groceries, why I'd showered before she did when I knew she had a 9:30 meeting, why she'd not folded the laundry last night, just once folded it, when I'd been doing it for weeks, and Bobby looked at both of us over his cantaloupe and quietly started whistling Bach's Toccata and Fugue in D Minor. Not just part of it—the famous opening—but the whole thing, start to finish, and when he was done he picked up his breakfast plate, took it to the sink, and left the room, as if his actions, including the verdict on our marriage, was just business as usual, something that needed to be done, and we should for God's sake get on with it.

We sat there staring after him. Of course, divorce had been on our minds a long time, but like most parents noodling along in the dry comforts of a dead marriage we'd convinced ourselves that our laziness was a kind of martyrdom, that staying together was the good thing to do—for the kid. But after that morning it was impossible. During every fight Rebecca and I had, Bobby would enter the room, cross his arms, and begin whistling the toccata and fugue.

When we finally told him it was over—the marriage—he let out a low sigh, and said, "Finally." Then he looked at Rebecca and said, "It's going to hurt for a while, but in the long run you'll both be a lot happier—and so, by extension, will I."

She never forgave him for that. It wasn't so much that he made our divorce so easy, so *possible*, but that he'd known what was best better than she did, he'd had more wisdom, been

brave where she'd been weak, been kinder and more for-
giving than either of us, taking the worst of the divorce on
himself, making us co-operate, continuing to exercise love
while Rebecca and I were free to finally hate one another—
and so she invented the Asperger's to explain it away, to turn
Bobby's greatness into a failing, a lack of control, rather than
something willed. Me, I was just happy to have her out of the
house.

It's no surprise, all things considered, that I got full custody. Rebecca disappeared into her happier life—off on
business trips to trade shows, conferences, sales meetings,
whatever it is they do in the world of smartphones—and had
Bobby over on the occasional weekend when she was at home
and unable to avoid having him around. Bobby always went
along dutifully, saying, "As distasteful as she might find these
sleepovers, Mom will one day be grateful to look back on
the time we spent together. The few memories she has will
somewhat mitigate her regret over all the fun things we *could*
have done." I shook my head to clear it, and then asked if he
wasn't getting anything out of it at all, and Bobby shrugged:
"No, it's boring over there. Run-of-the-mill mom and kid
stuff. I put it on for her, you know—Mom the big authority,
Bobby the little kid—to make her feel better. But I'd rather
be here working on our doomsday machine."

I kept doing my numbers, day in day out, at George Nix &
Associates Chartered Accountants. Sometimes Bobby would
sneak out of bed at night to peer over my shoulder at the figures and tables and code, shaking his head, saying he couldn't
sleep, sitting on my lap watching as I keyed in "all those boring numbers," as he called them, and sooner or later he'd

look into my face and say, "You know, you could do some-thing different with your life. It's not too late! So much of age is a function of the mind—an ingrained attitude." He'd wait while I smiled and hit the equation keys to complete a spread-sheet, and then I would ask if he'd like to sit with me on the couch with a bowl of popcorn and watch *The Omega Man* or any of those other bad post-apocalyptic movies he was always researching and asking me to buy. Bobby would nod eagerly and we'd sit down, his small body snuggled beside me on the couch, my arm up along the backrest and around his shoulders.

So it went, year after year, until Bobby was nine, and Otto Kovács knocked on the door—or rather just *before* he knocked on the door.

We were sitting in the kitchen eating breakfast, Bobby and me, the Saturday before Halloween. Bobby was more excited than usual, which is saying something, though it was a nervous excitement, hopping around the table, glancing out the window, checking the time on the microwave. I finished, pushed my plate away, and looked at him. "You want to do something today? Laser Quest? Maybe drive in to the Science Centre in Toronto? Take another trip out to the Conestoga Reactor and see if we can finally get past the guards?"

"Oh, we can't go anywhere," Bobby said. "Otto Kovács is coming."

"Otto what? Who are you talking about?"

He was talking about the Nazi nuclear program, that's what he was talking about. "Otto Kovács," he repeated, pronouncing the name with a very believable Hungarian accent. "He was a member of the original *Uranverein*."

"*Uranverein*?" My German, by contrast, was terrible. "What the hell is the *Uranverein*?"

Bobby put his hand on my arm. "The Uranium Club," he patiently explained. "German scientists who worked on nuclear fission. Some of them went on to form the second *Uranverein* in 1939. Kovács was a Hungarian physicist who ended up siding with Diebner against Heisenberg, when Diebner was administering the *Kaiser-Wilhelm-Institut für Physik* . . ."

"Jesus, Bobby, what the hell are you talking about?"

Bobby let out a long sigh. "Don't you know anything?"

"No, I don't know anything!"

"They were Hitler's physicists, early theorists of the atomic bomb."

I looked at Bobby like I was looking at some dark hole just prior to sticking my hand in.

"Some of them fell into American hands after the war," he said, "but Kovács went back to Budapest in 1944, when it became obvious—to him at least—that Germany would lose the war."

"Back to Budapest." For some reason this didn't sound like a good career move.

"He survived the siege of the city at the end of the war." Bobby shook his head. "I could tell you about that."

"I'll bet you could."

"Afterwards, when it looked like the Soviets weren't going to leave—this was 1948, in case you don't know—he

got out fast. But for some reason," Bobby paused a minute, "well, some reason I haven't figured out yet, he never
caught on in the west—like Heisenberg, von Laue, Hahn,
von Weizsäcker, and some others—and he ended up tutor-
ing high school and university physics students in Toronto.
We're lucky it was Toronto." He stared at me. "I mean, if he
was anywhere else, he wouldn't have the money to come out
here." Bobby kept looking at me. "What?" he asked. Then
he dropped his head. "I wrote him a letter, sent him some bus
fare I saved up from my allowance. I thought since he'd been
forgotten, it might make him feel better." Bobby waited for
me to say something, then made one last attempt to justify
himself: "He's one of the forgotten greats!"

I sat there, completely speechless. "So this guy is coming
here? Today?"

Bobby got up from the table, walked out of the kitchen,
and returned with a folder he pushed under my nose,
marked with the words "Doomsday Machine Project—Otto
Kovács," in thick felt marker on the tab. I pushed my plate
to one side and leafed through it, skimming Xeroxed copies of articles showing pictures of Kovács in Berlin in the
1930s and early 1940s, even a few from after the war, when
he'd worked briefly for the Soviet weapons program. Mostly
the file contained articles about other people—Heisenberg,
along with the other scientists Bobby mentioned—with the
name "Kovács" highlighted whenever it came up, notes
along the margins in Bobby's precise handwriting, and, at the
end, a translation of the "open letter" Kovács wrote for the
June 1947 issue of *Nemzet-talanság*, a short-lived anarchist

newspaper published out of Miskolc (Bobby had remarked: "Three issues published, no extant copies of number two").

This last article was the reason Bobby had contacted him. Kovács was definitely of the right-wing anarchist persuasion, hating government not because it prevented organic community, but because he didn't want *anyone*—especially government—telling him what to do with himself, or his wife, or kids, or property (not that he had a wife or kids or property). The letter was ten pages long, more like an autobiographical essay, written in an attempt to justify where he'd ended up. He talked about Germany during the war, how the Nazis had failed to "properly fund" the "super-weapon" they'd been developing, how everything was constantly bogged down in "ideology and bureaucracy," how various scientists had decamped to the Soviet or American authority, and who among them had "betrayed the principle of disinterested scientific inquiry by contaminating the laboratory with moral questions." By this point, I could tell the letter was a long farewell, the last words of a man who knows he's vanished into obscurity and will not get another chance to put into words his vision of life (or, in this case, his vision of the *end* of life).

Kovács finished with a description of what was awaiting him when he returned to Budapest in 1944—months of siege, soldiers looting the city, dead bodies in the streets, starving civilians, places so devastated you could no longer tell if you were standing on a street or on top of some fallen building. It was all there—rapes witnessed, throats slit over wristwatches, fires burning people alive. But what was truly remarkable was his fascination with the machinery of war—the tanks, the guns, the airplanes, all of it—set down in complete reverence, as if in addressing them he was addressing some higher intelligence, even a god. It was here that the words "doomsday machine" made their first appearance. Bobby, reading over my shoulder, said, "It had something to do with evolution." He pointed to the relevant but vague passages, and then read verbatim, "'Not the National Socialist understanding of Darwin, not the emergence of the super-man, the Aryan master race. This is not evolution as the siege made it known to me,'" wrote Kovács, "'rooted in that absurd organic determinism. When I speak of the machinery of evolution I am not using a metaphor.'"

I looked at Bobby, one eyebrow raised, then went back to the letter. "The siege," Kovács wrote, "radically altered my opinion of our labours." For the first time, he was happy not to be working under Nazi guidance, for while Hitler would have used the super-weapon to rid the world of certain races only to have *other races* take their place—which had seemed like an okay idea to Kovács back in the day—Kovács now wanted to get rid of *all* races, period.

"Equal-opportunity genocide," Bobby said, clearly in disagreement with Kovács.

"You say he's coming here?" I asked, coming up from the depths of the file and the information it contained. Without waiting for Bobby's reply, I continued, "So he wants to destroy all humanity, and you just want to destroy most of it—what's the difference?"

It was the first time I'd done that—seriously taken up what Bobby had been doing all these years—and I could see in his eyes that I'd broken some rule, transgressed some code in which my indulgence, my humour, my forbearance, acted as a counterweight to his own behaviour, keeping it all in the realm of play. But this wasn't play anymore. Otto Kovács was coming, and I had no idea what to expect.

"I never said I'd actually go through with it," Bobby quietly replied.

"You just want the power? Is that it?"

"Yes." He laughed maniacally. "Yes, that's it! I just want the power!"

"Seriously?" I said.

"No." He shook his head. "Power's no good unless you can use it. I'd have to use it."

I could not for the life of me tell whether he was kidding or serious. But I had to laugh. The way he said it, the whole thing, was so ridiculous.

Otto Kovács showed up early that afternoon, around one o'clock. Bobby ran to the door and had it unlocked and open before I'd had a chance to come in from the kitchen and peer out the window to see what Kovács looked like, whether he'd brought along any henchmen, whether the sky had suddenly darkened on his arrival, the wind begun to blow, forked lightning in the sky. He stepped into our home on a sunny autumn day looking indescribably old, worn out, broken, a tattered black overcoat hanging off his bony shoulders, a white goatee trimmed short, hair missing in patches, a twig-like cane in one hand and a creased leather suitcase in the other. The look in his eyes was neither mean, nor wary, nor embittered—none of the things you'd expect from a mad scientist. Instead, he looked grateful, and in fact the first words out of his mouth were directed at me and Bobby both: "It's so nice to finally meet you," he said, his Hungarian accent thickening every word, "and thank you very much for inviting me to your home." He looked around. "It's been a while since anyone let me inside."

I could see how that might be the case. There was a smell on him you got from month-old beer bottles not properly rinsed. I could picture him in one of those drippy apartments in Toronto's east end, broken furniture propped up with outdated phone books, scarred coffee tables with the veneer peeling off, drawers full of mismatched knives and forks, dishcloths duct taped around the handles of frying pans. It was all there in my mind, along with the room dedicated to Kovács's work—the tin filing cabinets, the cardboard file boxes, the shelves of books stacked haphazardly to the ceiling, charts and diagrams and mathematical formulas pinned to the wall, the very small dossier, not much bigger than Bobby's, filled with clippings on Kovács's career. And spread across the floor were the blueprints for the super-weapon that he'd sit down to every day, and which were no further advanced than they had been in 1948. But what flashed through my mind, more than this, was an image of Kovács walking out of his apartment every day, past the whores on the front steps recovering from a hard night, through the park, Allan Gardens, drug dealers bopping alongside asking if he wanted pot, meth, crack, keeping up their pitch until another potential customer came along, across Church Street heading west, three or four blocks during which the city shed its homeless and overnight shelters and bedsits and took on business towers, gaslit restaurants, and finally the hipster scene along Queen, its boutiques and sparkling electronics and restaurants overflowing with *mojitos* and brie burgers and fresh sushi and designer coffees and the clientele to go with them. But it was all the same to Kovács no matter where he walked, the things he'd seen in Budapest during the winter of 1945 had not ceased—there were still those who scrambled in the ruins because of those others who soared above—as if the siege stretched right across history, as if the siege *was* all of history, and the only way to end it was to reach the threshold and refuse to carry anything human across. Kovács was never out of it, he knew better than to even *want* out of it, and he'd take relief from Queen Street, from the way it made the siege real, and then turn and walk home again to sit in front of his blueprints, dreaming of the new elements, the new radiation, that would finally allow him to pass from theory to practice.

And now he was in my house.

Kovács reached into his bag. "Dom Perignon," he said, smiling at both of us, "1996."

I looked at him, at the bottle, at Bobby who was grinning. "That's an excellent vintage," my son said, "though some claim the 1985 is better."

"Assholes," Kovács replied, then looked at me. "I'll prove it to you. That is, if your father doesn't mind. You see, it's a very special day for me: I've been remembered."

Bobby looked at him and frowned. "That's surprising," he said, and I could it hear it already, that tone Bobby used, for instance at the junkyard, whenever he realized he was dealing with an imbecile. "Surprising because I thought the whole point of what you were doing—and correct me if I'm wrong—was to be forgotten. Isn't that right? If what you want is an end to human history, then surely 'being remembered' is no concern of yours."

"True," nodded Kovács, looking at him grimly. "I hadn't thought of that." He reached into his bag again and brought out three champagne flutes made out of what looked like stainless steel, gave one to each of us, popped the cork right there in our entryway, and poured two huge glasses for him and me, and a small one for Bobby. "To nothingness, then," he said.

I took a quick sip before Bobby did, thinking that if it tasted funny, if it was poison, I'd still have time to reach over and stop my son from drinking. But the champagne tasted amazing. We drank up, then Kovács refilled my glass and his own, and, after a glance at me, gave Bobby a little more.

There it was in my son's eyes as always: that same fearlessness, that command, that air of being two steps ahead of whatever we were thinking.

"So, uh, how did you two meet?" I asked.

"I wrote him a letter care of CSIS," Bobby replied.

"Ah," I said, abandoning my previous vision of Kovács in Toronto, "you work for CSIS?"

Kovács shook his head. "Nooooo," he replied, looking at Bobby as if I'd just said the stupidest thing. "They just know where to find me."

"Nazi atomic scientist," Bobby added. "CSIS would be interested in keeping tabs."

"Of course," I muttered, feeling like an idiot.

"Well," Kovács said, smacking his lips and taking from us the champagne flutes and putting them back into his bag. He nodded at Bobby. "You want to do this here?"

I looked at my son, then back at Kovács. "Do what?" I asked.

"Examine the prototype," Bobby said.

"Prototype? Bobby, what the fuck . . . ?" I stopped talking immediately, never having sworn in front of Bobby before, and Kovács was looking at me and shaking his head as if I was the worst father on Earth. "You brought a prototype into my house?"

Kovács appealed to Bobby for help. "The basement," Bobby said, glancing at the windows as if at this very moment CSIS agents were hiding in the hedge, peering into windows, crawling headfirst down the chimney with high-tech eavesdropping gear. "The basement," he said again, pointing, and Kovács put his hat back on and followed my son down the stairs.

It was damp down there, smelling of cinderblock, kitty litter, too much humidity. Bobby cleared a spot on the Ping-Pong table with a sweep of his arm, sending our junkyard scraps clattering to the floor, then indicated a spot where Kovács could lay out his gear. The old man reached into his bag, groped around blindly, rejecting one thing after another before his eyes widened and he pulled out what looked like a long looping horn, almost a trumpet but with more twists and only a single red button on top. He held it a while, and looking closely I could see how delicate it was, almost as if it were made of silver foil origami, carefully folded, and so thin that touching it too hard would tear a hole.

"It's actually pretty tough," Kovács said, seeing the look on my face. He shrugged. "You were expecting something big, right? Ironclad? That's the mistake they all make. Simplicity is the essence of good design," he whispered, "even—no, *especially*—in doomsday machines." He held up the horn. "Steve Jobs is a big hero of mine."

"This is stupid," I said, blurting it out. I looked at Bobby, who grimaced and held out his hand for the device. But Kovács shook his head and gripped it to his chest.

"You should go," I said to Kovács, stepping in front of Bobby, who looked like he was going to pounce on Kovács, rip the device from his hand, and press the red button or blow into it or whatever you were supposed to do. Kovács was tapping his fingers on the rim of the bell, staring at me now with eyes popping, lips stretched tight across his teeth. Then he held it out to me. "Why not take it?" he said, though I could barely make out the words, as though he were muttering to nobody at all. "You of all people," he snarled. "Take it!" I looked at it and shook my head. "You have sacrificed your life," Kovács continued. "Since your divorce you have not slept with a woman." He jabbed the horn in my direction, trying to get me to take it. "You have not spent time with your friends. You have no friends! Not anymore. You spend every hour of every day either at work—a job that bores you to tears, I might add—and the rest of the time trying to shore up your . . . crazy child's fantasy world. At night you've barely got the energy for a glass of whiskey." He continued to hold out the horn, though his arm was trembling. "By the time your son is old enough to leave, what's going to be left? Or perhaps that's when you're going to need this?" He jiggled the horn, and I finally reached over and ripped it from his hand. It was unbelievably heavy, like an anchor, and almost pulled me to the floor. I'd had some grand gesture in mind, breaking it over my knee, but it was all I could do to stay on my feet.

Bobby stepped in and grabbed the device, moving so fast I was startled and stepped back, and even though he quickly grabbed on with the other hand he still had to squat to keep from being pulled over, and ended up dropping it. The whole movement took about one second, which was long enough for Bobby to register the betrayal in my eyes, and for me to see the understanding in his. I knew what he'd done—detailing my pitiful life in those letters to his mad scientist pen pal, Kovács.

"My world would be beautiful," Kovács said. "It would be evolution," he continued, not interested in Bobby and me or what was going on between us. "None of that stuff you see in books and movies—where humanity has disappeared, and in its place trees and flowers have taken over the cities. All butterflies and blue skies and no factories or cars or over-crowded apartments anywhere." Kovács snorted. "I'm talking about true evolution! In its essence!" Bobby crossed his arms and looked at Kovács with an eyebrow raised. "Why does everyone assume that evolution is so clean, so untech-nological?" Kovács whispered, squatting down to speak to my son. "Who's not to say that all of this"—he indicated the world outside—"all those oil spills, radiation leaks, tar sands, spewing factories, cars by the billions, aren't exactly what nature intended for humanity? It let us have these brains and abilities, didn't it? Maybe all this industrial waste is a ful-filment of our evolutionary destiny. Maybe it's our natural purpose to wipe out biological life as we know it. I'll bet you environmentalists haven't thought of that, have you?"

"I'm not an environmentalist," said Bobby, offended. "Or at least not in the sense you're thinking of. Anyhow, what's your point?"

Kovács went on as if he hadn't heard him. "No! And that's because at its heart environmentalism is really a kind of ultra-conservatism. What you people want, more than anything, is for *nothing to change*—no species lost, no land masses drowned under rising tides, no alteration in the ecosystem as it stands. Or maybe you're even more conservative than that! Maybe like all conservatives you want to return to some mythic golden past! Bring back the dodo! Restore the rainforest! Let's have dinosaurs! You see, on this planet nothing is what it is, everything's constantly becoming (from the perspective of geological time, of course), and that's evolution—continual transformation with no end in sight. It's neither good nor bad, it just *is*."

"Jesus," said Bobby, "I had no idea you were such a fucking pedant." He looked at me and tilted his head as a way of saying sorry for using a swearword.

"Think of what we could bring about," Kovács said. "All those chemicals and isotopes and ozone-corroding gasses we're leaking everywhere. Bizarre hybrid plants! Dogs with ten eyes! Whales with massive prehensile legs! Or it could be so much more! By which I mean less!"

"More?" Bobby was skeptical.

"Less?" I asked.

"Maybe it's not a question of new *organic* life forms," said an exultant Kovács. "Maybe the next evolutionary leap is beyond biology. Maybe our destiny is to wipe out all biological life—us included—in order to bring about this next phase!

Maybe where this planet is headed, what we've evolved to bring about, is *machines*—robots, inorganic lives of steel and microchips and isotopes wandering across a planet reduced to plutonium dust!" Kovács stood up again. "Why not?" he said. "If evolution is about adapting to environment, and we're poisoning the environment, then that would be a logical development. What if that's nature's grand design, and we're just doing our small, humble part to enable it?"

Bobby shrugged, bored. I looked at my hands, preparing to throw out Kovács.

The old man lifted the device from the floor with one hand as if it weighed nothing. "That's what I saw during the siege," he said. "I'd get up in the morning, go out for water, and right in front of my door there was some soldier, his head run over by a tank. Crushed flat. Brains everywhere. And it occurred to me that rather than building machines to destroy ourselves we were destroying ourselves to build machines. That was our inescapable purpose."

"It sounds like *Battlestar Galactica*," said Bobby.

"First or second series?" Kovács asked.

"Second of course," replied Bobby, snorting. He nodded toward the device held in Kovács's hand. "So that's it?"

"This?" Kovács lifted the device to his lips, blew into it, and a horrible squawking sound echoed throughout the basement. "I thought I could improve the trumpet," he said. "What would Steve Jobs do? He'd take out the three valves and just have one." He pressed the red button down. Nothing happened, but despite myself I looked around, expecting the basement walls to quake. "Now I just have to figure out the causing-doomsday part of it."

There was a moment of silence, and then Bobby spoke: "Otto," he said, "please tell me you haven't come in here under false pretenses—telling me you've perfected the . . ."

"In theory!" the old man protested. "I've perfected it in theory!"

"You insult my father," Bobby continued, "never mind that what you say is true. But most importantly, I'm afraid we have deep philosophical differences regarding doomsday. For one thing"—he got up, dusted off his pants, and then looked the old man right in the eye—"here are some people, a small remnant, whom I would save. You see, I'm firmly rooted in the humanist tradition when it comes to the apocalypse."

There was a second of silence as Kovács looked at my son—and I could see something forming on his lips, arguments, counter-arguments, questions as to who Bobby planned to save, and why, and what the point of *that* would be—but before he could say a word I started to laugh, and I kept right on laughing as I grabbed Kovács from behind, causing him to drop the device, and pushed him up the stairs and out the front door.

"I sure was a weird kid," Bobby says, sitting beside me at the table and looking at the device. He's visiting with his wife, Anna-Marie, and their son, *my grandson*, Lucas, as they do twice a year, once at Christmas, and once in July for the week of my birthday. Bobby's a million miles away from me. In fact, you might say that Bobby—the Bobby this story's about—is long dead, passed away with all the other lives your child leads, all the people he is, from birth to adolescence to adulthood, each child I loved buried away and inaccessible to me in Bobby as he is now. I'm marking it again in Lucas with every visit—the kid he is, and the kid he will not be the next time they fly all the way from Australia to visit me.

"All that doomsday stuff," Bobby says, opening a beer, "very weird." It sounds like an apology, and I look at my son in his jeans, his blue shirt, the sneakers he's kicked off on the floor beside the kitchen table, where most nights we sit around drinking wine or playing cards, trying with all my might not to ask them to stay another week, a few more days, making up stories from a life I'm not living, all that stuff I'm not really busy with—buddies, lady friends, trips to the track or the opera, junkets to Las Vegas—the life I've invented so that Bobby can be at ease with the choices he's made, as I've done every step of the way.

"No," I say, "you weren't weird at all. You were perfect."

Acknowledgements

Some of the stories in this book were first published (a few of them in earlier versions) in the following places:

"The Animals of the Budapest Zoo, 1944-1945" appeared in *Raritan*.

"The Restoration of the Villa Where Tíbor Kálmán Once Lived" first appeared in *One Story*, and was subsequently published in the *PEN/O. Henry Prize Stories 2011: The Best Stories of the Year*.

"The Beautician" appeared in *The Southern Review*.

"Days of Orphans and Strangers" appeared in *Fiction*.

"Rosewood Queens" appeared in *The New Quarterly*.

"The Encirclement" first appeared in *Granta*, and was subsequently published in *The Best American Nonrequired Reading 2010*, and then translated into Esperanto by Einar Faanes and published in *Beletra Almanako*.

"The Miracles of Saint Marx" appeared in *Alaska Quarterly Review*.

"The Selected Mug Shots of Famous Hungarian Assassins" appeared in *Camera Obscura*.

I can't overstate my gratitude to the editors, staff, supporters and readers of these journals (and others) whose advice, interest, and encouragement kept me from quitting through seven otherwise lean years. It's still the purest publishing experience I know—done neither for fame nor money, only the love of the story. A huge thanks to Pei-Ling Lue for extraordinary editorial commitment and believing in the work more than I did, and to Cara Blue Adams for making an exception.

Mónika Fodor and her father helped clear up my uncertainties around PRO, the ÁVÓ, and the ÁVH at the eleventh hour. Thank you to both of them. (Naturally, the mistakes are mine.)

Special thanks to Ben Barnhart, Daniel Slager, Wendy Thomas, Janice Zawerbny, and Marc Côté for making this book happen.

And to Marcy, Benjamin, Henry, Molly, and Lucy for all the rest of my world.